WAITING *for* WHITE HORSES

a novel

NATHAN JORGENSON

Flat Rock
Publishing
www.flatrockpublishing.com

Flat Rock Publishing
P.O. Box 166
Fairmont, MN 56301
www.flatrockpublishing.com

Front cover photography by Denver Bryan, www.denverbryan.com
Cover and interior design © TLC Graphics, www.tlcgraphics.com

Text is taken from *Stories of the Old Duck Hunter*, by Gordon MacQuarrie. Reprinted by permission of Willow Creek Press, Inc., (800) 850-9453 www.WillowCreekPress.com

Text is taken from *The Singing Wilderness*, by Sigurd Olson.
Reprinted by permission of Random House, Inc.

Christian Island, by Gordon Lightfoot
© 1972 (Renewed) Moose Music Ltd.
All Rights Reserved, Used by Permission
Warner Bros. Publications U.S. Inc., Miami, FL 33014

Never Too Close, by Gordon Lightfoot
© 1972 (Renewed) Moose Music Ltd.
All Rights Reserved, Used by Permission
Warner Bros. Publications U.S. Inc., Miami, FL 33014

Ribbon of Darkness, by Gordon Lightfoot
© 1972 (Renewed) Moose Music Ltd.
All Rights Reserved, Used by Permission
Warner Bros. Publications U.S. Inc., Miami, FL 33014

Fifth Printing 2005
Printed by Bang Printing, Brainerd, MN

Softcover: ISBN 0-9746370-0-9
Hardcover: ISBN 0-9746370-1-7

DEDICATION

For my dad. The only real hero in my life ... he was my best friend. I wish he could have seen this.

For Dave Jones. I still smile at the mention of his name. He changed my life in so many ways ... I'm a better man because of our friendship. He was my best friend, too.

For my wife. She believes in me when she probably shouldn't. She is my last best friend.

~

chapter O NE

Silent and still, the gray sheet of water and the forest that surrounded it lay as quiet as death in the autumn overcast. He'd lost his way out there somewhere, and oddly enough he'd never really left home. Love and grief had swirled over and through him like the chill in November's darkest winds ... and left him here.

His legs dangled from the small pier as he stared across the lake. He was stranded, but he was finally home.

His eyes slowly lost focus and followed only the mercurial shine of the water's surface. Somewhere beneath it, or beyond it, he began to see the soft yellow light of his bedroom reading lamp. His wife lay next to him, warm under the covers, reading before bed on a cold winter night. She called to him. She wanted to read something for him. It was a quote from Shakespeare, and he saw her smiling as she read it. He'd heard it a hundred times before; she read it to him and smiled every time she came across it:

> *There is a tide in the affairs of men*
> *Which, taken at the flood, leads to fortune*
> *Omitted, all the voyage of their life*

Is bound in the shallows and miseries
And we must take the current when it serves
Or lose our ventures.

Before the image vanished, he wondered if he'd taken the tide as he'd always assumed, or escaped it … for all his life.

chapter Two

A steady west wind stirred the water and rocked the duck boat gently while two middle-aged men sat quietly in the darkness before dawn, hiding from ducks. Perhaps on this day they were hiding from the rest of the world too. Together alone, like little boys at play, they waited beneath the blind they'd built on the small boat. This place had become a sanctuary for them. It was the adult equivalent of the forts they'd built in their back yards as children. Just as they'd been safe from bad guys in the forts of their playtime, they were safe here…from the problems of their grown-up lives. Little boys choose places like this to share secrets about girls, dreams of the future, and fears about the dark things that trouble them. So do grown men.

"The boat stinks."

"Somebody left a dead crappie under your seat a few weeks ago."

"Hmmm?"

The mixing smells of musty burlap and wet dog filled their senses and sent visions of other days, some long ago, drifting through their memories like autumn leaves on a warm breeze. Each of them knew the joy that the other man brought to times like

3

this, and there was a sense of accomplishment, or maybe it was relief, that they had found their way to another opening weekend of duck season.

The friendship, which brought the men together in duck ponds as the seasons had passed for going on three decades, had always filled them with the joy that only children seem able to hold on to. Mourning, and an agonizing reappraisal of life, had tempered their friendship over the past year, but that was all put away for the moment. Today they seemed to be returning, albeit briefly, to the old ways, the easy ways of old times. Today they were happy to be reunited in this familiar old place and eager to embrace the memories that this little boat offered up for them. Everything was ready... and ducks would soon be riding the wind to visit them.

"You got the coffee back there?"

"It's in the duffel ... behind you."

Will Campbell, a forty-six-year-old oral surgeon from Duluth, sat in the middle seat of the boat. Six feet tall and lean, Will wore a thin mustache and there was some graying at his temples. He always had an easy, pleasant way about him. When he wasn't smiling he looked as though he was about to. A crooked front tooth set in a devious grin gave his angular face a warm look that attracted strangers and energized friends. As he fumbled through the gear on the boat seat, he held a small flashlight in his right hand. When the broken beams of light bounced around inside the duck blind, all that could be recognized amongst his camouflage-colored waders, jacket, and hat was a crooked smile on his narrow face. He reached into his duffel, found an old thermos, unscrewed the dented cup, and filled it with coffee. After he'd taken a sip, he let out a satisfied "ahh" and handed the cup to his partner.

Grant Thorson, a forty-seven-year-old dentist from Walker, Minnesota, held the cup to his face and let the steam warm him. Also a shade over six feet, Grant had a heavier build. His broad shoulders and the confident way he moved made it clear that he used to be an athlete. He was a handsome man with a square chin and dark blue, almost gray, eyes. When angered, his eyes could pass a cold, menacing presence across a crowded room. But those same dark eyes revealed the other side of his nature, for they could send waves of kindness and reassurance with a simple glance. Always the guy in charge, Grant sought order in all things. Slowly, as he observed and approved people, he let them into his world. His salt-and-pepper goatee seemed to add an air of intimidation when he spoke to strangers. Also dressed entirely in camouflage, he thought Will's face looked like a flashing beacon, certain to warn ducks of their presence, as he got his own face mask ready.

Taking the cup from Will was a simple enough act, but it had acquired a special meaning for these two. It had grown into a silent gesture of affection, an affirmation of their unique friendship. It had just evolved over the years. One would pass the other a half-empty beer or soda, a hamburger with a bite out of it, perhaps a cigar with spit all over it – it didn't matter. Each cigar or coffee cup was now like a handshake or a hug: It only reaffirmed their friend-ship. They shared all things like that. But not with anyone else.

As he rested his left arm on the outboard motor, which he always insisted on controlling, Grant took a long sip and swallowed. Then, while the darkness still hid the twinkle in his eye, he turned and said calmly, in a tone of voice that he intended to sound serious, "Tastes like shit. You still let the cat use your coffee first?" He took another long sip and passed the cup back to Will.

Over the years, criticizing the other man's coffee, food, pipe tobacco, hunting skills – whatever – had become one of the rit-uals of their hunts. During a morning in the boat, there would be an intermittent flow of criticism and insults. The whole idea was simply to be as obscene, deceitful, or sarcastic as was neces-sary to draw a smile from the other man. Grant Thorson adored Will Campbell and thought he was wise, warm, insightful, and hilarious. Will just made him laugh. Even talking about Will when he wasn't around made Grant laugh. It made him feel proud when he heard other people refer to him as Will Campbell's best friend.

Will said nothing, just smiled silently. By the time he'd taken the coffee cup again, Grant was fumbling with his pipe and lighter. It would be light enough to see ducks in a few minutes and both men wanted to pass the pipe before the action started. The boat was anchored in a fine spot that they'd hunted together for years. They'd named the place Christian Island after the first season they'd visited it. It was a rocky, brush-covered little island about one hundred yards off the tip of a long point of land in the northwest corner of Spider Lake, in northern Minnesota. The decoys were set in the exact formation that a couple of lifetimes of experience dictated, and the rolling surface of the water gave them life. The burlap and swamp grass that had been used to build the blind hung over the little green boat and deflected the chill wind while the two men hid.

Grant lit his pipe while Will sipped at the coffee and began to peer out over the dark water in search of ducks. Each of them carried a pipe and tobacco, but at times like this they usually lit one and then shared it, like the coffee. That way one of them was always free to pour more coffee, load a gun, pet the dog, look for ducks, or perform any other duty while the other guy functioned as boilermaker for the pipe.

When the aroma of Grant's tobacco reached Will, he kept his gaze out over the lake. But his nostrils flared and he breathed in deeply to be sure Grant could hear him inhale. Then, in a very matter-of-fact tone of voice, he inquired, "Smokin' inner tubes or dog shit today?"

Unable to hide a smile, Grant sensed his cue to defend the pipe tobacco. "I purchased this stuff in the 'fine tobacco' section of the gas station in Nevis. The tobacco technician – I believe her name is Brittany – pointed out that it said right on the pouch that this stuff is 'delightful.' And Brittany appeared to be a sixteen-year-old fat girl who really knew her pipe tobacco."

"I know her!" Will said sarcastically. "Nice tattoo! She's also in charge of all the jerked products, chips, coffee, and beer in the health food section of that gas station."

Both men smiled gently. There was a pause in the conversation while Grant took another draw on the pipe. He changed his tone and asked somewhat philosophically, "Ever notice that the expensive tobacco that tastes good usually smells like shit, and the stuff that smells good usually tastes like shit? Well, this is a special blend — inexpensive, tastes like napalm, and smells like the time you pissed on the campfire." His voice tapered off once again.

"Boy, that really stunk, didn't it?" Will chuckled at the silly memory.

"Want a hit?" Grant extended the pipe.

"Absolutely." Both men relaxed and settled into the conversation.

Will was aware that Grant was looking at him, waiting for him to take the pipe. But instead of reaching for the pipe, he stood up and brought his right thumb to his face. He pushed his right nostril closed with his thumb and then blew his nose as hard as he could. A cone-shaped spray of snot disappeared over the side of the boat.

That was it for Grant and he burst into laughter. "Nice one, doctor!" He chuckled.

He had no idea why it was so funny to watch his friend blow his nose, but it was. Will had always enjoyed a strange hold over Grant. He could pull a sick, childish laugh from Grant whenever he resorted to bathroom humor or bodily functions. Grant was totally unapologetic about his weakness; he enjoyed it, too. The men reveled in the ridiculous nature of their behavior — in the boat and out of it. They knew it was a little odd that two highly educated men found humor in such childish things. But as often as not when they were here, they found themselves talking about love, death, friendship, or God. Neither of them had ever had a friend quite like the other.

Grant took one more draw and then leaned to his right to pass the pipe. Suddenly, from behind them came the unmistakable sound of wings – many wings – whistling past them so unexpectedly and so noisily that both men flinched. Instantly, their necks shortened like turtles. Both men forgot about the pipe and reached for their guns. They tried to look for the silhouettes out over the water in front of them and load their guns at the same time. The ducks had certainly seen their decoys and would be making another swing over them soon.

The hunters sat motionless. The wind was at their backs, blowing out over the decoys and the open water beyond. They knew that the ducks would make another pass in order to have a closer look at the decoys. Eventually, after a couple of cautious, high-altitude passes, they just might decide to stop here. If they made such a foolish decision, they would adjust their flight so that their final approach would bring them straight into the wind...and straight into the hunters' deadly fire. All hunters learn early on that ducks prefer to land into the wind in order to let the air rush under their wings and suspend them for a soft landing.

The only sound or movement in the boat came from Nellie, Grant's tireless nine-year-old black lab. Her nose was pushed out through the peep hole that had been prepared for her in the burlap duck blind. As she wagged her tail, it made a rapid swishing noise when it brushed an empty decoy bag behind her. She was excited; she knew very well what it meant when the hunters flinched, grabbed for their guns, whispered to each other, and blew on duck calls. Grant Thorson thought Nellie was the finest hunting dog ever to take the field. He doted on her and wanted for others to notice her skills. Will saw her as what she really was: an always competent, sometimes exceptional gun dog with an unusually affectionate personality.

Once again there was the rustling, ripping noise of many wings. It was somewhat closer this time. Ever so slowly, Will turned his head sideways – only an inch or two – and peeked under the bill of his camouflage-colored hat through the brush on top of the blind. He knew that if the ducks detected any sudden movement near the decoys, they'd flare off and never return. Grant sat motionless, staring straight ahead, and let Will do the spotting. Only one of them needed to know the path the ducks were taking. There was no sense in his moving and risking being noticed by the ducks.

"They're straight up above us, takin' a good look," Will whispered. "They're too high but I think they might do it on the next pass."

As the ducks turned gracefully in a wide arc out across the gray surface of the lake, both men now had them clearly in sight – and they recognized the same thing. "Mostly mallards!" Grant whispered.

The sweeping turn the ducks made on their final descent carried them out over the lake about three hundred yards from the hunters. While the wide circle of the ducks' path took them away from the boat and decoys, both men quickly loaded their guns and adjusted their feet so they could stand and shoot at just the right moment. They watched from behind the burlap-and-grass blind as the ducks began to swing around. The hunters were totally prepared for what they knew was about to happen. But when it actually happened it made their hearts race, just as it had every time for so many years.

The two dozen or so mallards treated the hunters to the stuff their dreams were made of. The big ducks turned into the wind and streamed back toward the decoys, lower and slower. With cupped wings, they sailed silently, unafraid, into the decoys, rocking gently as they steadied themselves to sit on the water.

It was the magic moment – the opportunity that brings men to the marsh. Most waterfowl art depicts this instant in one way or another. Old men, too old to hunt anymore, close their eyes and see this sight in their daydreams. Grant was sure that when Nellie laid by the fire and twitched and whimpered in her sleep, she was reliving the moments like this one in her life.

At a distance of about twenty yards, all the ducks had their feet down and were fluttering toward the open water in the midst of the decoys. They were sliding directly into the kill zone that had been prepared by Grant at optimum shotgunning distance when he'd placed the decoys an hour earlier.

"Take 'em now!" Grant whispered unnecessarily. Both men stood up quietly and took aim over the top rail on the framework of the duck blind. The silence exploded and Grant's Browning side-by-side thundered twice before Will had fired. Immediately after the second blast from Grant's 12-gauge, Will fired three times with his ancient Browning autoloader. The final empty shell ejected from Will's A-5 had just hit the floor of the boat when Grant barked, "Nellie, back!" The old black dog erupted over the side with a great leap.

The loud splash Nellie made was like an exclamation point, putting an end to the several seconds of incredible chaos and noise just as violently as it had begun. Suddenly, eerily, the lake was very quiet again. Only Nellie's gentle splashing could be heard as she swam between the decoys.

Four drake mallards lay amongst the decoys. All were face down and stone dead. Nellie had the one nearest to the boat in her mouth and was returning to the boat when Will said, "Great way to start the season, huh? Like a message from God...OK boys, go back to your lives!"

Grant said nothing. Will's comment seemed to silence everything in him, and Will sensed it. During the past year, Grant had suffered greatly. Will had waited for Grant to open up and share something, but recently Grant had bottled everything up inside him even more than usual and shared little with his best friend. Grant bent down and reached over the back of the boat, near the outboard motor, and took the duck from Nellie. As she released the duck to him, Grant pointed at another greenhead in order to give the dog direction and said briskly, "Back!" She spun and was headed toward the second duck instantly.

Grant sat upright on the back seat and briefly inspected the duck. It was a fine, full-breasted male that had nested nearby — a "local," as hunters called them. It was the first weekend of the duck season, and all the ducks harvested now would probably still be locals. Grant knew it would take some serious cold weather in Canada to move the northern ducks down into Minnesota. And the typical mallard in the northern flight was much bigger. He tossed the bird gently to Will. As Will began to place it on a leather stringer in the front of the boat, Grant spoke softly, to no one, without looking up. "Locals are gonna get a lesson in foolish behavior. They won't be so trusting when a few of their friends get shot up." Among waterfowlers, it's well known that ducks start out the season unafraid of decoys. But as they've been shot at repeatedly while approaching decoys, they get smart, wary — "decoy shy," as the hunters say.

Will thought it was odd, though, the way Grant spoke. He sensed that Grant had more to say. Maybe he felt it was time to talk about the events of the past year? Will waited silently. Grant let the moment pass, as he usually did now.

Nellie returned to the boat with the second mallard. Grant was expressionless when he relieved her of the duck and pointed, "Back!" She spun in the water and was off again.

Will had noticed that Grant was now prone to lapses in conversation; he just stopped talking and seemed to be far away. After these pauses, he sometimes spoke about re-examining his expectations of life. Occasionally, he'd merely change the subject when he re-entered the conversation.

"Remember the time you shot my decoy?" Grant said, still not looking up.

"No!" Will lied, trying to sound innocent.

"Bullshit," Grant smiled, turning to Will. "It was a foggy morning. As the fog lifted, you thought you saw movement in our dekes. You slowly took aim and whispered 'swimmer!' and you pointed."

"Wasn't me." Will looked away, in false protest now.

"Then you crushed my new Herter's decoy — looked like a ship wreck." Grant still stared at Nellie and began to smile as he remembered the silly look on Will's face when he realized he'd shot a decoy. He could see that Will was searching for an excuse for his miscue and just couldn't find one. When Will had lost the urge to continue the denial, his face widened into a broad smile and he came forward with another confession.

"Did that with my dad once too, but I missed on the first shot — missed a stationary *decoy* on a still day!" Will was laughing now.

Both men looked at each other and laughed out loud. The somber expression on Grant's face had given way to a huge smile now. Only Will Campbell could make himself the butt of an embarrassing joke and then laugh just as hard as everyone else.

"No kiddin'. I was sure a mallard had paddled into our decoys. I stood up and fired ... missed 'em by a foot, and then when he didn't fly away I remember thinking, 'What a dope' — and then I blasted him."

"Frank pretty impressed?"

"Oh, yeah," Will chuckled. "He just couldn't believe it ... didn't know if it was worse to shoot at a decoy in the first place or to miss it at ten yards!" Will leaned back in his seat and pointed at Grant. "I tell ya what, he had the same look on his face as the time when I opened the driver side door on the old Nash Rambler and then backed it out of the garage ... took the door off the car and then knocked the garage door loose so it fell down on top of the Rambler. He just stood there with his mouth open." Will had not stopped chuckling the entire time he'd been talking.

They were both still smiling about Will's confession when

Nellie climbed into the boat with the fourth duck in her mouth. She released the bird to Grant and shook the water off her coat. Water splashed everywhere inside the boat and the hunters turned away from the shower. "Good girl, Nellie! You're still the best!" Grant said as he scratched her ears and rubbed her belly. It was always clear to Will that Grant thought Nellie was the best dog he'd ever owned, the best hunting dog he'd ever seen. Ducks, pheasants, grouse, it didn't matter – she *was* blessed with a great nose and a relentless attitude. But she really aimed to do only one thing with her life: please Grant Thorson. Will looked out over the lake, trying to spot more ducks, while Grant put his forehead on Nellie's and talked baby talk to her.

"Hey … before you stick your tongue in her mouth, why don't you pour me some more coffee?" Will asked.

Grant kept talking to Nellie as he reached for the thermos and started to pour. "He's an asshole, Nellie. Don't talk to him!" Grant said sarcastically. He brought the cup slowly to his own lips and took a sip in order to draw Will's attention to himself and Nellie. He knew his ridiculous conversations with Nellie drove Will crazy, so while Will looked on and waited for the coffee, Grant intentionally failed to pass the cup. He just continued his obnoxious baby talk with Nellie.

"OK, keep it. I don't think I can drink coffee and puke at the same time anyway!" Will thought that Grant just might actually make him sick. "God, I hate it when you do that!"

Will briefly glanced away from Grant's performance, and as he did he spotted a drake wood duck about two hundred yards away and moving straight toward them. The duck didn't appear interested in visiting their decoy spread but it looked as if its flight path might take it directly over the boat. Normally he would whisper something like "ducks" or "incoming" and both men would repeat the neck shortening and gun grabbing behavior while they planned their shot. But a devious idea came to him in that instant.

It would take extraordinary timing. Will just didn't know if the timing was right but ... maybe. "Payback is a bitch," he thought to himself and grinned. He decided not to tell Grant about the incoming duck. He'd try to shoot so that it would drop right beside the boat, as if on cue.

"So ... hey pard ... what do you suppose is the longest retrieve Nellie ever made?" he said very slowly, trying to mask his growing excitement. He was struggling to hide his own apprehension and at the same time push Grant deeper into his preoccupation with Nellie. He knew Grant couldn't pass up an opportunity to brag about her. The whole thing began to unfold for Will as the wood duck moved closer. He just hoped he hadn't piqued Grant's curiosity enough for him to peer over the side of the boat.

Grant was quite distracted by his own performance and still thought he was entertaining Will. He kept his face close to Nellie and eventually interrupted his own baby talk so he could answer, "That's a hard one, because she's made so many fine retrieves, haven't you?" Grant rubbed his own forehead on Nellie's and then continued. "But she ran down that wounded mallard over there." He pointed to the southwest. "That day she crossed open water and chased the bird around in the cattails for a while. I'll bet she went half a mile after that big boy ... didn't you?" He put his face on Nellie's again. It had worked. He hadn't guessed that Will had anything planned. He was just answering the question and still oblivious to the approaching wood duck.

The duck sailed closer now, almost straight above them. Will dragged his boot a little on the bottom of the boat in order to cover the subtle "click" noise that his gun made when he took off the safety. That noise always alerted Nellie, which would have alerted Grant, that he was about to shoot. He raised the gun quickly and silently. **BOOM!** Grant and Nellie both jumped. It had been a perfect surprise, a perfect shot.

The drake wood duck tumbled from the sky, heading – miraculously – directly into the boat. Grant and Nellie both had had only enough time to flinch violently and then turn toward Will when the duck crashed into Grant's right arm. The coffee cup flew and the thermos fell over, spilling coffee everywhere. Grant remained hunched over and barked, "*SHIT!*"

In the quiet moment that always follows commotion, Will said calmly, "Should be no trouble for her to bring that Woodie over here then … should it?" and he held out his hand. The plot had worked, and far better than Will could have imagined. Both men howled until their sides ached. Grant needed no explanation of what had happened. But after several minutes of laughter and cursing, he sat smiling while Will recounted and re-enacted every detail of the action. Eventually the pandemonium in the boat subsided and the two grown children decided it was time to resume the hunt. Grant held the empty thermos in one hand. Nellie had knocked over a box of shotgun shells when she'd jumped at the arrival of the wood duck, and Grant now used his free hand to place the shells back into their box on the boat seat in front of him. As he finished with the shells, he turned to his right and watched Will place the wood duck on the leather stringer with the mallards. He couldn't help but think how much he liked his boat and how much he liked to be there for times like this. The little boat had been the center of hundreds of great hunts, of good times over the years.

Twenty years earlier, a patient in Grant's office had been struggling to pay for his wife's new dentures and he'd offered to barter for the teeth. Said he had a "really nice" Lund boat he'd like to trade. Grant knew better but agreed to the deal anyway. When he went to the couple's farm to pick up the boat, he was more than a little surprised by the condition it was in. It was far worse than what he'd expected. An aluminum hull greeted him as he walked behind the old man's barn. Weeds had grown up all around the boat and had almost hidden it from view. There was an immense pile of junk and rusted farm implements nearby. The boat was structurally intact, but it had been colonized by several families of mice who had chewed all the flotation material from under the seats. All of the wooden parts were rotten and needed to be replaced. The boat had been beaten up, stripped naked, and left for dead – Grant loved it. All he saw was a vision of the restored boat, which he knew would serve as the perfect duck boat for Spider Lake!

Grant spent an entire summer restoring the old boat. He stripped off all the paint and replaced all the wooden parts. He primed and painted the shiny hull with olive drab paint, and built a removable framework of half-inch aluminum conduit on which he could hang the burlap-and-swamp-grass blind material that would hide him from wary ducks. When the boat was completely restored and ready for her maiden voyage, Grant waited until Will was in Walker for a few days of fishing on Leech Lake. During a cool, steady rain shower one summer evening, he brought Will into his garage for something of an inspection, but it was really just one little boy showing his friend a new toy. While the rain streaked past the street lights and pelted the sidewalk, Grant and Will walked around the green boat, which was sitting on its trailer. They walked and talked and sure enough the inevitable happened – they climbed into the boat and began pretending to shoot imaginary ducks.

Sometime after their pretend hunting trip had begun, they realized that Kate was standing by the door watching them. Grant's wife had a special beauty that came from way down inside her. Grant always said her smile was like drugs; you couldn't get enough. She was tall, with very long, very dark hair. But she had a light complexion, with eyes that held the light blue of the summer sky. Strangers often stared when they first saw her inviting eyes and warm smile, but then they looked away when they noticed her imperfection. Kate had been stricken with polio as a child and her left leg was withered. She wore a steel brace from her foot to her hip, and she walked awkwardly, with a stiff leg.

In their enthusiasm, the boys hadn't seen her when she'd come to the garage and stood still, just outside the side door, watching them play for several minutes. Grant was embarrassed when he finally noticed her, and he tried to pretend that the playtime she'd witnessed was actually some sort of check for seaworthiness. But she knew better. Grant had never forgotten the look on Kate's face at that moment. Her eyes told him once again that she not only loved him, but also, that she liked him and she'd always been his best friend. She shared his enthusiasm, his passion for so many of life's small pleasures, and she was proud of the man he was. She said nothing. She just held their eyes in hers for a moment.

As it turned out, she'd brought three beers to the garage and planned to join the party. Her full lips parted in a huge smile and exposed perfect white teeth when she raised the bottles to show them. That night as always, when she stood there in the doorway of the little garage, her posture and her smile made her one of those uncommon women who could create the illusion of grace even while standing still. Then she moved toward them. She swung her stiff leg awkwardly along and a vision of grace vanished into the summer night. But Grant saw only the smile … and his wife gliding over to take his hand. When the boys climbed out of the boat, she stood with her arm around Grant's shoulder and listened and laughed at the smart talk while she shared a beer with them. Grant had always felt something soothing in her touch. He'd always remember how close he felt to her in that moment. He smiled now at the memory of it. Then the pain washed over him again and his face twisted into a grimace with another memory: Kate had been dead for nearly ten months.

chapter THREE

Smoky gray clouds shifted in the breeze and tried to hide the blue October sky as the fifteen-horsepower motor pushed Grant's little boat back across the lake, toward Spider Lake Duck Camp. The sun was trying to break through and turn a chilly morning into a bright autumn afternoon.

"Be careful what you wish for ... you just might get it," Grant said to himself under the noise of the motor.

Spider Lake Duck Camp was Grant's favorite place on Earth, and now it was his home. He liked it almost as much for what it used to be as for what it had become. Originally, it had been a five-thousand-acre hunt club established in about 1890, by some wealthy St. Paul businessmen. The rail line stopped in Akeley in those days and then a twelve-mile walk was required to get to Spider Lake. This site for the hunting club was chosen because it lay on the edge of the spectacular hardwood forest of northern Minnesota. About forty miles to the west, the prairie pothole country, which stretches most of the way across the Dakotas, begins to open up. About fifteen miles to the east lies enormous Leech Lake, which remains one of the finest fisheries in the world. The area around Spider Lake is dotted with small, pristine lakes and many swamps and wetlands. This country was ideal habitat for almost all species of game animals, deer, ducks, grouse, and most species of freshwater fish.

Around the turn of the century, an immense log lodge had been built high on the sloping west bank. During the 1920s, another, smaller log cabin had been built for the gamekeeper about five hundred yards south of the big lodge and about two hundred feet into the forest from the lake shore. After World War II, the hunting club broke up. Victor Ordway, a St. Paul millionaire and Will Campbell's maternal grandfather, purchased the property. Both of the main buildings still stood, along with several other log buildings. Only about one hundred acres had been kept with the property. Some of the land to the north was now a waterfowl production area, managed by the state government. Some was a state forest and some had been sold to private landowners. But Spider Lake Duck Camp still looked the same to returning duck hunters as it had for almost one hundred years.

Grant scanned the shoreline in search of ... actually just searching. He seemed to be always searching now. The rickety chimney on the old wood-burning hot tub was visible through the trees now that the leaves were falling; 'the little boat house by the pier would be needing some paint in the spring,' he thought. He noticed a man in a brown fedora walking out on the small pier where the boat was kept tied. It was Franklin Campbell, Will's father. Wearing a bomber jacket and khakis along with his fedora, at seventy-five, Frank Campbell was still a handsome man.

Nellie stood in the very tip of the bow, facing home while a mound of decoys rested behind her. Will sat in his familiar seat in the middle and inspected the ducks on his lap. It had been a fine morning hunt – ten ducks – taken over decoys. They could do no better. Will held a drake mallard in his hand and gently stroked the feathers. Then he raised the duck to his face and breathed in deeply. He lowered the duck to his lap and brushed the exquisitely soft feathers once more. He closed his eyes and raised the bird to his face again. This time he touched the soft feathers to his cheek and just held the drake there for a moment. Grant knew that Will was honoring the mallard for being part of the hunt. He knew the ritual meant something to Will; Grant did the same thing himself with all the birds he took.

In addition to the four mallards and the stray wood duck, they'd taken five green-wing teal. They'd both been surprised at the number of teal they'd seen. A half-dozen times, small flocks of teal had come ripping directly above them, very low and from behind them. The teal were moving so fast that their wings had made a violent whistling noise, like a fastball coming straight at their heads. Each time, the two men had flinched involuntarily and then smiled at each other. They thought it was funny to be spooked by something they'd heard a thousand times before.

Several times, after Grant made difficult crossing shots, Will put his face in his cup and mumbled about how the real shooters drop the ducks *in* the boat. Grant couldn't stop his face from bending into a smile each time.

Grant steered the motor with his left hand and straddled the back seat of the boat. His favorite toys surrounded him and his old friend was here. The cool air felt good on his face. He was glad to return to this old adventure, this familiar place. But he felt strangely disappointed, too, because the adventure was incomplete. The good things in life were still good, but reclaiming the past was proving to be difficult. Perhaps he'd been wrong to expect so much healing from such a simple thing. Instead of being "back to normal" as he'd hoped, he began to think that it might take a long time to find his life again. His life had taken a turn he really didn't want to follow.

Frank stood with his hands in his jacket pockets until the boat was about one hundred feet from the pier. He raised his right hand in greeting and flashed a warm smile. Nellie was wagging her tail so hard it was thumping a decoy. When the boat pulled alongside the pier and Grant killed the motor, the first thing Frank said was, "Hi, Nellie," and she leaped from the boat to greet him. He hugged her and scratched her belly while she nuzzled up to him enthusiastically. When he stood up to take the bowline from Will's hand, Nellie stayed close at his side. Frank was a dog lover, and he'd known quite a few good ones through the years — but never one he'd enjoyed as much as Nellie. He spoiled and pampered her whenever he could, and she always sought him out because of it.

As he moved the boat into position, he said, "Must have been some birds moving, we could hear you shootin'! Hi, Will. How ya doin', Grant?" He extended his hand to both of them. "We got in late last night and saw you were both bunked at the cabin, so I just slept in this morning and had coffee with Evie. What a great morning, huh?"

Frank had planned to open the season with Will and Grant but, just as he'd warned them, business had kept him. They had instructions to go on without him if he wasn't at the cabin by the appointed hour. And so they had.

Frank Campbell was a wealthy, well-connected man. He and Will had always had a solid relationship, but it had been tested to its limits during Will's college days. Frank had recognized early on that his only son was blessed with great intelligence and personal warmth. He'd just assumed that Will would join his law practice and then do great things in business or politics. He'd envisioned an Ivy League education followed by law school. Perhaps a few years in practice to learn the ropes and make the connections Frank had planned for him. Then who knew how far Will could go?

Will just saw himself taking a different path. He wanted to attend the University of Minnesota at Duluth so he could live at home, be near his girlfriend, and hunt and fish as much as he wanted. Will Campbell understood from the outset that he was quite capable of achieving financial and professional success — those things would simply come to him, because he was better, smarter, than others. No matter what he chose for a career, he just knew he'd be a "master." Insomuch as he viewed success as guaranteed, he simply felt inclined to stay in Minnesota with his friends and enjoy the life he loved. In the end, Frank's significant powers of persuasion prevailed and Will wound up at Harvard. He was probably the only kid in his class who didn't want to be there. But he prospered. While in college, Will proved to possess that rare character that his father had always recognized. He got outstanding grades. His communication skills blossomed. He was witty, intelligent, insightful, courteous, and well liked by everyone. He fit in well with all the affluent young people surrounding him. But perhaps that was to be expected since he, too, came from some serious money. His mother was an Ordway from St. Paul and represented the old money in the Twin Cities. His father had been attorney general of the state of Minnesota, and his paternal grandfather had been a United States senator after he'd made a fortune in the logging business. By Midwestern standards, Will was aristocracy.

Something special set Will apart from other young men, however; he found a way to connect with almost everyone. While he was completely at ease chatting with men like the Minnesota Supreme Court justices his father sometimes socialized with, he was just as likely to strike up a conversation with the bartender or the guy cleaning the pool. Regardless of who he talked with, when the conversation ended the other person always felt as if he or she had just made a new friend — someone who cared. Everyone liked Will Campbell. You just couldn't help it.

Frank was very disappointed, even angry, when Will chose dentistry instead of law. Frank saw dentistry as a boring, limiting profession that was filled with glorified technicians. He felt it was not unlike one of the Greek tragedies that his son would break with tradition and turn away from all that had been planned for him just when the world was at his fingertips. Will, however, saw dentistry as the perfect niche for himself. He could make a decent living with very structured office hours and virtually no travel, so he'd be home to enjoy his family and his love of the outdoors. He married his high school sweetheart shortly after he started dental school, and when Frank realized how much Will was enjoying his life and career choice, he gradually – though reluctantly – gave up the plans he had for Will. In fact, he began to get sort of a vicarious kick out of his son's life experience. Will was the guy people met on the street and greeted with "Hi, Doc!" and a big smile. Will loved it. Frank had never experienced anything like it in his life. On a day-to-day basis, he only dealt with other highly educated people or businessmen with power and status. He didn't know the name of the man who serviced his car or coached his children's soccer teams like Will always did. He'd really begun to get a charge out of the man his son had become. Their friendship merely survived at first, then thrived, despite Will's career choice.

"We had a fine day, Dad," Will said as he hoisted the ducks for Frank to admire. They stood on the dock and made small talk about the weather and the local duck population. Will and Grant were both glad that Frank had finally made it to the cabin. They enjoyed his company. He wasn't a very good shot anymore and he passed up a lot of easy shots now. On good days, when ducks were moving, he took a pop at decoying ducks when they sailed in with their flaps down, but mostly he liked to sit in the middle seat and talk smart and drink coffee. Frank always had a story to tell or some new insight or information, regardless of what the topic of conversation was.

Eventually, Grant started moving up the shoreline, toward the little shed where ducks were to be cleaned. "I gotta get these waders off and then clean the ducks. Will's got a story for you, Frank!"

While Grant set off to clean the ducks, Will gathered the guns, ammo boxes, and duffels and set them inside the screened-in porch on the side of the cabin while he stripped off his waders, hung them up to air out, and told his father about Nellie's shortest retrieve. Will laughed all over again as he told the story, and it was already clear that the story would be repeated, by Will, with increasing gusto and significant embellishment for years.

Grant finished cleaning the birds and placed all but three mallards and one teal in the freezer. The four birds were plucked and then cleaned with the skin on before Grant brought them into the kitchen. Will was pouring Frank and himself a cup of coffee from the big white enamelware pot filled with cowboy coffee that Grant always kept on the stove.

Grant placed a slice of an apple, an orange, and an onion inside the body cavity of each duck and covered them with spices. He wrapped them each in a double thickness of aluminum foil and put them in the small electric oven. Then he glanced at his watch while he set the temperature at 250°.

"OK. It's one o'clock. Perfect. Dinner at six! We'll cook 'em low and slow. Potatoes go in at five and you're makin' the salad, Will. Frank? Evie's in charge of the wine as usual. OK?"

"Sounds good," Frank replied.

Grant poured some coffee for himself and walked slowly toward his favorite chair. The leather groaned softly as he settled into it. He looked out the window at the lake and the grounds around the cabin. There were chores to be done — wood to be stacked before winter and other such jobs. 'Maybe later,' he thought as he sipped his coffee.

"Pretty good start to the season, huh?" Grant asked softly.

"Not bad," Will replied into his coffee cup. They all settled into the old place briefly.

The great room dominated the cabin. The place oozed tradition and was a direct link to the old times. The logs were red pine. They'd darkened with age and given the place a very rustic feel. It was actually one large room that was a kitchen, dining area, study, and living room all in one. The kitchen still had the original cast-iron, wood-burning stove from the '20s, but Grant had had a new electric oven put in about two months earlier. The kitchen cupboards were knotty pine that had clearly seen some years, and the kitchen table and chairs were also made from rough peeled logs. The living area featured three large leather couches and two large leather chairs, all encircling a log coffee table covered with magazines. On the walls hung snowshoes, old photos, fishing lures, a couple of canoe paddles, and two large bookcases. There were three doors along the wall farthest from the kitchen. Two opened into small bedrooms and the other into a bathroom; the bathroom had been added after World War II. The ceiling was vaulted with log supports, and a moose head was mounted on the wall facing the kitchen. The only real noticeable modern convenience was a TV/VCR sitting on the small, knotty pine end table. Grant thought it was a textbook illustration of what every man should want his home to look like.

Frank had sold the cabin and five acres to Grant after Kate had died. Friends had advised him not to sell any part of the property, but Frank had reasoned it to be good for everyone if Grant owned the cabin. He'd seen the character of the north change somewhat in recent years. Vandals and thieves were far more mobile now with snowmobiles and four-wheel-drive vehicles. Grant would live there year round now that his daughter, Ingrid, had gone off to college. Having Grant Thorson near the Ordway House would provide security. Also, Grant revered the place and would never be anything but a good neighbor and a good steward of the land. Perhaps most important of all, Frank was moved by compassion for Grant. He liked Grant very much and sensed his immense feeling of loss at the death of his wife, which was so quickly followed by his daughter's high school graduation and departure for college. The move to Spider Lake was like medicine for Grant, and Frank knew he was grateful for it.

Frank also knew that Will was the only one of his children interested in keeping any of the Spider Lake property, and that the

Ordway House would be his someday. Will had never been especially interested in keeping the gamekeeper's cabin for himself. He thought it made perfect sense for Grant to live on Spider Lake. Grant could live in his dream home and still have only a twenty-minute drive to his dental office in Walker.

When Frank leaned forward with his empty cup in both hands, Grant thought he was going to stand up. But Frank stopped with his forearms resting on his knees and looked intently at Grant. "How's your dad, Grant?" was all he asked.

Warmth and concern registered in Frank's voice, but Grant could tell by the look in his eyes that he already knew the answer he was about to hear. "Not so good, Frank." Grant looked down and shook his head. "Good days and bad, mostly bad. He's really having a hard time with the move."

After nearly sixty-two years of marriage, Big Ole Thorson had been forced by old age to leave his wife, Gladys — the love of his life — and move into a nursing home. Advancing Parkinson's disease had robbed him of his dignity and wrecked the end of his life. He was losing the ability to chew and swallow, and to speak. He fell down more and more all the time, and when he'd begun to lose control of his bowels, Grant and his mother had made the painful decision to place him in a nursing home not far from the farm he'd lived on for eighty-four years. Big Ole's mind was still sharp, and he, along with everyone else, knew the implications of a move such as this. All of his hopes and dreams, all of the days of his life, had led him to this end — a little room where he sat all day holding hands with Gladys while some stranger came by periodically and helped him with his bathroom chores or put a bib on him and fed him.

The image of his father sitting in his wheelchair, trying to eat nursing home mashed potatoes while Gladys held a spoon up to his mouth, made Grant's face contort visibly.

Grant rose to his feet and looked away. "I'm gonna take Nellie for a walk along the lake. She rolled in something while I was cleaning the birds. She stinks ... needs a bath." It was clear he just didn't want to talk about his father anymore. He stepped onto the porch and took Nellie's rubber retrieving dummy off its hook. Dealing with his father's illness was difficult enough, but taken on the heels of Kate's death it was sometimes too much for Grant. The woods or the lake had always offered him a return to his past, his childhood, and the simplicity of the happy times of his life.

When Grant reached the porch, Frank turned to Will and raised his eyebrows. "What did I say?" Frank mouthed the words but said nothing.

Will stood and whispered in his father's ear, "Tough time for him, Dad. Despite all the bluster and tough talk, you know that boy has a soft heart. And it's breaking – still. He'll talk when he's ready." Both of them followed Grant onto the porch.

"Evie's got a long list of odd jobs for me. I'll see you boys later." Frank set his cup on the railing along the porch screen and started up the trail to the Big House.

"Later, Frank," Grant called.

"See you later, Dad." Frank didn't turn around. He just waved his right hand and kept walking.

"Hold on for a second and I'll walk Nellie with you, pard. I just have to get something." Will ducked into the cabin quickly and then reappeared with a pouch of chewing tobacco.

"Chew?" Will offered.

Will always liked to chew tobacco while he and Grant walked. He'd picked up what Grant now thought was a disgusting habit because, as a seventeen-year-old, he thought it made him look like a grown-up. Like Grant, he'd played baseball in high school. He'd started his tobacco habit because all the guys did it. He pretended to enjoy it until he actually did enjoy it. As a younger man, Grant had also tried to enjoy a chew while hunting, but it was never right for him. He knew now that he'd tried it – off and on – for several years only because he wanted to be like Will. He'd stumbled and then swallowed a plug of Beechnut one day a few years earlier, and wound up lying beside a trail throwing up in a mud hole while the woods spun violently around him. That was his last chew. Nowadays, Will would place a leafy glob of tobacco in his mouth and then extend his bag of chew toward Grant and raise his eyebrows mockingly. He knew Grant would have none of it. Grant usually just offered to do the surgery for Will when it was time to remove the oral cancer. Today he shook his head slowly and squinted when he said, "That black shit between your teeth looks really nice."

"Thank you, Doctor!" Will said with exaggerated cheeriness as they continued to walk.

Nellie was wagging her tail and bouncing excitedly at Grant's heels, begging him to throw her dummy so she could retrieve it. The dummy had duck feathers tied to it and Grant swung it at the end of a twelve-inch section of rope. He spun the dummy around several times and threw it as far as he could toward the cattails along the shore. When he hissed "back!" Nellie raced after it.

Grant and Will continued to walk along a little trail by the lake.

"Nice throw!"

"Thank you, Doctor."

Nellie crashed around in the cattails looking for her dummy.

"What do you hope for, Will?"

"Huh?"

"You heard me. What do you hope for ... dream about?"

"What do you mean – like ... things?"

"No, you have every thing that any man could want. What do you dream about?"

"Well, let's see. The nymphomaniac Amazon woman from outer space appears in front of me. She thinks this is about ten inches." He held his thumb and index finger about two inches apart. "She finds listening to hunting and fishing stories to be very erotic and she has no parents. Is that what you meant?"

Nellie returned with the dummy and Grant threw it again.

"That's good, but I was serious. What do you see when you close your eyes at night, or when you have a moment to day-dream?"

"Well, to be honest," Will paused, "even after all these years, I still think about the next time June and I are gonna make love. I dream about that *a lot*, still." Will turned and smiled. "I *do* it less and *think* about it more than I used to. No, that's not possible! But you know, I think about her in a different way now. I actually like her better now than I used to. I just think about her more, dream of being with her. That sound odd?"

"Not at all. Good answer!"

"I think about ducks, too. I see them gliding right toward me with cupped wings. But I never shoot 'em. Sometimes I try to but my gun won't fire!"

"Oh, jeez, man, there are some Freudian red flags there! You should get some couch time for that one!" Grant laughed and threw Nellie's dummy again, this time far out into the lake.

"So what do you dream about, asshole?" Will chuckled. "Solving the deepening economic crisis in Eastern Europe?"

"No. Same things as you, 'cept I kill the ducks." Grant smiled a huge smile. He always liked these talks with Will. Grant had hoped that time spent with Will would accelerate the healing of his heart. He'd always treasured the laughs and good times with Will Campbell.

Their friendship had begun twenty-five years earlier. They met on their first day together in dental school. They often referred to their time in dental school as something resembling a four-year fraternity hazing. That experience, like combat for military veter-ans, had sealed a deep friendship, the kind few grown men ever know. It seemed to them that someone at the university had decided that the way to produce better dentists was to persecute and harass dental students; if they could take the pressure, they'd be fine when they got out into the real world. The idea struck both of them as ludicrous. They bristled at first when they felt they were being asked ambiguous or misleading questions on exams simply to trick them into incorrect answers in order to create a bell-shaped grading curve. They felt they were graded in a subjective manner by men who resented the superior skills of their own students. Will saw through the lunacy soon enough and simply came to tolerate it. In fact, he learned to laugh and then "jump through the hoops" in order to please the faculty. Grant could never do that.

Their first meeting had had an unusual twist, which set the tone for their friendship. One afternoon early in their freshman year, Grant presented a laboratory project to an instructor for a grade. After several minutes of silent study, the instructor began to criticize, berate, and try to embarrass Grant. He even asked Grant if perhaps he hadn't understood the assignment. He gave Grant a C. When Grant returned to his seat at the laboratory bench, he was crestfallen.

Will appeared from behind Grant and sat next to him. Grant had seen Will around school, and he knew from the freshman directory that Will Campbell had attended Harvard. Grant was intimidated by Will, and now he was surprised that the stranger was sitting next to him.

"I heard that prick talking to you. Man, he really wiped his feet on you! Gimme your project. It looks pretty good to me," Will said with a smile. Grant slid the assignment across the table and watched while Will presented it to the same instructor, as if it were his work instead of Grant's.

Grant couldn't believe his ears: The instructor raved about the quality of the work and said it was the best project he'd seen from a dental student. Will received an A+ on the exact same work for which Grant had been given a C- only minutes before: And it was *Grant's* work on top of it all!

Will returned to Grant's lab bench and sat beside him. He raised his eyebrows, smiled a wicked smile, and slid the project back to Grant. "Told you it was nice work!" Will held a Styrofoam coffee cup in one hand and continued to smile. He hadn't even introduced himself yet.

Grant began to slide his chair back to stand up. "I'm gonna go stuff that clown in a beer bottle and make a wish!" he said coldly.

"Gonna tell him you cheated – handed in the same work as me?" Will asked calmly. "You oughta sit down and think about that."

"You saw what he did! He needs to have his ass kicked!" Grant shot back.

"Yeah, that's probably true, but the guy is either an asshole or an idiot – I'm guessing idiot. It will serve no purpose to kick his ass. Look, you do good work, you're gonna be fine. You know what they're gonna call the guy who graduates last in the class, don't you?" Will asked. His voice was calm once again, but it also held the hint of laughter.

"No." Grant made a face and shrugged.

"Doctor!" Will said and then paused. Both men smiled. Will raised his eyes as if to say, "Get it?" He took a sip of the coffee and shrugged. Then he extended his right hand and introduced himself.

"Hey, Sigmund! Your dog is over there eating deer turds. Did you teach her to do that? How bout a big kiss *now*?" Will had interrupted Grant's memory of dental school. Grant glanced quickly into the woods, and sure enough Nellie had dropped the dummy and was harvesting the forest floor.

"Ahh! Nellie! Quit that!" Grant's face was contorted when he looked back at Will. Then he tried to hide a smile. "I tried to teach her to chew, but she just couldn't keep that lump of tobacco in her cheek – just kept falling out."

He turned back to Nellie. "Come here!" Nellie came to him quickly. Her ears were pulled back now, though. She sensed anger in Grant's voice.

Grant sat on a stump and stroked her head. "Good girl, Nellie." Then he turned to Will. "So what do you suppose turns an otherwise pretty smart lab into a turd eater?"

"Who knows?" Will said as if he didn't care and it didn't matter anyway. "She's OK. All the good ones do that." Then he removed a densely packed, golf ball-size wad of tobacco from his mouth and offered it to Grant.

"No thank you, Doctor," Grant said.

Will threw the wad into the woods and filled his cheek with fresh tobacco. "Time for a rally chew," he said to no one.

Will arranged his tobacco inside his cheek for a moment while Grant scratched Nellie's ears. "So what do you hope for, pard? Will asked softly. "Tell me."

"That's the reason I asked *you* — I don't know anymore. I used to dream about Kate, in the way that you described. Before that it was other things. I do see ducks, too, really." Grant peeked up into Will's eyes and smiled. "I don't kill 'em either." He looked away again. "But it's just kind of ... blank, other than that. I don't have a dream like that anymore — wish I did."

chapter $\mathcal{F}$OUR

Small noises, like someone searching for something, were coming from the little shed by Grant's cabin when Will and Grant returned from their walk with Nellie.

Frank was fumbling amongst the old tools leaning against the back wall of the shed. The small log building had been converted from a garage to a bird and fish cleaning house many years earlier. It lacked running water, but the custom-made countertops were designed to ease the chore of cleaning ducks, grouse, and fish for the freezer. Screen windows had been added along one wall to let in fresh air and keep out the flies.

The wall next to the door was covered with dozens of old black-and-white photographs of men holding ducks and fish in their fists. In the middle of the old photos was a picture of a very young Will Campbell, barely able to hold up the stringer of ducks he was posing with. Frank had written "Waterfowl Processing Technician" across the photo years earlier, and now spider webs seemed to hold most of the photos in place.

Will and Grant stood by the door and looked through the screen at Frank as he re-arranged the tools along the far wall.

"What are you doing, Dad?" Will asked.

"Oh. Didn't hear you coming." Frank turned to face them. "Your mother asked me to put away a couple bird feeders." He brushed his hands together. "There's a lot of *old* stuff in here."

"Need any help, Frank?"

"No thanks. Got my whole list finished already." Frank walked to the countertop along the front wall and looked out at the others. He took a pipe from his pocket and filled it with tobacco. "We cleaned a lot of ducks and fish in here!" He spoke with the tone that old men use when they talk about the good old days.

"Your Grampa used to keep a bottle of blackberry brandy right there." He pointed to a small shelf above the door. "We were standing right here when I asked for your mother's hand."

"Really?" Will replied. "You never told me that before."

"Never told you a lot of things!" Frank smiled and puffed on his pipe.

"What'd he say, Dad?"

"Said he'd be thrilled to have me as part of his family!"

"Really?"

"No, not really." Frank smiled. "He *never* said anything like that. He just looked at me with those big old gray eyebrows all crunched up for a minute. Then he got that bottle of brandy down and we each had a pull from the bottle." Frank smiled a satisfied smile and watched the small clouds of smoke tumble away into the air.

Then he looked at his watch. "Oh, it's getting time to go get your mother. I'd better go."

"Stay here, Frank. I'll go get her. You make sure Will gets the salad done all right." Grant could hear Will and Frank talking as he walked up the trail to the Ordway house to pick up Evie and escort her to dinner.

He reached the porch on the Ordway house as darkness was gathering. October afternoons in northern Minnesota were growing short. Most of the natives loved the chill in the autumn evenings and Evie was no different. She sat in a wicker chair reading a paperback under a small lamp. She'd put on an old sweater when the shadows began to lengthen so that she could stay on the porch and enjoy her book in the cool, fresh air.

"Hello, Evie, time for dinner!" Grant called as he approached the porch steps. Evie had been waiting for an escort. She'd fallen the previous winter during a dizzy spell and she'd come to depend on someone else to steady her when she walked any distance. She was still a very attractive woman. Also seventy-five, the angle of her jaw, her cheekbones, and her pretty teeth still made people look twice at her. She still turned men's heads. She'd been born rich and beautiful and everyone could still plainly see the class and grace that guided her speech and movement.

Before Grant reached the top step of the screened-in porch, Evie had risen and begun to walk toward the door. She stopped in her tracks and exclaimed, "Oh, I almost forgot!" as she turned on her heels and went back into the house. She quickly returned with a big smile on her face, an apple pie in one hand and a bottle of wine in the other. "Anne Robertson brought this pie for you today. She came while you were out walking, and when she couldn't find you she brought it up here!" Evie was smiling a mischievous smile, and she raised her eyebrows with an obvious unspoken question.

"I told her Will was coming for the weekend. She's just being neighborly!" Grant said somewhat defensively.

"She's pretty, too!" Evie said, looking up at Grant and raising her eyebrows again. He took the pie in one hand and gave Evie his arm as if she were his prom date. "Chicks dig me, you know that!" It was all he would say in response to her questioning eyes, and she knew it.

"You're too young to be alone!" she pushed.

"Well, it's nice to be too young for something." He would say no more.

"Ornery kids!" She gave up.

Grant didn't want to talk about it yet, but he was beginning to feel something for Anne Robertson. They had dated in high school, and then while they were in college at the University of Minnesota they'd become very close and decided to marry. Anne got a job teaching high school English and coaching basketball at Wayzata High School after earning her degree. Grant started dental school on the same day Anne started teaching. They planned to marry after her first year of teaching and his first year of dental school. But Grant met Kate during his fall quarter of dental school and knew almost immediately that he loved her, not Anne. He felt terrible telling Anne that it was all over, and he knew he'd broken her heart. She wound up marrying another basketball coach and, in a twist that was a little uncomfortable for a few years, she and her husband had taken teaching and coaching jobs in Walker several years after Grant had moved there. Her husband had died of cancer almost exactly one year before Kate's death, and Grant sometimes wondered if he and Anne were meant to be together after all.

Evie and Grant didn't talk much on the way to dinner. Grant's knee was throbbing after a long walk in the woods, and Evie felt unsteady in the gray half light of early evening.

When they reached Grant's cabin, the quiet mood of their long walk together gave way to happy hour at Spider Lake Duck Camp.

Will was working in the kitchen and setting the dinner table. Frank was sitting on the leather couch opposite the VCR and rewinding *Jeremiah Johnson* to the beginning. Nellie lay on the couch next to Frank. She was on her back with her head in Frank's lap, reminding him with a nudge every time he stopped scratching her belly. There was a fire in the fireplace and Will and Frank were arguing about the Vikings' chances for the pro football season. The smell of roasting duck permeated everything. For a few brief moments during the final preparations for dinner, there was an atmosphere like a homecoming, like a small family about to sit down for Christmas dinner.

Grant reached for the brandy and water that Will extended to him. Evie noticed the exchange. Grant swallowed and returned the glass to Will. "I'll be needing one of those for myself. How 'bout you, Evie?" Grant asked.

"No thanks, but I'll take a hug from my boy." She and Will greeted each other with a warm hug and kiss. Will and his wife, June, lived in Duluth only a few blocks from Frank and Evie, but he sometimes didn't see them for weeks at a time. "I shouldn't have to come all the way to Spider Lake to see my son," Evie chastised.

"I know it, Mom. It's terrible. But we're so busy with the girls — soccer, basketball, choir, you know." Will's three daughters were twenty-two, seventeen, and twelve years old, and Will and June Campbell spent almost all of their free time attending events for their kids.

"You should call your mother more!" She didn't let up with Will. She shook her finger at him. Will looked at Grant, smiled, and shrugged his shoulders. "Sorry, Mom," he said sheepishly.

Frank and Nellie were alone on the couch. Nellie's paws extended straight up into the air while Frank stroked her belly and her neck. *Jeremiah Johnson*, the only videotape Grant owned was playing on the VCR when Frank called over his shoulder, "Hey, tell your mother about Nellie's retrieve!"

Will tried to explain the incident with the wood duck to his mother, but Evie just didn't get it. She had something of a blank look on her face after the second time Will told the story, like she was waiting for more.

"I didn't think it was funny either, Evie!" Grant said.

"I guess you had to be there," Will smiled as he brought the ducks to the table.

Dinner was elegant by any standard, but especially so for duck camp. Frank opened the bottle of merlot and they listened to pine knots crackle in the fireplace while they enjoyed a succulent duck dinner.

Whenever there was a group at Spider Lake Duck Camp, either at the Ordway house or at what was now Grant's cabin, there was an attempt to have at least one meal every day like this. The idea was to dine on duck, grouse, venison, or fish and simply to savor the event. Grant and Will had come to sense some kind of symmetry in these meals. The taking of the game had in many ways fed their souls; now the flesh of the animal would nourish their bodies. They appreciated the completeness of it all.

Grant had first begun to talk of the ethereal nature of these rituals years ago. He questioned Will about it from time to time, wondering if Will felt the same sense of completion in these formal meals. After one of their early hunts together, Grant had asked Will what he thought about saying a little prayer or blessing like the Indians did when they killed an animal, thanking the animal for giving up its spirit. Now they did it with every kill. At first, Grant had been reluctant to speak of it to Will for fear that Will would laugh at him. But Will was ready for the talk of these things, for he felt them, too.

Evie had nearly finished her teal when she quit. She took a deep breath, pushed her plate forward, and held an empty wine glass toward Frank. He tipped the bottle upside down and about an ounce and a half of the dark liquid slid into Evie's glass.

The bottle was empty, the meal done. Everyone was sated. "What time are you leaving tomorrow, Will?" Frank asked.

"Early. I'm seeing patients in the afternoon. Are you two gonna stay at the Big House for the whole week?"

"You bet!" Frank answered. He and Evie planned to spend a week at the Ordway house. Both of them felt October was a great time to be in the north woods, and they loved to experience autumn there. They'd rise early enough to enjoy the sunrise, have coffee, go for a walk, maybe go fishing, maybe take a nap, it didn't matter. The fresh smell of the pine forest after a rain, and the easy swooshing sound that the wind made when it moved gently through the tree boughs were what Frank and Evie still came back for after all these years.

"How 'bout you, Grant? Back to the salt mines?" Evie asked.

"Yeah, pretty much, but I've been taking Fridays to spend with my dad."

"Oh, how's he doing?" Evie's voice lowered.

"Struggling," Grant answered. Once again Grant didn't really want any more of this conversation, and the others read it on his face.

"We'll say a prayer for you," Evie let it go.

"Thanks, Evie."

"Let's go home, mother," Frank said as he stood up. "These boys have to work tomorrow." He was tired, and he sensed this was a good time to break up the party.

"Will, call your mother more! Grant, stop up to the Big House tomorrow night and I'll pour you a drink. Vikes are on Monday Night Football!" Frank shook hands and stepped out the door. He took Evie's hand and clicked on a flashlight to guide them along the dark trail up to the Ordway house.

Will and Grant did the dishes quickly. Grant was filling an old-fashioned glass with brandy and ice for each of them while Will was placing a CD in the CD player.

"Hey, put a little Gordo on there will you, Will? This evening calls for some Gordon Lightfoot." It seemed to both of them like a good time to have a breath of night air, and Grant leaned on the old screen door that opened onto the screened-in porch.

There were two oversized wicker rocking chairs on the porch and one big wicker love seat. The two men always enjoyed a few minutes like this at the end of a long day. They could see their breath in the cool night air as they sat slowly rocking in the dim porch light.

The instant he heard the music coming from the speaker by the door, Will felt he'd made a mistake. Lightfoot had always been the favorite of both men, and Will just hadn't thought about what might come spilling out into the night:

> *Ribbon of darkness over me*
> *Since my true love walked out the door*
> *Tears I never had before*
> *Ribbon of darkness over me*
>
> *Clouds are gathering o'er my head*
> *That kill the day and hide the sun*
> *That shroud the night when day is done*
> *Ribbon of darkness over me*
>
> *Rain is falling on the meadow*
> *Where once my love and I did lie*
> *Now she is gone from the meadow*
> *My love, goodbye*

Grant said nothing. Will said nothing. "Ribbon of Darkness," mercifully, was done, Will thought. Then things got worse:

> *I remember when best friends were jealous lovers*
> *Lying warm asleep beneath the covers*
> *Dreaming of belonging to each other*
> *So we tried, never too close*
> *Never too near, dying in time*
> *So we cried, but that is alright*
> *We meant no one no harm*
>
> *I remember when best friends were not mistaken*
> *Long before that freedom was forsaken*
> *Learnin' about all the good things*
> *In the world worth believin' . . .*
>
> *I remember when jealous lovers would stick together*
> *When the days were warm and the nights more tender*
> *When the bonds of truth were not made to measure . . .*

Try, try as you will
Following dreams never fulfilled

Grant took a drink and said nothing. Will wondered to himself, "What next?" as "Never Too Close" ended. Grant was a thousand miles away at that moment. As Will had feared, both songs had taken Grant's mind to thoughts of Kate. During the six minutes or so that the two songs had played, Grant had relived his life with Kate, like a dying man's life flashing before his eyes. It still happened to Grant frequently.

Will raised his glass and stole a glance at Grant Thorson. Grant's stare was fixed. In his mind's eye, he could see many images of Kate, but the one that came to him most often was the one he struggled most to understand. She'd gone to bed early one December evening complaining of flu symptoms. Instead of lying in bed with her and reading for a few minutes as he usually did, Grant had stayed up to watch an old movie. When he came to bed around midnight, Kate was gasping for breath and clutching her chest. He rushed her to the emergency room and held her hand for two days while the doctors did their tests. Some virus was destroying her heart. She was on the transplant list ten days later, and she died just after the new year. Grant still struggled to accept it all. He'd just assumed his life would always be happy and good and nothing like this would ever happen. He had no idea what a man might do to go about the business of getting on with life after something like this. Even before this terrible virus came along, Kate had suffered more than her share, and Grant had felt a need to undo that suffering as long as he'd known her. It bothered him tremendously that there was no order to it all. He had not prepared for it, and he could not fix it.

Several times during the long winter, he'd been walking or cross-country skiing by himself on moonlit nights. The sight of silver clouds sliding across the sky in front of a brilliant winter moon had made him stop and think that maybe she was out there —

somewhere in the night. He just stood there and stared at the moon and clouds and wondered. He wanted to ask out loud, "Honey, are you there? I miss you." But he never could do it. He often wondered just where she was and if she could see him.

The ringing of the telephone suddenly startled both men. Grant sprang from his thoughts and hurried to the phone. He hoped it would be his daughter calling from college.

"Hello?"

"Hi, Dad."

It was Ingrid calling from school. She often called on Sunday evenings now just to "check in" with Grant. He'd complained that she was difficult to contact because of her busy schedule and urged her to call him more frequently. He could tell by the tone of her voice that she was in a good mood tonight. He felt his own spirit rise when he heard the cheer in her voice. "Hi, honey, how's it going?" He looked at Will and raised his eyebrows while he talked to her.

Grant and Ingrid chatted pleasantly for about five minutes. Will could tell by the way Grant listened for long periods and then threw in a "yes" or "uh huh" that Ingrid was excited and was sharing some college experiences with her father. Grant periodically added the standard fatherly advice — "Well, study hard ... behave yourself ... eat good meals" — and then finished up with "I love you too, honey!"

When he returned to his chair, he was wearing what Will thought was the same sappy look that came to Grant's face every time he spoke to Ingrid. Grant leaned toward Will to emphasize what he was about to say. Then a silly grin came over his face and he said, "What a great kid."

The phone rang again just as Grant spoke. "She probably forgot to ask for money!" he said as he walked back to the phone.

"Hello, honey!"

"Dr. Thorson?" It was a woman's voice, clear and businesslike and definitely not Ingrid. She didn't sound like someone with a toothache or a telemarketer, either. Grant was slightly embarrassed.

"Yes." His tone was somewhat guarded now.

"This is Jessica Wickham, personal secretary to the President. Can you hold for President Hutchinson?"

"Yes!" Grant's face spread into an enormous grin. Will looked on, questioning Grant with his eyes.

The receiver clicked after several seconds and Grant was greeted with "Dr. Thorson I presume?" It was indeed Thomas Hutchinson, the President of the United States, a familiar voice to Grant Thorson, although the two men hadn't spoken for many months.

"Mr. President!" Grant said in a loud, clear voice. Will was smiling now, too. "Greetings from Spider Lake!" Grant smiled even more broadly as he spoke to his friend.

"How are you doing, Grant? I thought you two would be sitting around the fire telling lies about now. Did you 'while away the time of day in the lee of Christian Island'?" It was a direct reference to another old Gordon Lightfoot song.

"We certainly did! Wish you could have been here with us. It was pretty good shooting!"

Thomas Hutchinson had lived two doors down the dormitory hall from Will Campbell during Will's freshman year at Harvard. They'd become good friends, and Grant Thorson had been introduced to the future president when he and Will were dental students and Thom was in law school. Thom was still much closer to Will, still primarily Will's friend. But he'd come to like Grant Thorson very much. They'd made several trips together to the Boundary Waters Canoe Area during their time off from school in the summer months. Once they'd finished grad school and started their careers, they'd found time to hunt or fish together almost every year. Two years earlier, the young senator from Michigan had been selected as running mate for Democratic presidential nominee John Thorpe. Thom Hutchinson was a conservative Democrat and had been a compromise choice as his party's nominee for vice president in order to give the ticket "balance." Mostly out of curiosity, he'd run in several of the early primaries, just to see how he'd fare. He hadn't won any, but he'd generated some interest and come across well in the sound bites the media packaged candidates with. All of the other candidates who were interested in the VP slot would probably have given the Democrats a look that was too liberal. Thorpe/Hutchinson had won a narrow victory in November, and Thomas Hutchinson had become President of the United States when John Thorpe died of a heart attack twelve days after his inauguration. The new President had been struggling from the beginning. He was not a longtime Washington insider, none of the Republicans cared for him, and over half of the Democrats wanted someone else to be sitting in the Oval Office.

"Someday," Thom said in a somewhat wistful tone. "Actually, it sounds pretty good to me, but I don't think you could hide 250 Secret Service agents from the ducks." As if changing the subject he added, "But you had a good shoot today?" There was renewed cheer in his voice; he was truly interested.

"Yeah, it was a good day ... but we've had a lot better. Here, I'll let my waterfowl processing technician tell you all about it." He handed the phone to Will.

"Mr. President?" Will shook his head and crinkled his eyebrows. It still felt very odd to think of his old friend as the President of the United States. But then, as he'd reasoned once to Grant, "Hell, I'll bet even Richard Nixon had a couple of friends. We've gotta be at least as good as anyone he'd hang around with."

"Dr. Campbell?" President Hutchinson feigned formality with his old roommate.

"Yes, but this is oral surgery. You're probably looking for the psych ward or the VD clinic." Will smiled intently while he waited for the response.

"No, I was just confirming your address for some people at the IRS." It was hard to get ahead of Thomas Hutchinson.

Will laughed out loud. "So how is the President business these days, anyway?"

"Oh, you know, that same old 'leader of the free world' thing every day!"

Will and the President talked for several minutes. The nature of the conversation sounded positive and upbeat to Grant. Will looked at Grant with smiling eyes and spoke up. "Hey, Hutch. Nellie did the shortest retrieve in history today!" He then proceeded to tell the President the whole story of the wood duck. They laughed and chatted for a few minutes longer, and eventually Will said, " Here, I'll let you tell him. Take care, Hutch!" and handed the phone back to Grant.

The President of the United States then repeated his invitation to Grant Thorson. He'd called not only to inquire about the duck opener, but also to invite both of them to the White House for a party. He explained the formal party was next Saturday evening and that they should both bring their wives — or, as he'd said very deliberately, your "significant others."

When he said "significant others," he paused and then asked, very seriously, "How are you doing, Grant?" Grant sensed the concern in his friend's voice, and he could tell Thom wanted more than the standard answer of "good" or "fine." He knew Thom was asking if there might be some new romantic interest in his life.

"Life is good here, Hutch, but it's still one long day at a time. I just may bring a date."

"Great, but be here either way. I'm looking forward to seeing you guys!"

"OK, see you Saturday!" Grant was just about to put the phone down.

"Hey! Before you hang up … how's your dad doing, Grant?" Thomas Hutchinson had met Ole Thorson on a pheasant hunting trip years earlier, and he'd taken to Big Ole immediately, probably because he'd witnessed a rare and unexpected moment of candor. Grant knew exactly what the President was thinking of at this moment.

Will, Grant, and Thom had stopped hunting so they could pick up some lunch. They'd parked Thom's car in the center of Thorson's farmyard and were sitting on the rear bumper having sandwiches and sodas. Ole Thorson walked over to the young men and sat on the grass facing the boys. He just wanted to get to know his son's friends a little better, so he took a break from his farm chores and joined them for lunch. Ole had a blade of grass in the corner of his mouth, and he lay on his side and rested on his elbow while he talked to the boys.

In the telling of a little story, Thom Hutchinson had seen the sorrow and fear in Ole Thorson's eyes and the strength that had led him through it all. Grant's father had become an instant folk hero for Thom that day. Thom had even used the story Ole told him to introduce a book he'd written about Americans in combat. He also made it a point to get to know Big Ole after that, to chat with him at length about his life and times. Thom really was a man of the people, and when he met a compelling character, he studied that person.

"He's in a nursing home, Thom. Parkinson's, leukemia, old age. He doesn't talk much anymore. They say the Parkinson's sort of locks a person's thoughts inside. But you know, he never did have much to say anyway." It was more than Will had heard Grant say regarding his father for several months.

"I'm so sorry to hear that." Thom's voice registered genuine concern. "Please greet him for me!"

"Sure thing, Hutch." Grant didn't even know if Big Ole could acknowledge a greeting anymore.

They said their goodbyes and Grant hung up the phone. He returned to the cool, brisk darkness of the porch, found his empty rocking chair, and sat silently for a few minutes with Will. The ice cubes clinked in his glass as he drank the last of his brandy.

Grant shook his head and let out a big sigh. "What a day, huh?"

"Not bad," Will agreed.

"Listen to that," Grant said after a long pause.

"What?"

"The breeze blowing though the pines … isn't that fine?" Grant rocked in his chair for a moment and said to no one, "I wish the loons were still here."

chapter $\mathcal{F}$IVE

Ingrid Thorson had always been the apple of her daddy's eye. At every age, Grant had found his daughter's charm to be irresistible. A crooked smile or a laugh from Ingrid could usually pull him from a dark mood. Kate had always teased him about the silly look he wore as Ingrid argued her side of an issue. She was the one person that could always get right through Grant Thorson's tough, guarded exterior and appeal to the tender heart on the inside. Of course, Grant felt that her exemplary behavior just never needed confrontation or correction. For the most part he was right.

The resemblance that Ingrid bore to her mother was eerie. Whenever someone was introduced to the Thorsons, the stranger's first response would always be to exclaim how much Ingrid looked like her mother. When she'd graduated from high school in June, she'd been right at six feet tall with the same long, dark hair and blue eyes as her mother. Even close friends thought that Kate's high school graduation photo was a portrait of Ingrid. Kate had always loved it when people made the comparison. Ingrid did, too, although she tried to act as though she was offended by it.

The close relationship that Grant had with Ingrid had remained solid all along, but it had always taken a back seat to Kate's friendship with Ingrid. Mother and daughter spoke with each other about everything and always seemed to get along. Grant had felt his role change from the daddy who played games and read books with his small daughter, to the dad who coached his daughter's softball teams, to the father she seldom spoke to and who understood little of his teenage daughter. He saw his role as parent become that of disciplinarian and provider of rules and order. Although it struck him as fairly normal that Kate was closer to Ingrid than he was, he really didn't enjoy the way he found himself on the outside looking in during mother-daughter conversations.

When Kate died, it was understandably difficult for Ingrid. Grant's relationship with Ingrid changed again – it deepened as he became both father and mother, if that were really possible. During Ingrid's senior year in high school, though – before Kate's death and after – Grant had noticed Ingrid begin to separate from her family. She sometimes treated Grant with indifference and occasionally stared at him with contempt when he reminded her about who was still in control of the household. Her friends became increasingly more important than her father and she chose their company over his at every turn. Grant was satisfied that Ingrid's separation from him was a fairly normal child development. All things considered, he felt he'd done quite well as a "mother" to an eighteen-year-old daughter, and he missed Ingrid terribly when she went off to Concordia College in Moorhead, Minnesota.

During his first week alone at Spider Lake without Ingrid, Grant had quickly become aware of a strong sense of loneliness. He still missed Kate; she'd always been there for him to talk to. Then, just when he'd made friends with Ingrid, she'd left him – both literally and figuratively. Now he could talk to Nellie or read at night and that was about it. At first, it was a very difficult adjustment. But he responded by taking Nellie to the office with him and then working longer days. Nellie loved it, patients loved it, and Grant had less time to feel lonely.

When his father had moved to the nursing home, he'd decided to spend every Friday with Big Ole. He'd work at the office until 5:00 p.m. on Thursdays, and then he and Nellie would drive to his parents' home in Halstad. It had all worked out quite well from the beginning. He could stop and visit Ingrid as he passed through Moorhead on the way to or from Halstad, and the time with family helped with his own loneliness, too. Grant and his mother and Nellie would rise early on Fridays, be at Ole's room for breakfast, and then stay there for the day.

On this particular Friday, because of the President's invitation, he planned to leave his parents' place in Halstad a little early and catch a late plane from Fargo to Minneapolis, where he'd meet with Will and June Campbell and they'd all fly to the capital on Saturday.

Although this wasn't going to be a particularly busy week at the office, Grant felt the weight of a hectic schedule. The thought of the long drive to and from Halstad just before the flight to Washington seemed to add pressure at the end of the work week. He'd also wanted to visit with Ingrid on Friday evening, as he normally would have, when he passed through Moorhead on the way home. That visit would now have to be postponed if he planned to catch his flight out of Fargo on Friday night – but he reasoned that Ingrid certainly wouldn't be too broken-hearted if he missed a Friday visit.

Thom Hutchinson had been pretty clear about the dress code for the upcoming autumn party at the White House; the men needed to wear tuxedos. Since there was no place in Walker for Grant to rent a tuxedo, Will had offered to get one for him in Duluth. He didn't like the idea, but he'd have to trust Will with getting the tuxedos – and that, too, made him uneasy. Grant insisted on handling the airline and motel reservations as usual. That way he knew it would be done just the way he wanted.

There was also the business of bringing a date. To this point, he had not been compelled to start dating again; he just wasn't interested. In addition, before this he'd thought it was improper to begin seeing someone. It was just so odd to think of dating again. Who would have guessed that would be an issue in life at this age? He really had led a charmed existence; he'd never suspected he'd be dealing with something like dating at this point in his life. But he thought that maybe now it was appropriate for him to ask an old friend out for a special date. After all, he could sense Will Campbell and Thom Hutchinson cheering for him like a ballplayer that had just struck out.

He'd sat with Anne Robertson at a few high school ball games while her students giggled and pointed at them. He'd also asked her to lunch several times. They'd had long conversations at the grocery store or on the street when they'd crossed paths, but there had been no dating, no involvement. He sensed — no, he knew — that she had feelings for him, and for reasons he didn't understand he felt a vague fear or uneasiness because of it. Perhaps it was just the same old unwillingness to move on that he'd always struggled with. Deep down, he wondered if he was perhaps afraid to open any old wounds with Anne.

He called Anne Monday morning at school. She was in class at the time, but she returned his call about thirty minutes later. He could hear the excitement in her voice as she accepted the invitation to accompany him to the White House. She asked several questions about travel plans and what she should wear, but like most men, Grant was useless when it came to helping women dress for an occasion. Strangely, he wondered if he heard a bit of disappointment in her voice when he said he'd already made arrangements for her to have her own room in Minneapolis on Friday and in D.C. on Saturday night. Or maybe he'd hurt her feelings by verbalizing the fact that they each needed their own rooms, as if she didn't already know that. The little feeling of trepidation wouldn't leave him alone. He thought he should feel more excited about taking a date to the White House.

Anne had surprised Grant with a show of excitement he'd not seen from her in many years. He smiled to himself and asked her if she'd like to "go on a date ... and talk about our date."

They met at Emil's Leech Lake Café after Grant finished work on Tuesday. Anne had no idea that Grant was a personal friend of the President of the United States, and she smiled the entire time while he told her the story of their friendship. They agreed to meet at the Fargo airport on Friday evening after his visit with Big Ole and fly to Minneapolis together Friday night.

The week passed quickly in spite of the usual small crises that spring up every day in a dental office. In recent months, Grant had grown more and more cynical and even angry regarding his profession. It seemed that every bit of correspondence he received from the Minnesota state government had an adversarial tone about it, as though someone in St. Paul had decided that the dentists in the state needed to be threatened into compliance with state laws about infection control, hazardous waste, welfare programs, or employee issues. Grant did not like to be threatened, especially when he'd already spent considerable time and money to be sure he was in compliance with existing laws. He'd also begun to resent a growing third-party presence. Insurance companies were driving a wedge between him and his patients. He felt that all insurance companies were patently dishonest. He already saw most issues as fairly black and white, and in this case it was crystal clear to him that insurance companies were the embodiment of evil. The rapid changes in the framework for providing health care troubled Grant Thorson. He just wished it could be the way it used to be: he and the patient deciding just what treatment would be the best for the patient, without a self-serving insurance company or government agency interfering.

When his workweek ended Thursday afternoon, he was relieved to be on his way to visit his parents. Earlier that day, a mid-level bureaucrat from the state government had called to tell him that a "radiographic technician" would be stopping by the office to calibrate Grant's new X-ray machine, and that it would cost Grant $295.

"I just bought the thing last month and the manufacturer calibrated it at that time!" Grant had begun to lose his temper immediately when the person from the state followed Grant's reply with the threat of a large fine if he didn't comply. Wisely, he'd decided to stifle his anger. Now, as he drove west and began to relax, his frustration with the state government and various insurance companies began to wane. But it still triggered a string of memories as his thoughts turned to his dad. He remembered another time, several years earlier, when a dental insurance company had angered him and he'd complained bitterly about his career choice in front of his father. Later, Grant's mother had admonished him to never do that again because he'd hurt his father with his tirade. Ole Thorson valued his children's college educations as the true measure of *his* success in life.

Ole and Gladys Thorson were both second-generation Americans. They'd grown up on small farms around Halstad, and they'd known poverty. Actually, Gladys' family was affluent compared to Ole's. Her father ran the dray line in Halstad. He'd hitch up his horses every morning and haul freight from the rail station to wherever it was bound in the Halstad area. He'd kept his job and supported eight children during the Depression.

Gustav Thorson, however, had lost his farm to foreclosure in 1919, and then lost a second farm during the Depression. Big Ole's father was a tenant farmer for the next nine years and then took a job in a local meat packing house until he retired. Ole had seen heartache and had been poor during his entire young life. One day when he was in the ninth grade, he just turned around on his walk to the little country school down the road and quit. He took a job at the same local meat packing plant where his father worked that very day, and between that job and his own farm he didn't miss a day's work for sixty years. But quitting school was the one thing in his life he was ashamed of. He felt he was somehow less than other men who had an education. Now, Ole couldn't bear to hear his son voice any criticism of the education he'd worked his whole life to provide. Grant Thorson made it a point never to criticize his profession again in front of his father.

So, just like Will Campbell, Grant's presence in dental school represented a break with family tradition. No one in his family had any education, and they all thought it was extraordinary that one of their own should go off to dental school. Grant and his four brothers were the first on either side of his family to finish high school. Although he'd been a fair student in high school, sports were more important to him. When he started college at the University of Minnesota, he decided to try his luck and "walk on" the baseball team. He made the team as a pitcher but played only sparingly. During his three seasons on the varsity, he made several appearances each season as a reliever but never figured in any important games. He was a hard worker in practice, and each season he seemed on the verge of becoming a contributor, maybe a starter. But then someone would always show up who was just a little better than he was. Big Ole only got to see Grant pitch once – one inning of perfect relief ... that was it. When it was all over, Grant sometimes wondered if Ole was disappointed with him or ashamed of him because he never "made it."

During Grant's senior year, it turned out that one of the assistant baseball coaches was dating a secretary at the U of M dental school. His coach had been impressed with Grant's attitude and work ethic. He asked a few questions on Grant's behalf and then encouraged Grant to apply to dental school. Grant had nothing better in mind, so he filled out the application, took the Dental College Aptitude Test, and was accepted.

The road noise in the Suburban was a low drone as Grant cruised along the flatlands of western Minnesota. He remembered how he'd been motivated to study and make something better of his life because of his summer job. For five summers, he'd worked in the same meat packing plant that his grandfather and father had. He hated the stink, the noise, the hard work, and some of the hard cases who worked there. He knew for certain that this place was not his future.

On the last evening of the summer break before his freshman year at dental school, Grant was packing his car to leave Halstad for Minneapolis when Big Ole stepped into the garage. At first Grant thought he'd come to help, but Ole was wringing his hands and was clearly troubled by something. He wanted to speak but couldn't. He stepped closer to Grant and looked him in the eye. "I'm more proud of you at this moment than if you were going off to play for the Twins!" he blurted. Then he began to cry. It was the first time Grant had ever seen his father weep. It was the first time Big Ole Thorson ever gave those feelings a voice. "It won't be long and people will be calling you Dr. Thorson. I wish your grampa could see it." His voice still trembled in a rare show of emotion. It was in that moment that Grant Thorson first realized what an enormous thing he'd done. Ole Thorson wasn't ashamed of him! Quite the opposite was true, in fact. Grant could now see clearly that his father was overcome with pride at what Grant had accomplished. His four older sons were all good boys and very successful in their careers, but Ole Thorson — like so many poor, uneducated men of his generation — had immense respect for any doctor. The doctor was the most respected man in the community. Grant had completed the American dream for his dad.

Standing in the garage, watching his father weep, Grant had no idea what to do. He'd never seen such a thing before. He took several halting steps toward Ole and then put his arms around his dad. Neither of them spoke; it wasn't necessary.

Now, as he rolled along on the dark road toward Halstad, he wiped his own tears away. For his entire life, his father had been his best friend, his first hunting buddy. Big Ole was the only real hero of Grant's life, and lately he'd come to know that he was now his father's hero. That thought had weight, and it put a lump in Grant's throat every time it came to him.

With every visit to the nursing home, Grant could see that his father had lost something, and it made his heart ache. Invariably, Big Ole had given up or lost some subtle skill or abandoned some pleasure with each passing week. It seemed that it should be a joyful thing to spend these days with his dad, and in many ways it was. But Grant knew he was watching his father's life slip away. As he took care of Big Ole during his Friday visits, he knew he was also preparing his own heart to bear his father's death.

Gladys was waiting up for Grant when he arrived, just as she'd done thirty years earlier when he stayed out late while in high school. They spoke briefly and Gladys shared her concerns and frustration about Ole's steady decline since he'd been living in the nursing home. Grant was impressed by his mother's strength. She'd broken down and sobbed heavily a few times in the past months, but for the most part she was very businesslike as she went about taking care of Ole now that he didn't live at home anymore. Gladys now treated Ole just like she'd taken care of her boys when they were sick; all of her effort and attention was directed toward him.

Like Will's mother, Gladys was still pretty. But she had an entirely different kind of beauty. Gray-haired and beginning to stoop over slightly when she walked, she remained a doting mother for her children. She still prepared fried pork chops, fried potatoes, fried everything when her boys came home. She always had a jar of sugar cookies handy, and she made sure to plop it in front of any visitor to her kitchen. She fussed over her children and grandchildren. She fussed over Ole. Dressed in her cotton dress and working in her kitchen, she represented the classic little old grandmother as far as Grant was concerned. But in her blue eyes Grant could still see all the innocent playfulness of a little child, maybe the proverbial "girl next door." Grant loved to see that sort of light in the face of an eighty-year-old woman, especially his own mother.

They arose early on Friday morning and went to the nursing home in time to have breakfast with Ole. As Grant rounded the corner and stepped inside his father's room at six o'clock, he was once again surprised at his father's worsening appearance. Big Ole was sitting in his recliner, staring straight ahead and waiting for someone to come and help him start his day. He'd made it out of bed and into his chair but that was about all he had the strength to do. His hair was mussed up and his slippers were only part of the way on his feet.

When he saw Grant enter the room, Ole raised his arms as if to say, "Come here and hold me." He didn't smile; he never smiled anymore. He couldn't smile — the Parkinson's had stolen his great warm face and twinkling eyes. The doctors called it "loss of pallor;" a person's face just becomes blank, unable to show emotion. This was a special loss for Ole and those who knew him. He'd always been the typical stoic Norwegian with little to say in any situation. But he'd had a great face and he'd always been able to speak volumes with a mere glance. That was gone now; his face was just empty. Grant lifted Big Ole to his feet and embraced him. He held his father tightly and pressed his cheek against his father's. He kissed his father on the cheek and said, "I love you, Dad!" Big Ole was barely able to whisper, "I love you too, son." Gladys greeted Ole with a kiss and a hug while Grant steadied him on his feet before lowering him back into his recliner.

"Did you sleep all right, Dad?"

Ole shook his head to say "no."

"Are you hungry?"

Once again, the "no" signal. Gladys and Grant had begun to wonder whether Ole was just too stubborn to admit that anything was good at the nursing home or whether all of his complaints were indeed legitimate.

Ole pointed at something across the room now. "Yeah, what do you want, Dad?" Grant knew very well what Ole wanted, but he wanted to see if Ole would say the words. He pointed again.

"No, you have to tell me what you want, Dad." Grant smiled, challenging his father.

"I gotta piss!" Ole spoke fairly distinctly. He was angry at being pushed.

"OK, I'll take you." Grant smiled and sneaked a look at his watch as he helped his father to his feet and assisted his very slow walk to the toilet. Grant turned him, helped him get his pajamas undone, and sat him on the toilet. When Ole was done, Grant put him back together again and walked him back over to the recliner. It had taken eleven minutes.

Grant suggested that Gladys go get a cup of coffee in the kitchen while he got Big Ole ready for the day. He gave his father a sponge bath, washed his hair in the sink, and got him dressed. Then he wheeled Ole out to the dining room for breakfast.

When Grant proudly rolled his father down the hall and into the dining room, Gladys told Big Ole he looked nice. It didn't sound like something that a wife would say to her husband. It sounded like something a mother would say to a three-year-old, and the tone of it bothered Grant. He knew his mother meant only to cheer Ole up with a compliment, but he guessed that her comment hurt because it signaled another change. Gladys had never spoken to Ole like that. She meant it only to be nice, but to an observer it revealed a big shift in Ole's status: Somebody else was now responsible for getting him dressed, like a child. Ole finished about half a bowl of oatmeal and some orange juice and once again waited silently for a while before he pointed, this time down the hall toward his room.

"What do you want, Dad? Tell me."

"I gotta shit!"

"You have achieved a great economy of words," Grant said with a smile as he stood up. Ole hadn't always been so gruff, but he spoke from frustration now. He had told Grant two weeks earlier that he was tired of begging the young girls who worked there to take him to the bathroom.

Grant took him back down the long hall to his room and stood in the bathroom door after he'd set his dad on the toilet again. He got a newspaper and read while he stood in the door. "No hurry, Dad, lemme know when you're done and I'll help you with the paper work." Grant continued to read. Ole had told Grant that the nurses always treated him like a disobedient kid. They were curt with him and thought he was just making trouble with frequent requests for help with bathroom chores. His father had been a proud man throughout his whole life, and now he had to suffer the indignity of asking a stranger to help in the bathroom. Grant felt his heart break a little every time he saw this frustration in his father's eyes, but he tried to make Ole feel like he had all day to wait if that's what his dad wanted.

When it was time to clean up after the bathroom chores, Grant reached behind his dad with toilet paper and Big Ole winced. His bottom was blazing red. Either he or the nursing home staff wasn't doing a very good job of this anymore. Grant got some warm water on a wash cloth and gently cleaned his father. This sort of experience had been extraordinarily difficult for Grant at first. He'd always felt that bathroom chores were a pretty personal thing anyway, and he'd never imagined he'd be required to help his father in this way. He'd felt embarrassed, both for himself and for his dad, but strangely that all went away after the first time or two. Then, as time went by, he began to sense some relief or thankfulness in his dad. Big Ole had never been eloquent enough to verbalize the complex emotions he was feeling now, and the decline of his speaking skills made it certain that he and Grant would never discuss these things. But it was very clear to Grant when he was with his dad that Big Ole Thorson found it soothing that his son was the one who cared for him like this, instead of some stranger on the nursing home staff. Only once, when Grant had tucked Ole's shirt into his pants and washed up after a trip to the bathroom, had Ole said anything. He stopped during his painfully slow walk back to his chair and reached for Grant, hugging him and whispering, "Thanks son." In an unspoken way, these times in the nursing home were making them even closer. Grant couldn't help but see some symmetry in life. It hadn't been that long ago when Big Ole had done the same thing for him.

He returned Big Ole to his recliner. As he looked around the room, he saw a note card with the presidential seal on it. Thom Hutchinson had sent Ole Thorson a handwritten note! 'What a nice thing to do,' Grant thought. Thom had written a few lines about courage and the value of a loving family and told Ole he was thinking of him. When Grant finished reading the card, he looked back at his father. Ole was waiting for his glance, and he raised his eyebrows as if to say, "How about that?"

"Ever think you'd be personal friends with the Prez?" Grant smiled. "He likes you, Dad."

Big Ole raised his eyebrows and pointed at Grant. "He likes you!" he whispered.

Grant remembered once again how Ole had strolled up to him and Will and Thom Hutchinson and started a conversation. Ole had looked so relaxed all those years ago as he leaned on his elbow and talked with them.

It had just happened to be Veterans Day that day, and Thom Hutchinson had asked Ole in a very matter of fact way if he'd ever been in the service. When Ole answered that he'd been in the Air Force, Thom continued to ask about his military experience and the answers began to flow very easily from Ole. Grant thought it was odd that day; his father spoke so freely. Gladys had told Grant several times not to even ask his father about the war because of the terrible thing that had happened – and because just the talk of it bothered Ole. But Thom Hutchinson had such a comfortable manner about his questions that Ole began to ramble in a way Grant had never heard from his father.

"I was a side gunner in a B-25 bomber," Ole said with no emotion. "Stationed on Tinion for a while – you know, that's where the plane that dropped the bomb took off from."

Thom asked several questions about Ole's training and about the South Pacific. Then he asked Ole, "Ever get in a scrape?"

"Yeah, I got to fire my gun a couple times. I don't think I hit anything."

"So where were you when the war ended?" Thom asked.

"In a Japanese prison in Tokyo," Ole said flatly. Grant wondered if he should interrupt and try to rescue his dad from this conversation.

"No shit. What happened?" Thom was leaning toward Ole now. Thom Hutchinson had a strong sense of history, and everyone could hear the growing interest in his voice.

Ole Thorson began his story calmly. "We were bombing Tokyo at night, and our plane got picked up by a searchlight. The Japs had their anti-aircraft guns working along with their search lights, so when that beam of light locked onto you, you were in trouble. Well, the plane just lit up like midday, and we knew we had a problem. We started to take some hits. Shrapnel was ripping through the skin on both sides of the plane, and pretty soon the gunner on the other side got hit real bad." Ole paused. "He laid there in my arms and bled to death … asked me to help him … then called to his mother." Ole paused again and looked down. He was working hard to stuff the emotion that was swelling. His lower lip was trembling and he took a deep breath. "Next thing I knew, we were on fire and the captain told us we were going down, but not until we'd dropped our payload."

"Were you afraid?" Thom asked with a strange smile.

"Hell yes. My friend was dead and our plane full of bombs was on fire. We were going to jump out into icy darkness if we survived the next half-hour. We knew that if civilians captured us, they'd kill us. I was just a dumb hick and I was scared shitless." Ole smiled as if to ask Thom how he could ask such a stupid question.

"So what happened?" Thom returned an apologetic smile.

"I jumped ... landed in a rice paddy and pulled my chute up over me to stay warm. Next morning, I heard someone coming and stretched my neck to see who it was. Thank goodness it was the soldiers. They saw me and captured me. They had to turn their bayonets on the locals just to protect me. I found out later that two other crew members were beheaded by these people." His lip was steady now and his eyes were clear. "The soldiers took those of us who survived to a prison and starved us and tortured us until the war ended about six weeks later."

"Wow," Thom whispered. Grant knew the story. He'd just never heard his father tell it before.

"When I got to that prison that's when I knew I was gonna survive! For some odd reason, I just knew that no matter what they did to me I was gonna make it home ... and see my family." Ole's face tightened in defiance while he hosted the memories for a moment longer. "You can survive anything when you make up your mind, I guess." He paused, and as if he were looking through a tunnel he then finished his story. "It always bothered me though ... that I survived and my friends didn't ... didn't seem fair." All the emotion was gone when he looked up and shrugged.

The contrast between the survivor in the story and the withered little man sitting in front of him now was hard for Grant to understand. He let his breath out slowly and watched his father adjust himself into his chair.

Ole rested for a few minutes, then signaled Grant by raising his hand as if it were holding a cup. He was thirsty. Grant got him a glass with some ice and water, but Gladys stopped him. It was becoming too difficult for Ole to swallow, and he'd begun choking from time to time. She explained that the staff at the nursing home had provided some white powder, a thickening agent, to mix with his water so that the water would have the consistency of gravy and be easier to swallow. Ole was then supposed to drink the thick water through a straw. Grant paused and turned toward Ole as if to ask him if it were true. There was a rare flutter of emotion on Ole's face when he answered Grant's questioning eyes. Ole said nothing though; he only nodded.

Grant spooned some of the white powder into the water and watched it thicken into something like clear motor oil. He put a straw in the glass and held it up to Big Ole's lips. When Ole drew the solution into his mouth, he made a sour face, then looked into Grant's eyes again.

Grant wanted to do the right thing. He knew the doctors and staff at the nursing home were trying to help his dad, but he also knew that this was one of those times when he had to speak up.

"Tastes like shit, doesn't it, Dad?"

Ole nodded.

"Dad?" Grant took Ole's hand in his and spoke very softly and deliberately. "Life needs to be sweeter than this! Are you willing to take the chance that a swallow of cool water won't kill you, even if you choke a little bit? Does it seem to you that if you wind up with pneumonia and die from choking on a damn drink of water that it was just meant to be that way?"

Ole nodded "yes." Grant had hoped to see him smile, but there was no smile.

"OK, then we're gonna toss this shit and enjoy a cool drink."

"I'd like a Coke!" whispered Ole. Now Grant could see some strength in his father's face.

"Well, all right, now you're talking!" Grant exclaimed. He was thrilled. A little thing like going down the hall in a wheelchair for a Coke had the feel of a party after the past few weeks' experiences. Ole hadn't asked for a soda since he'd been in the home. "Hang on, Dad, we'll walk down to the pop machine and we'll all have one."

As he pushed his dad's wheelchair down the long hallway, his mother walked alongside him and put her hand on Grant's arm. When he looked down at her she nodded approvingly. He knew that in mentioning his father's death he'd taken a chance. But in offering to help his father defy death in this small way, he'd let everyone face it and maybe release some of the fear of it all.

While they sat in the lobby and sipped at their Cokes, Grant briefly began to feel good about the way the day was going, and he tried to tell Ole about the opening weekend at Spider Lake. But Ole just didn't respond. In a short time, Ole lost interest in his Coke and asked to return to his room for a nap. In spite of the sudden onset of the fatigue, Grant felt Ole had been strengthened by their conversation about death.

Several other times during the day, Grant began to share the details of his opening weekend with his dad. He wanted to tell Ole about the lake and the ducks; he thought his father would want to know. But Ole's face was just so blank, and he didn't ask any questions. In the past, his father had always been interested in Grant's stories after he'd been hunting or fishing. Now, there was only what seemed like apathy. Grant simply couldn't tell if his dad had lost interest in that part of his life because he was so involved with the simple chores of his own existence, or if the Parkinson's disease had just closed the window into Ole's heart.

Grant stopped trying to tell the stories he'd wanted to share. He found himself just watching his dad struggle through his own day. When he looked at his dad again, he saw a tired, sick old man — and it hurt him. His father was beginning to lose hope.

Somewhere, just beyond the reality of the dying old man who sat before him, Grant could see the man that used to be. For

Grant, his father remained fixed in time, and he was thankful for that. The image of Ole Thorson standing with a shotgun under his arm during an autumn sunrise was so vivid that Grant felt he could touch it. Square shoulders and black hair, tan canvas pants, jacket and hat with a red plaid shirt ... Big Ole's dark eyes sparkled when he spoke, and Grant could see his hero like this even now, despite all the changes old age had made.

There were several strolls in the wheelchair, what seemed like dozens of trips to the bathroom, two short naps, and a couple of small meals during Ole's day. By the time Grant tucked his father in bed that night, he felt exhausted. He kissed his father goodnight and said, "I love you, Dad, I'll see you next Friday." Ole squeezed Grant's hand and closed his eyes.

The drive to Fargo seemed to take forever. Grant was tired and depressed after the day with his parents. There had been no real physical labor, nothing to tire him out, but he felt nearly exhausted just the same. Nonetheless, he was glad he'd been there once again. He was also uneasy about the weekend. He just didn't know what to expect with Anne. Neither did he know what to expect during a visit to the White House — this was all pretty odd.

Grant sensed that he'd been waiting for something, anything, to come along and return his life to normal again. He knew now that no event or person was going to come along and undo the sorrow that life had brought his way recently, but his life experience had taught him to expect only good times and good fortune. His father and nine uncles had survived combat in World War II. His immediate family had sailed through the Vietnam years without incident. There had never been any real unhappiness, sickness, or death in his family until recently. So how could he, he thought, have anticipated the events of the past year? He'd just understood that his family would always surround him and his work would be fulfilling. Now his wife was dead, his daughter had gone away, his father was dying, and he was unhappy with work and lonely much of the time. He'd been thinking only of these dark, unhappy things as he parked his car and carried his baggage into the Fargo airport. He felt hurried, confused, and cold as he approached the entrance to the terminal.

The night was chilly. Grant noticed people and cars moving all around him as he walked along the sidewalk, but nothing was for him. All the world seemed to exist apart from him. Then, suddenly, his spirits lifted smoothly as though a switch had been thrown inside of him. Anne was waiting for him by the ticket counter. He saw her through the large windows before he entered the lobby and he couldn't help but smile. His pace quickened some. She was still a very attractive woman, but she looked even prettier than he'd expected tonight. She wore khaki slacks and a light green sweater under a leather coat. Her long, dark hair caught his eye the way it always used to, only now there were a few gray strands in it. Her eyes were large and brown and the skin on her face was still soft and dark. It made him feel very good to think that the pretty woman by the counter was waiting for him. Now there was something familiar – something warm and good – waiting for him.

When she smiled, her whole face lit up. Only the small crow's feet at the corners of her eyes gave a hint of her age. After he'd checked his bag and received his boarding pass, Grant crossed through the metal detector and walked directly toward Anne as though he couldn't stop. He did something crazy. He took her hands in his and kissed her on the lips. It was a full but soft kiss, and he held it for several seconds. When he stepped back he regretted it immediately, and he knew Anne could see that he was surprised and embarrassed by his own actions. It was an impulsive thing, the kind of thing he never did. He did it without thinking, and it surprised both of them. She'd still been smiling at him, waiting for something less of a greeting when he kissed her. He couldn't believe he'd done such a thing. It was an uncommon moment of spontaneity, and he was instantly afraid of what she might be thinking. Maybe she'd be disgusted and run for home. Maybe she'd take it as an understanding on his part that there was something more going on than a first date. In any case, he was losing control of the situation because of his own foolish behavior. 'Shit! Why did I do that?' he thought. "Hi!" was all he could say at first. He smiled a sheepish smile and tried to hide his loss of composure. "Been waiting long?"

"Just a few minutes." She smiled an odd smile.

They both tried to act as though they didn't feel something warm and good in the kiss. But just beneath the composed exterior they tried to show each other, they were excited now by what they felt.

But this was suddenly unfamiliar territory for both of them. Neither one of them had done any dating since they'd lost their spouses. Anne had thought about getting out into the world again, and she had given herself permission to meet other people and entertain ideas about romantic involvement. Grant, however, hadn't even thought about dating yet. Intellectually, perhaps, both of them were ready to try this, but neither of them really knew how to deal with the warm feeling in the middle of their chest that had been sparked by a single kiss.

Grant made a point to not let go of Anne's hand as they turned and walked toward their gate. He could feel her small hand returning his firm grip. Anne ended a clumsy silence with "How's your Dad?"

"Good," Grant answered immediately. His father wasn't good – he was terrible – but "good" had just jumped from Grant's mouth. After he'd had a few seconds to think, he realized he'd blurted it out because his thoughts had been only of the wonderful feeling of Anne's hand in his.

"Well, actually, he's not good, but he's resting comfortably some of the time." It was a clumsy recovery, but it was good enough for

Anne. She'd only asked the question in order to stem the uneasiness. Suddenly now, she wasn't concerned about much else besides the feeling of his hand in hers. They were able to board their plane immediately, and they went directly to their seats, still holding hands.

They sat silently for several seconds, her thumb gently stroking the back of his hand. She turned her face close to his and said, "That was nice." She had given her approval of the kiss in a voice that was warm and smooth as silk.

He drew in a deep breath and let it out slowly. He looked into her eyes, raised his eyebrows, and nodded his head slowly as if to say, "Me too."

The feeling of fatigue that had weighed on Grant since he'd said goodbye to his mother several hours earlier had been rolled away by a wave of excitement. He didn't know where this moment would lead, but he was aware that he felt something he hadn't felt for a long time. There was a beautiful woman sitting with him, and everything she told him with her dark eyes and soft hands let him know that she was glad to be with him like this. He knew he was feeling the same thrill that young people feel when they start to fall in love for the first time. He remembered the feeling because he'd felt it with the same girl thirty years earlier.

He wanted to speak. He wanted to say something profound. There was so much history between them, and much of it was painful or clumsy. It seemed to him that something needed to be said that would establish a new beginning for them. There was indeed something special between them that stretched all the way back to childhood. They'd been classmates in grade school, then high school sweethearts. They'd discovered sex together in college and shared all the pleasures of young lovers. They'd planned to marry and live happily ever after.

And now life had brought them back around to this moment. Grant had truly been in love with Kate all the years they were mar-

ried. He didn't feel that he'd suppressed any latent feelings for
Anne, although he'd revered her in the same quiet way that many
happily married men care for an old love. If he'd have been married to Kate for fifty more years, he'd still have had a special secret
place in his heart for his first love. He'd reasoned that everyone
savored young love in such a way. But Anne wasn't quite sure what
she'd done. She'd been forced to stop feeling anything for Grant
because he'd taken his love away from her. She didn't think she'd
ever be able to stop loving him. She'd just been forced to build an
emotional wall around that love in order to have a relatively happy
life with someone else. When she and Grant had begun visiting at
length and he'd asked her to come to Washington, she felt that wall
in her heart begin to crumble. And when he held her hand and
kissed her; the wall seemed to fall down a little more. She was a little confused, but she liked what she felt right now.

For one of the very few times in his adult life, Grant could not
find the words to establish control of the situation. He felt his
heart beating like a hammer. He took another deep breath and
leaned toward Anne. They both knew there were no words for this
situation. They kissed again and then simply looked at each other
while they held hands. When the stewardess passed them with
refreshments, they were sitting silently holding hands, wondering
what to say.

"Want a drink?" Grant finally spoke.

"Definitely!" Anne smiled.

Grant poured the contents of a tiny brandy bottle into a glass
for Anne, and then did the same for himself. He raised his glass
and nodded to her as he sipped at the brandy. Then he turned
toward her and leaned closer. "OK, we need to back up a little bit
here … how was your day?" he said with a smile designed to
acknowledge the unusual situation they found themselves in.

"It was a good day." Anne started out with a smile, as well, and
went on from there. They were able to begin a normal conversa-

tion, and they both seemed to understand that for now they needed to just reacquaint themselves through small talk. They held hands all the way to Minneapolis, neither of them wanting to let go of the feeling.

Will and June Campbell were supposed to meet them at the bar in the hotel where they were all staying at 12:30 a.m. for a nightcap. By the time Anne and Grant hurried through the small, dark door, it was a quarter to one and Will and June were waiting for them. They both felt a little odd entering the bar and joining friends as a couple. Silently, each of them wondered if Will and June could tell that something had happened between them. They ordered another brandy, and the two couples sat and chatted in the bar until closing time at 1:30 a.m. Will and Grant decided to meet for coffee at 8:00 a.m., but the women wanted to sleep in before doing some last-minute shopping, since their plane for Washington didn't leave until 1:00 p.m.

Grant held Anne's hand as they walked toward her room. There was nothing awkward in this moment for him; he had no intention of going into her room. When they stood by her door, he bent down and kissed her again. Then he put his arms around her and they just held each other for a few minutes. He whispered, "I'm glad we're here, like this."

"Me too."

They said goodnight, kissed again, and she went into her room and locked the door behind her. Grant went to the next room and opened the door. Once he was inside, he felt alone. He hadn't felt like this for a while, and it surprised him. He had grown accustomed to feeling alone — not that he liked it, but he'd just grown used to it or maybe grown stronger because of it. But now, he knew the solution to this lonely feeling was only a few feet away, and it felt strange to think that he could actually do something to make the loneliness go away. He sat on the bed and rubbed his face. He was tired but he didn't think he could sleep — there were so many thoughts whirring though his brain. What was Anne thinking? He didn't even have a very good handle on his own thoughts — how could he even guess what was going though her mind?

He wondered what Kate would think if she could see him now. He wondered if she could see him now. Then he told himself not to think like that anymore. He tried to imagine what Anne could feel toward him. After all, he'd hurt her terribly all those years ago.

He stared straight ahead and remembered how it had been when he'd met Kate and left Anne. For some reason Grant always had trouble explaining to others or understanding it himself. He'd known almost instantly when he met Kate that she would be his wife. Grant's future with Anne was destroyed before Anne ever knew there was a problem between them. Kate had been on the faculty at the dental school when Grant was a student. She taught a course in biomaterials in the dental hygiene department. Although he never had her for a teacher, he'd noticed her in the halls many times. She was difficult not to notice. She was 5-feet-11, and when she spoke it looked like she was always just about to break into laughter. Grant thought she seemed to give off an aura when she spoke. Grant found himself staring at her from across the lunchroom early in his freshman year. She was just another pretty girl until she started talking. The university hospital, the medical school, and the dental school were all filled with pretty young women. But when Kate began to speak, her eyes caressed whoever she was talking to. Her mouth curled into a knowing smile, as if she had some special thing in common with the person she was with. Grant could not look away from her. She'd been telling a story to Dr. Joe Ruminsky and Dr. Irvin Schaffer when he first noticed her. Ruminsky was the head of the operative dentistry department and Schaffer was the dean of the dental school. Both men had God-like status with the students. Grant remembered the look on both men's faces as they waited for her to finish her story.

She had their total attention. Both of them leaned forward and smiled with open mouths as they waited for the punch line. Judging from their reaction, it must have been a dirty story – and a pretty good one because both of them laughed long and loud. They also both touched Kate's arm when they said goodbye. She'd charmed two men that were forty years older than her ... and she was good at it.

Grant couldn't stop staring at her. There was no way she'd notice him from across the room anyway. And there was no way some guy like him had a chance in hell with a woman like that. The forty-, fifty-, sixty-year-old men with status and money were always talking to her, telling stories with her. He just kept staring.

And then she moved. She walked out into the hallway. Her head bobbed a little, and she swung her left leg awkwardly and bounced on her right foot so she could swing her left leg again. The steel brace was showing below her pant leg now. She smiled at someone else that Grant couldn't see. It was the huge, radiant smile he'd noticed all along.

Initially, Grant thought it was strange that with all the male students around, Kate was not attached. Now he knew why. Men saw her limp and discounted her immediately. Her imperfection – some would call it a handicap – made her incomplete and thus undesirable to most men. But Grant found himself more attracted to her each time he saw her. He watched her face as she talked with other men. She made them laugh, and she made them like her. They always left her smiling. They left with another woman or they went back to their job, but they always left her as though she was not to be thought of as a real woman, a girlfriend. He wondered if she was aware of what men thought, if she understood why men didn't pursue her like they otherwise would.

For weeks Grant worked to summon the courage to position himself in her path as she walked through the cafeteria. Finally one day, he forced himself to speak to her as if he'd accidentally blocked her path. She smiled the same smile at him that he'd seen her give to the others. He loved the way her words and her eyes pulled at him. She didn't know until months later that he'd stepped in front of her that day on purpose.

He found himself looking for her every day, hoping for a chance to step in front of her again so she might smile at him. Even though he could see that other men were overlooking a special beauty, he felt there was little chance she'd go out with him. She simply knew too many other men around the university who were smarter, richer — better than him.

She did decide to see Grant Thorson, though, when he asked her to go to a baseball game. After several short conversations around the vending machines and in the hallways at the dental school, Grant was drawn to her, not just because of her beauty but also because of her enthusiasm for everything she spoke about. He could feel her joy, or disdain for things, as she spoke. From then on, he simply wanted to take her someplace with a comfortable atmosphere and talk to her at length. She said later that she'd agreed to go out with him because he was so polite when he asked her. That one ball game spelled the end of his relationship with Anne. Although there had been no sexual contact between Grant and Kate, he apologized to Anne as though he'd been an unfaithful husband. They'd both cried bitter tears as they'd said goodbye at Anne's apartment door all those years before.

Seven years passed before Grant saw Anne again. He didn't think of her much during those years. But when he did, he felt no longing for her — only remorse at the way things had ended between them. Then Anne's husband, Aaron, had accepted the head football and basketball coaching position at Walker High School. Anne just walked into Grant's office and reintroduced herself. She simply wanted to be the one to tell him that she and her family had moved to his community. It was an awkward conversation, as were many of their encounters over the first year or two.

But gradually they just became two people who lived in the same small town and greeted each other as friends.

Grant had always thought that Anne had married "down" – that she'd let someone who was not as smart as she, and maybe just plain not worthy of her, choose her, and then she'd simply let marriage and the rest of her life happen. Grant thought Aaron was a nice enough guy, but he viewed Aaron as not very bright and a pretty average teacher and coach. Anne had always appeared to be fairly happy, but then he'd basically avoided her for most of the past twenty years. Kate knew all about Anne and never expressed any jealousy. She asked Grant a few pretty personal questions after Anne and Aaron moved to Walker, but Grant had answered honestly and she'd been OK with everything she knew. Kate had never been friends with Anne, but she liked Anne and commented many times that she thought Anne was pretty.

Grant's feet were on the floor and his hands were folded behind his head as he lay on his bed and stared at the ceiling. The relationship he'd had with Anne for the last twenty years had just changed incredibly. He wondered if, after all that had come between them, they might wind up together again.

Anne stood in front of the bathroom mirror and took off her makeup. She, too, was struggling, trying to find her true feelings. At one time, she'd felt Grant Thorson was the most handsome, special man in the world. But after he'd broken up with her, she'd put him aside and gone on with her life, hadn't she? She'd tried to hate him for a while, but she couldn't do it. She'd married a nice man and had two fine daughters. She'd always remembered that her mother had cautioned her not to marry "on the rebound," and she'd secretly wondered all her life if that had, in fact, been what she'd done.

No matter how she thought about it all, she knew one thing: She now felt something stirring deep inside of her that she thought she'd put away forever many years ago.

chapter SIX

Once again the next afternoon, as the plane roared down the runway, Grant took Anne's hand in his and said nothing. Just across the aisle, Will and June both noticed the small display of affection. June didn't speak when she turned to Will, but her eyes asked the question, "Did you see that?" Will's only response was to raise his eyebrows and smile a sinister smile. Grant had given Will no indication that he had any new romantic feelings for Anne while the two men had been chatting over coffee earlier in the morning. During the past few weeks, Grant had admitted to Will from time to time that he might like to call Anne and try to restore their old friendship because they'd shared so much when they were younger. Will had been encouraging Grant to call Anne for some time. Now he sensed that something was actually happening between them. June had been straining at her seatbelt and looking for an excuse to lean forward and crane her neck across the aisle for a few minutes. She was watching Anne's thumb as she softly stroked the back of Grant's hand. When June turned to Will, smiled, and nodded confidently, he knew for sure that something was happening between Grant and Anne … June was never wrong about this sort of thing.

Both couples visited quietly with each other during the flight, but there was no conversation across the aisle. Grant accurately sensed that Will and June continued to steal a glance at him and Anne whenever they could. He smiled at the fact that Will now knew that he'd been holding something back — he knew Will would want "details."

It was nearly 5:00 p.m. by the time they were able to check into their rooms, and there was a telephone message waiting for them when they opened the door to Will and June's suite. Jessica Wickham's voice was crisp and businesslike as she gave a number for them to call and let her know when they were in town. Then she told them there would be a car sent to pick them up around 7:30 p.m., if that was all right with them. Will called the number that had been given and made final arrangements for their car and driver. He hung up the phone with a shrug of his shoulders and said, "OK, what do we do now?"

"I'm going to unpack and start getting ready," came June's immediate response.

"Me too," Anne said.

Grant volunteered to walk Anne to her room, and as they turned to go Will spoke up. "I'll be over to your room in a second, Grant, and we'll have a drink — won't take us two hours to get ready!"

"No! You'll stay right here and help me get ready!" June said with that tone of voice that wives and mothers take when they feel their husbands or children are about to say or do something inappropriate. Will protested mildly but then gave up. He knew from years of experience when to do as he was told. Anne and Grant were in the hallway, just leaving Will and June's room, when Will caught Grant's eye, smiled a great smile, and called back across the room to June as she opened a suitcase on one of the beds. Will was smiling a wicked smile at Grant, but he was still talking to June when he said, "Say, honey?" His tone was that of a beggar. "We do have plenty of time before we have to go. What do you think?"

"IN YOUR DREAMS!!" June shouted, still looking through her suitcase.

Will kept a silent, devilish smile. He waved and raised his eyebrows several times as he closed the door.

As Anne and Grant left Will and June's room, Grant couldn't help but recall the way he'd felt toward June when they'd first met. He resented her immensely because he thought she was simply stealing his best friend. He resented the hold June had on Will. She could make him give up fishing trips or hunting trips that he'd planned for weeks. Grant felt that June did that sort of thing just to exercise her power over Will. He used to mutter accusations about "getting her hooks in" behind her back. After a while, Grant realized that June, in turn, resented the hold he had over Will. She felt Grant could make Will turn away from plans she'd made for herself and Will. She felt Grant was just a bad influence on Will — one of those "buddies" that make otherwise fine men behave like pigs. Eventually, June and Grant each decided that the other was probably here to stay, and they developed sort of a grudging tolerance for each other. Over the last ten years, that tolerance had developed into friendship. Neither of them had ever verbalized the hard feelings from the early days, but each knew the other had harbored them.

June was still pretty and petite, with green eyes and blonde hair. She'd been Will's girlfriend all through high school and college. Grant had always thought it was odd that their relationship had survived in spite of their separation while Will was at Harvard. Perhaps the reason Grant had let go of his negative feelings for June was that he could see that Will truly loved her. The first time he heard Will speak of her, he noticed the great respect Will had for her. Will just never intended to be with anyone else for his whole life. Grant thought that if Will cared for her that much, then he'd try to like her, too. As he matured, Grant began to reason that he'd probably disliked June in the beginning because he was jealous of her. Those childish feelings had all gone away long ago, and Grant was now a little embarrassed that he'd ever felt that way.

When he tried on his tuxedo, he was relieved to find that Will had picked out the right size. He'd always struggled to trust others when it came to handling the details. He'd been dressed for half an hour and he was sitting in an overstuffed chair watching football highlights on TV when the phone rang. "I'm ready," was all Anne said.

"I'll be right there," he said as he stood up and looked at his watch. It was 7:10. Anne swung the door open and stood there smiling shyly. She was stunning, and he was taken aback. Her long black hair hung down over her exposed shoulders and back. She wore an elegant black evening dress that gave perfect lines to her sexy figure. A pearl necklace lay around her neck, and small pearl earrings hung from her ears and swung gently when she moved. Her large brown eyes were warm and inviting when she smiled.

"Whoa! You look really nice!" Grant gasped.

She reached one hand toward him and took his hand. She pulled him forward and raised herself on her tiptoes to kiss him. "So do you," she said softly after a gentle kiss. He thought she smelled wonderful, too. Each of them felt the same familiar little warm rush inside. They were both aware of this same thrilling sense of anticipation that they'd felt all those years ago when he'd come to pick her up for a date. She held his hand tightly, and he returned the soft pressure. Each of them wanted to let the other know that they intended to hold on.

From Will and June's room, all four of them walked to the lobby to wait for their ride. A huge black limousine pulled up under the extended roof of the hotel while Will and June, and Grant and Anne looked out through the glass doors and waited. A serious-looking young man got out of the car and approached Will.

"Dr. Campbell?"

"Yes," Will answered.

"I'm agent Mike O'Neil, and I'm here to escort your party to the White House," the young man said politely. There were brief introductions. Then Mike O'Neil opened the doors of the limo for them. As they were driving down Pennsylvania Avenue, Anne reached for Grant's hand and he could feel her excitement.

"Do you talk to the President very often?" Anne threw the question out for either one of the men to answer.

"I've written to him several times and he's called me twice," Will responded. "He called about a month after he took office and then about six months ago. Both times I think he just wanted to hear a friendly voice."

"About the same for me," Grant added. "I send a card every now and then and he called me when … when Kate died." Grant's tone trailed off a little; he hadn't even realized where his answer was taking him. After a short pause, Grant turned to Will and smoothly left the subject of Kate behind. His voice rose somewhat when he said, "You know, I didn't really like Thom when we first met. He struck me as an arrogant rich kid. I was certain he'd never want to be around someone as poor as me and that he looked down on me. I think he just tolerated me because I was your friend." Grant shrugged.

"Yeah, that would be about right," Will said. "Thom did a lot of growing up after college. But he's told me many times over the years how much he admires you." Will stopped and looked out the limousine window. "Ever wonder what must happen to a man's personal life when he has some extraordinary thing happen to him – like becoming the President? Do you suppose he can be a great man and still have a private life … friends like us?" Will looked around as if waiting for an answer.

"Got to," Grant replied. "Greatness comes from our private lives."

When the limo pulled up to the White House gates, Agent O'Neil rolled his window down and a uniformed guard bent over and looked inside. He obviously knew the Secret Service agent driving the car, and he waved the limo through without comment. The White House grounds were spectacular as the October full moon rose over the Washington skyline. The crisp air of early evening, the moon, and the way the grounds were lit all combined to create a surreal atmosphere.

The young agent stopped the car beside a small stairway and let everyone out. He turned to Will and said, "Please follow me, Dr. Campbell." Everyone followed him into the White House through a small door, down a short hallway, and into a small room where two men wearing black suits were sitting in folding chairs. Both men stood up and nodded a greeting to them. One of the men said, "He's in the Lincoln sitting room" as he turned to look at Mike O'Neil.

"Are you still with me?" O'Neil's voice was pleasant and reassuring but very businesslike as he led them down a corridor that struck them all as opulent. They got on an elevator, and when the doors opened they were led down another extraordinary hallway. In spite of the beauty and rare quality of all the furnishings, there was a sense that someone lived here. Agent O'Neil rounded a corner and stopped. "Mr. President, your friends are here," he said as he stepped back.

Thomas Hutchinson was standing in the middle of a small study with leather chairs and fine fixtures all around him. He'd been waiting for them. "Welcome to the White House!" he said as he stepped toward them. Will extended his hand first but the President walked past it and embraced him firmly. "Great to see you, Will," the President said with some emotion. He then took June in his arms the same way and told her she looked beautiful. Then he turned to Grant and once again held his old friend in a warm embrace. "Thanks for coming," he said softly. Again, there was emotion in his voice. Finally he turned to Anne. He extended his hand and said, "Thomas Hutchinson."

Anne took his hand and blushed noticeably. "Anne Robertson" was all she said.

"You look splendid, Anne. I hope you have a nice time this evening in spite of your date's tendency to appease his antagonists." The sarcasm in his comment was obvious to everyone. Thomas Hutchinson had always admired Grant's willingness to speak up and challenge statements he thought were incorrect, or that were made by someone on the other side of an issue and were spoken as though every right-thinking individual would just accept them as fact. He liked that quality in Grant, but he knew it sometimes made Grant appear obstinate and impossible to get along with. "He tends to candy coat things — never says what he really means," the President said with a sly smile.

The President stepped back and asked if they would like to have a drink and visit briefly before they went downstairs and joined the party. Shortly, a young woman brought a drink for each of them, and as Will held his glass of scotch he raised it in a salutary gesture toward his old friend.

Then Will spoke a line of dialogue from *Jeremiah Johnson*. Thom tilted his head and repeated the appropriate reply, directly from the movie. In an instant, all three men were caught up in the old ritual: A quote from *Jeremiah Johnson* was a challenge — it had to be followed up with the next line from the movie. For just a moment, all of them wore the look of happy children playing a child's game.

Eventually, Thom Hutchinson turned very slowly with a huge grin, only raising his eyebrows when he caught June's eye. He enjoyed this repartee just like Will and Grant and he remembered all the lines from years of repetition. These lines, this game, had a special meaning for Thom Hutchinson, and that meaning was not lost on these men. He had come so far, and it hadn't always been easy. When John Thorpe died, it had been impressed upon Thom that he should appoint another liberal democrat to restore balance. He'd been pressured into choosing Connecticut congressman

Daniel Garski. Garski was young and handsome and popular with the party, but Thom didn't like him. In addition, party hardliners were leaning on Thom to cut military spending and champion a national health care bill. He was in favor of neither, and the stress of conflict was weighing on him. His physical appearance had even changed with the pressure of the Presidency; his face seemed to have aged ten years in the last two.

It seemed to Grant that fortune, or destiny, had carried Thom along to this point. He thought of Kate quoting from Shakespeare … of the tide that men ride or don't ride through life.

Grant held his drink in one hand and leaned forward slightly for emphasis. "Thank you for the nice note to my dad, Thom. It was a real treasure for my folks."

"I always liked your dad. He exuded strength. He looked like Vince Lombardi with a cowboy hat. Sometimes, when he looked at me and smiled, I just couldn't read his face. It seemed like he was either going to hug me or punch me in the nose. But I could see that whichever one of those two things he did, he'd know he was right." The President was smiling.

June Campbell quickly added, "Like father like son I guess, huh?" and they all had a laugh at Grant's expense. But strangely, Grant felt that June had just paid him a fine compliment.

They visited for a few more minutes, mostly about old times and old friends. President Hutchinson was very gracious with Anne and asked several questions of her regarding her life story, past and present. Grant supposed that Thom Hutchinson already knew the answers to the questions he was asking because the Secret Service would probably have provided him access to a personal history for any guest such as Anne.

While they were speaking, Ellen Hutchinson entered the room and all the greetings were repeated. Will, June, and Grant did not know Ellen as an intimate friend, the way they knew Thom. Ellen and Thom had met while he was in law school, and as a result she'd only been able to get to know Will and Grant on their occasional weekend vacations through the years.

After several minutes of pleasant conversation in the study, a serious-looking man in a black suit came and whispered something to Thom Hutchinson. Thom raised his hands and spoke up. "Ellen and I have some more 'mingling' to do now. I'll definitely see you all later. I've arranged for one of my staff to help you find your way around tonight. His name is Martin Walters and he'll be here in a minute ... no, he's here now. We'll see you again later." The President and First Lady disappeared around a corner as a small man with thinning, sandy-colored hair entered the room.

Martin Walters introduced himself to everyone and then led them downstairs to the party. As he walked, he explained that this party was one of several each year to which the President invited a few senators and congresspeople, some people of influence and money, and some of the media. Then he'd let his staff complete the guest list. The President knew very well that business and political games would be played tonight at this party. Martin said the President had specially requested to have Will and Grant there ... just because he wanted to see his old friends.

There was a string quartet playing on one end of the East Room. As they entered the room, they all stopped and stared. There was a large crowd of attractive, well-dressed people filling the spectacular and historic East Room of the White House, and Will, June, Grant, and Anne were now part of it all. They'd seen this only on the TV news or in the movies. Several large tables with food lined one corner of the room, and Grant guessed there were about three hundred people present. None of them had ever seen such splendor. Martin was amused at the way they'd all stopped in their tracks in order to take in the sight. Will leaned over and said. "Martin, we're all just thinking about how much this reminds us of the Ducks Unlimited banquet at the Bemidji American Legion Hall, that's all." Martin smiled and began to point out famous or influential people they might know. From time to time, Grant leaned close to Anne to say something into her ear. Each time he was close to her he felt the small stirring inside of him again. He loved the way her hair tickled his lips when he put his mouth close to her ear. He breathed deeply to draw in the smell of her perfume. This evening, this party, would probably be the social event of his life, but now Grant was thinking of this evening as a first date with Anne more than a special visit with the President of the United States.

Eventually, Martin left them and explained that he'd be right back. Will turned to Grant and said, "So, whadaya think? Are we missin' a good shoot on Spider Lake this weekend?"

"Nah! The second weekend is usually kinda slow. Hutch timed this little get-together pretty well. But you know, I was thinking — what if we were all set to head to D.C. and the bluebills started pilin' in to Spider Lake? Would you give up a sure thing bluebill shoot with wet snow and winter winds just to come here for some lame thing like this?" Grant smiled sarcastically and looked around himself in all directions.

"No way in hell!" Will's eyebrows were furrowed, and he was fighting back a smile. "My family is with me on that one, too! Honey, if you had the choice, you'd way rather stay home and clean ducks than come to some silly thing like this, wouldn't you?"

June just turned away from him.

"See? She's speechless! She's there!" Will was nodding and pointing at his wife. All four of them knew that Will and Grant actually might choose bluebills over the President.

Grant was smiling when he looked away from Will and glanced out over the crowded room. But his smile melted quickly when he saw who Martin Walters was bringing to introduce to them.

"Hey, what's the matter, pard? You look like you just stepped in something," Will said.

"I'm about to." Grant gestured toward Martin Walters.

Senator Myron Bently had been a college professor at the University of Minnesota before running for the state legislature. While in the legislature, he'd successfully sponsored health care legislation that he claimed made Minnesota a leader in health care reform. Health care providers had lobbied vigorously in opposition, but they'd lost. Now, the professional journals nationwide all joked about the restrictive environment for health care professionals in Minnesota and warned young doctors and dentists not to consider practicing there. Doctors, hospitals, pharmacies, dentists – all providers – felt that their civil rights had been violated by the legislation. Myron Bently had rallied support for the idea by arguing that the way to hold down health care costs is to punish the health care providers. Bently was now a United States senator. Grant's smile was long gone when Martin returned.

Martin Walters, however, was smiling as he began introducing Myron Bently.

"Senator Bently, I'd like to introduce you to several of your constituents. This is Will and June Campbell from Duluth, and Grant Thorson and Anne Robertson from Walker. This is Senator Myron Bently."

Bently shook hands with Will and June first, then Anne, then Grant. Grant actually considered crushing the little man's right hand briefly, then thought better of it. Bently talked continuously and waved his hands as he spoke. Grant found it amazing that Senator Bently never asked any of them about themselves but rather spoke of himself and his "vision."

Finally – mercifully, Grant thought – Senator Bently moved along to enlighten others in his obnoxious way. Grant leaned over and spoke into Martin's ear so no one else could hear: "It was all I could do to keep from stuffing that little prick into a garbage can!"

"He's a United States senator!" Martin replied with indignation.

"That guy is bad for America."

"In your opinion!" Martin added.

Grant's eyes narrowed, his brow tightened, and he turned toward Martin with a look that was as cold as death. His voice was even and low. "You're goddamn right it's my opinion, and I'll share it with any smart ass who thinks he has the right to lecture me about the 'way it is,' and I'll change it if someone can give me a good reason to, but I won't listen to bullshit and then nod my head and smile about it."

"You just did!"

"I didn't come here to embarrass the President!" Grant snapped.

Martin smiled through pursed lips as Grant looked away.

For the next two hours, things went much more smoothly. Martin introduced them all to a few of the President's staff. Will wandered off and struck up a conversation with a couple of Canadian businessmen, who, as it turned out, had hunted ducks at some of the same places as Will and Grant. June and Anne took the time to talk and get to know each other better while the men told hunting stories and laughed with the Canadians.

The ornate room had a warm, casual feel about it on this night, Grant thought, in spite of the large number of people there. A yellow quality in the lighting seemed to make the atmosphere very personal and close as the evening moved along. Anne and Grant took every opportunity to chat only with each other. They spoke of people they recognized and current events, and the mood was pleasant and comfortable. Each of them talked briefly about their nearly grown-up children. But the conversation never really came around to the life each of them had led since they'd last shared an evening together twenty-some years earlier.

The string quartet began to play a new piece of music while the two of them were chatting. Suddenly, Grant raised his head, reached for Anne's hand, and led her near to the musicians. They stood silently holding hands for several seconds and watching the musicians. Grant leaned close to her and put his lips by her ear.

"Do you know this music?" he asked.

"No."

"It's called "Ashoken Farewell" ... makes me feel something each time I hear it. Do you like it?"

"Yeah, it's OK," Anne said with only a hint of a smile. She didn't think much of it one way or the other. When she looked into Grant's face, she was surprised to see that his eyes were full of tears, though he was trying not to show it. He took his handkerchief from his pocket and wiped his eyes dry. He said nothing but tried to smile. This type of thing happened to Grant from time to time, and he always tried desperately to hide it. He viewed this show of emotion as a weakness, a serious flaw. This was still the same boy she'd known long ago, she thought. She could remember seeing him do the same thing several times while the National Anthem was being played before ball games, and now she also remembered one other event that had remained puzzling for her over the years. Once, when Grant had been coaching Ingrid's fourth-grade softball team, one little girl on the team, who was not particularly athletic, struck out several times consecutively. After her fourth or fifth clumsy strikeout, she began to cry as she walked back to the bench. Grant stopped her, dropped to one knee, and looked directly into her eyes. He said something to make her smile and then let her return to the bench while he went back to coach third base. Only one or two of the mothers who were at the game that day noticed what happened next: Grant stood silently and cried — sobbed — hiding while on the playing field, with his back to the crowd and his own team. The little girl's pain had crushed the big man. Anne saw his behavior as something that made him a good person, but she'd never understood the emotion, the passion Grant had for the small moments.

When the string quartet finished "Ashoken Farewell," Anne and Grant held hands and strolled around the room until they rejoined Will, June and Martin Walters.

Grant noticed a big, handsome man walking toward them. The man had gray hair and appeared to be about sixty. He was talking to a striking blonde woman in a long red dress. The woman's hair was shoulder length, and she, too, was tall but very thin. Grant guessed her to be thirty-five or forty. It appeared to Grant that this gray-haired man was showing off his trophy wife. "Who's that?" Grant asked.

"John Lewis III. Old family friend of the President from Michigan. Republican, too. How about that – family fortune in the auto parts business. I'll introduce you to him. He's coming this way." Martin said.

"Pretty wife!" Grant said.

"That's not his wife – although he's probably trying to get her in the sack. That's Susan Wells. Watch out for her – the bitch is poison." Martin seemed briefly agitated while talking about Susan Wells. "She's something of a rising star. She really isn't a Washington insider yet, but she knows the insiders and the powerful people." His demeanor flip-flopped abruptly when they drew near. "Hello John, Susan. I'd like you to meet someone." He was instantly cheerful and friendly.

After the introductions, it was clear that John Lewis III was drunk. Like Senator Bently, he talked only about himself. Grant looked on with mild contempt while Lewis rambled. He turned his eyes to Susan Wells and immediately had to force himself not to stare. She was not voluptuous or seductive; she was sleek and graceful. She was tall and thin. The word that came to Grant's head was "clean," and he thought that was odd. Susan's lips were thin and her facial features were fine. Grant thought she looked intelligent. He did begin to stare at her and found himself thinking that, strangely enough, she might be a woman who could become sexier by putting glasses on. He was puzzling at his own unusual sense of Susan when she turned her eyes to him. She'd caught him staring, and he confessed with a smile.

Grant moved his eyes to Will while John Lewis continued to talk. His facial expression never changed, but his eyes twinkled subtly when he glanced at Will. Something childish had passed, unspoken, between them. Lewis would not stop talking, and Will's right hand reached toward Grant. Grant smoothly extended the drink he was holding toward his friend. Will took the drink, then sipped from it several times as everyone listened to John Lewis. Grant was sure Susan's eyes had not left him, and he wondered if she'd noticed the glance he'd exchanged with Will. For some reason, Lewis interrupted himself and said, "Whadayou do for a living, Bryant?"

Without hesitation, Will stepped into the conversation. "My friend and I are both waterfowl processing technicians ... but we're here because we're pretty large campaign contributors of the President." His friends had seen this look on Will's face many times before. He was overacting badly and having fun with it. "Last year, each of us gave OVER ONE HUNDRED DOL-LARS to his campaign!" Will raised his eyebrows and nodded once to affirm his claim as he returned the drink to Grant. His face was totally earnest as he nodded again and reassured John Lewis, "It's true!" Grant tried to appear serious, and he nodded in agreement with Will. June and Anne were afraid they'd smile and embarrass someone, so they stared at their drinks.

Lewis had no idea what to say in reply – he just didn't get it – so he started talking about himself again. Martin smiled. Susan Wells was briefly puzzled with the conversation, but when she made eye contact with Grant she could read clearly the satisfaction in his eyes. Grant could tell now that Susan was something of an innocent bystander in this exchange. The dry smile and the way his eyes whispered to her answered all of her questions. Grant just wanted John Lewis III to go away.

A hand reached to Grant's elbow and a Secret Service agent spoke into his ear. The President wanted to have a word with a few old friends in the Green Room, right next to the East Room. The men excused themselves and were led to the Green Room, which was much smaller and furnished more like a den. Several men, all former hunting partners of the President, were gathered there for a drink and a few stories — sort of a boys-only experience. The two Canadians were there, too. The President was already talking with two other old friends whom Will and Grant had never met. As so often happened, they started to talk of the old days back home. Then, as everyone listened, one of the men began to tell of an old dog with special talents, and soon each of them had added some anecdote about an old dog or two. John Lewis began to ramble with a pompous lecture on how to select the best puppy from a litter when the President spoke up and said, "Grant Thorson's Nellie is the best I've known. How did you pick her from the litter, Grant?"

All eyes, including Lewis, turned to Grant.

Totally relaxed now and ready to have a little fun, Grant decided to continue where Will had left off with John Lewis III. He took a deep breath and decided to squeeze the moment.

"Well, I too believe it's very important to be careful in selecting a puppy." He paused and took a posture and facial expression that he felt looked cerebral, intellectual. "Like Mr. Lewis, I believe it takes experience and skill to select the pup that will prove to be the pick of the litter. Some dog men like to throw a feathered dummy and see which of the pups does the most enthusiastic retrieve. Others like to check the roof of the mouth for black spots; they claim that a black palate indicates a superior puppy. Still others have varied tests: Roll the puppy on its back and see how it gets up, or perhaps run away and see which pup follows the fastest. There are so many theories, and they all seem to make sense." Grant paused, looked around at his audience, and then sipped at his drink to add emphasis to what he was about to say. "When I selected Nellie from her littermates, it was a rainy Saturday morning. I took my eight-year-old daughter to the kennel to help me pick out our puppy. We played with all the puppies for a few minutes, and then Nellie did her business right there on the floor. I said, 'I'll take her!'" Grant shrugged his shoulders and stopped. Everyone was silent.

"What made you choose her?" Lewis asked.

"I figured she wouldn't shit in my car on the way home!"

Everyone howled with laughter except John Lewis III.

The small gathering lasted about fifteen minutes more. Several strangers approached Grant and Will with large smiles and introduced themselves. They all said the President had spoken of them for years and how they were glad to meet the "guys from Minnesota."

Eventually, the small gathering began to break up. Then the President said he actually had business to attend to and began to say goodnight to his guests. When it was time to say goodbye to Will and Grant, Thom Hutchinson took them aside and turned to Grant. "I have a favor to ask of you." It was spoken in such a way that Grant knew the President meant business.

"OK, what is it?"

"I want you to sit on the President's Committee to Develop National Health Care Policy.

Grant wrinkled his face and said, "This is just gonna be one of the bogus public relations things where somebody designs the project to prove what they already believe, isn't it? You know I think this sort of thing is all bullshit, Hutch!"

"Yes, and you know I do, too. But I'm caught in the middle here. The liberals in my party want to make hay while the sun shines — they want some national health care legislation while we have a majority in Congress. They'll see the work of a committee like this as an initiative on my part to push for national health care legislation. I want you to be part of this group. I'm not in favor of any national health care legislation. I think if we rush into something now, it could bankrupt our country. But I can't abandon my party. I must *appear* to want this legislation. I couldn't control all the appointments to the committee, but I do have the power to choose several members – and I want one of them to be you."

"What do you want me to do?"

"Be the voice of reason on this committee. Say things that need to be said!"

"I'll be a disruptive force and make everyone hate me."

"Yes. After a lifetime of developing that particular skill, the thought of using it to serve your country bothers you?" Will interjected with mock seriousness.

"You did fine tonight. I set you up twice and you passed both tests." The President smiled at Will's comment but still spoke to Grant.

"Bently and Lewis?" Grant asked with a smirk.

"Yes," the President said, still smiling. Then he looked at Will.

"I wouldn't mind, if I could just be in charge of the whole thing, I guess." Grant was trying to find a way to make it impossible for the President to appoint him to the committee.

"Doesn't work that way here," Thom said.

"Why me and not Will?" Grant was still looking for a way out.

"Because I asked *you*! Now you're gonna do this because I need you!" Grant could sense command in Thom's voice; his smile had vanished.

After a significant pause in the dialogue, Will spoke up once again. "Tell him you'll do it if you can carry a gun ... show the fairies you mean business!" Will turned to the President. "Maybe he could just shoot somebody right off the bat. You know, the first time some rat bastard says some bullshit thing, he can shoot 'em in the knee ... sort of establish his presence." He turned back to Grant. "That would make it better for you, wouldn't it?" Will nodded "yes" while raising his eyebrows to question Grant.

They all laughed out loud. It was Will's way of backing the President and encouraging Grant.

Grant kept his head down and nodded. "OK," he said reluctantly.

"Good, you'll do fine!" the President said.

"So what kind of gun does he get?" Will asked.

The President emerged from the Green Room smiling, with one arm around Will's shoulder and the other around Grant's. Susan Wells happened to be looking when the door to the East Room opened, and she thought for a brief moment that the three men resembled little boys walking down a county road, playing together on a hot summer day. She'd known the President for several years and had never seen him smile so completely.

The President then bid Will and June, and Grant and Anne a pleasant goodbye and said over his shoulder, "Jessica Wickham will be in touch with you, Grant."

Will called to him, "Keep your powder dry!"

Thom Hutchinson looked back over his shoulder and called, "And yours!"

~

Several minutes later, the President was seated, by himself, in the Lincoln room on the third floor of the White House when Martin Walters entered the room and sat down in the chair facing him. Martin and the President discussed the evening party and some of the day's business. As he rose to leave, Martin said, "Your friends from Minnesota were ... unlike your other friends."

"What do you mean by that, Martin?"

"Well, they seem to think with like minds. Their friendship is unique."

"Yes, it is." The President smiled.

"Dr. Campbell is universally well liked. Dr. Thorson has not learned the art of compromise."

"No, he has not." Thom Hutchinson was still smiling.

"Are you sure you're comfortable with him on the health care committee? What if he's an embarrassment to you?" Martin asked.

"Martin, I don't mean to offend you, but never question me on that score again! Grant Thorson has integrity and strength. I struggled to like him the first few times we met years ago. I know he's not perfect, but he's the real deal. He'll do fine." His smile had vanished.

"I'm sorry, Mr. President."

"Its all right. I do understand how others see him sometimes." The President smiled at Martin Walters again, and the tension of a moment earlier was gone.

"I saw them do an odd thing tonight. They both drank from the same glass several times. Don't you think that's a little odd, sir?"

"Well, Martin, years ago I saw them share a drink also," the President smiled. Martin had called back an old memory. "June Campbell turned to Will and said, 'Yuk, aren't you two old enough to have your own drinks yet?' Will said nothing to her. He just reached into his mouth and took out a wad of chewing tobacco and held it between his thumb and forefinger briefly." The President folded his arms and smiled. "Grant opened his mouth and stuck his tongue out as Will tossed his chew into Grant's mouth. It was just a stunt, a little nonverbal communication to let June know she could but out. It worked, too. June turned away in disgust and to my knowledge never mentioned that sort of thing to Will again. So, yes, it would be safe to say that their friendship is unique."

Martin raised his eyebrows, shrugged, and left the room, "Goodnight, Mr. President."

"Goodnight, Martin." Thom Hutchinson was still smiling as he thought about Grant and Will sharing a chew.

~

As Mike O'Neil drove Will and June, and Grant and Anne back to their hotel, the four of them each took a relaxed posture in the back of the limo and shared their own insights into their evening at the White House. "Not exactly your ordinary night out, huh Will?" June asked.

"We'd have to drive all the way to Bemidji to find such a dignified crowd around home," responded Anne. Everyone looked at her and stared briefly before they laughed. She seldom made a run at humor, and her comment surprised them all.

"Say, Doctor, did you enjoy your chat with Senator Bently?" Will asked, his question dripping with sarcasm.

"Oh, I could just feel the tension when he started talking. I was so afraid you were going to say something!" June was looking at Grant.

"Am I really that hard to get along with?" Grant asked.

"Yes," they responded in unison.

The ride back to the hotel took only a few minutes, and they all chatted briefly about the things that had impressed them during the evening: the elegance of the White House, the people they'd met, a private visit with the President. It had been a special experience for all of them. Grant was now glad just to be holding Anne's hand once again.

Will and June said goodnight and went directly to their room when they returned to the hotel. When Grant and Anne reached her room, they stood briefly in front of her open door. Grant took her in his arms and held her close. He stroked the small of her back softly with his right hand and then kissed her. He held her briefly and whispered, "I had the prettiest date there tonight." Then he backed away to let her close her door. She stepped back into her room and then looked into his eyes. She said "goodnight" and closed the door. He felt that disappointment must have registered on his face. He wanted Anne to ask him in; he wanted this evening to continue a while longer. He knew Anne had never been one to stand around and make foolish conversation, but he hoped she valued this moment as much as he did.

When she closed the door, Anne was disappointed that Grant hadn't followed her into her room. She knew he was only trying to be a gentleman, but she wanted to be with him for a while longer, too.

Five minutes later, there was a knock on Anne's door. She looked out the peep hole and saw Grant. When she swung the door open, he was wearing a gray sweatshirt, old khaki shorts, and sandals.

"Can I come in?"

She was now wearing a long, black silk robe with a red rose on the breast. Grant smiled sheepishly as Anne took his hand and pulled him into her room. When she looked at him now, she saw the handsome boy she'd been in love with so long ago. He sat in a big chair and gently pulled her onto his lap. She laid her head on his shoulder and put her arm around his chest. They held each other for several silent moments as they lay on the soft chair, resting their feet on her bed. He stroked her hair for a while and leaned his head against hers. This was all he wanted, to hold her like this. He couldn't remember any moment in his life quite like this one. But then, just how many people could have moments like this, he reasoned: The dark-haired beauty that he'd discovered love with had been restored to him. One of the very best things from his past had been gone for so long and now seemed to be his again. Anne reached her right hand to his face and softly touched his cheek. He let his right hand slide along the curves of her right side until it was resting on her hip, and then he gently rubbed his hand over the silk robe covering it. Still no one spoke. The moment had magic, and neither of them wanted to disturb it. Their feelings were becoming charged with sexual tension. Anne felt something building, surging inside of her that she'd been waiting, hoping to release for a long time.

"If someone had told you two years ago that you and I would be here like this tonight, what do you think you would have said?" Grant whispered, not really expecting an answer.

"I'd have been happy to hear it." The bluntness of her words surprised both of them.

Each of them suspected that the other was eager to stop restraining the passion that was swelling, but neither of them wanted the tenderness of this moment to end either. He slid his hand up and down along satin curves. He stroked her hair and gently touched her face. When he could wait no longer, Grant moved his mouth to hers. The moment did not vanish; instead it became more perfect. Each gentle stroke of her tongue on his made him want more. She shuddered as he slid his left hand inside her robe and began to explore her body. She was wearing nothing under the robe, and she gently turned to share herself with him.

Their lovemaking was slow at first; they intended to savor every second. There was no sleep for either of them until just before dawn — only quiet periods when they held each other and waited for another wave of passion.

The first rays of morning sunlight were moving across the wall of Anne's room when she awoke and realized that Grant's chest was pressed against her back and his arms were around her. She knew he was asleep. She wasn't sure how he'd feel if Will and June knew he'd spent the night with her, so she woke him.

The newness of this situation seemed odd but not really uncomfortable to either of them. When Grant was dressed, he held her close once more and kissed her. "This is a good thing!" he said as he rose to leave.

"Yes!" she replied.

"Call me when you're ready for breakfast, we probably should talk about all of this."

chapter SEVEN

In the week that passed after their visit to Washington, Grant and Anne had spent every evening together. The physical aspect of their renewed relationship was red hot, but their attempts to discuss their feelings had not been very successful. Anne had never been one to talk a lot, about anything, so it was understandable that she was having trouble sharing her feelings. Until recently, Grant had always been very confident that he understood his emotions, but now he, too, was struggling to verbalize or even comprehend just what he was feeling. They looked forward to each other's company — in fact, they found it difficult to be apart — and small talk and laughter came easily for them now.

Jessica Wickham had called Grant on the Monday after he'd returned home from Washington. The initial gathering of the President's Committee to Develop National Health Care Policy was to be held on the last Saturday of October at the Four Seasons Hotel in Washington D.C., in twelve days. Initially, Grant was upset that he was expected to give up another October weekend on Spider Lake — so much so that he briefly considered telling Ms. Wickham that he just couldn't make it. But when he remembered the tone Thom Hutchinson had spoken with, he knew he had to find a sense of duty in this whole thing. Grant resigned himself to do whatever Thom asked. He also thought there was a reasonable chance that Spider Lake wouldn't freeze over and put an end to the duck season for several weeks. He could probably spare another October weekend after all.

He really didn't know if it was necessary, but he'd sought Ms. Wickham's approval to bring a "significant other" once again. Since the committee was to meet only on Saturday, that left Friday and Saturday evening for personal time. Grant called Anne immediately to ask about a return trip to the capital. Plans had been made for another late arrival on Friday and then dinner on Saturday after the meeting.

~

It had been two weeks since he'd seen his parents, and tonight, as usual, the road seemed dark and long as he returned from another Friday visit with his father. Big Ole had been a little weaker and slower, as Grant had expected. But he'd had a pleasant visit with Ingrid at the campus coffee shop, and he'd been in good spirits as he said goodbye to her and set out on the last leg of the return trip to Spider Lake.

Normally, the last few miles of the drive home were tiresome and Grant had trouble staying awake. But tonight, he was excited because he knew Will Campbell would be waiting for him at the cabin with cold beer and something to eat. They'd planned to spend the weekend as they had so many times in the past: duck hunting on Spider Lake. Grant figured Will would be arriving at the cabin about an hour before he got there.

The dark woods around Spider Lake were silent and the lake was calm when Will arrived at Grant's cabin. He'd left Duluth a little early so he'd have plenty of time to talk with Grant when he arrived at Spider Lake. Frank and Evie had closed up the Ordway house for the winter, so instead of re-opening the place that would someday be his, he just bunked with Grant like he usually did on hunting weekends. He put his gear away, made preparations with the boat for an early-morning duck hunt, and then put a frozen pizza in the oven.

"Perfect timing!" Grant exclaimed twenty minutes later when he opened the back door of the cabin and was greeted by a warm fire in the fireplace and the smell of pizza. He took a beer from the refrigerator and dropped onto the leather couch while Will cut the pizza.

"So how's Big Ole?" Will asked as he walked around the coffee table and settled into the big chair. He was carrying a beer and several pieces of pizza on a paper plate.

Grant spoke slowly and looked straight ahead. "Didn't get out of bed right away today — that was a first — and he hardly ate anything. He fell twice last week and had some bruises. We spent most of the day doing bathroom projects." He paused, then turned and looked directly into Will's eyes. "Put a diaper on my dad today, Will!" His tone changed entirely with his last sentence. Initially, he'd been simply sharing his day with Will. Now he seemed to be pleading for understanding when he mentioned the diaper.

"Oh. I'm sorry, pard, that's gotta be difficult for everyone."

"Yeah." He spoke slowly now. "But you know, there's something about this that still seems to be drawing us closer together. It's ... OK, I guess." Grant sighed and his voice trailed off again. Then he reached over and took a slice of pizza off Will's plate. He took a large bite and followed it with a swallow of beer as he leaned back into the couch and put his stocking feet on the coffee table. "I never saw all this shit coming, Will!" Grant's eyes remained clear, and he paused for a while. Will admired his friend's strength, and then he thought briefly that for the first time in a year he was going to see Grant Thorson let down a little and share more of his feelings. Several long minutes passed while neither of them spoke.

Finally, Grant took a deep breath and raised his head. "Gonna ask me about the rest of my week?" Grant smiled now as his countenance lifted from the fatigue of a moment earlier. He wanted to change the subject.

"So how was the rest of your week?"

"Good. Thanks for asking!" Grant stopped. He was teasing now; he knew Will wanted information about Anne.

"OK, perhaps you could fill in the blanks between Saturday night and yesterday?"

"Don't you think this is a strange conversation?" Grant asked, deliberately stalling his answers.

"Not yet, but I'm hoping!"

"No, really, in one breath I'm telling you about my dad and all those difficult things in the nursing home, and in the next breath I'm telling you about this really fine thing, this old romance that has been rekindled."

"Oh, jeez, I knew it, there's gonna be some sex stuff coming here, isn't there? OK, so what was the sex like?"

"I suppose it was about like when you do it, except there were two people involved and quite a few more orgasms." Grant reached over and took another slice of pizza off Will's plate. "I'm so glad you encouraged me to call Anne," Grant started, then looked at Will. "When I held her hand, I felt the same excitement I felt thirty years ago when I went to her house to pick her up for a date."

"So what happened last weekend to change everything? You were a little leery about the whole thing in Washington."

"It was really odd. For some reason, I just walked up and kissed her and it was great, magic, like old times." Grant shrugged his shoulders.

"So you dropped some tongue down her throat and now she's in love with you?" Will's forehead wrinkled with the question.

"Yeah, that would be a sensitive, romantic way to put it," Grant smiled. The two old friends talked for several hours and drank way too much beer while they discussed Grant and Anne's relationship – and everything else they could think of. One of them would walk to the refrigerator and get two more beers. Then, a few minutes later, the other would make the trip to the refrigerator for another round.

While they continued to drink, Grant noticed that Will's hair got more mussed. It always happened that way. It didn't matter that he never touched his head; his hair got mussed when he drank. The more he drank, the more his hair got mussed – every time. It was a phenomenon Grant and June had been aware of for years.

Finally, Grant put an end to their midnight chat. "We're getting up at 4:00 a.m., I'm kinda drunk, and you look like shit. Let's get some sleep."

~

When the hateful sound of the small alarm clock smashed through his ears and filled his head, Grant thought there must have been some sort of mistake. He knew he'd just laid down in bed a moment earlier, and now the clock had exploded. He turned to his right and saw the red 4:00 flashing. He lay there for a minute and thought about turning the alarm off and rolling over. He could never really do that, but today his bed felt particularly warm and comfortable. He wanted to call to Will and wake him, but he feared that the noise of his own voice might make him sick.

His head hurt when he sat up, and the floor felt cold on his bare feet. He hated everything he was feeling. He had to force himself to stand up and get going. He walked past the guest room and slapped at the light switch. As he looked over his shoulder, he could see Will was having the same trouble getting started. They both stumbled around the cabin as they walked into their clothing and got their gear ready.

Will's gait was something between a shuffle and a stagger. He wore boxers and a gray T-shirt as he slid his red wool socks across the floor on his way toward the kitchen. His hair was matted, and his mouth hung open when he reached the coffee pot.

"We're gonna need two pots of coffee today, pard. Reach down under the cabinet and grab that other old thermos behind the colander would ya ... no, farther back." Grant gave directions in a scratchy voice as Will searched for the second thermos.

Will had not spoken since he'd risen, and he was obviously in pain. Grant was wearing long underwear, work boots, and an orange stocking cap while he sipped at his coffee and watched Nellie devour her breakfast. "Never start drinking Nellie ... unless you can hold your liquor better than Will!" Will Campbell found it too painful to reply, and the hunters finished their preparation in silence.

"OK, I've got ammo, jerky, Ding Dongs, chew, and both pipes in the duffel, and Nellie's been fed and walked. Grab the coffee and your piece and let's go." Grant groaned. As usual, he was going through his checklist to make sure everything was ready. Will always had confidence that if Grant said they were ready, then they were ready, and he followed along. When they stepped off the porch, the morning air was chilly. But there had been no frost that night. Neither of them wanted to say it, but they were both afraid there had not been enough cold weather to move new ducks south for them. The locals would probably all be decoy shy by now, and today's hunt might be slow.

They motored across the big open bay to set up their boat and decoys with the wind and Christian Island at their backs. There were many other good places on Spider Lake to set up decoys and hunt ducks, but they almost always came here. When they were freshman dental students, Will brought Grant to his family's cabin for a weekend hunt. They'd stayed in the Ordway house and had two days of outstanding gunning by this little island. Grant was smitten with the place, and he started referring to the little island as "Christian Island" in reference to Gordon Lightfoot's song about a boat and a place where he always found peace and happiness. When the snow melted and the lake's ice broke up in the spring, Will brought Grant north once again, this time for the opening weekend of the fishing season. They caught fish all around the little island – crappies and panfish in the weeds and shallows along the bar that stretched from shore to the island, and walleye in the deeper water off the point of the island. It was never anything but Christian Island after that. Lightfoot's song had become like an anthem for Grant Thorson; every time he heard it, it took him home.

The little motor had droned in their ears for several minutes when Grant cut the throttle and began scanning the shoreline with a flashlight as he looked for just the right place to set the decoys. "So whadya think?" he asked Will as he looked around.

"My fuckin' head hurts. Got any aspirin?" Will groaned. He had not looked up since he'd stepped into the boat.

"Always, in the duffel." Grant pointed the flashlight at the camouflage-colored duffel bag in order to help Will.

Will fumbled around until he found the aspirin. He took the top off the thermos and scooped some water from the lake to wash down the four aspirin in his left hand.

Grant cut the motor entirely and let the boat glide silently up to a weed-covered point of land. When he got out of the boat, the water felt cold even through his neoprene waders. He pulled the boat a little farther into the weeds and then leaned on the gunwale while he spoke to Will. "You gonna help me set the dekes or sit there and listen to your pulse?" he asked.

"Fuckin' head hurts" was all Will said as he climbed out of the boat. The water was about two feet deep by the boat and remained shallow around the weedy area where the men always set the decoys. They unwrapped the lead weights and decoy cords from around the decoys' necks and placed each decoy with a purpose. Old time waterfowl lore says that wise hunters should never place an even number of decoys, so Grant always kept fifteen in the boat. He usually kept a string tied to one of them and ran the other end of the string back to the boat. When ducks were circling the spread he'd pull the string and make the decoy appear to swim. At this stage of the season, the decoys were usually placed in two groups or perhaps a semicircle, with an open space in the middle for the ducks to land. This "kill zone" was usually about twenty yards from the boat, and these hunters usually preferred not to shoot at ducks that would not fall into this area.

Nellie rested her front feet on the gunwhales and wagged her tail as she watched both men place decoys and then check the look of their setup with flashlights. When Grant and Will re-entered the boat, she was pacing with nervous energy.

Once the blind was correctly placed over the boat, Grant stood up and shined his flashlight over the decoys again. Everything seemed to be in order now. Even with headaches, both men had always found joy in the rituals of setting decoys and preparing their hiding place. In fact, all the peripheral things that went along with the hunting had become very important to them. Last night's overindulgence, today's headaches, the correct placement of the decoys, the expectancy of whatever might come their way today, and the knowledge they could do it all over again tomorrow gave them a temporary, peaceful sense of satisfaction with their lives. They felt that if they had found their way to another moment like this, they must be doing something right. When they were here, they were somehow separated, or safe, from all the stress and troubles in the rest of their lives.

The darkness was beginning to lift now, and neither of them could see any shadows suggesting the movement of ducks through the sky. Each man found his own pipe and coffee cup today. Neither of them felt any need to speak. They just puffed on their pipes, sipped at their coffee, and enjoyed the quiet time.

"So how's your head?" Grant asked with a smile.

"Some better. Thanks for your concern," Will mumbled. "Can you still hear it pounding, too?"

Each man searched the sky for ducks as he spoke. The cold air and exercise and the expectation of ducks coming to decoys always seemed to clear their heads. Now, as they began to converse about the little things – the weather, the ducks, whatever – they began to turn their attention to each other and only peer over the top of the blind periodically.

"So what are you gonna do?" Will finally asked.

"About Anne? I don't know. I guess I don't plan to *do* anything just yet. If you're asking me if I'm in love with her, I'd have to say yes. But you know, it's odd, we don't talk about our feelings much. It's just difficult for either of us to find the words." It was as if Grant were talking to no one in particular. His sentence just trailed off into a silence of several minutes. When he spoke again, he uttered a question as though the answer should be kept secret. "Hey, you wanna know something else?" Grant's face seemed to be searching, as if he wanted to say something but he was uncertain. "Sometimes I feel like I'm being unfaithful to Kate. You think that's strange, pard?"

Will did not respond. He tightened his face and squinted. Will's look told Grant that he didn't want to hear that sort of talk, but he waited for Grant to continue.

Grant took another sip of coffee and then turned again to Will with a puzzled stare. "It feels as though Anne's been waiting for me all these years. I even wonder sometimes if I was supposed to marry Anne in the first place but I denied my destiny. Sound crazy?"

"Sounds ridiculous! Don't go down that road. Kate was the one for you. She made you a better man." The casual tone of a few minutes earlier was gone from Will's voice, "She was the very best – pretty, clever, fun for your buddies to be around. You two shared some sort of energy when you were together. You were both so lucky you found each other. Remember how it was? You were just a country boy who was floundering academically and personally, and when she came along you grew up. I was there, I saw it! I saw how you changed when you met her."

"Yeah, I know." Grant's focus seemed to be about ten feet beyond Will when he responded. "I took her to a Twins game in September of our first year in dental school, and I knew that night I was gonna love her forever. It was a nice autumn night at the old Met Stadium. I could only afford the two-dollar tickets in the left field bleachers, but the Twins were, as usual, about twenty-five games out of first place, so there were a couple thousand empty seats behind home plate. We moved over along the first base line in the third inning." Grant stopped and looked at Will. "Know what I remember the most? She brought a glove! She knew something about baseball, she liked eating ballpark food, she listened to me while I tried to impress her with my knowledge of the game. But she sat there with that glove and cheered like a little kid. She just held that glove and pounded her right hand into it like a little boy ... but she was this gorgeous, intelligent woman. I'll never get that vision out of my mind. She found joy in one of those things that women just never notice At one point, I was trying to describe the thrill of rounding third and heading for home, trying to beat the throw and knowing there was gonna be a play at the plate. Hmph." Grant pursed his lips and shook his head. "Know what she said? 'I guess I can run like that when I get to Heaven.' I was proud of her and embarrassed for myself at the same time. Silly, isn't it, but when I looked at her I knew then and there she was the one. She asked me, as we were walking to the car that night, how I felt about the brace on her leg. I told her I really didn't see a brace. I told her I thought I was already in love with her just watching her talking to other men ... before I ever knew she had it. I sure wasn't gonna let it get in the way now. I went to Anne's apartment and broke up with her after I dropped Kate off at her place. It was awful. Anne said she could smell Kate's perfume on me!" Grant smiled and shook his head sheepishly.

"She told June about that night a few years ago, buddy," Will added with a smile. "She told roughly the same story, but she added something. She told June that she knew you were the one that night, too. Kate told June that you'd said some things that no one else ever had, and that you'd looked at her in a way that no one else ever had."

"Really?" Grant said softly, staring at his feet and not expecting an answer. The boat was quiet for a long minute. Then Grant added, "I never thought my life would be like this, Will. I thought we'd be happy together for our whole lives ... and my dad would never get sick or die ... and all the good things in my life would just be there." Several minutes passed in silence while Grant looked at Nellie and scratched her ears. "So why do you think this stuff happens? Do you feel like you understand any of this?" Grant was still holding Nellie's ears.

"Well, I don't mean to be too literary or metaphorical ... is that a word? But I like the old analogy that life is like a long river that runs to the sea. The sea maybe represents Heaven, I suppose. We all get to start in the relatively placid, still waters of our youth. You know, something like Spider Lake, which eventually flows to the Mississippi and then to the sea. But then, soon enough, we run into rapids, and waterfalls, and rocks just beneath the surface that would smash our boats and pull us under. Some of us get swept into the current way too early and don't get to see the whole long river. Some of us just close our eyes and bang into every rock and somehow stay afloat and make it to the sea ... but we miss so much of life because we're afraid to look at it. Then, somehow, a few of us navigate the whole river and deal with every rock and waterfall and we reach the sea triumphantly."

"Like my dad?" Grant said cynically.

"Well, all metaphors probably break down somewhere," Will said, and then his tone became defiant. "And maybe there *is* some triumph there for your dad. How the hell do you know? Besides, he's still running that river!" Will smiled.

"What about the ones who get swept under?"

"They get to the sea, too!" Will raised his eyebrows.

Grant stared at Will. "That's good. I like that," Grant said after another long pause. Once again he remembered Kate reading Shakespeare's quote about the tide that carries men through life.

"Hey, pard, we got company," Will whispered, and once again the mood in the boat changed instantly. Both necks shortened as they reached for their guns. Nellie was soon wagging her tail and looking out her peephole; she understood. "Six mallards, way high and left." Will's duck call screamed a loud, long hail, and the ducks turned toward them.

"They're turning," Grant whispered. The ducks did turn, and they made several swings past the decoys. But they remained well out of range and then flew away. "I'm afraid that's what it's gonna be like today, pard," Grant said as he set his gun down once more.

"That's why they call it 'hunting' instead of 'shooting.' I guess the ducks win that one," Will said as he leaned back and unscrewed the lid from the second thermos of coffee. He poured some coffee into the dented thermos top in his left hand. "Ducks or no ducks, it's good to be here." Will spoke to no one in partic-ular. He appeared completely satisfied as he looked out over the lake and took a sip of coffee. A second later, he convulsed forward and spat out the coffee. Coffee and curses sprayed from his mouth like a shower. "This shit is really nasty! What the hell did you do to this stuff?" He was spitting, trying to clear all the coffee from his mouth.

Initially, Grant thought it was just the usual criticism of his cof-fee, though maybe a little overly dramatic. Will had an unpleasant look on his face, though, and Grant knew soon enough that perhaps he wasn't kidding. "It's the same stuff we've been drinking. *You* filled both thermoses from the big pot on the stove! Gimme a hit."

Will made a point to throw the contents of his cup over the side of the boat. "Probably kill the fish," he mumbled. Then he filled the cup for Grant and passed it. Grant sniffed at the cup and then furrowed his eyebrows slightly. He took a sip and swished it around like mouthwash. He immediately lurched forward and spit it out on the floor of the boat.

"Whoa! This stuff *is* kinda foul! Lemme see that thermos!" Grant took the thermos from Will's hand and began to pour the coffee onto the floor of the boat. The boat was always strewn with dirt, swamp grass, candy wrappers, rainwater, and empty shotgun shells; the coffee would make no difference. A stream of brown coffee ran from the container. As the flow began to lessen, Grant flicked his wrist to raise the bottom of the thermos above the top. As he moved his hand, something sped out of the bottle and tumbled to the floor. It made a noise like a wet dishrag when it hit — "splat." Nellie jumped back in surprise.

"AHHHH, SHIT! It's a fuckin' dead mouse!" Will hollered and leaned back, away from it, disgust and revulsion etched on his face. "Didn't your mother teach you to wash the dishes? Shit, I'm gonna puke!" Will's face was twisted, and he looked as though he was about to gag.

Grant was disgusted, too, but he thought Will's response was hilarious. "Well, what do you *think*?" Feigning disgust, Grant tilted his head and raised one eyebrow. "Gee, I scrubbed and scrubbed ... but I just couldn't get the old dead mouse off my thermos ... so I just put it away like that. Of course I wash my dishes! The poor bastard probably fell in there last summer and couldn't climb out." Grant raised both hands like claws and began to make scratching motions, as he thought a mouse trying to climb out of a thermos would do. He was looking right at Will and still clawing at the imaginary thermos. "Then you re-hydrated the little mummy this morning when you put the coffee in!"

"Nice fuckin' tea bag! God, get that thing outta here!" Will begged. His face was still contorted and almost fearful, as though he thought the dead mouse might attack him. Grant picked up the squishy gray mouse by its tail and flipped it out of the boat. Will put his hands to his face and rubbed his eyes as he began to chuckle. He couldn't stop laughing.

"Now there's a first," sighed Will as both men laughed out loud for several minutes. "Got any soda or water in your duffel? I'd like to rinse now, Doctor."

At no time during the next two hours did any ducks threaten to disturb the discussion in the boat. The conversation continued to lurch back and forth from the sublime to the ridiculous.

"Patient called me at home ... at about supper time, two weeks ago. You wouldn't believe what happened." Grant said as he fumbled with his pipe.

"Try me."

"Said his gold crown had come off while he was eating – and he swallowed it." Grant continued, "Then it gets better. When I explained that we could make a new one *or* he could wait for it to pass and then we could re-cement it, he asked how much for a new one. I told him, and he said he'd recover it himself." Grant started to smile. "So he shows up at the office with his crown about three days later and starts telling us about crapping on a screen window out behind his garden and then panning for gold, has my whole staff in stitches."

"Did you re-cement it?"

"Sure. Ran it through the sterilizer ... good as new! I told him I didn't usually do such shitty work though."

Will groaned and then smiled. "I got called to the ER about two months ago ... I think I've got you beat here, pard. Some local high school principal had arrived about an hour earlier, with a carrot stuck in his ass ... didn't know how it got there."

"Probably just loves his vegetables." Grant's face contorted as he spoke.

Eventually, several comments were exchanged that were filled with sexual innuendo, and Grant turned to Will with a question. "OK, what would you do if you found out that June had been having an affair with someone?" He thought he was being something of a straight man in asking the question. He expected a clever retort about "throwing the bitch out" or some such response. Instead, Will got quiet for a moment.

"I'd forgive her if she wanted me to. I wouldn't trash everyone's life over that." The tempo of the conversation turned on that answer.

Grant had heard many other men answer that question through the years, and everyone he'd ever spoken with had answered quickly and made it clear that they wouldn't tolerate such a situation.

"Ooo, good answer," Grant said quietly. He should have known Will would express his love for June in such a way. It was the kind of answer that drew him to Will.

"Thank you, Doctor!" Will smiled. "So what about you?" he asked.

"Huh?"

"What would you have done if Kate … you know?"

"Humph." Grant smiled. "That thought never occurred to me. I think the idea of her wanting someone else was … impossible." Grant leaned back in his seat and stroked the whiskers on his chin. He smiled a bigger smile through his left hand. "Sounded bad, didn't it?"

"No! Not at all. I can understand how any woman who had you could never think of another man!" Will agreed sarcastically. "Or, she'd be so disappointed with sex that she'd lose interest forever."

"I didn't mean it quite that way." Grant continued to hold his hand over his mouth and smile. His eyes cast a sheepish look, and his hand covered the silly grin. He'd been able to share virtually every secret of his life with Will, but now he seemed reluctant to let something out. When Grant started to speak again, Will knew he was about to learn something from deep inside his friend.

"Remember how Kate used to look at me, after we started ... dating?" Grant still smiled the goofy smile through his hand. He looked like he wasn't sure yet if he wanted to continue the story.

"Dating? Yes, I remember."

"Remember how you always teased me? You said she was hot for me?"

"Yeah. But that was because she was practically grinding herself on you around school."

"Not exactly. You still exaggerate just a little. But she did look at me ... that way. Wanna know why?"

"Is a pig's ass pork? Absolutely! This is gonna be good, isn't it? Gimme some more coffee. Even the stuff with the dead mouse in it is OK. So go ahead." Will leaned back and tilted his head, listening intently.

"Well," Grant started slowly, "we weren't 'active,' if you know what I mean, for a while. But then it became clear that it was going to happen." Grant stopped suddenly. "You want me to keep going?"

"Please do, Doctor." Will didn't smile.

"Well, one Friday we went out to a movie and then went back to my place. One thing led to another and pretty soon were both standing there naked looking at each other." Grant paused again. "It was her first time!"

"No!"

"Yeah." Grant's smile covered his entire face.

"I s'pose you were sportin' quite a shiner, huh?"

"Yeah, a real blue veiner, harder'n Chinese math. Anyway, she'd look at 'things' and then get this strange, wide-eyed smile. But you know what was really something? When I looked at her, naked, you know ... there was a lot going on in her head. She was *really* self-conscious about her leg. It was about half the size of her right leg, and it sort of rested there. Her right leg was muscular and hard from doing all the work, I guess. Anyway, I could see that it was really difficult for her to share that with me. She was also very self-conscious about the naked thing. She liked it, but she felt she was going way out on a limb sharing all of this with me.

"Well, it was pretty easy for her to see that I thought she was beautiful, and that I was enjoying the view, if you know what I mean. And she *really* liked that — the way I was looking at her. Nobody had ever looked at her quite like that, and she loved it. And she liked for me to see that in her eyes, know what I mean? She was a little embarrassed to be standing there like that, but then she was liking it, too." Grant shook his head. "I can't believe I'm telling you this."

"It's OK. I'm a doctor."

"Anyway, I lifted her onto my bed and began to ... touch her. I went really slow at first. I didn't know what 'limitations' she might have because of the leg." Grant leaned forward and in a very reassuring manner he continued with his finger pointing at Will. "Absolutely no limitations!" He smiled as he had before. "She made these funny noises ... kind of giggling when I touched her. Man, did we unleash some pent up sexual energy! We didn't leave my apartment until Sunday night."

"How many times?" Will squinted when he asked.

"Let's just say that if we'd been hunting, I'd have come home with more than my limit. But that's not why I told you all of this. Remember how she used to look at me around school? Well, that was the same look on her face the first time we got naked. She always smiled at me like that ... remember?"

"Yeah," Will nodded. The memory of Kate's smile was bittersweet even for Will. He could only imagine how his friend felt at the sharing of his story.

~

They waited oddly enough, mostly in silence, for two more hours, but still no ducks appeared. So they returned to Grant's cabin about noon. Grant took two ducks from the freezer and prepared them with apples, oranges, and onions as he always did. As was their custom, they set out along a grouse trail while the ducks were cooking. They walked for four hours, all the way to Stump Lake Boy Scout Camp, and flushed five grouse, but they killed none. In their younger days, this would have been a disappointing day – no ducks and no grouse. But as they'd matured, they'd come to realize something that most lifelong hunters do, at the end of the day, it really didn't matter what was in the bag; it mattered that life was better, richer, for having spent another day afield, in God's creation, with a fine friend.

Two tired men lit a fire in the stone fireplace and were about to sit down to a meal of roast mallards and wild rice about 6:00 p.m.. They were tired from a long night and a long day; they would definitely be in bed earlier tonight than the previous night. But in this moment, there was only joy for Will and Grant as they celebrated their day, their friendship. This place and the things they did together here allowed them to expel all of life's troubles and distractions for a little while. Now, if Grant thought about it, his loss of Kate, his anguish over his father's health, his longing for Ingrid might snatch this moment of happiness away from him. But that was the beauty of Spider Lake Duck Camp and his friendship with Will Campbell; trouble would go away sometimes when he was here.

As Grant carried the ducks to the table and Will took a beer for each of them from the refrigerator, all that lay before them was an evening of laughter and another day on Spider Lake. The yellow light from the fire danced across the old logs in the cabin.

Will raised a bite to his mouth and pointed to Nellie. She was lying by the fire and sleeping. "She worked hard all day and came home with nothing to show for it."

"Hell, she had a great day. She got to play with her best friends all day and then sleep by a warm fire at night," Grant replied. But as he looked at Nellie now, he was reminded of his first night at the Ordway house. A big smile crossed his face, and he said,

"Remember that big old lab your dad had – was it Sam?"

"Yeah."

"The first night I stayed up here when we were freshmen, I bunked beside the fireplace on the couch at the Big House, and I thought it was the most classic thing I'd ever been a part of. A big fireplace, guns leaning against the wall, and a dog curled up by the fire. Just like all the artwork at DU banquets, you know? I went to sleep with that image in my mind. Then I woke up about 2:00 a.m. with a terrible choking sensation."

"Really?" Will said in surprise.

"Yeah. Damn dog had his tongue about halfway down my throat." Grant was laughing as he finished. "That was bad enough, but the worst part was that just before I went to sleep, I looked over at the fireplace and Sam was layin' there licking his nuts like nobody's business!"

Will thought it was hilarious. "Sam probably just thought your mouth smelled like rotting carrion or road kill ... just wanted a taste. So which is worse – dog nuts or dead mice?"

"It was a toss up ... so to speak!" Grant said with a sick smile. "Great table talk, eh!"

"Dog nuts and dead mice?" Will said as if he were puzzled, try-ing to remember something. He paused in the middle of his ques-tion and took some more wild rice. "Didn't Joan Baez have an album by that title when we were in school?" he finished.

"I think that was Carol King. Grab me another beer, will ya? OK, remember the time ... ."

So many of the best moments, the best days of their lives, had passed like this. Each of them found something better within themselves because of the other. Maybe sometimes it was humor, sometimes insight or understanding. And they were better men because of each other.

When Grant slid under the covers that night, he lay on his back with his hands folded behind his head and watched the firelight from the other room flicker on the walls. He thought about Will's analogy of life as a long river and he smiled — he liked that thought. He felt he'd spent the day both literally and metaphorically on some calm water.

As he drifted off to sleep, he thought of Anne. He wondered why she felt like a new friend, one who didn't quite fit in with the rest of his life, instead of the old friend she was. That would all change with time, he thought.

chapter 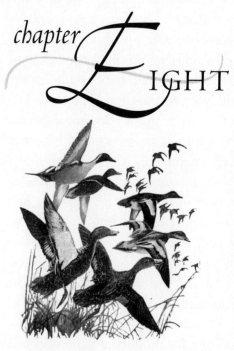 **E**IGHT Stacked neatly on the table in front of Grant were several three-ring binders. They were filled with material concerning the state of health care in America, and they'd been sent to him by Richard Bailey. All Grant knew of Bailey was his reputation as a very liberal president of a very liberal East Coast university, and that he'd been selected by President Hutchinson to chair the committee.

Eleven places had been set at a large oval table in the center of the large meeting room at the Four Seasons Hotel. Grant had come earlier than all of the others and taken his place as soon as he'd found his assigned seat. When he arrived, there didn't seem to be anyone around yet except hotel staff.

As he leaned back in his chair and looked across the mostly empty room, he raised a coffee cup to his lips. He'd been very cynical about this committee since the President mentioned it. Grant suspected that the President's Committee to Develop National Health Care Policy had been stacked with people who already had an agenda. That agenda was to provide a framework for a National Health Insurance program that would advance their own careers or the career of the person who had them placed on the committee, while they positioned some well-heeled and generous lobbies to profit handsomely from any healthcare legislation that might emerge.

Grant lowered his coffee and watched as people began to mill into the room. He'd promised himself that he'd hold his tongue and let others define this committee before he spoke up. Other committees like this one had been assembled by previous administrations, ostensibly for the same purpose. Various experts had been calling for the government to get into the health care business for some time. The topic of national health care had always triggered emotional debate, and there was still substantial opposition to any sort of National Health Insurance. Grant doubted whether any legislation would be forthcoming during the next several administrations, regardless of the recommendations of committees such as this one. However, he'd seen what he felt was bizarre and short-sighted legislation emerge from the Minnesota legislature only a few years earlier, and he did fear what might come from this committee.

Everyone seemed to arrive at once. Richard Bailey entered the room with something of an entourage. He had three assistants, all of them carrying documents. Men and women began to wander around the table, apparently looking for their name on a placemat as Grant had done. Eventually, a small, disheveled-looking white man with a scraggly reddish gray beard took the seat next to Grant and nodded hello. He was dressed in a dark, gray tweed sport coat and brown pants, with a beige plaid shirt and red plaid bow tie. Grant's face bent into a smile as he said hello to the man. He remembered an angry comment Kate had made in one of their first conversations by the vending machines at the dental school cafeteria all those years ago. She'd been upset by something that one of the other professors had done. "Rinky dink lame ass 'lifer.'" She was really angry when she'd said it. She never talked like that, which made it even more difficult for him not to smile every time he remembered it: "Thinks if he dresses like a clown, smells bad, and wears vinyl shoes everyone will think he's an intellectual!" Grant began to feel more certain that he knew what the mood and makeup of this committee would be.

Then an Asian woman, who looked to be around forty, took the seat on the other side of Grant. All the other people with a seat at the table appeared to have assistants or secretaries, and there were people sitting at the other smaller tables in the room. Grant couldn't tell if the others were observers, support staff or media.

As the noise and commotion in the room grew, Grant also began to feel intimidated. He'd certainly brought no staff along with him, nor had he prepared in any way. He began to wonder if he'd missed something in the instructions he'd received from Jessica Wickham.

Richard Bailey stood up to begin speaking, and the room became still. Bailey was a very articulate man. He was well dressed and smooth. Grant thought he *looked* like the president of a university. He introduced himself and listed the impressive credentials that qualified him to chair a committee such as this one. He said he'd been in contact with the President and leaders of Congress, and they were waiting for a study of the health care crisis and recommendations for health care legislation.

A quick glance around the table heightened Grant's cynicism. There were four whites, three blacks, two Hispanics, one Asian, and one Native American. The split with regard to gender was six men and five women. This group was politically correct. Everyone here was a "token" representing some demographic group. Grant was one of three white males.

Each member stood in turn and shared impressive credentials. Four members were physicians, three had doctoral degrees in the social sciences, one was an insurance expert, one was from an East Coast think tank," and Grant was the only dentist. He felt like an outsider immediately; he knew he didn't belong with this group. They all seemed to be experienced with gatherings like this one.

Several of the committee members seemed to Grant to be merely intellectuals — university gray hairs who were here simply to try to share their knowledge because someone had asked them. A couple of them seemed to be the types who really enjoyed listening to themselves talk and assumed others did, too. The others, in varying degrees, struck Grant as single-issue types who had an ax to grind — access to medical care by inner-city minorities, or the plight of the rural poor. When they spoke, it sounded to Grant as if they wanted to punish someone more than help anyone. Not surprisingly, the rumpled-looking man sitting next to Grant mentioned proudly that he had been working closely with Myron Bently, whom he described as a "leader in health care with experience in drafting meaningful health care legislation." His name was Darrell Osterquist, and he came across immediately as condescending and abrasive to Grant.

The introductions were done alphabetically, and Grant Thorson's name came up last. He felt he'd heard enough by then. Everyone else seemed to have the solutions to the health care problems — at least they hinted at that during their introductions. Most of the others sounded as if they had an agenda that would identify those responsible for the problems and fix the system. He made sure his introduction was the shortest. "My name is Grant Thorson. I've been practicing dentistry in rural Minnesota for twenty-two years. Minnesota — the home of Myron Bently's "Minnesota Health," an annual $600 million boondoggle that pays for nothing and provides coverage for no one. It simply siphons the working poor onto welfare while it keeps hundreds of bureaucrats — who know and do nothing — on the government payroll. I'm here because I'm the only person in this room who's had his hands on a patient at any time for the last two decades. I'm a health care provider, health care consumer, and an employer. I write a check each month for health care insurance coverage for my employees. I live in the real world."

Richard Bailey rose and assumed control over the committee when Grant sat down. The entire room was silent. As usual, Grant had taken a position and almost certainly offended some of those who had spoken before him. He sipped at his coffee and wondered if he'd been too blunt with his introduction. 'Ah, what the hell!' he thought, "I just can't listen to bullshit like that and not speak up." The president *had* told him to say the things that need to be said – whatever that meant.

The morning meeting broke for lunch after Richard Bailey had spoken for almost three more hours and detailed what he felt were the causes of and the cures for the health care crisis. He stated that after lunch, the group would break up into smaller groups. Each member would then receive an assignment so that each person could be responsible for some particular part of the next committee meeting in one month.

For lunch, they all moved to a restaurant on another floor of the hotel and sat at several smaller tables in order to get to know each other more easily. Grant was pleased that several of the committee members spoke to him as though they were interested to get to know him and not angry with him for speaking so bluntly. But as lunch ended and everyone began to push themselves back from the tables and relax for a brief minute, Grant began to think of Anne. She'd wanted to do some sightseeing and then stop by the committee meeting and watch for a few minutes at the end of the day. They'd planned to go out for a drink after Grant's meeting, then return to their room and change clothes for a formal dinner at a fine restaurant.

Grant's afternoon was spent listening to Richard Bailey once again. Bailey made assignments to each of the members and explained each assignment so that everyone could understand the other's charges. The small talk around the table began to irritate Grant. He heard exactly what he'd expected to hear: people who viewed themselves as enlightened or already on a mission, confidently discussing the solutions to the nation's health care problems. Grant had arrived with little enthusiasm for this project, and now he could feel what slight interest he had left ebbing away from him. His assignment was to report on the duplication of expensive diagnostic equipment and the effect it had on health care costs. He felt it was a tired, worn out topic. In fact, he'd written a paper on that very topic while in dental school – and he'd thought it was a tired, worn out topic then.

Grant was now confident that he understood how this game was to be played. A committee was set up by the party in power in order to study some "crisis." Committee members were then chosen by those in power precisely because their interpretations and recommendations were predictable. Politicians from the party that formed the committee in the first place would then quote the findings of this impressive committee as they argued for whatever legislation they wanted.

As the meeting closed, Richard Bailey spoke with force. "The President has assured me that he views it as imperative that we return a specific plan for National Health Insurance as soon as possible so that Congress can begin drafting legislation to ease the health care crisis."

"Whoa, that's about a 9.5 on my Bullshit-O-Meter!" Grant whispered to Darrell Osterquist, seated next to him. Osterquist did not smile or say a word in reply. Grant felt it was a fine way to end the day.

With the day's meeting at an end, he found himself enveloped in a large overstuffed chair in the hotel lobby. He sat with his legs crossed while he drifted through an easy flow of daydreams. He thought of Spider Lake and tried to picture just what the day might have been like at home. He assumed Will had been grouse hunting somewhere around Duluth, in Minnesota's Arrowhead Region, and he wondered what the hunting was like. A slow replay of the comments from the committee meeting passed through his mind's eye from time to time. The Asian woman sitting next to Grant seemed very intelligent, and he'd enjoyed speaking to her. The Native American woman struck Grant as a humorless antagonist; she spoke of "her people" several times and didn't seem to understand that this wasn't a racial issue. One of the black men across the table had written several books, and Grant wished he could have spoken with him for a while. He wondered just how well he'd ever get to know any of the people on this committee.

And now, as he was waiting for her at the end of the day, he thought of Anne. He was eager for her to arrive. She'd returned to Washington with him just to have this night together, and both of them were now anxious for a long romantic evening before tomorrow's flight home. She'd called about an hour earlier because she was running late, and Grant had assured her that he'd simply wait for her in the lobby if she hadn't arrived by the time the committee meeting had broken up.

Staring vacantly at his own left shoe, which was resting on his right knee, he became aware that someone was standing beside him. At that same instant, he heard a woman's voice: "I didn't think the President would have any waterfowl processing technicians on the health care committee."

Mildly startled, he looked up and saw an attractive woman dressed in a dark business suit. "Pardon me?" was the best he could do in response.

"Dr. Thorson? I'm Susan Wells. We met two weeks ago at the White House. You said at the time you were a waterfowl processing technician, whatever that is, so imagine my surprise to find you here today." Her face was playful, and she wore a broad smile. She thought he was handsome and that he carried himself like an athlete. Based on what she saw in his eyes that night, she guessed he had a sense of humor — and she was attracted to him on both counts.

Grant stood up and shook her hand. "I'm sorry, I didn't recognize you at first." Only the faint suggestion of a smile in his eyes as yet, Grant remembered her now as the pretty blonde who was with John Lewis III. He remembered Martin Walters' comment — "the bitch is poison" — as he began to speak. "Actually, I'm fully licensed in the dental and waterfowl processing arts in several Midwestern states," he smiled. "And I never introduce myself as a dentist."

"Why not?"

"Because people always put their finger in their mouth and start talking about some horrible experience ... and they think I must be a geek because dentists are basically geeky."

"Well, that's true," she agreed sarcastically.

His face now slid into a silly, apologetic smile as he continued. "I hope I didn't offend you that night, Miss Wells. I was merely having some fun at your date's expense."

"My date?! Now that's offensive! The only time I spoke with him that evening was during those few minutes when we met you and your wife and friends."

Grant's opinion of Susan Wells improved greatly as he learned that she'd not been with John Lewis III that evening. "Well good! I'd have been disappointed to learn that such a beautiful woman was with such a toad." He was immediately embarrassed at what he'd said. He felt he'd informed her — in a very clumsy, sexist way — that he found her attractive. He had no business telling her that anyway. He was sorry he'd said anything, and he worried that she'd think he was stupid. At the same time, he worried that she'd think he was trying to hit on her. But still, he was impressed by her beauty.

"Now I *am* sorry!" he continued immediately, while incredibly he started to blush! The heat and the color rose quickly from under his collar. Grant could not believe what was happening to him, and he tactfully resigned himself to it. He simply looked at Susan and flashed a smile that consumed his whole face. "I can't remember the last time a girl made me blush."

Susan laughed out loud while Grant continued to smile at her and shake his head in disbelief. "I can't remember the last time someone called me a girl." She was struck by the way he just stood there red-faced and smiled at her.

He looked her directly in the eye and watched her laughing as he waited for his head to stop burning. He didn't like it that this beauty was laughing at him. But he could see in her eyes that she was flattered by it all. He also thought he saw something more in her eyes — kindness, perhaps, maybe a sense of humor?

When she'd stopped laughing and he felt his normal color return, he added, "The woman you met isn't my wife. She's my ... friend, and she's due here any minute. Please stick around and I'll introduce you." Grant looked over Susan's shoulder and saw Anne entering the lobby. He waved until he caught Anne's attention. When Anne reached them, he took her hand in his and kissed her gently. Anne was already looking at Susan when Grant spoke up. "Anne, I'd like you to met Susan Wells, again. Susan, this is Anne Robertson, again." Anne smiled a confused smile.

"We met at the White House two weeks ago," Susan offered.

"I thought you looked familiar!" Anne's confusion cleared and she relaxed noticeably.

"So really, Dr. Thorson, how did you wind up on this commit-tee? You seem to be cut from a little different cloth than the others."

"Really? Why do you say that?" He knew exactly what she meant. He wanted her to say it.

"Well, you're the only one in there who's not an academic, you don't seem to have a cause to champion, and you could just as well have given Mr. Osterquist a knee to the groin during your intro-duction."

"Yeah, I would have enjoyed that, too." He smiled again, then looked at Anne and added "I'll tell you later," in a matter-of-fact way. Then he turned back to Susan Wells. He remembered again what Martin Walters had said of her, and although he could sense no poison, he decided not to give her too much information. "I represent the concerns of the rural health care providers, I guess."

Grant paused and tilted his head to return a question. "And how did you find your way into that meeting today?"

"I thought you knew. I'm a correspondent for *The Washington Post*. I cover the White House and write a weekly column." She was very matter of fact with her explanation.

"Oh, yeah, Martin Walters did hint to us that he admired your work, but that was all he said," Grant smiled.

"I'll bet! Now speaking of toads, there's a dandy!" Susan wasn't smiling now.

"I've been pretty critical of the President recently, and Martin is thin skinned and overly protective of the President." She re-adopted a businesslike posture.

Grant did not want to deal with any issues now, and he wanted to let Susan's remark be the end of it. He pretended to put his fingers in his ears and said calmly, "I've heard enough of Washington politics today." Then he smiled at her and added, "I thought all Washington reporters were gray-haired, cigar-smoking curmudgeons who hung out in dingy bars."

"Well, some people think I'm working my way that direction, but I think of myself as a journalist, a woman of letters." She relaxed again, smiled, and tilted her head back to emphasize the distinction between herself and some of the old-time journalists. "And I also teach a class at Georgetown University," Susan smiled again.

"OK, so whadya teach?"

"American Literature and the Art of Composition." Another smile.

"Really? I wanted to be a writer at one time also. But I discovered that the two greatest writers in the history of the English language had already said everything I wanted to say!" Grant shrugged, raised his eyebrows, and dared her to guess.

"OK, I'll take the bait on that one. You're referring to William Shakespeare and Robert Louis Stevenson?" Susan smiled.

"Who?" He looked at her with such innocence that she wondered briefly if he had, in fact, not heard of Shakespeare or Stevenson. Then his face curled in indignation and he put his hands on his hips.

"Gordon MacQuarrie and Sigurd Olson!" Grant appeared incredulous that she would not think of these two first. He was enjoying this conversation. It reminded him of his discussions with Will.

"Who?" She didn't have to feign ignorance; she'd never heard of Gordon MacQuarrie or Sigurd Olson, but she wanted Grant to be absolutely sure she'd never heard of them. "Oh, are they the guys that wrote *Mad Magazine*? No, that was Alfred E. Newman!" She thought the reference to *Mad Magazine* was a pretty good retort, but she held back her smile.

"Jeez, didn't they teach you *anything* at college — no MacQuarrie, no Olson?" He pretended to be appalled. "Well, apparently you did read *some* of the classics. I'm referring to *Mad Magazine*."

Anne watched while Grant and Susan sparred for a few more minutes. She thought Susan was pretty, and it was obvious to her that Susan enjoyed Grant's wit. Grant seemed animated, and his eyes twinkled as he teased and joked with Susan.

Their brief conversation ended when Susan suddenly looked around and then apologized for disturbing their date. Then she announced that she had to catch a ride back to her office. Sensing that three had become a crowd, and that she might be stealing someone's date, she decided to take her leave. She said pleasant goodbyes but excused herself as though she'd remembered she was late for another appointment.

As she walked away, Susan was aware that she was very attracted to Grant Thorson. Both her personal and professional dealings with men had caused her to become cynical about the selfish nature of most men. But she was aware that she'd lowered her guard right away when Grant had begun joking with her. The strength he'd spoken with early in the day had impressed her, and now she'd seen humor and personal warmth in him. "This is an interesting man," she thought as she left him alone with Anne.

The instant Susan was gone, Grant took Anne's hand in his and asked about her day. She took a deep breath and told him she was somewhat tired. In a moment, they were holding hands in the twilight of a warm autumn day as they strolled along the sidewalk for the short distance back to their hotel room. Anne described some of the things and places she'd seen. Grant joked briefly about the committee. They decided to forego the drink they'd planned and just return to their room and change clothes before dinner.

As the door to their room closed behind him, Grant switched the lights off. Beams of light from the street poured into their window, and Anne stood with her back to Grant and looked at the city outside. He found his way to her in the dark and stood close behind her with his chin next to her ear. He reached his hands around her waist and held her silently for a moment. She could feel his excitement, and when she could wait no longer she took his hand and led him to the bed. They made love twice during the next hour. Several times during their lovemaking, she brought both hands to his face and gently touched his cheeks before she brought her mouth to his. She had not held him in such a cautious, questioning manner until that day, he thought.

They lay together for about half an hour, nearly sleeping with their arms and legs entwined. He began to run his hand up and down her bare leg for awhile before whispering, "Still want to have dinner?"

The answer came swiftly. Anne turned to face him and touched his cheek once more. She kissed him on the lips and then jumped up and hurried into the bathroom. "Get dressed!" was all she said.

The restaurant they'd chosen was elegant. Arches of bleached stucco separated the rooms, and white pillars seemed to be everywhere. Grant thought the place had a Mediterranean feel about it. He would have preferred someplace else, but Anne held his hand and smiled as they walked through the reception area. She loved it. When the waiter told them he had a table for them, Grant asked, "Should we go look for some place with moose heads and dead fish on the walls?"

"Not tonight!" She smiled and squeezed his hand.

Men turned to look at Anne as she and Grant walked across the restaurant to their table. She wore a long satin dress of a deep cardinal color. Her earrings were silver with teardrop-shaped onyx set in them, and she wore a matching pendant. As Grant slid her chair under her, he said softly, "Everyone's looking at my date. Just like it used to be." He kissed her on the cheek and took her hand in his as he sat next to her.

Anne was slowly stroking the back of Grant's hand with her thumb, once again, when the waiter brought a bottle of wine. Grant poured each of them a glass and then gave one to Anne. He raised his glass and looked at Anne. "Here's to us." They touched glasses and took a drink.

"You bought me a bottle of wine once before ... remember?" she smiled.

"How could I forget? You hurled all over my '62 Ford." Both of them were smiling huge smiles now. "Of course, it could have been the lime vodka, the cherry sloe gin, or the rum and Fresca you drank first."

"My dad was really mad at you!" Anne had not stopped smiling.

"*Your* dad? It really hit the fan when Big Ole woke up the next morning! Turns out when I got home, I threw up in my closet and passed out on the floor. But not before I'd left my muddy shoes on the kitchen table. The really impressive thing for my dad, though, was that I'd left my car running, with the doors open, right in the middle of the barnyard. When he woke up and saw that, he came to my room and got me at 6:00 a.m. Made me clean up the puke in my closet and then took me to the pasture on the north side of the farm. We made fence until noon! I pounded steel fence posts into the ground with a sixteen-pound pile driver while I was dying with a hangover. He was so angry he never said anything except where to put the next post and to 'get the lead out!' Then, at noon, he sent me to your house to apologize to your dad." Somehow, the passing years had caused Grant to remember that day with a smile now.

"My dad was ready to clobber you, too. But when he saw how terrible you looked, he actually felt bad for you. He laughed about that for the rest of his life."

"I didn't read much compassion, or humor, in his face that day." Grant could not stop smiling either. "I never did that again, either!"

The waiter began to bring the various courses of their meals, and they continued to recall events from their shared past. They talked about grade school bullies, junior high dances, classmates they'd had and hadn't kept track of. "Remember when Miss Anderson came into the classroom crying and told us that President Kennedy had been killed?" Anne asked.

"I'll never forget it." Grant paused. "Remember when I caught hell for bringing a transistor radio to school so I could listen to game seven of the World Series when the Twins lost to the Dodgers?"

"No, I never cared much about that stuff. But I remember the time you got in trouble for beating up the Laskey brothers on the playground."

Grant flashed at a memory from a generation earlier. "Those rotten little bastards were picking on the little Babcock kid. That poor little kid had something wrong with him. He walked funny and looked retarded — remember? — and those damn Laskey boys teased him until he started to cry. If those two sons-a-bitches walked in here right now, I'd beat the hell outta both of them again." Grant was angry all over again, and he actually looked around the room as if trying to find the Laskey boys.

The anger had streaked across Grant's face with the memory of a forty-year-old injustice. It passed quickly also. But in that moment, Anne saw once again the face of the boy, the man, she'd loved her whole life. Anne reached a hand up to his cheek and touched it softly. Grant thought she had a faraway look on her face. "I love you, Grant Thorson." She smiled. Her facial expression was calm but somewhat mysterious.

"I love you, too." His reply was quick, and he smiled a warm smile. It was the first time he'd said those words to her since all those years ago. It was the first time either of them had said them. Anne felt a gentle wave of satisfaction that the words had been spoken. Grant sensed something odd and immeasurable in the exchange. It wasn't that he didn't love Anne, because he did, but in a very strange way that he could not understand, he wondered if something had turned with those words.

With each course of the meal, the wine bottle grew lighter. Anne continued to recall incidents from their childhood through their college days. Grant enjoyed hearing her recollection of events he'd not thought of for many years. He thought it was the first time she'd really relaxed since they'd begun seeing each other again.

Many of the tables throughout the restaurant were empty when the waiter brought the chocolate cheesecake dessert they intended to split." Ah, Cabernet Sauvignon and chocolate cheesecake ... a fine combo," Grant said as he poured the last of the wine into each of their glasses.

"You used to lie on the couch and eat peanut M&Ms and drink beer. That was gross."

"I still do that. I didn't even think to check the menu and see if we could have had *that* for dessert! Oh well, next time."

"You haven't really changed in all these years," Anne said.

"Well thank you, I've tried not to." It sounded like something he'd say to Will. He smiled a self-satisfied smile and thought he was clever for a moment.

Her hand rested on his as she looked across the table at him. "You were a good boy. My parents always liked you." As Grant studied her face, he was happy to see that she took some pleasure from her memories of their past.

"Your dad didn't always like me."

"No, not always, I guess."

They finished the cheesecake and chatted quietly while the restaurant emptied. After dinner, they held hands and strolled around the lobby of the hotel for a few minutes, just walking and watching other people go by. The woodwork was stained a dark walnut color and all the furniture was leather. After a few moments of walking, they settled onto a leather couch that afforded them an excellent view of the human traffic in the lobby. There were several businessmen crossing in front of them. The men carried cell phones and spoke impatiently to someone at the other end of the call. But most of the people milling around in front of them were couples. Some of the couples seemed to be merely tolerating each other, almost ambivalent toward one another. Some of them spoke quietly and appeared to be on their way to some other place. But most of them appeared to be on the town for an evening, dressed in their finest and looking for a good time.

A dark-complexioned man crossed the lobby quickly with a very young, very attractive blonde woman on his arm. Both the man and the woman took long, hurried steps, and the woman's long dress and hair fluttered behind her as if a breeze were blowing in her face. The man rang for an elevator, and then his right hand slid down to the woman's butt. By the time the elevator door closed and hid the couple from view, Grant and Anne had watched them kissing, probing each other with their tongues for almost a minute. Grant turned to Anne and raised his eyebrows.

Anne squeezed Grant's hand. She looked up at him with a hungry smile and said softly, "Let's go up to our room."

Their bed was still torn up from before, and they never turned the lights on when they entered the room. They tumbled into bed with their clothes on and kissed and groped each other as impetuous young lovers would. They laughed as they kicked off their shoes and threw articles of clothing across the room one at a time. But their laughter quickly turned to impatient, urgent groans of ecstasy when her long dress was pulled above her hips. Grant still wore his white shirt and tie and they'd already had sex once before the last of their clothes had been thrown onto the floor.

Grant thought that Anne held him differently, kissed him differently after that. When they had finally removed the rest of their clothing and thrown it to the floor, Anne put her elbow on her pillow and then rested her head on her hand so she could look at Grant. She touched every inch of his body, very slowly and gently. Occasionally, she brought her face close to his skin and sniffed at him. Sometimes she kissed the place she'd moved her face.

Gradually, as Anne moved up and down his body, Grant sensed that Anne was looking at him differently than she ever had before. He watched her move about him, and he began to sense that she was looking at him for the very first time. She would pause and stare at him from time to time. And then it seemed that maybe she was looking at him for what would be the last time, as if she were trying to make a point to remember everything. His wonder about the unusual nature of her touch was washed away soon enough as its powerful effect restored him. He was carried off once again by his own lust; he could think of nothing but sex.

She continued to touch his face softly from time to time. She was slower and more passionate during their sex after that. When they lay close to each other and talked, or slept, between lovemaking, she held him more closely and seemed always to keep her arms around him.

As morning light began to brighten the edges of the curtains, neither of them wanted this night to end. Just as it had happened so many years earlier, the morning sun peeking into a window only seemed to change their small room into a new place, a new situation for them to carry on with their lovemaking. The morning lasted until they had to hurry to catch their plane home.

chapter *N*INE

The smell of popcorn filled Grant's cabin when the phone rang about 8:00 Wednesday evening. Anne and Grant had spent every evening together since they'd returned from Washington three days earlier. Tonight they were sitting together on the couch, watching a video, when the phone startled them. Grant had suggested *Jeremiah Johnson*, but she said he'd seen it. And so they'd settled on a "chick flick," as Grant still referred to all romantic movies. He hit the pause button on the VCR and walked to the phone.

"Hey, Grant. How's it going, eh?" It was Dennis Taylor, a forest ranger from the Minnesota DNR. Taylor lived in Baudette, Minnesota, on the huge Lake of the Woods, and he was a long-time friend of Grant's. He'd called to let Grant know that there was a big storm brewing on the central Canadian plains, and that he was beginning to hear of heavy duck migration just to the north of him, on the cusp of the storm.

"Ducks ought to be to your place by Saturday at the latest, eh?" Taylor said. "Should be the big flight all at once again this year. Hope you'll be able to catch 'em on the way through. Just thought

I'd call and let you know to get ready. Maybe we'll see you this summer for some fishing, eh?" Grant loved the way Taylor talked. Although he was from Minnesota, he added "eh" to the end of all of his sentences just like Canadians did.

When he hung up the phone, Grant said with childlike excitement, "Ducks are comin', eh? Gotta call Will!" Immediately he began dialing Will's number, and they made arrangements right then for Will to be at the cabin on Thursday night this week instead of Friday.

Once again he called out to Anne, "Ducks are comin', eh? Gotta call Mom!" He started dialing his mother next. He begged her forgiveness because he now planned to skip Friday's visit with Big Ole in order to catch the finale of the duck season. Gladys put him at ease when she told him that Ole had asked her just that day if Grant had mentioned how the hunting had been. Both of them took it as a sign of good health that Ole was interested in something outside his now very small world. Gladys added that she thought Grant should stay there and enjoy the hunting since the roads would be bad due to the coming storm anyway.

Once more Grant called out, "Ducks are comin', eh? Gotta call Ingrid." He called his daughter but could only leave a message on her machine that he wouldn't be there for his usual visit on Friday evening.

When he returned to the couch, Anne was rewinding the video and feeding Nellie the popcorn Grant had spilled on the couch. She'd been unusually quiet for the last couple of days, ever since they'd returned from Washington. Now she was preparing to go home early.

"Hey, are you OK?" He lifted her chin up so she would look at him. His eyes still held the question.

"Yeah, but I have to work tomorrow, and it sounds like you have things to do," she said with little conviction. They'd been together every night since Friday's flight to D.C., and Grant noticed now that her mood had changed. She'd become more withdrawn during the past two days.

"Ducks are comin', eh?" He raised his eyebrows and smiled.

"Yeah, you and Will have a nice time. I'll see you in a few days." As she spoke, Grant thought he recognized a maddening little trait that he'd seen and disliked in Kate also. Anne appeared to be angry or disappointed with him, but she would not address her feelings. He thought she was doing what all women do from time to time: expecting her man to read her mind and act accordingly to make her happy.

But Grant also felt sadness, as though he'd hurt her feelings. "Hey, this is what I do, it's what I am!" He smiled again and tried to coax a smile from her.

"I know. I'm just tired." She put a hand on his cheek again and kissed him. She put her arms around him and held him for a few minutes, silently. She kissed him again. "I love you," she said quietly. She held eye contact with him for several seconds.

"I love you, too! Hey, dinner at my place Sunday night?" He pointed to the kitchen. "This whole thing will be over by then ... you'll see."

She nodded her head. "Sure," she said as she walked out the door.

Anne had never shared Grant's enthusiasm for the outdoors, or for so many other things for that matter. He hoped she was just tired and not really angry with him for spending so much time with Will. He turned and said to himself, "Ducks *are* comin', eh?"

~

A sense of change hung in the air Thursday after work as Grant walked across the street to start his Suburban and head for home. The sky in the north, out across Leech Lake, was gray and steely, and the swirling gusts of north wind carried the first real chills of winter. Autumn was almost over in northern Minnesota; the witch of November was coming.

Grant went to work in earnest to prepare for the arrival of the proverbial northern flight when he got home. Above the rafters in the old garage hung several dozen decoys that were only used at times like this. Grant retrieved them all and placed them in the boat. They were heavy old bluebill decoys made of wood. They'd once been his father's, and he cherished every opportunity to use them. These relics had been there for hundreds of days of classic duck hunting through the years, and Grant wished they could talk to him. Big Ole had told Grant how he'd stacked them in his wooden rowboat and paddled across open water on Leech Lake to hunt ducks before World War II. As Grant handled the antiques and smelled their musty smell, he listened to the sounds they made as they bumped into each other inside their decoy bags. Grant could see his father as a young man once again. The use of old decoys and old guns and old hats always made him feel connected to a colorful past, and he liked that.

Cold snaps during autumn always stimulate ducks to begin their migration. Each cold wave brings a few new ducks south. Then, one day, winter rolls down from the far north and pushes the last of the ducks out. Oftentimes one late autumn cold spell turns into the first winter storm. In the last bunch of hardy ducks that pass through just in front of the storm, there will be some large, fat northern mallards, which are much sought after by hunters. But another prize, which for some hunters goes unclaimed for a lifetime, is the greeting of the northern bluebills. The bluebills will always make up the last of the ducks to migrate through at the end of the season. The image of wave after wave of greater scaup or "big bills" strafing a decoy set in blustery, foul weather is the sort of memory that makes hunters' eyes glaze over when they tell of it. Anyone who has ever seen it never forgets it — and speaks of the sight in a reverent voice. Usually this northern flight seems to move through suddenly, on a day or two when hunters just can't get to the marsh quickly enough. Sometimes the weather that pushes the last of the ducks is so foul that it's foolhardy for men to expose themselves to it.

Grant was filled with nervous energy when he prepared all the gear for an early start. He and Will would set extra decoys tomorrow, maybe a hundred of them, in the form of a huge fishhook. Blue bills apparently use the long arm of the fishhook to guide themselves into the curved part of the hook, which would be located just in front of the shooters. Bluebills fresh from the far north have absolutely no fear of decoys and seem to sail in toward decoys as if they were sliding on a string.

At about 7:30 p.m., Grant called Anne to tell her that it looked to be a great day tomorrow and that he was waiting anxiously for Will. She was less than overwhelmed; she just did not share this enthusiasm or understand it. She simply said to be careful and to call her tomorrow. Anne's uninspired response hurt Grant's feelings. He wanted her to be excited, too, to feel the things that moved him. He tried not to think about it, but he also heard something in her words that he didn't want to. He knew that she'd wanted him to cancel his plans with Will in order to be with her. She expected him to set aside this thing he'd loved his whole life. He chose to block out the little feeling of resentment that was rising. He'd just stuff it, not think about it.

Jeremiah Johnson was playing on the VCR when Grant noticed headlights in the yard. It was about 9:00 p.m., and there was a cold wind blowing from the northwest. When the door by the kitchen opened, Frank Campbell stepped in. "I hope three's not a crowd!" he said with a smile.

Will was just behind his father and carrying all their gear. When they had brought all their warm clothes and gear into the cabin, Grant offered them a drink.

"No, thanks," Frank said. "I'm gonna sit by the fire for a minute and then hit the sack if we're gonna get up at 'oh dark thirty,' like they say!" He rubbed his hands together and smiled.

Grant and Will each had a brandy, and the men sat by the fire and talked about the weather and the ducks and their expectations. In a short time, Frank was ready for bed. He stood up and excused himself.

"So how was the trip to Washington?" Will asked as he leaned back into the couch.

Will listened while Grant shared his experience with the President's Committee and explained his immediate frustration with the mood and makeup of the group. Health care, however, held only moderate interest for Will tonight; he really wanted to know about Grant's time with Anne.

Before this, Will had always felt complete confidence in Grant's appraisal of any situation. He knew Grant could recognize and read the big picture very well. Straight talk was about the only way Grant knew how to share his feelings, but tonight Will felt that Grant was vague and uncertain. Grant described what he said was love; Will thought he heard about something less or something else. Grant talked about looking forward to life with Anne; Will wondered if he was hearing about resignation to the future.

After listening to Grant for an hour or so, Will abruptly changed the subject. "So, Dennis says the big bills are comin', eh?" He smiled to imitate Dennis Taylor's Canadian accent. He did not want to listen to the conflict in Grant's words any longer, but he didn't want to confront it just now either.

"Yeah, he said a buddy of his from the Manitoba Ministry of Resources told him that Lake Winnipeg was covered with divers and they were moving south. Dennis said he was seeing new ducks yesterday ... mallards. We just might hit it right on the money this year!" Grant smiled. "The decoys are in the boat, the gas can is full, the coffee is ready, no mice! Let's hit the sack and be ready early."

Next morning, Frank was sitting at the kitchen table reading and having coffee at 3:30 a.m. when Grant arose. Frank had made biscuits and started some bacon frying. "Morning, Grant. Coffee's hot. The local radio weather guy says it's thirty-two and not gonna get any warmer today; northwest winds at twenty-one miles per hour."

"Perfect!" Grant smiled. He fed Nellie and took her out. She always knew when she was going hunting. The guns, the gear, the early start — she could tell when a big day was coming. She moved like a puppy now as she ran around the yard and did her morning business.

When Grant burst back into the cabin, he slammed the door behind him. "Colder than a well digger's ass! This is gonna be good!"

Sunrise today was to be at 6:48 a.m. Hunters cannot legally set decoys until one hour before sunrise and cannot start shooting until a half hour before sunrise, but the three men wanted to be anchored just off Christian Island at 5:00 a.m. so they could claim the place, just in case someone else had plans to hunt there, too. Few other hunters ever came to Christian Island this late in the year. It was a long ride across open water from the public landing, and then the other hunters had to cross several treacherous, rocky channels, like the cemetery, just to get to the bay where Christian Island awaited.

The little boat was loaded almost to the point of being unsafe. When Will stepped into the boat and pushed it out from the pier, he lifted a bag of the bluebill decoys to clear himself a place to sit. "Jeez, these old boys are heavy! No wonder the gunwales are just above the water!" He let Grant hear the concern in his voice. Grant shared his concern and chose a longer course, close to the north shore, in order to avoid the really rough water in the middle of the big bay.

When they arrived at Christian Island, Grant took them directly to the ideal spot to set up the decoys. They'd built a permanent blind here many years earlier, but wind and waves and ice had taken a heavy toll on it every year. Eventually, they'd grown weary of the repairs on the old blind, and over time they'd come to prefer hunting from the boat. The water around the boat was still, but the north wind raced over the island behind them and roiled the open water just outside the cattails where the boat would be hidden.

Grant steered the boat while Will and Frank began to open decoy bags and toss decoys over the side. When the curved part of the fishhook had been created with decoys along the shore, Grant briefly anchored the boat in the shallow water. "OK, I'm gonna lift the anchor and leave the motor in neutral. As the wind blows us straight out, we're all gonna drop these decoys along the line where the wind blows us in order to make the long arm of the fish hook. Ready?" Both men answered and Grant lifted the anchor into the boat. The wind pushed at the boat and it began to move immediately. All three men started dropping the old bluebill decoys over the side one at a time. By the time all of the decoys were bobbing and swimming on the waves, the boat had been blown about eighty yards into the lake and the water was getting rough.

"That's it!" Frank said when the last decoy hit the water. Grant put the outboard motor in gear and they returned to the small opening in the cattails just along the shore. Grant took one more look to be sure he liked the way the decoys were set. It was always a little hard to tell what the setup looked like with only a flashlight to illuminate things, but he felt satisfied. The blind was hung over the framework on the boat in only a few minutes, and the men were pouring coffee soon after.

From the darkness of the middle seat came Frank's voice. "I hunted here in 1950 with your grandfather, Will. Victor was an old-time shotgunner. He didn't really care much what the daily bag limit was; he just shot until he was done. In those days, the limit was fifteen ducks per shooter though ... can you imagine thinking that fifteen wasn't enough?" Frank began to ramble about Spider Lake and the old days. Occasionally, Will or Grant would ask a question and Frank would take off on another long narrative.

As the sky began to grow lighter, Grant peered over the top of the camouflage that was covering the boat and scanned the lake for moving ducks. Frank continued to tell stories while he drank coffee. "President Eisenhower stayed here once, you know," he said to both of them.

"Yeah, I'd heard that from some of the old timers in Walker. Did you meet him, Frank?" Grant did not look into the boat, instead keeping his eyes along the skyline.

"No, Evie and I had just started dating. I really wasn't part of the family. But she and her parents came up here and hosted him for a week. He wasn't the President when he stayed here, but I guess he was quite a celebrity. Ike was a friend of one of Victor's business associates, and Victor invited a group of fishermen up here shortly after he bought the place – they used to bring a lot of big groups up here in the old days, they say. They took Ike over to Leech Lake for a couple of days and then fished here for the rest of the week." Frank talked about the Eisenhower visit for a while longer and then went on with more stories.

It was now mid morning and there had been no duck sightings. Grant had been standing up and turning in all directions to look for them for some time. "Does this make you guys a little nervous? We're duckless at 10:30 a.m., and we thought we'd be all done by now. So where are the ducks? What the hell, they couldn't all just migrate around us, could they?" He reached for the coffee cup in Will's hand as he sat down on the boat seat. Will and Frank looked at him as he tried to warm his hands on the coffee cup. He looked at Will and shook his head in frustration.

Nellie had come to his side and rested her chin on his leg. She was ready for some action, too, and even she seemed to be asking the same questions that Grant had verbalized. As Grant raised the cup to his mouth, Nellie turned her head quickly and raised her ears. Before Grant could react, he heard several "quacks" followed by the sound of splashing water.

Reflexively, Grant and Will stood up to look at the decoys. Six mallards jumped from the surface of Spider Lake and flew away. The inactivity of the morning had lulled them all, even Nellie, to the point that they'd given up their vigilance. "They always seem to know when it's safe to do that!" Will laughed. "Usually they wait until I'm trying to take a dump somewhere back in the cattails though." Will now looked back to his left, out over the open water.

"Jeez, there's ducks moving all over!" The neck shortening and gun grabbing activities started immediately. Grant pulled some camouflage over the top of the boat and then put his eyes close to the peephole he always used while he watched circling mallards. "Jeez, they're all over the place!" Will repeated. "They must have all come together!"

"OK, we got ducks at about twelve o'clock ... you guys ready?" Will whispered. He gave several soft calls with his duck call. "God! They're coming straight in!" He waited for a moment. "OK ... take em ... now!" All three men stood and fired at once. Seven shots had been fired; three ducks lay dead and one was wounded. Grant reloaded quickly and killed the wounded duck.

"Nellie, back!" Grant snapped, and Nellie was over the side after the nearest duck. "Boy, we're gonna hafta be careful today. I don't want that old dog chasing some wounded diver across open water on a day like today." All of them knew that many hunters had lost dogs on days like this one.

Today they would be shooting mostly "divers" as opposed to "dippers." Diving ducks have the ability to dive several feet below the surface of the water and oftentimes will feed on small fish or aquatic invertebrates. Dippers, or puddle ducks, usually just turn upside down and feed on aquatic vegetation that they can reach while suspended from the surface of the water. Dippers can be found on any size body of water, from prairie potholes to wet spots in grain fields to rivers and lakes. Divers, on the other hand, prefer bigger bodies of water like large lakes and rivers.

Occasionally, when a dog goes to retrieve a diver that's wounded and can't fly away, the duck will merely dive under the surface of the water and leave the confused dog behind. Then the duck will resurface about fifty feet away and the dog will then swim almost close enough to catch the duck; then the duck will dive again. When the duck resurfaces again, the dog will continue to pursue. Sometimes the dog wins. But other times, the dog is led into rough water and blown so far from shore that he drowns trying to return.

"If you can't take a kill shot with their flaps and their feet down, then let 'em go." Grant's instructions were meant to be taken seriously. The men knew Nellie was putting her life in jeopardy with long retrieves today.

"So, where the hell did all the ducks come from? Look around! I can see two hundred ducks moving right now!" Will was pointing along the eastern skyline. "This is amazing!"

"They're riding along on the front edge of that big arctic air mass. Looks like we picked exactly the right weekend!" Frank answered with a smile.

Nellie returned to the boat with the first duck, a hen mallard. Grant put his bare hand in the water and took the duck from Nellie. "Back!" he ordered as he gave her direction with his other hand. "Well, OK! Maybe we'll have some northern mallards just in front of the bluebills — if they're all coming, that is." Nellie retrieved two large drake mallards and another hen, and the men quickly covered up with camouflage again while Nellie shook the cold water off her coat.

"We got more ducks comin'!" Grant said almost as soon as they'd covered themselves. He started to call and then stopped. "Hell, they're comin' in with or without anyone talking to them. This bunch looks like divers. I'm not shootin' this time. Frank and Will ... you take 'em now!" When they stood, each man picked the closest target and shot once. Will's duck fell and Frank's didn't. Nellie made the retrieve. Then the men hid immediately once again.

A third time, ducks were turning toward them as soon as they were hidden. "Ducks!" Grant said out loud. "Frank, this bunch is yours. We're not shootin' again until you show us how to do it." Grant was showing deference to the senior hunter in the boat. It was now clear to all of them that there would be plenty of shooting on this day, and Grant planned to honor Frank by letting him be the only shooter to raise on the next flock of ducks. "OK, old man, show us how whenever you're ready." Frank said nothing — which Grant knew meant "thank you." Will and Grant exchanged smiles.

When the ducks were almost on top of the decoys, Frank stood and fired three shots. Nothing fell; he'd missed all three times.

"Jeez, Dad, maybe you should wait until they land!" Will was smiling. "You could ground pound 'em."

"Don't be a smart ass!" Frank sat down and reloaded, never looking at Will.

"OK, Frank, got another bunch turning, way out there!" Grant called loudly on an old, beat-up-looking duck call. Nellie raised her ears and looked out her peephole. "This bunch is yours, too, Frank! Don't screw up again!" Grant smiled at Will again.

The ducks were sailing straight toward the boat when Frank stood. He fired three times again … and two ducks fell. One was a large drake canvasback, and it was dead in the decoys. The other was a redhead. It had a broken wing and was now swimming near a decoy. Will stood immediately and shot in order to kill it quickly.

"Whoa, nice shootin', Will! You got 'em both!" Grant called. Frank and Grant were both laughing now. Will had killed the redhead, but he'd hit another decoy, too. "Look, if you shoot any more of my decoys you're gonna hafta eat one." Will smiled at his shooting now, too. He had no reply. He just stood and chuckled.

Several more times as small bunches of birds approached, Will and Grant deferred to Frank and allowed him to shoot by himself.

There were so many birds moving in bunches that ranged from five to fifty ducks that the hunters seldom had time to rest or chat between shooting opportunities. These ducks on the cusp of the winter weather were totally unafraid of decoys. They'd probably never seen hunters before. Several times, bunches of ducks landed in the decoys while Nellie was retrieving and the men were standing up waiting for her to return to the boat.

"OK," Will said. "We've got fourteen ducks. We need one more and we'll each have our limit of five. Dr. Thorson, I believe you're up." For the next bunch of ducks, Frank and Will would defer to Grant.

In short order, one of the flocks moving in the distance turned toward the men's giant spread of decoys when Grant called to them. "Looks like about a dozen birds. There's a nice big one on the left side. I'm gonna take 'em ... now!" When he stood to shoot, the birds flared to the left. Grant fired once and folded the big duck on the left. "Nellie, back!" he called, and Nellie was gone. "Jeez, is that some sort of mutant hen mallard? It's nearly as big as some of the geese we took a couple of years ago!" Grant said.

The bird was big and dark, and when Nellie was halfway back to the boat with it, Frank stood up. "It's a black duck! I haven't seen one of those around here in thirty years!" he exclaimed. When Nellie brought it to the boat, Frank held it up and spread its wings and talked again about the old days while Will and Grant cased their guns.

They had their daily bag limit. It was now time to quit and go home for the day. "No ducks at 10:30 and fifteen by noon. Unbelievable! And we could take another fifty or a hundred if we wanted to," Grant said as he looked around.

"I think we saw something today that we may not see again," Frank said slowly. "I'm seventy-five years old and I've hunted my whole life. I've never been sitting on a fine spot with decoys set and watched the last of the northern ducks arrive. This is amazing!"

He looked at Will and shook his head. "And I think the front is moving slow enough so that they'll be here tomorrow, maybe in greater numbers!"

Picking up and bagging the decoys took them about twenty minutes, and they were carrying the last of the wet gear and decoys into the garage at 1:00 p.m. "Dad, why don't you take Nellie into the cabin and stoke up the fire. Grant and I will clean the ducks and be in shortly."

Forty minutes later, all of the ducks were cleaned and placed in the big freezer in the garage. When Grant and Will stepped into the kitchen, the cabin was quiet except for the faint noise of a football game on TV. Frank was sleeping on the couch with his feet on the coffee table, and Nellie had crawled onto the couch and curled up next to Frank for a nap.

"That's the way it's supposed to be," Grant said quietly as he pointed to Frank and Nellie. "We had a helluva day so far — mallards, cans, bluebills ... a black duck! And now we can sit by the fire and watch football while we sleep. Screw the grouse, I'm gonna take a nap!"

All of them were slouched in the leather furniture and sleeping when the phone rang at 5:00 p.m.. Evie was calling to see how the day had gone and to ask about the weather. She said the weather reports all called for some snow and very cold winds for the next two days. Frank ended his conversation with "No, I don't think I will!" and then said goodbye.

Supper was ready about an hour later. Grant put some frozen chili in a big pot and stacked a few bowls and some crackers on the table. Tonight's meal would not be elegant. The hunters simply wanted a hot meal that required little preparation and little cleanup. When supper was finished, they did the dishes quickly and then prepared their gear for the next morning's hunt.

The clock said 8:27 p.m. when they decided to sit down for a nightcap and plan the next day's hunt. Everyone was tired. Will leaned back in his chair, sipped at his drink, and summed up every-one's feelings. "Feels like it's about 3:00 a.m. I'm ready for bed. So what's the plan for tomorrow?"

"I'm gonna sit it out tomorrow. You two shoot 'em up. I'll get up and make breakfast for you." Frank's face seemed apologetic to Grant.

"How come, Dad?" Will asked as he leaned forward.

"I'm tired. I was cold today. I had a great day today, and I'll just finish the season on that note."

"That's OK, Frank, it's supposed to get nasty tomorrow after-noon ... could freeze everything up for the winter." Grant knew what he'd really heard from Frank, and he let it go.

~

The smell of bacon and coffee woke Grant up at 3:30 a.m. When he pushed his bedroom door all the way open, Will and Frank were sitting together at the kitchen table, talking quietly. When Will heard Grant shuffling across the wooden floor in his stocking feet, he raised his hand to the back of his father's neck. He stood quickly and then gently stroked his father's shoulders. Grant knew he'd interrupted a private conversation between the two of them. Will turned to Grant. "No change in the weather, pard. The lake's still open and it's still thirty-two degrees. Coffee's hot, too. You look like shit, by the way!" It was too early to smile. Grant shuffled to the stove, poured himself some coffee, and sat down at the table with the others.

Breakfast was finished a little earlier than the previous day, and the hunters set out slightly earlier, too. On this day of all days, they didn't want someone else to get their spot on Christian Island.

Grant steered the same longer, smoother, calmer course to the island as he had the day before. Rough water was particularly scary in the dark, and neither man wanted to brave the open lake. They were relieved as always when they got to their special place and found no one else there. They did, however, have to break some ice along shore in order to get the boat into the weeds. Today had the look of the last day of the season. A cold blast now would lock all of the shoreline, if not the entire lake, in ice. "We gotta think about getting this boat out of the lake today, too! We'll have to keep a close eye on the weather this afternoon."

They pushed the little boat back into the weeds in order to get out of the wind for awhile. It was still dark enough to pass for the middle of the night. "Let's just have another hit of coffee before we put out the dekes." Will was almost asking if it was all right to take a break. As he poured the coffee in the darkness, he said slowly, "That was a great day for my dad yesterday. Thanks!" He took a sip and passed the cup to Grant. The only light in the boat now was a small flashlight in Grant's hand.

"It was a great day for all of us." Grant's response had the tone of a rebuttal.

"No, I know you were trying to make it special for my dad, and you did. He was scared to come today, you know that?"

"Yeah, I thought so." Grant's voice trailed off. He'd heard the fear in Frank's voice the night before. He had indeed been trying to make yesterday special for Frank. "Maybe if we were a little smarter, we'd be afraid to be out here, too." Grant returned the cup to Will and there was a long pause.

"My dad is *never* gonna hunt with me again," Grant halted. "He's never gonna come and see me again, he's hardly ever gonna talk to me again." After another pause, Grant raised a steely look toward Will. "Ever tell your father you love him?" Grant's question caught Will by surprise.

"No, my family isn't ... like that," Will stumbled.

"Well, mine wasn't either until a short time ago. But you know, I'd always remembered looking at my dad's face when we buried Grampa Thorson." Grant spoke slowly. "Dad just stood there and tears ran down his face ... no crying, really, just tears. I couldn't help but wonder if some of the pain I saw on his face was because of something left unsaid between them. I carried that thought with me for a long time, just couldn't get away from it. When Dad got sick, I went to him one day and kissed him on the lips, like when I was a little kid. Then I hugged him for a long time and eventually I said 'I love you, Dad' into his ear. Know what he did?" Grant smiled an odd smile. "He wouldn't let go of me! Pretty soon, he reached his hand up behind my head and stroked it and said, 'I love you, too.' For me, it felt just like when Ingrid used to cry and then I'd hold her. Remember how that felt, Will, when you held your children when they needed you? Well, I know Dad felt the same thing. I just could tell. He wouldn't let go! Can you imagine how it must have felt for him? It had been almost half a century since he'd held anyone like that, and he'd *never* spoken the words! He just wouldn't let go! That's how we greet each other now, every time." Grant was glad that Will couldn't see the tears welling up in his eyes. He quickly began to stuff the emotion that filled him.

"You gotta tell your dad, Will," Grant said quietly.

Nothing was said between them for a few minutes. They just passed the coffee cup back and forth.

"Let's put the dekes out," Will said finally. "You ready?" He reached for the decoy bags and started to open one. He didn't want to think about what Grant had said any longer.

"My mother called me last night." It sounded as if Grant had something more to say.

"Yeah?" Will understood that Grant wanted to talk some more. He stopped fumbling with the decoys, reached for the thermos, and poured some more coffee. Will halted and turned toward Grant. The gesture made it clear to Grant that Will intended to listen to whatever he was about to say.

"Dad told Mom what kind of funeral arrangements he wanted. Told her who he wanted for pallbearers, what music he wanted, all that stuff." Grant stopped. "No feeding tubes, no life support, none of that."

"Whoa," Will said quietly. "I guess that's a conversation you don't forget, huh? How did your mom handle it?"

"She cried a little when she talked to me, but she said Dad was just fine with it all." Grant paused. "You know, it's kind of odd ... having your mother share a conversation like that with you." Grant halted again while he prepared to speak. "I don't know, Will." Grant leaned forward and rested his elbows on his thighs. He was facing the floor as he said, "If I ever really thought about it at all, I guess I thought my Dad should have a Viking funeral. You know, where they put the body of a Viking warrior in a boat and fill it with fire- wood and set it on fire – that's the way they honored great Vikings. I told Mom that, too. She laughed a little and said Dad was pretty specific about the fact that he wanted to be buried in the little Lutheran cemetery out by the farm." Both men let the quiet of a dark morning surround them.

"I like that Viking thing, that's good," Will said with a faraway look in his eye.

Grant leaned back in his seat once again. "I guess we'd better put the dekes out now." Will knew that Grant was done with talk of Ole's funeral. Grant started the motor and drove slowly while Will began tossing decoys over the side once again. Then, when the decoys nearest the weeds were set, Grant put the motor in neutral again and dropped the anchor.

"You ready to let the wind blow us out so we can set the shank of the fish hook?"

"Yep."

Grant lifted the anchor and the boat began to move with the wind again. Both men dropped decoys steadily until all the boat was empty again.

"OK, let's get back in there and put the blind up. I'm freezin'," Grant said as he plunked the motor back in gear and opened the throttle.

In only a few minutes, the boat was tucked neatly into the weeds just a few yards from the curved end of the fishhook formed by the decoys. When the blind was finished and the boat covered, the men felt warmed immediately by the way the camouflage blocked the wind.

"That's better, but I'm still cold. Pour me some more coffee, will you, pard?" Will asked while he slapped his hands together. "It's a good thing we brought extra coffee, huh? Hey, if you're gonna open a new thermos, you taste it first, will ya? You know, to check for mice."

"Why don't you just light up another bowl of that Dr. Assmouth pipe tobacco ... a couple draws on that stuff and you wouldn't notice a dead skunk in your coffee."

It was only five minutes until legal shooting time would start, but the overcast weather made the darkness far too deep to consider shooting. The men could just begin to make out silhouettes passing above them. Grant set two full boxes of shotgun shells on the seat in front of him. Will was also setting shells out in front of himself as he stashed the empty decoy bags in the bow by Nellie's peephole.

"Hey, I'm still cold. Hit me one more time with the coffee, would ya, pard?" Will said as he passed the dented thermos top back to Grant. Grant obliged him but took a sip himself before he returned the cup. They could see each other, although not too clearly now, as the dawn was breaking. Will held the cup to his face with both hands and tried to draw the heat from the coffee into his nose. Grant rubbed Nellie's ears.

Neither of them was paying attention when six ducks splashed into the decoys. They looked at each other and smiled while Nellie scrambled to her peephole and started whining when she saw the ducks. Both hunters also peeked through the blind. "Jeez, it looks like the sky is filled with ducks! We're not gonna shoot ducks on the water today!" Will said. Then he stood up and hollered,

"GIT!" and the ducks flew away. "Today we don't shoot until their feet are down, hangin' there like kites!"

"Damn right, numb nuts, you'd just shoot my decoys anyway. Just be sure that today you only shoot the ducks that can swim *and* fly."

Both men stood up and watched as dozens of small flocks of ducks circled above Spider Lake. They'd never seen anything like it before. There were hundreds, maybe thousands of ducks in sight as they looked over the lake.

"Wow! So this is the northern flight," Will said as he turned his head slowly right and left. "If we both stand and shoot at every bunch that comes into our dekes, this day is going to be over way too soon. Maybe we should do what the old timers talk about ... alternate turns at decoying birds and call your shot, one duck per flock," he suggested.

"Sounds good to me, but let's cover up and get to it. We've got ducks lookin' at us right now." Grant pulled the camouflage back over himself as he sat down on the boat seat. "You first, Will. There's a small bunch turning into us right now. You take 'em when you're ready."

The hunters watched as the approaching bluebills dove directly toward them. The white bellies of the large bluebills seemed to disappear as the birds flapped their black wings to push themselves into the wind. The ducks looked black, then white, then black. Then, suddenly, their white fronts stayed exposed as they cupped their wings to glide into the decoys only a few feet from the boat.

"The big boy in the middle," Will said calmly as he stood up and pushed the top of the duck blind open. The big drake folded with his first shot, and Grant sent Nellie immediately.

It had been raining off and on during the previous day and this morning, but now the rain had turned to snow. The snowflakes were huge and heavy and wet. Grant could hear them hitting the boat. The woods around the lake were beginning to look white as the snow formed an even layer on the ground and piled up on tree branches.

"OK, you're up!" Will said as he reached for still another cup of coffee. "There's a small bunch circling low, coming from right to left. God, I'm gonna hafta piss real soon!" The sentence struck Grant as absurd, and he was laughing as he stood to shoot. He missed badly and he turned to Will still laughing.

"Not fair. It's a do over. You were trying to distract me!" Grant covered up again and continued to laugh.

Grant was peeking out through a hole in the blind when he saw another small bunch of about ten bluebills flashing black and white and moving their way. "OK, here's the deal." Grant began speaking fast; he knew he didn't have much time to complete this thought before he'd have to shoot. "Remember in the book *The Pathfinder* by James Fenimore Cooper ... oh yeah, you don't read books without pictures. Well, anyway, the guy who was Hawkeye in *Last of the Mohicans* is called Pathfinder in this book, and he gets into this shooting contest and loses on purpose so that the young chick will fall in love with the other guy in the shooting contest ... he's trying to do a noble thing here." The pace of his narrative quickened. "Well, anyway, after he loses this shooting contest on purpose, the guy who won it says something to Pathfinder about being a loser, and it makes Hawkeye mad. So he reloads Killdeer — that's his gun's name — and then raises Killdeer and points it at a seagull while the gull is flying around. He waits until the gull crosses paths with another gull and then he pulls the trigger. Both gulls fall down dead, and everyone knows that he really could have won the shooting contest and had the babe if he'd been that kind of guy." He took a quick breath and began speaking as fast as he could. "Well, I am that kind of guy, and I'm gonna take the bird in the middle of this flock. And when I stand up the birds will flare. Then I'm gonna drop the one in the middle *and* the one behind it when they cross." The birds were approaching now, and Grant positioned his feet.

"Thank you for that brief narrative, Dr. Tolstoy. Now I really have to piss!" Will said just as Grant was standing to shoot. He was trying to distract Grant again. The birds flared and Grant waited to fire. Will could see that Grant was smiling, trying not to laugh again. Then, as Grant fired once, two birds fell dead. Grant sent Nellie, then turned to Will and laughed from deep in his belly. He put his gun down and signaled a touchdown with both arms in the air. Just like a hundred other times, both men laughed out loud for several minutes and joked about what they'd done.

By the time Nellie had the second bluebill back in the boat, Will was standing on Nellie's platform on the bow of the boat and loosening his waders. "I really gotta piss," was all he said.

Grant was opening a package of beef jerky when he noticed the sound of running water.

"You know, if you took one step forward, some of that urine might actually go over the side of the boat!" Grant's nose was crinkled in disgust as he spoke. Will had pulled his waders to his knees and exposed his naked rear end to Grant as he urinated, like any six-year-old would do. The stream of urine was striking the inside of the boat and running steadily from the bow to the stern, where Grant sat chewing at the beef jerky. The boat was always a mess by this time of year; mud, wrappers, weeds, feathers, and empty shotgun shells covered the floor. There was already about a half inch of rain and melted snow in the boat, so a little urine was not really a problem. Pissing in the boat was an old trick. Will did it about once a year, and both of them actually thought it was still pretty funny – they'd never stopped being crude little boys.

"No way! If I fell over the side with something this big and heavy in my hands, I'd go right to the bottom and drown. You wouldn't want that, would you?"

"No, you're wearing my waders."

"Yeah. I just pissed on 'em a little bit, too. Sorry, eh?"

"You have pimples on your ass!"

"Yeah, my complexion has been *so* bad lately, and I forgot to put my makeup on this morning." Will began to dress himself again. "It's cold out here. You just don't know how cold it is until you grab your weenie with frostbitten hands. We're talkin' some serious shrinkage here." Will was talking to himself, but it was all for Grant's benefit.

Grant was chuckling as he counted the ducks on the leather stringer. "Eight ducks!" he said, "all Bluebills. We need two more." Several minutes later, a bunch of five came sailing into their decoys, and Grant missed an easy shot.

"Nice one, Pathfinder," Will groaned, and they covered up again.

"OK, before you have to piss again; we have two ducks coming in together. You take the one on the right and I'll take the one on the left ... you ready?" Grant said. Grant secretly planned to shoot the one on the right – Will's duck – first. Then he intended to shoot the one on the left – the one Will would leave for him – second. The trick seemed like a fitting way to end the day – and the season.

"Yup, you stand when you're ready!" Will said.

Grant stood and Will followed quickly after him. Grant swung his gun to the bird on the right – Will's bird. BOOM! They both fired at once, and both ducks fell.

They both whipped their heads quickly to the side, staring at each other briefly in disbelief. "YOU CHEATER!" they both yelled at once, then burst into laughter. Each of them had had the same idea. They'd both shot the other man's duck.

"Been huntin' with you for twenty-five years. I guess I've seen that one before," Will smiled.

The decoys all had ice forming on them, and the men's hands were painfully cold after plucking dozens of slippery wooden decoys from the frigid water and then tying the anchor ropes around the decoys' necks. It was 9:30 a.m. and they were through for the day, maybe the season. As they motored back across Spider

Lake, they noticed that the snowflakes had changed from the big wet kind that "splat" when they hit to the little hard flakes that almost burn when they strike the skin. Thousands of ducks still swarmed over the lake, and they couldn't help but notice that the north shore of the lake was beginning to ice up. They knew now that today would be the end of the season.

When they reached Spider Lake Duck Camp, they carried all the gear and decoys up to the old garage, then winched the boat into the boat house and removed the motor and carried it, too, up to the garage.

Frank helped them carry the gear. When the work was done, they all stood on the shore of Spider Lake for one last farewell to the ducks ... to the lake. For all of them, this moment was like bidding an old friend farewell. The lake they would certainly see again, but all the good times they'd had during the previous spring, summer, and fall seemed somehow about to be locked up under the ice.

Grant Thorson stood silently as the snow slashed through the red pines on the north end of Spider Lake and across the gray surface of the water. He could just make out flocks of ducks circling around Christian Island way out there though the white streaks of snow. The imminent freeze up of Spider Lake filled him with a sense of loneliness.

"So why do I feel so bad? I know I'll be out there catching crappies through the ice and cross-country skiing before long."

"Because you know there's an old friend who won't be talking to you again for a long time," Will answered as he kept his stare out over the lake.

The men spent the rest of Saturday putting away decoys and all of the other gear. They cleaned the bluebills and prepared one last duck dinner at Spider Lake Duck Camp. The talk ran high at dinner as they discussed the arrival of the northern flight. They didn't bother to go to bed early. Rather than retire early, they extended the season a few more hours with several drinks and a rehashing of the season's finale on Spider Lake. Grant had showered and changed clothes before dinner. Will, however, had chosen to remain in his flannel red plaid shirt, long underwear, and heavy red socks during the afternoon and throughout dinner. One of his shirttails was tucked into his long undies, and his hair was a little mussed from the beer he'd been drinking. Grant knew it was only Will's way of squeezing the duck season a little longer. His arms waved and he stood up repeatedly as he described all the day's action for his dad.

The temperature had continued to plummet all day Saturday and Saturday night. When Grant woke up Sunday morning, it was nearly dawn. He shuffled, as always, scratching and yawning, to the old white coffeepot on the stove. Once again Frank was sitting at the kitchen table before anyone else was awake. Now he was staring out across the lake and scratching Nellie's chin. It was zero degrees Fahrenheit. The wind had stopped blowing and the sun was shining along the tops of the pine trees on the eastern shore, but it was very cold. The lake was frozen most of the way across, although there were patches of open water in the middle. Frank turned slowly toward Grant and shook his head sideways.

"Season's over!"

chapter *T*EN

The woods around Spider Lake Duck Camp should have been dark and forbidding on a moonless night. But the white snow on the forest floor sparkled like the stars in the clear northern sky. Anne drove cautiously along the winding lane that had been cut through the tall pines many years earlier.

Grant was bent over the fireplace, rearranging the embers with a poker, when Anne walked in. "Hi," she said as she took her coat off and hung it by the door. "How was the weekend?"

"It was awesome!" he said, still looking into the fireplace. "It was as good as it can ever be! Just like it used to be!" He put two more logs on the fire and turned toward her. "It was perfect. You know … the cold, the hard work, the fear, the darkness, the thrill of playing the game correctly — God, that's how you know you're alive."

If he'd been looking directly at her face, he might have noticed a tiny grimace and seen her shoulders drop a little at his words. She didn't want to deny him the joy of his weekend, but she wanted for the joy in his voice to be because she'd arrived, not because of his passion for something else.

Grant crossed the room quickly and greeted Anne with a kiss, then held her for a moment. "How was your weekend?" he asked, stepping back from her.

Her reply carried the distant hint that her weekend would have been better if he'd been with her. "Oh, it was nice. I did some reading and got some things done around the house. I went over to the Native American Art Festival in Bemidji on Saturday morning before the weather got too bad. It was nice!" Now he thought he could hear something he'd heard in her voice years ago. She'd mentioned the Art Festival several times during the previous week, and she'd hoped he would spend the day with her there on Saturday. But when Dennis Taylor called with news of the duck migration, she understood immediately that he'd be hunting with Will instead of attending an art festival with her. Now she was leaving her frustration out there for him to notice. He wasn't totally sure, but he began to remember that he'd been involved in discussions like this before. Was she trying to undo his weekend? If she couldn't make him choose not to do the thing he loved, maybe she was trying to make him feel guilty now for having done it. He chose to ignore the feeling.

"Yeah? Did they have a good crowd?" Grant turned his back to her now and walked to the refrigerator as he spoke.

"It was fair ... starting to see some Christmas shoppers," she replied as she walked to the fire.

Grant opened the refrigerator and then turned toward Anne. He was holding a bottle of wine for her to see. "Wanna celebrate the end of the season?" he asked with a smile. He knew what her answer would be.

"Definitely!" she replied. Anne actually liked the excitement that she saw in Grant's eyes when he spoke of his love for the hunt, but she was envious of the enthusiasm and joy he showed for his times away from her. She had expected him to give up more of his time in the outdoors in order to be with her. Now, her relief that he would have more time for her spread across her face, and she was glad to let him see that, too.

Grant stood at the log table and leaned forward while he twisted the corkscrew into the cork. He wore faded jeans and a gray T-shirt that said "Muskie Days" across the front. Except for some gray at his temples and a few gray whiskers, Anne thought he still looked as he always had. When the cork made the low thud that it makes coming out of a wine bottle, Grant looked at Anne and raised his eyebrows. Then he threw the cork into the fire. When he'd filled two glasses, he brought them to the fireplace and held one out for Anne to take. As she reached for it, he pulled it back. "Nope, gotta have a kiss first."

She smiled, stood on her toes, and kissed him as he handed the wine glass to her. Grant pushed the old coffee table out of the way and then sat on the floor in front of the fireplace. He was leaning back on the couch and looking up at Anne while he patted his hand on the floor and raised his eyebrows again, inviting her to sit.

When she sat on the floor next to him, he put his arm around her. They both leaned back on the couch and sipped at their wine several times while they looked at the flames dancing in the fireplace. "You're still a pretty girl," Grant said softly. Anne loved it when he said things like that. She put her hand on his thigh and gently rubbed the inside of his leg. Grant always liked to stroke her long hair, and after he'd run his hand along her soft black hair several times, he touched her face ever so gently with his fingertips. He touched her ear, her cheek, then her eyelids and her lips while she rested her head on his shoulder. He sipped at the wine and continued to touch her softly.

As it happened almost every time they were alone together now, their desire for each other quickly became urgent, unstoppable. Grant brought his mouth to hers and began fumbling with the snap and the zipper on her pants, pulling himself toward her as they began to undress each other.

When their lovemaking was finished, they lay beside the fire with their arms and legs entwined as lovers do. They were both soaked with sweat. Sex had seemed absolutely urgent for both of them, and now they lay together holding each other close. Anne wanted this closeness never to end. Grant rolled onto his back and extended an arm to the side. "Wow," he sighed. "So what are you thinking?"

"Nothing. I just want it to be like this forever," she whispered. She did not ask Grant what he was thinking. She brought her face close to his and kissed his cheek.

"Yeah, me too," he said softly. Grant was beginning to notice that during sex, and during the excitement that was always a prelude to sex, was the time he felt closest to Anne. Maybe it was the only time he felt close to her. More and more now, as soon as sex was over, something always made him feel somewhat distant from her once again. Now, other thoughts swirled and floated through his mind while he lay there. Somewhere just behind his eyelids, he saw things drifting across his conscious mind. He saw water and sky. He saw Will smiling and he saw his father as a young man. He saw Ingrid as a small child and as a young woman. He saw Kate as she'd been when he held her as he was holding Anne now. He saw the farm where he grew up. He saw his little boat with ducks gliding around it. Grant smiled a faraway smile as he thought of all the things of his life.

In the flickering light of the shrinking fire, Anne pressed her body against him again. Grant tried to tell himself that it was the heat from the fire that made him feel closed in.

~

During the month or so that Grant and Anne had been seeing each other again, Grant had basically become comfortable with Anne back in his life. He felt he loved her. He enjoyed her company. But sometimes when he was with her now, he felt a vague tension growing between them. Anne had always been slow to voice her feelings. Grant knew that and actually admired that quality in her, but he sensed she was holding something back from him. He wondered occasionally if she had some misgivings about their new relationship. Sometimes she would start to say something and then stop herself. He'd noticed that from time to time, she would lose interest in their conversations. When he questioned her about it, she'd reply with something like "I'm just tired" or "I was just thinking of something else — it's nothing."

He thought about her recent quiet periods all during work on Monday morning and decided to call her at school over the noon hour. "Hey, you wanna have dinner out tonight?" He made sure to let her hear an upbeat tone in his voice.

"Sure, but most of the seasonal places are closed. Where should we go?" Grant was glad to hear some excitement in her voice, too.

"Well, Emil's, of course." He let her hear exaggerated joy and anticipation when he said it; he knew what her response would be. There really weren't many restaurants to choose from in Walker this time of year, and they both knew it. If there had been something more to her liking, he would have suggested it. She groaned, but only in mild protest. She'd tolerated Emil's Leech Lake Café, but Grant's fondness for the place had become a running joke between them.

"I'll pick you up after work. Oh, I don't think I'm gonna wear my tux, just in case you wanted to plan your ensemble." Grant thought he was clever when he hung up the phone.

Emil's had remained a unique establishment through all the years Emil had operated it. When Anne and Grant entered from the street, the little bells hanging on the door announced their arrival. Grant looked at the ancient wood-and-glass cabinet on his left. Inside the old display case next to the cash register were cigars, fishing reels, shotgun shells, fishing lures, and a price list for the live bait that Emil also sold. Behind the old display case hung camouflage jackets and hats along with large landing nets and minnow buckets. There was a sign directly behind the cash register that read, "Nobody beats Emil's meat."

In order to get to the tables and booths and the breakfast counter in the back of the restaurant, all customers had to walk past this display case in the front. Some extraordinarily poor taxidermy adorned all of the walls along the way. The fish and ducks mounted on the walls had a tortured look to them. Grant and Will had joked for years about whether the taxidermist was merely incompetent or perhaps a little twisted.

As they entered, Grant turned to Anne and nodded. "Now this is a classy place! Would you like to take the window booth by the northern pike, or the corner booth by the missing link?" Poised above the corner booth, there was a mammal of some sort with a hideous snarl on its face and a contorted posture. Grant smiled a huge smile, and Anne shook her head with a practiced disdain as she led him toward the window booth.

While they slid into the booth, they both looked out at the big, dark expanse of Leech Lake. Only a handful of lights were visible across Walker Bay tonight.

Grant lifted his left hand in a silent greeting to Emil Krause.

"Hi, Doc!" Emil called out over the noise and conversation in the restaurant.

In a familiar gesture, Grant raised his left hand again to order dinner. He showed Emil two fingers on his left hand to order two hamburgers. Then he put his thumb and forefinger together and rotated his wrist once to order coffee.

Emil Krause nodded, smiled, and called out, "You got it, Doc!"

"You eat here too often," Anne said as she watched Grant order their meals.

"No such thing," Grant smiled and leaned back in the booth.

During the previous weeks since Anne and Grant had begun seeing each other again, they'd spent almost every night together.

Most evenings, they had been at Grant's cabin. But sometimes they'd stayed at Anne's house in town. Tonight's meal at Emil's was a bit of a change of pace for them.

As Grant raised his arm to rest it on the back of the booth, Anne put her elbows on the table and leaned toward him. "Ever wonder where all of this is leading?"

He knew she was asking about the future — their future … together. He'd suspected that it had been on her mind for a while.

"Every day," he replied.

"So what do you think?"

"Well, I don't think about all of this with an end in mind. I think I'm pretty happy and comfortable for the first time since I lost my wife. I think you're my old friend from long ago, and you're back and that makes me feel good. I love you. What do you think?"

She wanted him to talk of more, of a future together, of commitment, of marriage. He could see she was disappointed with his answer, but he would not apologize for it or change it.

"Anne, Kate has been gone for less than a year. You've been alone for twice that. It's best if this kind of thing has time to play out … know what I mean?"

"Yes." She was somewhat embarrassed that she'd brought it up now, and she looked away.

He reached across the table and took her hand in his. "Hey, I love you!" he said reassuringly. He understood now that she'd had so many quiet times recently because she was checking herself, holding back questions like this about the future. He could see the frustration in her eyes. It was clear she wanted to press the issue.

Anne leaned forward and spoke up only enough to be heard over the background noise behind them. "So what if we got married? You'd want to live in my house on the golf course, wouldn't you?" There was an edge to her voice. She felt that need to push the issue of commitment. Grant wished that he wasn't hearing it. Anne was compelled to address it.

Grant let go of her hand and leaned back in the booth. "I'm pretty happy where I'm at." He almost looked away from her, but he knew that would make a strong enough statement to hurt her. He held her eyes with his and continued. "I just moved to the lake. It's my dream home." He chose not to address marriage.

"Well, I just thought ... you know ... my house is so close to the office, and to school. And it's so new." She didn't look away either, but she was uncomfortable with Grant's response.

"Yeah, it's pretty nice," he conceded. He nodded slowly and let his eyes drift to the coffee cup in front of him.

"Hey," he raised his face again, "did you hear that the Gronwald place on Big Sand Lake sold?" He had to change the subject.

"Oh?"

"Yeah, $400,000, and the lake access isn't very good either."

They ate their dinner and talked of other things. Marriage and moving weren't mentioned again, but the weight of their conversation never lifted.

chapter ELEVEN

With the hunting season over, Grant did little else than work and be with Anne. On his visits to Halstad, he tried to stay with his mother from Thursday night through Saturday afternoon and then return for Saturday night with Anne.

Gladys was beginning to show the stress of her constant supervision of Big Ole. Occasionally now, Grant began to insist that his mother stay home and rest for a day while he stayed with his dad. He found it to be surprisingly difficult to be a continuous caregiver for an elderly person. His father needed direct supervision for meals, bathroom chores, walks in the wheelchair, even a drink of water. By the end of the days alone with his dad, Grant was exhausted. He didn't know how his mother could do this.

On one November weekend, Grant could not leave for Halstad until Friday afternoon, and Anne decided to accompany him for his weekly visit with his parents. On that weekend, Anne Robertson caught a glimpse of the Thorson family that she'd never seen before.

Several times, when she watched how Grant's mother acted when she was around Big Ole, Anne saw the little things that had become the measure of love. Gladys would carefully spoon oatmeal into his mouth and catch his spills with the spoon, just as she'd done for her five sons and all of their children. She put his slippers on his feet when he was cold; she cut his fingernails because he could no longer do it himself. When he had to rest, which was often, Gladys would sit on a hard wooden chair next to Big Ole's recliner and hold his hand while he slept. Sometimes she'd read and sometimes she'd just hold his hand and watch him sleep.

When Ole slept in his reclining chair, Grant and Anne would sit on Ole's bed and read while they waited for Ole to wake up. Dozens of times each day, Anne watched Grant's father's right hand emerge from under his blanket and reach for Gladys' sleeve. When he tugged on her sleeve, Gladys would turn and smile. Then, always, he would tug again and she would lean over to him. When her face was almost touching his, he would whisper something, something Grant could never hear. Then Gladys would kiss him on the lips and reply very softly, "I love you, too!" She'd sit up again and look at Grant and Anne with a sheepish grin, as if she were a little girl who'd just been caught kissing her boyfriend on the way home from school. Sometimes she could manage to turn her face away from them before her smile dissolved to tears.

On that last Saturday of November, Grant explained to his parents that he had to return to Washington, D.C., the next weekend for another meeting of the health care committee. He told Big Ole that he'd be back in two weeks instead of one, and he tried to joke with his dad a little bit. Grant couldn't tell if his father was disappointed with the news or just tired, but Ole made it clear that he wanted to go to bed early on that particular Saturday. Grant and his mother washed Ole for bed, brushed his teeth, tucked him in, and said goodnight. "I love you, Dad. I'll see you in two weeks!" Grant said as he walked out the door to Ole's room. Anne stood in the corner, apart from it all, and watched silently. Ole made no reply.

Grant planned to take his mother home and then return to Spider Lake. But when they were in his Suburban and heading for the farm, Grant stopped and told his mother and Anne that he had to go back to the nursing home. "I'll be right back, Mom," he said as he left them in the car and walked quickly to his father's room. Quietly, he knelt beside Big Ole's bed and looked at his father. Grant's face was close to Ole's; he could hear his father's shallow breathing. His father lay before him now, in this nursing home, waiting to die. Grant felt the back of his throat tighten once again, and he began to cry. He wanted to change all of this; it hurt him so badly to see his father, his hero, reduced to this. Now, his father couldn't even die in his own bed. His family had to leave him here every night and return to their lives without him. Grant felt like he was abandoning the one man who had always been there for him, always loved him, always been his best friend.

Grant's face was contorted as he tried to be quiet, but his crying woke his father. Ole's eyes opened into sharp focus immediately, and Grant was surprised to read the concern in his father's expression. Ole showed so little emotion on his face anymore. But now Ole's eyes were asking, "What's the matter?" He was puzzled about Grant's tears, but he figured out soon enough that the tears were for him. Their eyes met, and each of them returned a lifetime of love to the other with a simple glance. Grant reached over and stroked Ole's forehead gently. "I just had to come back and look at you one more time, Dad," Grant whispered. He could say no more as he choked with emotion.

"So how do I look?" An absurd smile flickered across Ole's face when he spoke.

His father's face and the silly question now struck Grant as funny, and he was laughing and crying at the same time when he said, "Damn good, Dad!"

"Yeah, that's what all the nurses tell me, too." Ole almost seemed to smile. Grant laughed out loud and held his father's face close to his.

Ole's face was expressionless for a moment. Then his dark eyes passed a look of reassurance to Grant. He reached a thin, trembling hand to his son's face and touched the whiskers on Grant's chin for a moment. "You're a good boy, I'll see you in two weeks," he whispered, then closed his eyes again.

When Grant left his father's room for the second time, he was surprised to find his mother and Anne standing just outside the door to Ole's room. They'd followed him and heard and seen everything. For a brief moment, no one knew what to say, and they just stood there looking at each other. Then Grant took Gladys in his arms and hugged her. There were no tears and nothing was said. They all knew that the only thing Ole Thorson had left was the love of his family.

~

The snow along the shore of Spider Lake crunched under their boots. Anne and Grant walked slowly along the frozen surface of the lake. Nellie circled them, searching for grouse with her nose to the ground. "I'm glad I went with you last week," Anne ventured after a long silence.

"Me too."

"Your parents have a special love."

"Yeah," he kept walking slowly.

"Sixty-two years is a long time. They're still devoted to each other." Anne had been moved by what she'd seen at the nursing home.

"Yeah."

She turned to Grant and asked bluntly, "What happened?"

"Huh? Whadya mean?" He didn't know what she was talking about.

"What happened when you broke up with me?"

"I told you everything then." He shrugged his shoulders. He wondered what had made her change the subject.

"No, you didn't. You said you'd met someone else that you had strong feelings for and you felt you had to tell me. It was pretty clear that I was being dumped, but all of a sudden you just left my life, like that!" Anne snapped her fingers. "I thought we were planning our wedding. And after that night, you never spoke to me again until I walked into your office." It was the first time she'd spoken of their breakup, and he could tell she wanted to know what had happened. There was no anger in her voice, but she was demanding an answer.

Grant sat on a fallen tree and looked up at her. "You really wanna know?" he asked seriously.

"Yes."

He put his hands on his knees and looked down. "I'd seen Kate around school, and I thought she was pretty. Young men notice that sort of thing," he shrugged. "Then, one day, I bumped into her by the vending machines and we had a brief exchange – you know, 'Food here tastes like shit! Ha ha!' Then I saw her around the halls a little more often and we spoke briefly. I didn't think too much of it."

Grant had started his explanation with an apologetic tone. But as he spoke now, Anne began to hear excitement, passion in words. "Each time I saw her, I was drawn to her. She was tall and pretty, and she was always talking and laughing with older guys and professors. Our small conversations got longer, and I began to look for her, wait for her. The way she walked ... you know. The way she talked ... I loved it. There was something vulnerable there, hidden underneath the self-confidence. Those blue eyes, her smile ... she just took hold of me like she'd been waiting for me." Grant stopped and looked up at Anne. He took a breath and continued.

"I began to feel conflict inside me. Sometimes when I was with you, I'd think of her." Grant looked at Anne again. "Want me to keep going?"

"Yes."

"One night, I made up some story about studying so you wouldn't be suspicious, and I took her to a ball game. That was it for me. That night, I knew she was the one. I knew when I spoke to her that I loved her, felt something deep and undeniable for her. I came to your apartment and told you. I know we weren't married or anything, but I felt committed. I felt awkward and terrible. I never cheated! Well, maybe what I just told you was cheating, I don't know. That's about it."

Grant's confession had regained the feel of an apology. As he'd spoken, Anne had felt a weight lift from her heart and then settle back again. After so many years, she felt some sense of completeness in the whole thing now. Even after all these years, she'd still needed to hear it all from Grant. But the pain of it all was still there.

Anne felt jealous of Kate all over again, almost angry with her. She was the athlete with the great legs and figure. She was beautiful and had everything going for her. But Grant had chosen to love someone else. She'd been over this so many times, and it always came around to the same realization. Intellectually, she knew Kate was a good person. After all — she'd done exactly what Anne would have done: she'd married Grant Thorson. Anne was really just jealous of the spark in Grant's eyes when he spoke of her. She wanted to see it in his eyes when he held *her*; she wanted to feel it on his lips when he kissed *her*.

"Do you feel for me what you felt for her?" Anne was serious now. She wasn't begging for an answer, but she was intent on getting one. Her eyes were fixed on him. She asked the question in the same way a cop might try to prompt a confession from a suspect. Then tears began welling in her eyes.

Grant stood up and said sternly, "I love you, Anne! You can't know me as well as you do and question that. Our life experiences are fairly unique, I think you'd have to agree. You can't ask me to compare the feeling of infatuation I had as a twenty-two-year-old with what I feel for you now. It's not fair." Even as he spoke, though, Grant Thorson knew that it had been a fair question, one he just did not want to answer now. He felt comfort with Anne, but it was not the joy, the laughter, or the excitement he'd known with Kate. He'd waited for that, assuming it would come, since the first trip to Washington. But now it seemed that the more she pressed, the more he retracted. She wanted him to hand over the passion in his heart ... and he had no control over that.

"It's just that sometimes, I see something flash in yours eyes or hear it in your voice. I saw it in your father's eyes last week when he looked at your mother ... even after all he's been through. Maybe it's passion, excitement, or love – I don't know. But I want it. I see it when you speak of Kate, Ingrid, your father, or Will. I think I even saw it when you spoke to Susan Wells. That's what I want from you."

Grant knew exactly what she was talking about. "I don't know what you mean," he said as he looked away. He didn't want to go any further down this road. He didn't have to – Anne understood now as she watched him struggle and try to hide it all from her.

chapter TWELVE

Thomas Hutchinson was slouched in the small rocking chair he kept in the Oval Office. The chair reminded him of John Kennedy, and he would have kept it around for that reason alone. But it was also comfortable, and he found that it helped him relax if he could empty the Oval Office from time to time and sit in the old rocker while he took a cup of coffee or a diet soda.

It was 6:00 p.m. now and his afternoon's work was done. He had two more appointments scheduled for after the supper hour, but they would be informal visits with congressmen regarding proposed legislation. Martin Walters had just finished briefing the President regarding the day's business when a woman knocked and then entered. She walked quickly to Martin Walters, handed him several pieces of paper, then excused herself.

As Walters read the papers, he began to smile. "Looks like Dr. Thorson brought a bit of an attitude with him from the Land of 10,000 Lakes!"

"Oh?" the President said. He smiled and looked up at Walters, who was now sitting on the arm of the couch in the center of the room.

"Yeah. Janean just brought this in. I sent someone over to the health care committee meeting today. I wanted to know just what, if anything, was going on over there." Walters smiled and held the papers up for the President to see. "It seems that Richard Bailey assigned every member a topic to research before this month's meeting. Each member was to show up with some information about his or her topic and then share it with the committee so they could hit the ground running, as it were."

Walters raised his eyebrows and continued. "Your guy starts off the meeting this morning with this: 'There is no health care crisis in this country! We have the finest system of health care in the history of the world. But we do have a greed crisis in the health insurance business, and the insurance companies would like the government to make their problem go away so they don't have to do the difficult things. We also have a *health* crisis in this country. Our culture has almost delivered us to the point where we as individuals, believe we can take a pill or have a surgical procedure done to restore our health after we've destroyed it with an unhealthy lifestyle or perhaps simply a long life. We seem to believe that as long as we have good insurance, or benefits, then we can simply buy more health! We can buy a pill to help us lose weight. We can buy some surgery to restore our eyesight, or heart valves, or hips and knees, whatever. Cosmetic surgery can provide better chins, eyebrows, calves, boobs, you name it. So what exactly is the crisis here?

'We are at a dangerous point with this committee. We're about to start proposing a myriad of solutions to the subtle problems involved in what some would call a health care crisis. But first we need to ask ourselves some hard questions: Is it safe and wise for us to assume that the course we've chosen for our health insurance system in this country is the correct one? That all we need to do is get the government deeply involved in the management of it and everything will be fine? That's a scary thought where I live!'"

Walters then flipped a page and looked up at the President before he continued reading. "Then the good doctor finished up with this: 'Dr. Bailey, the report you asked me to submit regarding the duplication of expensive diagnostic procedures is right here. You'll forgive me if it's a little dog-eared and yellow around the edges? I wrote it twenty-five years ago when I was a freshman dental student, but I think it's as relevant now as it was then. My professor gave me a B- — he said I presented a far too liberal look at the issue.' Then your man smiled what he would probably call a shit-eating grin and sat down. This guy is good!"

Thom Hutchinson smiled and said nothing.

"Are you going to call him tonight while he's in town?" Walters asked.

"No, maybe next time. What else have you got there, Martin?"

~

The small crowd of committee members, their assistants, the media, and the hotel staff had walked slowly toward the lobby of the Hilton Hotel, talking and joking quietly shortly after the health care committee meeting had ended.

Grant lingered at the large table by himself. He had nowhere to go and nothing to do until his return flight to Minneapolis the next day at noon. Anne had decided not to accompany him this time. She said she had some things to do, but he felt she'd decided to stay in Walker in order to have some time alone.

Grant felt all alone at the moment, too, but he didn't really like the feeling now. He thought it was similar to the way he'd felt during the first few months after Kate's death. He was placing loose papers in some folders and stacking them on the table in front of him when someone approached from his right side and moved the chair next to him.

"Hello, Dr. Thorson!" It was Susan Wells. She smiled and extended her hand as she stood beside him. Grant had looked around for her earlier but had not seen her. He assumed she'd lost interest in the committee and was covering some other story. When he realized that the pretty woman had sought him out and come to greet him, his mood changed quickly. He was relieved that someone had made a friendly gesture. The only feelings he could remember similar to it were the times as a child when he'd felt alone in a strange place and a friend had appeared to claim him.

"Hello, Miss Wells," he said as he stood to shake her hand. "But nobody calls me 'Doctor' — well, my parents like to — it's just Grant, though, OK? It's nice to see a friendly face." He hesitated. "You are friendly?"

"It's just Susan, too, and yes, I'm friendly." She thought it was charming that he said his parents liked to call him "Doctor," and she smiled. She'd arrived late, during the afternoon meeting. A writer from another newspaper had told her of Grant's comments in the morning meeting and of several more things he'd said during the day. The only reason she'd come to this meeting today was because she'd enjoyed her brief conversation with Grant the previous month, and she was curious about him. As the other newspaper correspondent had related the conservative nature of Grant's remarks, though, she began to wonder if she'd been mistaken in her first impression of Grant Thorson. Maybe he was just another ultraconservative "cowboy."

"I just got here. How was the meeting?" Susan asked innocently. She didn't intend to let him know what she'd heard about the meeting already.

"Well, I guess I made everyone angry right away this morning," he answered as he sat down again and gestured for her to do the same. "You know, each of us really has only one perspective from which to view an issue, and my entire life experience causes me to see this issue as I do."

Susan thought he sounded as though he was asking permission to feel as he did. He rubbed his eyes and reached for the water on the table. When he'd taken a drink, he leaned back in his chair and looked into her eyes.

"It's funny, the way people think," he paused, "or don't think." Grant continued. "The liberals out here all take this arrogant damn posture that anyone who doesn't think like they do is just plain stupid or they'd understand the issue better. And they think they're so clever when they make fun of anyone who disagrees with them." He was looking right at her, and Susan felt as though he'd been reading her mind. She said nothing.

"And you know, the conservatives are just as bad. They'll assume the same arrogant, self-righteous attitude that anyone who would disagree with them is obviously immoral or else they'd be conservative. And once you get to that point, you're stuck. You know, there were a couple of pretty intelligent people sitting here today who see the health care picture totally different than I do … and not one of them was interested in why I feel the way I do. All they wanted to do was tell me why I'm all wrong. You know, I don't think any of these people who disagree with me are immoral, but something in their life experience has led them to a totally different view of the world." She had been looking, just a few minutes earlier, for signs that Grant Thorson was just another redneck. But in a short time, he'd exposed a vulnerable side of himself and impressed Susan that he was actually pretty insightful.

Grant sat back and rolled his eyes again. "Oh, hell. What do I know? I'm just some dentist from the north woods. I'm also doing all the talking." He smiled broadly now, and she liked it. His mood seemed to change now. "Thanks for talking to me. It is nice to see a friendly face. How was your day?"

"I'm guessing it was a lot better than yours," she said with a smile. She felt compelled to help him. She hoped he wouldn't feel as though she was "talking down" to him. She paused before she continued. "Grant, one thing you must remember about this city is that everyone here has an agenda. Right and wrong get a little blurry, they don't matter too much, and people's feelings only get in the way most of the time." She was trying to relieve some of his frustration; she'd seen it a thousand times before on the faces of people new to Washington politics. Her impression of Grant Thorson had changed considerably during the short time they'd been talking. She could see he was thoughtful and intelligent, and that he probably was not cut out for this place. She decided to change the subject.

"Do you have dinner plans for the evening?" She raised her eyebrows and smiled. "Is Ms. Robertson meeting you somewhere?" Now she hoped to draw him out from any more discussion of Washington.

"No." Grant shook his head, and the way he curled his lip told Susan that she'd struck a nerve. She'd moved from one depressing topic to another.

"Did I ask a clumsy question? Sorry." Susan could sense immediately that something had happened between Grant and Anne. She felt good inside briefly; maybe this handsome man wasn't as attached as she'd thought. She was surprised by her own feelings.

"No. But Anne isn't with me this time ... it's a long story, but it's OK," Grant smiled.

Susan felt very awkward for a moment, and then she remembered something. "Hey, I did some research on the great writers of the English language!" She pointed her finger at Grant and smiled. She knew he'd like what she had to say.

"Gordon MacQuarrie was born in 1900, in Superior, Wisconsin. He was an outdoor writer for the Superior newspaper for years, and then he moved to Milwaukee to work for a bigger paper. He wrote clever stories for outdoor magazines also. Many of his best stories have now been rounded up from all over the place and compiled in three books called *Stories of the Old Duck Hunters Inc. (Incorrigible) and Other Drivel.*" She smiled. "He died young in 1956. The current generation of duck hunters reveres him. I thought his stories were charming, like Norman Rockwell paintings only in print." She took a breath and continued. "Sigurd Olson was born in 1899. He also lived in northern Wisconsin. He taught at some small college in Minnesota or Wisconsin. He was a naturalist and a conservationist way ahead of his time. He wrote several books about the beauty of the north woods. He is revered more by conservationists and nature lovers. He died in 1982. I personally enjoyed *The Singing Wilderness* more than the other books of his that I could find. It's hard to compare the two writers. I liked them both." She smiled an enormous smile.

"Wow, that's pretty good!" Grant was clearly impressed with her effort, and he couldn't help but smile. Then his face slowly tightened with a look of frustration, his eyebrows furrowed, and he said, "I couldn't find *anything* on those two guys you mentioned, though." He held the serious façade briefly, then smiled as they both laughed out loud. Grant could not hide the surprise and the satisfaction he felt that Susan had actually researched MacQuarrie and Olson. He smiled a silly smile while she described her research and trips to several bookstores. She was surprised, too — surprised that she'd been motivated to continue the game even in his absence. He was obviously not someone who would ever have any power or a voice in her world. She just liked him.

When Susan finished speaking, Grant leaned back in his chair and pointed at her. The meeting room was now empty except for the two of them. "Any woman who appreciates Gordon Mac-Quarrie and Sigurd Olson would have real value in my world. You wouldn't happen to own a boat, would you?"

"No. Why?"

"There's an old joke that we tell at home. It's about a guy who puts an advertisement in the newspaper classifieds. The ad goes something like this: 'Wanted: Attractive woman about thirty years old. Should have her own boat, motor, and trailer. Please respond with photo of boat, motor, and trailer.'" The look on his face asked, "Get it?"

"But I'm over thirty," Susan said, still grinning.

"How much over?"

"Way over."

"Oh well, you're still not bad!" There would be no blushing for Grant today. He was truly enjoying the conversation with this pretty woman. When he heard himself tell her she wasn't bad, it was as if he could see the look in his own eyes. He knew he was smiling broadly. He knew then exactly what Anne had been talking about, and he could feel himself laughing and talking with Susan in a way he'd never done with Anne. Now that he was aware of his own behavior, he was compelled to end the conversation so as not to validate the things Anne had said. But he continued anyway; he felt himself being drawn to Susan. With every word she spoke she became more attractive. He couldn't remember a conversation being this much fun in a long time. Only Will Campbell made him smile like this. He understood that this was just how he'd met Kate, and he felt something familiar.

"So, all I know about you is that you work for the *Post* and you don't own a boat. Can you fill me in with some biographical stuff?"

"Like what?"

"Married?"

"Twice."

"I was expecting a yes or no, indicating current status."

"No."

"Where you from?"

"Hometown?"

"Yes."

"Ithaca, New York."

"College?"

"Columbia."

"Why Columbia?

"Scholarship."

"Must be smart?"

"Yup."

"Parents?"

"Yes." She smiled and nodded.

"More, please." Both of them were enjoying this.

"Dysfunctional family, battered mother, alcoholic father, both gone now."

"Jeez, I'm sorry." Grant was embarrassed that their little game had led to that answer. The conversation ground down now.

"It's OK. I grew up with my mom, hardly knew my dad. Both of them died while I was in college." Susan had no difficulty in sharing any of this with Grant.

"Tough start in life!"

"Yeah, maybe, but things have worked out well." She smiled.

"OK, married twice?" he started over, raising his eyebrows, asking for more information, and trying to put some cheer back into his voice.

"First time in college. We were stupid kids. It lasted for about eight months. Second time shortly after college. He was an attorney, seemed like the thing to do at the time. He turned out to have no character, a jerk. OK, it's your turn."

"Pretty boring. Raised on a farm in Minnesota. Loving family. Married a girl from school. Happily married for twenty-three years, and she died of heart disease. One daughter, Ingrid, she's eighteen, she's perfect. I live a small life on a small lake in Minnesota." Grant smiled when he finished, and Susan could see he was very proud of his family, his life. She liked that.

They talked for a while longer. They were enjoying themselves as they began to get to know each other, and they were flirting a little. Grant was beginning to wonder if he should ask Susan to dinner. He had no intentions beyond dinner and a pleasant conversation, but the thought of asking made him feel awkward. He was afraid she'd say "no" for whatever reason, and he didn't want that. He felt something good inside, but he denied it.

Susan had been hoping that he'd ask her for a drink, or dinner also, and when he didn't she began to feel as though she needed to invent a reason to leave. She'd seen something joyful and innocent in his eyes tonight. She'd seen it all along, actually, even the first time they'd met at the White House. Now she wanted to sit close to him and touch him while she talked with him. But she denied herself, too. She didn't want it to be awkward for him if he wanted to go now and couldn't because she wouldn't shut up.

"Oh, it's getting late and I have another appointment in a few minutes." She didn't, but she felt she needed to get going. She'd invented a reason to excuse herself.

Grant stacked his papers and carried them under his arm as they walked across the empty meeting room and into the hotel lobby.

"Thank you for talking with me, Susan. It's been a pleasure getting to know you!" Grant smiled a warm smile and extended his hand. "Maybe we'll see each other again next month if they don't kick me off this committee."

"That would be nice. I'll be looking forward to it. Good night, Grant." She shook his hand and walked out the door. She was tempted to turn around and confess. She thought she could see in his eyes that he liked her and wanted her to stay. She had no place to go, but just in case he was still watching she wanted to look as if she was in a hurry. As she walked she thought, "He thanked me twice for *talking* to him. I wish he'd have asked about dinner or a drink!" Her skepticism regarding Grant had vanished quickly, and she was already looking forward to seeing him again.

When Grant entered the lobby of his hotel, he walked directly to the desk clerk and asked, "Who makes the best pizza around here?" When the desk clerk answered, Grant said "thank you" and walked to his room. He kicked off his shoes, picked up the phone, and ordered a pizza to be delivered to his room. When he'd popped open a beer, he stood in front of his window and looked out at Washington. But his thoughts were far away. He thought of

Ingrid, Big Ole, his mother ... and Spider Lake. He smiled to himself when he thought of Susan Wells. He wanted to call Will and talk for just a while. 'Maybe later,' he thought. Then he began to think of Kate. He thought only of the good times and laughs they'd had over the years. Kate was the only other woman he'd ever laughed and joked with as he had today with Susan. Tonight, he smiled at the memories.

When the pizza was delivered to his room, Grant turned the TV on and found a ball game to watch. He put his feet up on the bed and ate his pizza. Tonight, it seemed all right to be alone again.

chapter T HIRTEEN

S now was falling gently on a quiet December night when Grant switched off the TV and let the cabin settle into darkness and quiet. All he and Anne could see out the windows were white streaks just outside the window glass. As usual, the light from the fire gave the cabin a yellow hue as the soft light flickered on the walls.

From the darkness next to him came a question that surprised him. It shouldn't have.

"Do you think we should move in together?" Anne asked.

He knew what his answer would be, but he tried to wrap it in reason, then hesitation, so it wouldn't sound like "NO!" "We both have daughters in college that would break our hearts if they moved in with someone. I guess that sounds a little hypocritical in light of our present situation, doesn't it? I guess this is sort of a special situation though ... I don't know. I think it would be best not to set that example for our children."

"This example is better?" she asked cynically. She was pushing the issue.

195

"Yeah, I know what you mean," he conceded. "But at least they don't know about this, do they? Doesn't this sound like the same discussion we had a long time ago?" Grant's tone changed, and he laughed gently as he spoke. "Only then we were talking about our parents instead of our kids." He was trying to joke with her, and change the subject.

Anne was embarrassed that she'd mentioned the future again, but she was frustrated, too. She felt Grant's answers were always evasive when she mentioned it. For now, though, she chose not to press the issue. She sat next to Grant in the darkness and held his hand.

Earlier in the evening, she'd walked past him while he sat at the kitchen table looking at a calendar. She stood behind him and looked over his shoulder for a moment while he studied the month of July. When he marked off four days with big X's, she asked what he was planning. He'd responded with a big smile, "Fishin' with Will." The moment had been doubly frustrating for her because she'd felt for some time that that particular weekend stood out as the perfect time for their wedding.

She wanted to let it all go away for the night, but she just couldn't. "How do you think our kids would feel if we told them we were getting married?" she asked from the darkness. She tried to adjust her voice so that her question came across as rhetorical, but Grant heard the edge on her words.

The phone rang before Grant needed to respond, and he got up to answer it immediately. "Thorsons'." He paused, then exclaimed, "Doctor!"

"Great," Anne thought, "it's Will Campbell. This conversation is over for about forty-five minutes!" She got up and walked to the bathroom to start taking off her makeup and getting ready for bed. Grant saw the frustration in her movements and decided to postpone his chat with Will. She'd been there only a minute when she heard Grant say, "Yeah, I'll call you tomorrow."

He walked into the bathroom and pulled her close to him as if he wanted sex. Anne turned her face away from him and her body stiffened.

Now, for the first time, she could feel anger in Grant. "All I wanted was to kiss you." He released her and stepped back. "We're way too far along to be playing the old 'sex is a weapon to get what I want' game." His eyes were dark and hard now. She hadn't seen this in his eyes before.

"Just what do you want, Anne?" He was trying to be sincere, but there was an air of contentiousness not far below the surface when he spoke. She heard anger in his tone.

"I need some commitment." Now she seemed to be pleading.

"I gave someone complete commitment twice. Kate died and left me. The other time I broke someone's heart — you remember that? For now, all I can give is to tell you I love you."

"We need to move on from here," she said.

"What's wrong with here?" He hung his head and said softly, "I don't know, Anne."

She knew she'd seen that anguish before, many years before, when he stood on her doorstep and broke up with her. She stepped toward him quickly. "We'll talk about it some other time" was all she said as she held him for several minutes. She had been frustrated that he would not give her that special passion or a commitment to their future. But now, for the first time since they'd begun seeing each other again, she was afraid he was actually taking something back instead of merely balking at the next step.

When they lay in bed that night, they were "spooning" while they waited to fall asleep. Anne lay on her side with her back to his stomach and his arms around her as they both watched the snow fall outside the window. As he lay close to Anne, his eyes were wide open. But he could see Will's face and hear very clearly something Will had said jokingly a thousand times: "Women don't want to *marry* the perfect man, they want to *create* him." He'd thought that was funny, until now. Both of them watched silently for most of the night as they waited for sleep to come.

chapter $\mathcal{F}$OURTEEN

During his last visit to Halstad before Christmas, Grant saw that his father was smaller and weaker, as usual. His mother was more worn down. His life felt heavier when he returned home. When he arrived at Spider Lake on Saturday, he hadn't seen Anne since the Wednesday evening when they'd argued about the future. They'd made plans for her to have dinner with him Sunday evening, but when he'd returned home from Halstad on Saturday night he hadn't called Anne. He assumed she'd be hurt by that, but he neglected to call anyway.

Anne arrived at Grant's cabin shortly after dark Sunday night. The air outside was clear and calm, and Grant could hear the car approaching from the long, wooded drive. As always, a yellow glow from the fire illuminated the cabin. But there was no delicious smell of roast duck. Grant had just not been motivated to prepare the usual Sunday dinner. He planned to make supper after they had had a chance to talk for a while.

The moment Anne walked in the door, Grant sensed something unusual. She took her coat off and laid it over a kitchen chair. Her face looked tired and drawn as he went to kiss her. She kissed him gently and held him for an extra moment longer than usual. She seemed stiff, distant.

"We need to talk," she said firmly. Grant could feel something in his stomach tighten.

"OK." He looked at her and raised his eyebrows.

She was looking at the floor now. She took his hand in hers and said quickly, "I took a job in Minneapolis ... I'm leaving tomorrow ... I don't want to see you anymore." She looked up into his face.

He could feel his stomach tightening more every second. He had not expected this. "What happened? I thought you loved me?"

She held his hand but made it clear that she did not want him to put his arms around her. As she began to speak, her voice trembled, and she had to let go of his hand so she could use a handkerchief to dry her eyes.

"That's just it. I love you. I've loved you since we were children. But I know it's never going to work for us."

"Why do you say that?" He reached for her and she stepped back.

"When all of this happened between us a few months ago, I thought you were going to be the love of my life. No, you are the love of my life. I loved you when we were kids. I loved you while I was married to someone else." Her face contorted and she sobbed briefly, then regained her composure.

"But Anne." He reached for her again, but again she stepped back.

"No! I have to say this." She stepped back quickly. She sobbed again for a moment, then took a deep breath. "I used to watch the way you looked at Kate when I saw you together around town. I saw something in your eyes ... other people around town talked about it, too. I see it when you're with Will. I see it when you speak of your father, your family. I see it when you tell me about the things of your life. I know I saw it when you spoke to Susan Wells. I wanted so much to see that in your eyes when you were with me. I never have seen it when you're with me. I know I never will. I've been fooling myself. I thought I saw it **once** … on that one special night. That will have to be enough for me."

He said nothing but reached for her hand. She pulled back once again.

"No. Let me finish." She wiped her nose and breathed deeply again. "You have passion for so many things of this life." She looked around the cabin and pointed. She was referring to the things of Spider Lake, his family, his friends. "You have such passion for a piece of music that you get choked up; you still want to beat up the bullies of your childhood; you want to fight the good fight in your profession! But you just don't have that 'feeling' for me. It all came into focus for me after our time in Washington two months ago, and then more and more over the past weeks."

"Anne, we can be happy together here … " He tried to plead with her.

"Don't do this to me!!" she yelled. There was anger in her voice now, for the first time. "All we have is the past! And that just won't carry us through!"

Anne stood quietly and looked at her feet for a few seconds while she wiped her nose. "You know, I needed all of this to happen. It seems funny that a thing like this could be so pleasant and so painful at the same time. If we hadn't had this time together, I never would have had closure with you. I'd have spent my whole life dreaming of something I could never have. I know now what I should have known twenty years ago.

He started to speak, but she raised her hand to cover his mouth.

"Grant? … Honey? … You know exactly what I mean, don't you? You know I'm right?" Anne's face was totally calm now, and her tone was similar to that of a mother comforting a small child.

"You know we're not going to make it together, don't you?" Now she wanted for him to answer.

He wanted so much for things to work with Anne, but he knew now that his relationship with Anne was based in no small part on his desire to restore order to his life by bringing back part of the past. She said she didn't see that special light in his eyes when he spoke to her. But that was because she lacked the passion he longed for — she just didn't share his excitement for the other things of his life. In this brief moment while he stood in front of her, he understood something about himself: *Something* was missing in all of this. He knew that the sights, the sounds, the smells of the duck boat or the ballpark, or even this cabin stirred something in him that tied him to his childhood, to his past, to all the loves of his life, and he wanted that connection. He'd been willing to try to make a life with someone who did not share that passion but only reflected the past, and that was wrong. They would not be happy together — that was once again true, as it had been twenty years earlier.

"You know I'm right, don't you?" Anne repeated.

"Yes," he replied with his head down, facing the floor. When that one little word left his lips, he knew part of his life had just ended.

Anne began to sob heavily and then she put her arms around his waist. The back of Grant's throat felt tight. He was empty of all feeling. The words she'd spoken had crystallized all of his thoughts. She'd verbalized exactly what he'd known all along. But still, he wished this could all be different. He wanted her to stay and hold him, though, and he sensed she might if he pleaded for her to keep trying. But he did know that she was right about everything, and that it would be wrong for him to mislead her.

They held each other for a moment longer until Anne had stopped sobbing. They both knew that the next minute would be one of the most painful moments of their lives. She took another deep breath and let go of him. She put her coat on without another word and moved to the door. When she'd swung the door open, she turned and looked at him.

"I do love you, Anne," he said softly.

She reached her hand to his cheek and then kissed him. "I know you do … " – and she was gone.

When the door closed behind Anne, a part of Grant wanted to run after her and try to make her stay. But a stronger force compelled him to remain where he was and let her drive off. Grant stood in the little kitchen, looking at the door for some time after he'd heard Anne's car crunching the new snow. She drove away slowly, through the tall pines, along the narrow path to the main road about a mile away.

The cabin was quiet – more quiet than he'd ever noticed it could be. Finally, he moved away from the door. He filled the fireplace with wood and sat on the soft leather couch. The yellow light from the fire still cast a glow around the cabin now. As the fire jumped to life, shadows moved along the walls again. Grant could feel the warmth of the fire on his stocking feet as they rested on the coffee table. The heat and the flames were all he thought about as he stared into the dancing fire. Their love had been like a fire, he thought. Just like a fire. It was a pretty sappy analogy, like something from a movie, but it fit. It had burned hot once, then been neglected until only the smallest coal remained. Then it had been rekindled by something. Some fuel had caused it to burst back once again into a hot fire, and then that fire too died quickly. The fuel was like the paper of birch bark: It burned hot and fast but faded the same way. The real, lasting fuel was the solid wood in the middle of the tree. They'd never had that solid fuel, and you needed both to build a fire. Now, in his heart, he felt sorrow at the loss of an old friend and sorrow for all the pain he'd caused her. Grant just sat quietly in the small cabin and watched the flames dance.

~

The shrill noise of the telephone startled Grant. He looked quickly at the small clock on the kitchen countertop. It read 9:30 p.m. He'd been feeding the fire and staring at it for several hours.

"Hi, Dad! How was your week? We got a lot of snow here, and now it's really cold!" It was Ingrid, and he was very glad to hear her voice. However, in the moment that he'd been uplifted by the recognition of her voice, he'd become aware of a strange contradiction of feelings inside him. His initial thought when he'd heard the phone ring was that it might be Anne wanting to talk to him again. He knew instantly that he didn't want that, and he'd been briefly afraid to answer the phone. He knew Anne was right in what she'd done earlier, and that if she called him now, perhaps crying and wanting to talk, nothing good could come of it. The agony of their breakup would only be drawn out.

As Ingrid spoke about her week at school, Grant hid his feelings from her. He listened to her, he spoke to her, but as he stood with the phone to his ear he was distracted by an avalanche of feelings rolling over him. He struggled to concentrate on what Ingrid was saying.

When Grant realized that it was Ingrid on the phone and not Anne, he was also immediately disappointed that Anne hadn't called. He knew it made no sense to feel that way. He didn't know if it was a good thing or a bad thing, but something inside of him wanted Anne to miss him, to still want him.

Ingrid talked about her week at school for some time. Grant was listening, but not very well. Then she asked her father how the hunting had been. "The hunting was really good, honey. We had a great season. The lake is all frozen up, though!" His voice gave no hint that anything out of the ordinary had happened, and they spoke for a while longer.

When Grant had first told Ingrid that he was seeing Anne Robertson, Ingrid hadn't known what to think of it. She naturally thought of her father as belonging, forever, only to her mother.

But in a short time, she'd grudgingly accepted that maybe her dad was entitled to have a woman friend. Grant assumed Ingrid had been so wrapped up in her own life that she had no idea that her father and Anne had been quite serious. Both of them knew that their conversation was winding down when Ingrid asked her dad, "How's Anne?"

Grant looked around the silent cabin and said quietly, "Oh, she's fine."

chapter *F*IFTEEN

A blustery, cold wind swirled off Leech Lake as Grant walked across the street to the small coffee shop. His feet were cold, and a chill crept under his collar. He lowered his head into the wind and tucked his chin under the collar of his coat as he walked. When he reached the door to Emil's Leech Lake Café, he stomped the snow off his feet and stepped in. Emil Krause heard the little bells on the front door tinkle and looked up to see Grant Thorson walking in. "Hi, Doc!" he called out.

"Hi, Emil. Cold enough for you?" Grant smiled and walked to a booth by the window overlooking Walker Bay on the south end of the lake. Grant loved this life. He knew the name of everyone in the café at that moment, employees and patrons alike, and he knew where most of them lived. "Just coffee!" Grant said as he sat down.

"They're catchin' crappies through the ice over on Red Lake already!" Emil said with a smile as he set a cup of black coffee on Grant's table. If Emil didn't strike up a conversation with him, then one of the waitresses or another customer would, and that was one of the things Grant loved about his little town. But today he wanted only to sit in the quiet café and look at the big lake.

"I wouldn't be driving my truck too far out on the ice just yet," Grant replied with a smile. He didn't want to invite any more conversation, though, and he turned quickly toward the window and opened up a newspaper. He had no intention of reading the paper, but he hoped his friends would allow him some privacy if he appeared to be reading it.

It was mid-morning Wednesday, and a patient had cancelled her appointment, leaving Grant an hour with nothing to do. He'd told no one yet of his breakup with Anne. His staff had stopped asking questions about Anne on Tuesday, so Grant assumed they'd heard via the very short grapevine around Walker that Anne Robertson had quit her job and left town. The women who worked at his office had talked of little except Anne since she'd come into Grant's life again. Now, there had been no conversation about her for the past twenty-four hours, and Grant sensed that his staff was waiting for him to confirm what they already knew but were afraid to ask. He'd decided he wouldn't discuss it with anyone at the office; he just didn't want to talk about it with his staff.

He was glad he'd been able to function at work without any emotional distractions during the week so far. As long as he was busy at work, he didn't think about Anne. But when he was at home at night, his thoughts turned to her all the time. He missed her presence in his life, and he felt he loved her. But he still knew that she'd been right in what she'd said. All they had was the past. He knew he'd tried to think of her as a replacement for Kate. He understood that was wrong and would have caused problems later, but the empty feeling he'd felt in his stomach when she'd walked out the door returned to him every time he thought of her.

While he sat in the little café staring out the window, he thought back over the previous few weeks and all that had happened. People always said there was a plan to it all when something bad happened.

He thought about how they always said, "God has a plan, whether we understand it or not." Grant took little consolation in the idea that whatever it was that had happened with Anne was part of some plan. It was still impossible for him to understand how the death of his wife or the painful decline of his father could be part of a plan. Today he just thought Leech Lake looked very big and cold ... that was enough to think about for now.

That evening, when he'd finished the supper dishes, Grant took Nellie for a walk along the edge of the woods by the cabin. The night was cold and still, and the moon shone brightly behind some thin clouds. Grant liked nights like this. While Nellie chased around in the woods, Grant looked into the sky. He just took in the beauty of the night and wondered about his life. He remembered his evening walks in the days and weeks just after Kate's death. He thought that little had changed. He wondered if Kate was out there looking down on him, or if she had any idea where he was.

Grant wished he could guide the direction of his life to be exactly like he wanted. All he really wanted was a return to the way it used to be. The woods were silent, and the trees cast moon shadows as he looked around. He began to wonder just exactly what his life "used to be" like. He wondered just what part of his life that "used to be" he would want to return to. Would he return to his childhood? Was he happiest when he was in high school? – college? – when he was a young adult? He truly didn't know the answer. He only knew that the past was easier.

When he went into the cabin, he threw several small logs into the fireplace and then walked directly to the phone. He dialed Will Campbell's number and dropped heavily into the big leather chair by the fire.

"Campbell's," Will answered.

"Doctor?" Grant tried to sound serious.

"Doctor!" Will recognized Grant's voice immediately, and Grant imagined the grin on his face as he spoke.

"Got a minute to chat, old buddy?" Grant asked. He was smiling now also. As he spoke, Will always made him smile. But Will Campbell knew that his friend was troubled. He could hear fatigue through the telephone, and he knew Grant needed to talk.

"You bet, pard. What's up?" Will answered.

Grant told him everything. He began with his trepidation over the first flight to Washington, then related every experience and feeling he'd shared with Anne since then. There was no built-up emotion or anxiety that escaped with the story; he just gave Will the facts.

"I guess that's about it, Will. Whadya think about all that?" Grant said when he finished. With the possible exception of the night several weeks earlier when they drank too much, it was more than Will had heard from Grant since Kate died.

"Well, I have to ask you this, Doctor, so please consider the question before you answer." Will had spoken slowly at first. He paused and then blurted, "Do you think the bitch was after some payback for leaving her on the altar, as it were, all those years ago?" Just in case it was time to choose sides and lend some support, Will wanted Grant to know for certain just whose side he was on. "I gotta tell you, buddy, I've wondered from the very beginning if she might not have been waiting for a chance to stab you in the heart. Sorry if I offended you. But you know what else? Maybe she was making some sort of a preemptive strike. Maybe she knew you were just gonna drop the bomb on her again and she couldn't take it."

"You know I'd be lyin' if I told you I hadn't thought about that stabbin' me in the heart thing, too," Grant replied immediately. "And I'd have to give you a definite 'no' on that one, Will. Anne just wasn't like that. Nothing between us ever had *that* feel to it." Grant paused and started again. "It may have been some sort of protective thing on her part, though. The strange thing is, I knew all along that something wasn't right. But then I got to where I *wanted* it to work between us. I just wanted it to be like it used to be ... maybe like I thought it was." He paused again. "Do you think you can love someone, Will, and know that you're not meant to be with them?"

"I guess you've done it twice now," Will said firmly. "With the same woman."

"Yeah," Grant sighed very quietly and waited for a second. "So what about a plan? What about God's plan for my life? Do you see a plan here with all this stuff?"

"No, I surely don't. But I do see my friend floating down that long river and bangin' into every damn rock right now. Maybe it's just that you haven't hit many rocks in your life until now and you're reeling — you don't know how to deal with this kind of stuff yet. I still like the long river analogy."

"Me too. I can live with that for now," Grant answered.

"But you know, old friend, it could just be that you can't see the plan yet because you don't want to." Will waited for a reply, but none came.

"Or what if — and I want you to think about this for a minute — what if you're just a rock in somebody else's river?" Will added.

"Huh?" Grant replied after a short silence.

"Maybe everything isn't about you. Ever think of that? Maybe Anne's canoe just keeps bangin' into you." Will waited for a response once again. None came.

"You still there, pard?" Will waited again.

"That was good, Will. You kinda surprised me with it, though!"

They talked for only a few more minutes and decided to get together again for some ice fishing in a couple of weeks.

"You're a good guy. You're gonna be fine, Grant Thorson!"

"Yeah, I know. I just wanted to talk to you." Their conversation ended the way it usually did.

"Keep your powder dry!" Grant called out.

"And yours!" Will replied.

Both men wore broad smiles when they hung up their phones.

~

The following Saturday dawned clear. The morning sun lit the snow so brightly that it hurt Grant's eyes to look across the white expanse in front of him. A blanket of snow about two feet thick had covered Spider Lake since before Thanksgiving. The storm that had frozen the lake and ended the duck season had been the first of several early-winter blasts from the north. Spider Lake was locked in ice all the way across the big bay now, as it had been for weeks. When Grant stood at the picture window in his cabin, Spider Lake appeared as a pure white sheet between the tall pines that framed it on either side and along the eastern shore.

The air was very cold and still. The snow crunched under Grant's feet when he stepped outside, and he could see the vapors from his warm breath as he carried firewood into the cabin. He'd cut and stacked an enormous pile of wood alongside the garage, and he kept a fire in the fireplace whenever he was home. It was a quiet, sunny morning – the last weekend before Christmas, and Ingrid would be home from college for the Christmas break later in the day. Grant had cleaned the cabin and was excited to spend several days alone with her before they went to celebrate Christmas with Big Ole and Gladys. All five of Grant's brothers and their families planned to return to Halstad for the holidays. Everyone had sensed that they might be spending their final Christmas with Big Ole, and several of Grant's brothers had even verbalized the thought. Nonetheless, there was an air of anticipation as Grant planned for the Christmas week.

Today there was a warm fire crackling. Grant had two mallards ready to place in the oven around 1:00 p.m. so they'd be perfectly cooked for supper. He'd set Ingrid's and his cross-country skis and boots by the garage door in preparation for an evening ski around Spider Lake. This was to be their first Christmas without Kate – their first Christmas at Spider Lake – and Grant wanted everything to be perfect when Ingrid came home.

Grant poured himself a cup of cowboy coffee from the battered enamelware coffeepot that was always on the stovetop. Corny music played on the TV while two guys caught lake trout somewhere in Canada on one of the TV fishing shows Grant loved. He closed his eyes and held the steaming cup under his nose while he breathed in the aroma. Then he remembered the dead mouse falling from their thermos to the floor of his boat and he smiled. "Ah, no mice!" he said just under his breath while he walked toward the closet by the back door, stepped into his boots, and reached for a heavy coat and hat.

Nellie had been sprawled out by the fire, twitching and moaning in her sleep. The instant that the familiar sound of Grant's boots crossing the floor woke her, she scrambled to her feet and looked at him. Her head was turned sideways in the manner that dogs all tilt their heads and seem to ask, "What's up?"

"Wanna go for a walk?" Grant asked. Instantly Nellie's tail was wagging and her front feet were bouncing up and down on the floor. "Well, OK, let's go!" Grant said as he opened the door, and the two of them stepped into the cold, still air of a Minnesota morning. Grant still carried his coffee cup as they walked through the tall pines and toward the trail that led to Stump Lake Boy Scout Camp.

The woods were silent. Grant thought that he and Nellie must have sounded like a pair of elephants crashing along the trail. The noise they made alerted most of the deer to run away, but Grant and Nellie flushed several ruffed grouse and saw some small birds. Grant always enjoyed the long walks in the woods, but today he was especially in need of something to help burn off some nervous energy, Ingrid was coming home.

He could hear the sounds of car doors closing and women's voices echoing through the woods as he returned to the cabin along the trail. Melanie Willette, a high school classmate of Ingrid's, had been a close friend for years, and the two of them had gone off to college together. Melanie had planned to drop Ingrid off at the cabin today, and Grant could hear them laughing as he stepped up his pace to hurry around the last bend in the trail.

Ingrid was lifting a large duffel from the trunk of a small car when Grant and Nellie emerged from the woods. Nellie sprinted to the car and greeted Ingrid. "Hi, Dad!" she said with a smile.

"Hi, honey!" Grant answered; he was thrilled to see her at home. She was beautiful, just like her mother, and now she was home to be with him for a while. Grant thought it was a fine day now – the sun even seemed to shine a little brighter.

"Hi, Melanie."

"Hi, Grant," Melanie smiled.

"Well, let's get your stuff inside. Are you two hungry?" Grant talked continuously while he hugged Ingrid and then Melanie.

Melanie had left the car running and soon explained that she wanted to go straight home.

"See you later, Ingrid," she called with a smile as she drove away.

Grant opened the door for Ingrid and she stepped into the cabin. Before she'd taken her coat off, she turned to Grant and said, "Looks nice, Dad, but it still sort of lacks a woman's touch." And she smiled a huge smile.

"It's perfect like it is!" He recognized what she meant about the place: It had the feel of a men's club.

"Well, it's you!" she smiled and hugged him again.

"Good to have you home, kid. Are you hungry?" he asked.

She unzipped her duffel and threw a handful of dirty laundry into the small laundry room behind the corner of the kitchen where the washer and dryer sat. "No, I'm not hungry, but I'm pretty tired. We were up late last night ... big party to celebrate the end of the semester, you know!" She carried her duffel and a second bag to her room and returned.

They chatted for a while about Walker and some of her friends from home that she hadn't seen in the six months since her high school graduation. She spoke about the frustrations and stress of her freshman year and how much more difficult her classes were than what she'd had in high school. In short order, it was clear to Grant that she'd been up late and was still tired. She was leaning back in her chair and closing her eyes between sentences.

"Why don't you go take a nap. I'll stoke up the fire and keep the place warm," he suggested.

"Sounds good to me, Dad," she said as she stood and walked directly to her room and closed the door. Grant retrieved the coat she'd left on the back of a chair and hung it up in the closet before he fueled the fire. He thought it felt so good to have her back, safe and warm, under his roof once again.

~

The last hint of gray daylight was disappearing through the pines when Grant heard Ingrid stirring in her room. It was 4:41 p.m. on December 21st, the shortest day of the year. The sun had begun to disappear behind the trees on the top of the hill behind Spider Lake Duck Camp at about 4:15, and the dark shadows of the big pines had been racing back across the lake since then.

The cabin smelled delicious. The aroma of roast duck filled the place once again. Grant had baked potatoes and squash in the oven, and two places were set at the table. He'd rented several videos for the night, hoping that Ingrid would be excited to see at least one of them.

Nellie had spent the afternoon on the couch, napping and retrieving ducks in her dreams. Grant had been up and down from the couch all afternoon, watching a ball game and preparing something of a welcome home dinner for Ingrid. Everything seemed to be ready now, and Grant was excited at the prospect of spending the evening with Ingrid.

The door to her room opened, and when she emerged she walked directly to the bathroom. Forty minutes later, the bathroom door opened and Grant could hear her hair dryer click on.

When she was done with the hair dryer, Ingrid remained in front of the bathroom mirror combing her hair and putting makeup on her face.

"Hey, Dad!" she called out. "Melanie is coming to get me at 6:00 and we're going to a movie, then there's a party at Willette's house ... I'll be home at 1:00. That OK with you?"

"I've got dinner for you, honey." Grant felt crushed, and it sounded to him as though he was pleading with Ingrid to stay home. He could hear the frustration in his own voice.

"That's OK, we'll get a pizza." She had no idea she was breaking his heart. Grant could tell by the tone of her voice that she had not noticed all the plans he'd made for them. She was concerned only about her friends and herself.

Grant decided not to pressure her to stay home or make a big deal of the fact that she hadn't wanted to spend more time with him. He'd just try to pretend he wasn't upset about her leaving him alone tonight. Ingrid continued to get ready for a night out while Grant quietly went to the dinner table and put one place setting back into the cupboard.

Later, after Ingrid had disappeared out the back door, laughing loudly with her friend, Grant slumped into his chair at the dinner table. He picked at one of the mallards for a while and then turned to Nellie. "So that's the way it's gonna be, huh? Just you and me?" She raised her head off the couch and looked at him. "You still love me, don't you?" Nellie raised her ears now.

"You want a treat?" Nellie recognized the word "treat" and was off the couch and at his side instantly. Grant fed Nellie the duck he'd prepared for Ingrid. He gave it to her one small morsel at a time. She sat and wagged her tail and watched his hands intently.

"You see, Nellie, that's the way life is – people just break your heart." He held a piece of duck for her and she snapped it from his hand. She looked at him intently, waiting for more.

"But you never do, do ya?" Another piece of duck was snatched from his hand.

"You always love me. You're always there for me." He held another piece for her and it disappeared as her dark face flashed past his hand.

"Course, it's easy to understand why. I'm a helluva guy, and a fine friend, too, right?" She took another piece from his hand and held her intense posture.

Grant looked at his old friend now. A long string of drool extended about five inches from her mouth, and her eyes were begging for more duck. "Jeez, you are a slob, Nellie. I really didn't think I'd be spending tonight watching my date slobber all over. Take this and git." He gave Nellie the last piece of duck and motioned toward the couch. Nellie put her ears back as though she was ashamed and tiptoed back to the couch.

"Now, don't act like no one loves you – you know that isn't true. It's just that your table manners are so bad, even worse than Will's." Grant smiled as he mentioned Will's name. He decided at that moment to call Will and talk about fatherhood for a while. As he was dialing the phone, he turned to Nellie and said, "Hell, Nellie, I guess you shouldn't feel too bad about your manners. My other friend here is the one who likes to pee in my boat."

"Campbell's!" Will answered the phone.

"Doctor?" Grant leaned back in his chair at the kitchen table, smiling with pleasure, now that he was talking to Will Campbell.

"Doctor?" Will replied, with all the feigned reverence he could muster. He knew Grant's voice and was glad to hear it.

"Me again! Sounds like you have a party going there, Will." Grant could hear laughter and commotion at Will's house. If he'd been talking to anyone but Will, he'd have felt like a nuisance for calling so frequently.

"Yeah, a bit of Christmas cheer. So what's up, pard?" Will took the cordless phone and walked to a quiet room.

Grant explained that he'd called because he was looking for a shoulder to cry on, and he related the way Ingrid's first Christmas home from college had begun. He shared his hurt feelings and his sense of loneliness and abandonment.

"Ah, hell, buddy, she's the same great kid she always has been! She's got to grow up, you know, separate … cut the apron strings. She needs to be independent. They all do. Wouldn't you be worried if a beautiful young thing like that had nothing better to do over semester break than sit home and watch *Jeremiah Johnson* with you?"

Grant turned instantly to the stack of videos by the VCR. *Jeremiah Johnson* was on top of the pile. "Maybe," he replied.

"I remember when Molly was that age. She thought I was so stupid she wouldn't talk to me." Will paused.

"That's what June says about you, too."

Will ignored Grant. "She thought I was invisible about half the time too — unworthy of any recognition. I wanted to take her by the scruff of her neck like you would a naughty puppy, but June just kept telling me to give her time and she'd grow out of it."

"Did she?"

"Sure!"

"I never saw her behave badly," Grant said.

"You're not her father." Will paused again. "Every kid has to find their own way, and it will always involve leaving their parents behind in some ways. It's gonna be OK. Just be there when she needs you. That's one thing you do real well." Grant knew the last words from Will were heartfelt.

"Yeah, I guess so," Grant sighed. "But I don't remember feeling that way about my parents."

"That's because your memory is even shorter than that other little thing of yours that you admire so much. How do you think your dad felt when you spent every spare minute playing ball or chasing girls or huntin' and fishin' with me? I even heard you rail several times about that packing house where your father worked his whole life as though it was hell itself, and I don't know anyone who loves and admires his dad more than you do. S'pose your folks liked to hear that? You had to become who you are at some point, too, and you did it by separating yourself from your parents' lives. You know, that's the hard thing about being a parent: You can't give your kids your life experience. You have to watch them go out and get their own. Sometimes you watch your kids get hurt, but it always hurts you when they leave … for a while.

"Yeah, I guess you're right again … you always are. Hey, I'll let you get back to your friends now. Thanks for talking to me, old buddy!"

"Yeah, I'd better get back to the party. There are some guys who asked if I'd tell them again how I shoot ducks and have 'em drop in the boat." Will had heard the despair in Grant's voice and wanted to end the conversation on a lighter note.

"Tell 'em about the decoys you've killed, too!" Grant was smiling now, because he knew Will was too. Then Grant's tone changed entirely; he was totally serious now. "Hey, Will?" Before he hung up the phone tonight, he felt a need to share something much deeper with his friend.

"Yeah?"

"*You're* the one who's always been there for *me*. I love you, Will. I never would have made it through the past year without you." Grant's words surprised Will Campbell. It was one thing to say the words "I love you" to your father or your wife or your children. But your hunting buddy? Will knew, both from the words and the solemn way they'd been spoken, that Grant was acknowledging a milestone in their special friendship. It was more — much more — of a declaration than Will was used to from Grant. Taken on the heels of their conversation about their fathers the previous autumn, Will understood Grant's need to leave nothing unspoken between the two of them, either. Will knew what Grant felt for him, and he had the same feelings for Grant. They had shared a lifetime of laughs and a few heartaches. They'd grown up together and they were poised to grow old together. Each of them had contacted the other one first whenever something good, or bad, happened in his life. Each of them sought the counsel of the other frequently.

"Yeah, I love you too, pard ... my best friend!"

Grant interrupted a long pause. "Hey, you better get going! Merry Christmas to your family! I'll talk to you in a week or two!"

"Hey! Wish Big Ole and Gladys a Merry Christmas, too."

"You bet. Watch your top knot."

"Watch yourn."

chapter SIXTEEN

Big Ole Thorson was still sleeping in his small room at the nursing home on the morning of Christmas Eve when his five sons crept into his room. It was just before 7:00 a.m. when John, James, David, Paul and Grant paused and stared at their father as if he were an exhibit in a museum. They began to smile and glance back and forth between themselves as Grant made his way to his father's bedside.

Grant knelt on the floor and softly placed his hand on his father's forehead. He gently pushed the thin strands of gray hair back across the top of Ole's head. Ole opened his eyes with the second stroke from Grant's hand and recognized Grant immediately. Then he moved his eyes to the other forms behind Grant. The older boys had all arrived late the evening before, and today was the first time they'd all been together in three years. It took a minute to register, but momentarily Ole realized that all of his boys were there. When Grant could see that recognition in his father's eyes, he said, "Merry Christmas, Dad! You're going home for a day!"

Ole Thorson smiled as though it was his *first* Christmas! At least Grant knew that the faint look of recognition in his father's eyes was today's equivalent of a broad smile. The others thought Ole's face seemed blank. But Grant thought the joy in Ole's eyes was unmistakable. Grant sat his father up in bed and helped him get his balance so that the other boys could take turns and say hello to their father. John and James had not seen Ole in the nursing home yet, and both of them tried to hide their feelings of surprise as they embraced their father. They spoke to him as if they could see no change since their last visit months earlier. But they could scarcely believe the man in front of them was their father. When they made eye contact with Grant, they begged silently, "Why didn't you tell me it was this bad?" Ole whispered "hello, son" and "I love you" to each of them, and it seemed he made a special point to hold his arms around each of them and touch them as much as he could.

The boys gave their father a shower, dressed him, fed him breakfast and had him ready in half an hour. They laughed and joked with each other and their father as they had all through their years together at home. The camaraderie they shared had always been nourished by a rough, relentless banter. The little bathroom in Ole's room had only enough room for Grant to enter and help his father with bathroom chores, but the other boys stood just outside the door and kept up a running commentary about body functions and noises coming from inside the bathroom. Today, even bathroom chores were funny for Ole Thorson. The commotion that had filled his home for years had found its way to this little room, and he was pleased.

Suddenly there was a small disturbance just outside the bathroom door. Grant and Ole could hear feet shuffling hurriedly, then a shower of laughter. The door to the bathroom opened just a crack, and John's face seemed to be pushing though.

"You guys better hurry up!" John was trying to sound serious. "Paul's having a problem this morning." John reached up and grabbed his own nose. "He's gonna need to get in there pretty soon."

"Shut up!" Paul called from behind John. "You're still trying to blame others for your bad behavior."

"It wasn't me!" John laughed as he pulled the door shut and returned to the commotion in Ole's room. For just a moment, the nursing home had the feel of Ole Thorson's home a generation earlier.

Ole looked at Grant and shook his head sideways, then rolled his eyes and a tiny smile creased his face.

"They're your kids," Grant chuckled as he buttoned his father's shirt and pants.

As the boys rolled Ole's wheelchair down the long hallway toward the kitchen and the nurses' desk, the banter and joking followed behind Ole like a small storm. When they reached the front desk, the nurse who seemed to be in charge confronted them and asked if they had permission from the nursing home staff for a home visit.

John Thorson, Grant's oldest brother, turned to the nurse. John hadn't been home in six months; he lived in Los Angeles and had been very busy with his career since Ole had moved to the nursing home. Far more than the others, he was shaken by the diminished state of his father. He did not intend to let anything interfere with his father's Christmas. "I don't think you understand. My father is coming home for Christmas. We're not asking for permission. We'll have him back tomorrow afternoon." There was no malice in his demeanor, but there was no mistake in his intent. The boys rolled Ole out the front door and lifted him into the van they'd borrowed. Ole waved silently at the nurse when he passed by her. She returned a sly smile.

"Grampa's coming, Grampa's coming!" several of the small children called as they pointed out the window when the van turned into the driveway. When the door to the white house opened, the

Thorson clan stepped out into the cold air and waited on the front steps as Big Ole's wheelchair was lifted into the house.

It was clear immediately to everyone at the Thorson home that this Christmas would not be like all the others in their lives. For all the grandchildren, this would always be remembered as "the Christmas that Grandpa was in the wheelchair." "Hi Grampa, hi Grampa," everyone greeted Ole individually. The small children were afraid of something – they'd never seen Grampa like this, and their voices showed the fear. The older grandchildren tried to comfort their grandfather when they spoke. Some of them touched him. His daughters-in-law hid their sorrow and sounded perky when they greeted him. Only Sarah, John's wife, wept when she said hello and kissed him.

Big Ole was up and down from naps several times. It took all five boys to keep up with Ole's demands for transportation, drinks, and bathroom chores. In a very short time, it was obvious to all the family that Ole would not be returning home ever again after Christmas Day. The realization that this would be Ole Thorson's last Christmas, his last visit home, began to take hold early on Christmas Eve.

In addition to the boys and their wives, there were seventeen grandchildren and three great-grandchildren around the old farm-house. The house only seemed crowded during meals, when the kitchen and dining room were packed and raucous. The Thorsons had remodeled the small house during the early 1970s, when all the farms in the valley seemed flush with prosperity. Each member of the family sought out a few quiet moments with Ole whenever they could. It became clear early on during this visit that his family, at least the ones who lived far away, might be saying goodbye to him. Every conversation seemed to contain the odd paradox of laughter followed closely by tears as old memories were shared. Early in the day, Aaron Thorson, Big Ole's youngest great-grandson, was placed by his mother into Ole's lap for a photograph.

Aaron began to cry and reach for his mother. As so often happens at just such a time, a silent pause emerged. Aaron's two-and-a-half-year-old brother, Teddy, pointed at Big Ole and called out, "Who is that guy?" Everyone laughed out loud, and once again Grant felt certain he could see a smile in Ole's eyes.

Ole, too, seemed to know that these small conversations were goodbyes. He pulled his children and grandchildren close to him and touched their faces, held their hands. He whispered "I love you" if he spoke at all.

That evening, John and Grant carried Big Ole to the bedroom he'd slept in for sixty-two years, and when Gladys shut the door behind them, John turned slowly toward Grant. "Penny for your thoughts?" John's eyes twinkled.

Grant rubbed his face with both hands. He smiled back at his older brother. "S'pose there's any brandy left behind Mother's china, where the old man used to hide it?" This day, like so many other days in the past few months, had been more stressful than it should have been, and now it seemed almost surreal to Grant and John. All the Thorson boys and their wives sat around the small living room and chatted very quietly for an hour, about nothing really, after their children had been tucked away in bed.

After church on Christmas morning, John grabbed Grant's arm and gestured for Grant to join him in a walk around the farm. They put their coats on and stepped out into a cold, clear Christmas day. They hadn't walked far when John asked, "So how long is it gonna be?"

"Don't know," Grant shrugged; he knew what John meant. "He seems to be slipping faster all the time. But you know, he has some good days, too."

John kept his hands in his pockets when he walked. "Only saw Dad cry twice," he offered.

"Yeah?"

"Yeah. I was just a little kid when he got back after the war, but I do remember how he cried. We thought there was something

wrong with him. We didn't understand how he must have felt."
John continued to walk. "And then he broke down the day he
came home for the hospital and told us you'd been born. Put his
face in his hands and cried ... really unusual."

"Really?" Grant furrowed his eyebrows.

"I think there was always something special there ... between
you two."

Grant did not reply.

"Or it could have been because you were so ugly."

Grant smiled but still did not reply.

"Mom seems to be holding up OK?" John asked.

"Yeah, she's pretty strong, huh?" Grant nodded.

"How you doin'?" John asked after they'd walked around the
barn and the rickety old corncrib. Of all his brothers, he'd always
been closest to Grant, and he wanted to know just where Grant's
life was leading nearly a year after Kate's death.

"I used to stand over there," Grant pointed with a glance of his
eyes. "Dad would hit me fly balls. The implements that he kept
sitting there by the corncrib were the monuments in centerfield of
Yankee Stadium." Grant stared at the old buildings. The breeze
carried the smell of manure and hay bales from the barn. It was a
good smell to both of the men. "I was never better than when I
played here."

Grant pointed again, this time with his right hand. "See those
nails in the wall of the shed? Remember how we used to hang our
dead ducks there for a few days to let them age? Mother hated
cooking ducks. She used to cook the hell out of 'em, so they tasted
like shoe leather. Little Ole Hokanson made ducks the right way."

John could see that his brother was lost in his own thoughts.
Then a smile leapt across Grant's face and he turned to John.
"Remember when that old bull of Little Ole's got frostbite on his
nuts?"

John's only response was a belly laugh.

"Dad and Little Ole tied that bruiser in his stanchion with a one-inch hemp rope, as tight as they could get it." Grant continued chuckling as he spoke. "Then Little Ole went around behind him with a bucket of warm water." Both of them were chuckling now. "Remember the sound that bull made when Ole raised that water over his nuts?"

"Sounded like a freight train hit the barn!" John said as he lost control of his laughter. Both men were bent over with their hands on their knees while they laughed.

"I just remember fragments of rope and splinters all over the inside of the barn when I went in there the next day," Grant added, still bent over and laughing.

"You know, Dad laughed out loud every time that got mentioned for thirty years after." John was wiping tears from the corner of his right eye and still laughing as he talked.

When John looked back at Grant once again, Grant was scanning the white building and the farm implements scattered around the farm. Grant turned and stared into John's eyes. "We don't get to have many friends like Dad or places like this in our lives, do we?"

John didn't reply; he knew the question didn't call for an answer. But after they'd walked a few yards, toward the grove of trees by the stockyard on the side of the barnyard, he asked, "Mom said you were seeing Anne Robertson again?"

"Yeah."

"Mom said you broke up with her last week?"

"Yeah." Grant looked straight ahead.

"Good. I never liked her."

"You always said she was nice!" Grant scowled and looked at John.

"Well, actually, I do think she's nice — too nice for you, as a matter of fact. I just wanted to say something to make you feel good," John said with mock sincerity.

"Keep tryin!" Grant put his arm around John's shoulder as they walked back to the house.

A huge Christmas dinner came and went, along with all of the activity and commotion of a large family Christmas. Big Ole presided over one final Christmas dinner and ceremony around the Christmas tree. Someone found the eight-millimeter movies and the bulky old Bell and Howell projector. The movies were charming in spite of the shaky quality that everyone's home movies seem to have. The grandchildren called continuously to have their parents and aunts and uncles identified, and they laughed out loud at how foolish their family used to look. Each of the Thorson boys was moved by the changes in their family that had been brought on with the passing of time.

Everyone was laughing at Grandma's hairdo and ugly glasses as she drove into the driveway behind the wheel of a pink and black, 1950-something Chevy and waved. But the talk and laughter all subsided quickly when the next scene flashed onto the wall. Standing in the yard, wearing his high, laced boots, his tan pants and jacket, a tan hat and red shirt stood Big Ole Thorson. He was a fine figure of a man. His eyes were dark. He smiled to show a row of teeth and then put his hands on his hips. Surrounding him were his boys. John was a skinny kid of about fifteen. James, David, and Paul were arranged in decreasing order of height, and each of them held up as many ducks as their small arms would allow. It was probably opening day sometime in the mid 1950s. Grant sneaked a look at Ole ... the old man stared at the image on the wall as if it was impossible for him to comprehend the changes the years had made. "Wow, look at Grampa," one of the grandchildren said.

Then the camera wobbled slightly, and from the bottom of the screen emerged a toddler. Each step was unsteady as a young Grant Thorson waddled toward his father. Big Ole picked him up and turned him toward the camera, then waved his boy's hand. Grant thought he might cry, but he stuffed his emotion and the movie continued. The laughter and jokes resumed. Ingrid cast a glance to her father but didn't dare touch him for fear he might break.

When the movies ended, the younger children began playing with Christmas toys and the older ones played board games. Ole never spoke; he only touched those who came close to him. And as the afternoon shadows began to lengthen, all of them began to prepare themselves for Ole's return to the nursing home.

When darkness began to close in on Christmas Day, Ole's boys dressed Ole in warm clothes and prepared him for his return to the nursing home. The family gathered into a quiet crowd in the kitchen as the boys tucked a scarf around his neck and buttoned his coat. He stopped at the door and another round of goodbyes began. Every one was personal and painful. Then Gladys said her goodbye. She was last. She kissed Ole on the lips and said, "See you tomorrow, Ole. It was nice to have you home." She was just saying goodbye, goodnight, to her husband, but the scene by the back door of the old house now suddenly was so wrong. There in front of them sat the strongest man in their lives. He was wrapped in warm blankets. His family could hardly see his frail little face behind his scarf, and his sons were taking him to a strange place so he could wait to die. Gladys put her hands to her face and cried when she heard the words she'd spoken. "It was nice to have you home" – it sounded terrible ... final. She reached her hand toward Ole as the boys took him away. Then she ran to her room and cried. No one in the little kitchen that night would ever forget the agony on Gladys' face. To be sure, in spite of the Parkinson's, resignation and sorrow were there in Ole's eyes for all his children to see. The grandchildren stared at their mothers and wondered why they were crying.

When the boys had Big Ole tucked into bed that evening, each of them took a quiet, private moment to chat with their father. Each of them ended their visit with "see you tomorrow, Dad. I love you."

Grant was the last to bid his father goodnight. His brothers were waiting for him in the lobby. When he knelt beside his father's bed, he put his face close to Big Ole's. He put the palm of his hand on his father's forehead and stroked it gently. Ole reached up and touched Grant's whiskers again.

"Are you afraid to die, Dad?" Grant asked calmly. He looked directly into his father's eyes. He'd come to sense that his father drew strength from him when they spoke together like this.

"I'm not afraid of being dead," Ole answered quickly, in a voice that was much stronger than his usual whisper.

"But I'm afraid it's gonna hurt to die," Ole added. He was holding Grant's hand between his own frail hands – no fear in his voice, just logic.

Surprisingly, Ole's words coaxed a smile to Grant's face. "Good answer, Dad!" he said slowly. As usual, Big Ole had come right to the point, and Grant was moved by the candor in his father's reply. Grant was well aware of his father's unwavering faith that Jesus would be right there to take him away to Heaven the moment his life ended, but Ole had never verbalized any anxiety over a painful end.

"You'll be fine, Dad. Don't worry about stuff like that. Heaven is filled with souls who felt just like you do."

"No feeding tubes, no life support." Ole stared at Grant. "Just let me go!"

"Get some sleep, Dad. Merry Christmas!" Grant stroked his father's head until the exhausted old man drifted off to sleep.

When Grant said goodbye to each of his brothers the next day, there was an unspoken certainty that they'd all be together again very soon ... for a funeral.

~

On the last night before Ingrid was to return to school, she and her father put on their cross-country skis and went out to ski around Spider Lake. The night was clear and calm. A nearly full moon lit the sky in front of the cabin, and pines along the eastern shore cast long shadows onto the snow-covered lake, almost as though they were hiding a sunrise, not a bright moon. A new sheet of snow glittered in the moonlight, like a billion diamonds had been spread over it.

Christmas break had come and nearly gone now. Grant had asked Ingrid to reserve this one night of her time at home to be with him. Ingrid was a better athlete than her father now, and he simply followed behind her in the tracks that her skis made. Several times he stopped and looked back at the trees and the stars. The night was growing brighter as the moon rose, and it seemed that the stars had never shown more brightly.

Ingrid was far ahead of him, perhaps a quarter of a mile, when she noticed he had dropped way behind her. She reversed her direction and skied toward him on her own tracks.

"You OK, Dad?" she asked when she was close enough.

"Yeah."

"What are you doing?"

"Just enjoying the beautiful night."

"You're not getting much of a workout!"

"Don't want one." He stood with his hand atop his ski poles and looked around. "I'm just thinkin' about love ... and death ... and feeling good ... and feeling bad ... and why I love this place so much."

"Sounds like you're writing a song for the Nashville Network!" She made a face like she had a mouthful of something bitter.

"You asked me!" Grant smiled at her answer.

"If I'd known you were gonna say something like that I wouldn't have asked anything."

"You used to be such a cute kid."

"You used to be taller and smarter."

"Wanna race back to the cabin?" Grant asked.

"Why?"

"Loser makes the popcorn! Gimme a decent head start!" Grant was off.

"OK, but I'll need a sundial to time this head start," she called to him.

'What a great kid,' Grant thought to himself. 'At least I got one evening with her over Christmas break. Maybe that is more than I gave my parents.'

Ingrid pulled even with her father about one hundred yards from the little boathouse by the cabin. She skied effortlessly and stayed even with Grant for a few strides. Then, as she pulled away, she said, "No butter, please." She never turned to look at him when she skied up the hill to the cabin.

Grant bent over the popcorn popper on the kitchen countertop and drew in a deep breath. He loved the smell of popping corn. Ingrid stood next to him and began to pour some Coke in a glass. "Do you get lonesome, Dad?" She was looking into his eyes when he raised his glance to her.

"Well, I sure did for the first few months after your mother died. I got angry at her for dying sometimes, too!" Grant smiled and shook his head. Then, for the first time, he told Ingrid all about his feelings and his recent experience with Anne.

"She wasn't right for you, Dad. It wasn't meant to be." Ingrid reached in front of Grant and sprinkled salt on the popcorn.

"Really?" Grant stepped back and smiled.

"Mom told me about you and Mrs. Robertson a couple of years ago." Ingrid smiled a sheepish smile.

"Really?" Grant let his surprise show.

"Yeah, she told me everything." Ingrid paused for a moment and looked away. When she spoke again she couldn't look at her dad. "When she got really sick, she told me something else, too." Ingrid looked into the fireplace when she spoke.

Grant crossed his arms and waited. "Yes?""

"She told me to make it easy for you to love someone else — she knew she was gonna die, Dad." Ingrid began struggling to hold her tears back.

Grant took his daughter in his arms and said nothing while she sniffled and sobbed quietly. Then Ingrid continued haltingly. "She said eventually you'd meet someone who'd bring a light to your eyes." She paused again. "What do you think about that, Dad?" she asked as she rested her head on her father's shoulder.

"I guess that's the nature of love — that a dying woman could concern herself with something like that and know that your approval would be important." He took a deep breath. "Your mother was the very best, just like you." He stopped and took another deep breath. "How are you getting along?"

Ingrid stepped back and wiped her eyes. "I still miss her. I think of her every day."

"I suspect you always will," Grant sighed. "I do, too."

"You know, I read in one of my classes that a child's personality is almost completely formed when they're eighteen months old, and that by age six a child's parents have already had their most significant impact on him or her. I was eighteen when she died. Sometimes now, when I think about it, the way she was at the end … I wonder if she didn't know that she'd done everything she was put here to do."

"What about me? I wasn't ready for her to die. I'll be losing my father soon, too, and I'm not ready to be without him."

"I don't know, Dad." Ingrid shrugged her shoulders. She seemed ready for the conversation to be over.

The phone rang and Ingrid answered it quickly. "Yeah, yeah, yeah. Well, my dad and I are just having some popcorn, then I'll be right over," she said enthusiastically.

Grant was immediately disappointed. He knew that tonight, once again, Ingrid's friends were more important than he was — and she was leaving.

chapter SEVENTEEN

Grant had always enjoyed the air of excitement that he felt on a university campus. Now, as he walked along the sidewalks of Georgetown University, he could feel the energy of the place, just as he remembered the campus at the University of Minnesota when he'd been a student. Two college boys called loudly to each other, and Grant couldn't help but recall beer parties and hockey games and nights just like this one many years before.

It was a chilly evening. The temperature was hovering around freezing, and there was a heavy mist in the air. Grant thought it was almost tropical, though, compared with the minus ten degrees in Minnesota that he'd seen on the weather map in the newspaper that morning. He kept his hands in his coat pockets and curled his shoulders forward in order to raise his collar over his neck as he walked through the Georgetown campus. He was looking for McDonough Hall now as his eyes moved from one building to the next. There were several small groups of students walking in random directions across the grounds, and he was about to ask for directions when he found McDonough and made his way inside.

All day during the committee meetings, he'd looked around trying to find Susan Wells. But as far as he could tell, she had not made an appearance. During a break in the afternoon session, Grant had noticed that a photographer who had been in the meeting room for about an hour after lunch was preparing to leave. He'd stopped the photographer and talked to him long enough to learn that he worked for the *Post* also, and that he knew Susan Wells. The man told Grant that Susan had decided to spend most of the day at the White House because of a press conference scheduled for about 3:00 p.m. Then he added that Susan was planning to speak to some group at Georgetown University in the evening. Grant then called Georgetown and found that Susan Wells was scheduled to speak to the Daughters of the American Revolution at 8:00 p.m. at Hart auditorium in McDonough Hall.

As he entered the ornate building, he raised his eyes and took note of the gray stone arches across the front of the structure. He noticed several handsomely dressed groups of people standing and talking quietly amongst themselves near the entrance. It was 8:35 p.m. now, and there was no sign of anyone taking tickets or checking for registration by those in attendance. Across the granite floor of the foyer were two large doorways about thirty feet apart. Each doorway had two very large wooden doors, which were closed. Grant assumed these doors opened into the auditorium. When he looked farther to the left, he noticed a smaller wooden door that he guessed also opened to the auditorium. He made his way to the small door and opened it slowly.

He was relieved to see Susan behind a small podium. 'At least I'm in the right place,' he thought. Grant guessed that about 250 of the three hundred or so seats in the auditorium were taken. He stepped into the large room and let the door close quietly behind him. He took a seat near the door and relaxed. He enjoyed the sense of anonymity he felt at the moment; no one here except Susan had any idea who he was, and for some odd reason he liked that.

Susan immediately impressed him as articulate and scholarly. She was discussing the writers of the pre-Revolutionary War period and the effect their work had in moving the American people toward revolution. She obviously had great command of the subject matter. She was able to draw on knowledge of obscure facts and a thorough understanding of the political and personal motives of the people of the Revolution. Grant could tell that Susan was not merely intelligent, but that she truly enjoyed what she was doing.

Grant had found his way here because he wanted very much to see Susan while he was in Washington. When she'd missed today's health care committee meeting, Grant had actually felt bad, disappointed, at her absence. He felt drawn to her. Susan was a beautiful woman, but some thing in her eyes had invited him, he thought. And now he was willing to take a chance and come looking for her. He'd enjoyed their laughter and conversation during the previous months, and he was curious about her.

Grant had listened to Susan for an hour when he realized she was nearly finished with her speech. He'd been taken into her presentation by her skills as an orator and her passion for the topic.

The time had flown by, and now Grant found himself wondering just what to do when she was finished. Initially, he'd planned to speak with her afterwards as she'd done with him after the committee meetings. Now he wasn't so confident that he should approach her here. He was intrigued with her beauty, her brains, her presence, and he began to feel a sense of intimidation. After all, this was her world – and he was definitely out of place here.

Grant began to fear that, if he approached her now, perhaps Susan would see him as some sort of hick or out of towner who had stalked her to this place. What if she didn't remember him? Or what if she gave him a quick and obvious brush-off?

'If she really wanted to talk to you, she would have contacted you,' he thought to himself.

'Maybe she's dying for you to call her,' he argued with himself.

When Susan finished her presentation, there was a short period for questions. She handled every question with wit and insight; the audience loved her. One man asked several long, rambling questions that were so long and obtuse that they seemed to contain the answer the man was searching for. Susan handled his questions with great respect and then gave answers that were far more succinct than the questions had been. Grant chuckled to himself; there always seemed to be some pseudo-intellectual who just liked to hear his own voice asking questions. Grant thought the man would do well on the President's health care committee. When Susan thanked them, the audience gave her a long round of applause and then began to move to the exits.

While Susan remained at the podium organizing her papers, several people made their way up to her and began to ask questions. From Grant's seat, Susan appeared to welcome the personal questions and comments. She stood chatting with the small handful of individuals while Grant also made his way cautiously to the podium. He'd decided to say a quick "hello" and then leave.

Six people remained at the podium as Susan placed her papers in a small leather briefcase. She appeared to be working her way to the door, as though ready to go home. Grant had been hiding behind another man, hoping to be the last person to speak with her. It was clear to him now, however, that if he didn't reveal himself to her soon, it would be too late.

Grant turned around and took one step sideways. He was about five feet from Susan when she recognized him. Her eyes widened and her mouth actually fell open slightly with surprise. Before she could say anything, Grant nodded politely and said, "Hi, Susan. Enjoyed your speech, you're very good!" through a very guarded smile.

"What are you doing here … no … I mean …what are you doing here?" she stammered uneasily.

"Well, the police left that small door unguarded so I came in there." There was nothing else for him to do but point and smile.

Susan's face registered complete surprise. "Thank you ... and hello," she said as she recovered from the surprise and extended her hand.

"I didn't expect to see you here tonight," Susan added.

"Apparently not," Grant smiled again.

Almost everyone from the small crowd around the podium had dismissed themselves when Susan had recognized Grant. An older woman and another man stood looking at Susan while she spoke with Grant now. Susan seemed somewhat uncomfortable, and Grant understood why immediately: She was with the other man.

The man had short, mostly gray hair and delicate features. He was handsome and well dressed, and he appeared slightly irritated at Grant's presence. Susan was still flustered by Grant's appearance, but she gained control of the situation by starting the introductions.

"Grant," she said as she held her hands together, "this is Jason Vincent." Susan gestured nervously toward the man. "Jason is a professor here at Georgetown, head of the English department!"

"Jason...," she held her hands together again, still somewhat anxiously, Grant thought, "This is Grant Thorson. Grant is my ... dentist."

Jason Vincent smiled now and extended his hand. "Nice to meet you, Dr. Thorson!"

"Nice meeting you!" Grant replied. He turned slowly to Susan. When he didn't think Jason could see it, he blinked both eyes at Susan, as if something had splashed in his face. He knew she would understand the gesture. It begged the question, "What the hell was that?"

"And this is Petra Vanderhoft, my editor at the *Post*. Petra, this is Grant Thorson," Susan continued, still somewhat unsteady with herself.

As soon as he'd shaken Petra Vanderhoft's hand, Grant stepped back and said quickly, "Well, I'd better be going. It was nice to meet you Jason, Ms. Vanderhoft." Grant was walking backwards now. He pointed at Susan and exaggerated a wink; it looked like an intentionally atrocious attempt to impersonate Elvis. "See you in six months, Susan ... be sure to floss 'em!" He knew he'd walked into something uncomfortable between Susan and Jason – that much was unmistakable. He also thought the panic on Susan's face was uncharacteristic of her, but he didn't need to be asked to leave.

The entire exchange between the four of them had lasted less than two minutes. Grant did not know what he had been part of a moment earlier, but as he reached the wooden doors to the auditorium he couldn't help but smile. The whole thing had been so bizarre. 'Well, I'd have to say that she did remember you though!' he said to himself as he walked back out into the night and hailed a cab.

When Grant returned to his hotel room, there were two messages waiting for him. The first one was from Jessica Wickham at the White House; Grant was supposed to call her whenever he got the message. The second was from Susan. She'd left it early in the afternoon. She sounded warm and friendly, and she was explaining that she wanted to see him during this weekend's visit to D.C. but that, because she was busy with other obligations, she almost certainly wouldn't be able to. Then she gave her phone number in case he wanted to call. "Shoulda listened to that one earlier," he said to himself.

He sat down at the little table in his room and immediately called the other number he'd been given. An operator asked if he could wait for a moment when he asked to speak to Jessica Wickham.

"Jessica Wickham," she answered momentarily. Her voice was firm and professional as always.

"Miss Wickham, this is Grant Thorson. I'm just returning your call. Don't you ever go home?"

Grant doubted that she was used to being joked with, but she obviously enjoyed it. "No, my foot is chained to this desk. Can you hold for the President?"

"Jeez, Miss Wickham! Don't wake him up just to talk to me. I can call back some other time." Grant felt suddenly embarrassed that she might impose on the President because of him. "I'm just returning a call, I don't even know why I was supposed to call."

"Wake the President? Now that's a good one!" she chuckled. "I just spoke with him a minute ago. Please hold."

Momentarily, the President's voice came over the telephone line. "Grant?"

"Hello, Thom!"

"So, another weekend in Washington? How are things with the committee?"

"Just like we both knew they'd be — political, biased, unproductive, buried in bullshit, but other than that, pretty good."

"Yeah, that's probably about right." The President added calmly, "I tried to reach you earlier. Were you out on the town?" he asked.

"Well, not really. I went to Georgetown to see Susan Wells speak. She's pretty good!"

"Yes, she is. She's been pretty critical of me lately you know."

"She told me that a month ago. I said I wasn't interested."

Thom Hutchinson laughed out loud. "She's not used to people talking to her like that."

"I wasn't rude. I just said I trusted my friend to do the right thing, and that was the end of it."

"Well, thanks, Grant, that's nice, but it's not why I called tonight. Your name came up in conversation earlier today."

"Uh oh," Grant interrupted.

"No, it was good. I told Martin Walters that I'd like to celebrate the walleye opener with you and Will on Spider Lake. A short vacation for Ellen and me, like old times. Would that be all right with you?"

"I'd be honored!" Grant said with a smile.

"Great! I'll have my staff start some preparations for a trip to Minnesota in May. I'll work it out with Will, too." Grant could tell that the President was pleased with the thought of a day fishing with old friends.

Then Thom changed the subject once more. "Will wrote and told me you and Anne had broken up. I'm sorry. She was nice."

"Yeah, but it's OK. I don't think we were meant to be together. Maybe when you get to the lake we can sit around and talk like we used to. Do you still do that kind of stuff?"

"Not as much as I'd like!" Thom paused. "I'd better be going, Grant. I'll talk to you again soon!"

"Keep your powder dry!" Grant called out.

"And yours!" Thom replied. Then the line clicked.

~

Martin Walters stood up in front of his chair in the Lincoln Room when the President re-entered.

"Sit down, Martin, it's too late in the day for that. I just talked to Grant Thorson. Please begin making plans for an overnight stay at Spider Lake with Dr. Thorson and Dr. Campbell on the opening weekend of the fishing season in Minnesota. OK?"

"Sounds good, Mr. President. We can get some photo ops of you fishing in the north woods. Voters still like that rugged, outdoorsy stuff that they saw during your campaign."

"Yes, that's OK Martin. But remember — most of all, this is to be a two-day vacation for me. I could use some time fishing, relaxing." Thom Hutchinson sat back in his chair and looked away from Martin Walters. Martin could see the faraway look in his eyes, and he knew the President was imagining himself rocking gently in a summer breeze and fishing with his friends. "By the way, Mr. President," Martin said raising his voice, "did I tell you what Dr. Thorson said today at the health care committee meeting?"

"No?" The President spoke the word "no" slowly, as if it were a question.

"You know how we talked about this sort of committee providing sound bites for the media? Well, Dr. Thorson served one up today." Martin took a breath and smiled at the President as he took a piece of paper from his pocket. Then he started again.

"A TV crew rolled into the meeting this morning and just happened to start shooting as Dr. Thorson began to speak. Your boy did it again, and I quote: 'The shortsighted pseudo-intellectuals in the legislature in my home state of Minnesota decided to target health care providers as the cause of the problems in the health-care system, and they enacted punitive legislation designed only to hurt the health care providers in our state. Most legal experts agree that this legislation, which entitles some citizens to the services of others, violates the civil rights of the others. It all kinda makes you wonder just where the ACLU hides when someone other than a dirtbag or a murderer needs their civil rights protected.'"

Thom Hutchinson smiled and shook his head.

"It gets better. This guy gets truly obstinate when Bently's mouthpiece, Darrell Osterquist, gets up to speak. Osterquist rambled for a while later in the day, bragging about the cost containment measures in the *Minnesota Model*. Instantly when Osterquist finished, Dr. Thorson rose and said: 'Please excuse me. I don't like to be too anecdotal, but I believe I can clearly illustrate the cost containment of the *Minnesota Model*. A friend of mine at home is a physician. He's been doing vasectomies for thirty years now. The hospital's fee for a vasectomy has risen 1,280 percent in those thirty years, and the doctor's share – the amount he actually receives – of that fee has been reduced from thirty years ago. Sound management in the *Minnesota Model* ... a 1,300 percent fee increase in order to do one thing, to support a bloated bureaucracy.'

"Both of those sound bites made the evening news. Sure doesn't sound like he's trying to get elected to any office, now or ever!"

"And that was the whole idea in having him here, on the committee – wasn't it?" the President replied.

~

Susan Wells walked briskly across the lobby of the Four Seasons Hotel and asked the clerk for Grant's room number. She knew the clerk wasn't supposed to give out that information. She was surprised at how easily she was able to turn on the charm and convince the clerk that Grant was waiting for her. She said thank you, turned quickly to hide her satisfied smile, and walked toward the elevators.

Her intent was to apologize in person for her strange behavior earlier in the evening. Although Susan had initially suspected that Grant was something of a cowboy, a political ultraconservative, she remained very curious about him. She'd thought he might be the embodiment of the arrogant, ignorant, right-wing conservative she detested. But she'd seen something deeper – maybe a little mysterious and more insightful – in him during their earlier meetings, and she found him intriguing. She was drawn to him because she enjoyed his wit, and she felt he exuded a confident strength that she found attractive. And she thought he was handsome; when he smiled at her she felt like she had in junior high when the older boys smiled at her. Not many men made her feel like that anymore.

When she reached Grant's room, she was just about to knock when she thought better of it. "A personal apology is in order here … but he might think I came to his room for the wrong reason," she mumbled to herself just as she was about to knock on the door.

She reached into her purse, found her cell phone, and called Grant's room while she stood outside his door. When she heard his room phone ring, she moved away from his door slightly so that he wouldn't hear her voice in the hall if he answered the phone.

Grant had changed his clothes and was brushing his teeth when the phone rang. It was 11:30 p.m. now, twenty minutes after he'd spoken with the President, and he assumed the call would be from Jessica Wickham. Perhaps Thom had forgotten something. When he answered, the voice on the other end was clear and friendly.

"Hello, Grant, this is Susan Wells. I'd like to talk to you."

"Do you have a toothache, Susan?" He was pleased with himself that he'd thought quickly enough to come up with something better than "OK," and he was glad she couldn't see him smile.

"No," she replied.

"Perhaps you'd like to talk to my receptionist and schedule your next appointment? Have you been flossing?" He sounded very serious. He wouldn't let go of her false claim to be his patient, and he made sure the sarcasm in his questioning was obvious.

"Look, I came all the way over here to explain myself. Don't make it any more difficult for me."

"You're in the hotel?" She could hear the surprise in his voice.

"I'm in the lobby," she lied.

"Well, that's great! I'll be right down." He'd wanted to see her all day, but after the incident at Georgetown he'd resigned himself to the fact that he wouldn't see Susan during this trip to D.C. As he'd thought about her during the past hour, he'd come to feel that he probably had been right when he'd argued with himself that she certainly wouldn't be interested in his friendship. Now, however, she was in the lobby, waiting to talk to him. He found her attractive in every way. He knew she lit a spark in his eyes. But just now, he felt himself on a bit of an emotional roller coaster with her. He didn't bother to try to hide the excitement in his voice when he said he'd be right down.

Instantly, Susan began to feel panic rising in her. She began backpedaling away from his door. What if he burst out of his door now — especially now that she'd lied and said she was in the lobby when, in reality, there she was standing just outside his door when he walked out? She'd look like a fool. She knew she couldn't stand the embarrassment of such a scene.

Then, as she turned and ran from his door, she said the thing she knew she had to say but didn't want to, "OK, c'mon down." She turned off her phone and sprinted for the elevators. She pressed the little green triangle that pointed down and looked around for an elevator door to open.

"Shit, shit, shit," Susan whispered as she waited for an elevator. She could feel the desperation rising in her now. She thought all the elevators must be broken. Finally, she heard the "ding" announcing that one of the elevator doors was about to open. But immediately after the ringing of the small bell, there came another noise. The door to a nearby room had opened and then closed.

"What if it's his door? And he's walking this way now? What if I get on the elevator and the door hasn't closed yet and he walks into the elevator and there I am? What if I'm still standing here waiting for this damn door to open when he walks around that corner? Shit!" She was driven by a panic now. She did not want to be found out. She raced around another corner and hid behind the ice machine when she heard footsteps drawing near to the elevators.

Susan wasn't even sure if she was hidden from view when whoever it was that came to the elevators entered the open door and disappeared. She wondered if she should wait for a while longer in case it wasn't actually Grant who had come to the elevators ... he might come now if she returned to the elevators. What if he was walking around the lobby looking for her now? What if he was waiting for an elevator to return to his room when she got off the elevator in the lobby? "Shit!" she whispered as she ran to the elevator and pressed the green triangle again.

Her eyes darted right and left while she waited for an elevator door to open again. Finally, there was another "ding" and the door in front of her opened. She breathed a sigh of relief when she saw that no one was inside the elevator, then stepped inside quietly and pushed the button for the lobby.

"Thank God!" Susan thought when she stepped cautiously out of the elevator and noticed Grant wandering across the lobby, walking calmly with his hands in his pockets and looking for her.

"Grant! Over here!" she called out as she waved to him. "I did it!" she whispered to herself while he was still far across the room. "He'll never know I was up there."

She saw Grant's face brighten when he noticed her waving at him. Once again he felt like he had as a little boy when he'd been lost in a crowd and someone had appeared from out of nowhere to rescue him. Other than Thom Hutchinson, Susan was the closest thing he had to a friend for about two thousand miles. She was very pretty, she was nice, and she was smiling at him — and that was all he needed just now to feel good.

After they'd exchanged greetings, they found a quiet corner of the hotel bar and ordered a drink.

"So just what was it that I walked into tonight?" Grant asked with a smile.

"Well, that's a difficult one to explain," Susan began. She went on to tell Grant that Jason Vincent was in charge of an entire lecture series sponsored by the university, and she'd planned to meet with him afterward to discuss the project. She said that when Grant had appeared, she'd felt compelled to invite him to join them afterward but she knew she couldn't do that. She said he'd surprised her so by his sudden appearance that she'd just panicked and made up the "dentist thing" in order to expedite the end of a clumsy situation that she couldn't fix anyway.

Grant allowed what he thought was a pretty thin cover story to pass because he enjoyed Susan's company. He wanted to believe that what she'd said was the whole story, so he didn't question it. "So then you came over here to talk about great authors again?" Grant smiled.

"Well, yes, but mostly to apologize for the way I acted. And also to hear about the committee meeting today." She smiled and moved on.

"Well, thanks. My day was ugly. I managed to irritate almost everyone with my ignorance, but you already know about my ignorance. So what did you do while you weren't at the health care committee meeting?"

"Well, in case you didn't know, there are other interesting stories developing around town. I was busy with a couple of them. The President announced he'd be traveling to Europe in April, and I was at the White House for the press conference. The health care committee is pretty much old news now," she smiled.

"Oh, really?" Grant said sarcastically. Then he added, "Is everything out here buried in bullshit and politics, like that committee?"

"Yeah, pretty much."

"So what do you do for fun?" he asked.

"I talk to you." Her eyes locked onto his. She was surprised at the bluntness of her own answer, but her eyes never gave it away.

"Oooo," Grant said softly. "That was good." The thing he saw in her eyes now reminded him of Kate. In no way did Susan resemble Kate, but the way her eyes pulled at him made him remember the excitement that only Kate had made him feel. "I wish we had tonight to do over again."

"Me too." She touched his hand. "But I have to go. It's late."

"Next month?" he asked.

"Yeah," she answered, reaching for her coat.

Grant wanted to tell her that Anne was out of his life. He'd waited for the right moment, but it never came.

When Susan stood to leave, she extended her hand to Grant. He pushed it aside and put his arms around her. He hugged her gently and put his lips by her ear.

"Thanks for coming to talk to me. It's been nice to have a friend out here these last couple of months." Then he squeezed her gently once again and stepped back. She noticed strength in his voice.

"Me too. See you next month?" Susan smiled, walked out the door, and hailed a cab. She wanted to stay.

Grant stood with his hands in his pockets and smiled as she walked away. He wanted her to stay.

chapter *E*IGHTEEN

The inside of the cab smelled like ... well, 'it smelled like the inside of a cab,' Grant thought. He hated to admit it to himself, but he was crestfallen after two months of almost no contact with Susan and then a final failed attempt to contact her. Now, a gray March day had surrendered to a rainy evening, and the depressing cab was taking him from the depressing airport to his depressing room at the Four Seasons Hotel in Washington. Grant had booked an early flight from Minneapolis in the hopes he could invent a reason to see Susan Wells tonight. But when he'd called her on Wednesday to see if she could join him for dinner, he'd been told by Susan's voice mail that she would be out of town for the weekend. He chose not to leave a message.

At least he was in town for the sixth and final health care committee meeting – that was reason to celebrate. He had never really understood the point of this whole exercise in Washington. The committee, he supposed, would grind along and do whatever it was going to do regardless of the objections of people like him.

His role on this committee had never been very clear, either. The President had told him to say the things that needed to be said. He'd supposed all along that Thom Hutchinson had expected him to voice the concerns of conservative middle-class Americans. In that way, the President could expose the other members of the committee to a conservative point of view without stating it himself. From the beginning, Grant had been willing to confront the committee — he knew it was one thing he was quite good at.

In that light, the February meeting had been something of a letdown for Grant. The committee had seemed to lose its way at about that time. The discussions had become less spirited. Even for Grant, the arguments had become less acrimonious and therefore less enjoyable. Everyone had seemed to sense that this issue was too big, with too many different concerned parties and too many varied viewpoints.

A more personal disappointment had come when the President had made a last-minute trip to New York and Susan had followed. Grant had looked for her all day at the meeting and waited around for her to find him afterwards as she'd done before. He'd tried not to appear crestfallen when she'd failed to show. He hadn't called her in the month prior to the meeting because ... well, because he was a little intimidated by her, and then he didn't want her to think he was pursuing her. But he had thought of her often, and he was very much aware of the little spark he felt when he spoke with her. She had called his hotel room on Saturday night and they'd spoken briefly. That was nice of her, too, but their telephone visit was far less exciting than any of their previous conversations.

He looked out the window of the cab and watched the strangers walking quickly in the drizzle. His ride pulled up under the awning in front of the hotel, and he just sat for a brief moment. 'Great, I came early so I could have two nights by myself with nothing but the committee to fill my time,' he thought to himself. He stepped out, dragged his luggage onto the sidewalk, paid the cabby, and trudged inside.

When he reached his room, he dropped his bags, kicked off his shoes, and reached for a beer in the little refrigerator all in the same motion. Then he flopped onto his bed, opened the beer, and began searching for a hockey game with the TV's remote control. A few minutes later, he was watching the game – but his thoughts were somewhere else.

He was embarrassed that he'd had such high hopes for a visit with Susan. Obviously he'd misunderstood whatever it was that he saw in her eyes before. 'What in the world would she see in me anyway?' he thought. 'I'm a geek ... a dentist from geek city. She ended our last phone conversation, which was weeks ago, with 'talk to you soon.' What the hell does that mean?' He sat on his bed and drank beer until he fell asleep.

~

Richard Bailey greeted everyone and then assumed control of the final committee meeting with a stirring opening address – a call for every member to do the right thing, to unite, and to recommend at least the basis, the format, for further study of sweeping health care legislation.

It all sounded like the same old rhetoric to Grant. He let the steam from his coffee warm his nose and face before each sip as he listened.

In a few minutes, however, Bailey was rolling. 'Damn, he is pretty good,' Grant thought. Bailey was convincing. If anyone in his audience did not already have strong feelings to the contrary, Grant knew Bailey would quickly win them over to his way of thinking. Even though he didn't like to admit it, Grant knew that some of the things Bailey said made sense even though Grant disagreed with them. Bailey began to cite statistics and bemoan the health care crisis once again. He turned the page on the speech he was reading, and Grant lowered his face to his coffee.

When Bailey began speaking again, Grant sat up straight in his chair and made a puzzled face. He looked around the room – at the reporters, at the other committee members – but only Charles Sanders returned his glance. As he listened, Grant became more and more agitated. His old, contentious nature rose to the surface quickly. Finally, he stood up and interrupted Richard Bailey. "Dr. Bailey? You're quoting a survey done in Russia! By Russians! You're telling us, and the media …," Grant gestured to several reporters at one of the tables, "… that the Russians, have a lower infant mortality rate than we do here." Grant's tone was incredulous. The room was deathly silent. "I just don't believe it! You shouldn't, either, and you know it isn't true. Those sons-a-bitches haven't told the truth about anything for seventy years. Shame on you for trying to sneak something like that into a forum like this … to insinuate that Russia has a better health care system than we do! You should be able to make your point well enough without having to use information that you know is untrue. You're too good for that!" Grant sat down. "OK, please continue."

Richard Bailey glowered at Grant Thorson. He then turned several pages of his speech and continued, obviously angered by Grant's interruption. When he reached the end of his opening speech, he folded his papers and addressed the group informally. "I had intended to start this, the last of our meetings, by having each of us make a comment for the record and simply forwarding our remarks to the President and to Congress. I still intend to do that. I'd planned to proceed in alphabetical order, but since Dr. Thorson seems to have a lot to say today, I'd like to start with him and proceed in reverse order. Dr. Thorson?"

Grant rose to his feet. He felt good. He was ready to accept the obvious challenge Dr. Bailey had extended. "Thank you, Dr. Bailey. I should apologize for interrupting you earlier … well, no, I shouldn't. You had it coming." Grant paused. He put his hands in his pockets so no one would be distracted by any movement he might make.

"We have not done the hard work here. None of us have. And we all know why, too! There will be no consensus among us …

never! We all want something different. We all value our own individual well-being more than the good of the country. Some of us have a political agenda." Grant paused and gestured to Darrell Osterquist. "Some of us have a moral reason for proposing national health care." He gestured now toward Richard Bailey. "If I'm to be intellectually honest, I must admit that I'm guilty of thinking about my own self-interest, too. We need to ask ourselves some hard questions if we are to consider a national health care policy, and we don't bother to ask these questions because we know we'll be passionate in our disagreement.

"Most of the issues we need to examine exist out there at the place where medicine and philosophy meet. Whose rights are more important – the mother's or the fetus'? Should a person faced with a certain and painful death be allowed to choose a doctor-assisted suicide? Is there a point when it is financially unfeasible to continue or to initiate medical treatment? Is there a time when it is morally objectionable to discontinue life support for a patient? Are citizens entitled to the services of doctors? There are hundreds more questions like these. Which of you wants to allow the person sitting next to you to answer for you? We even argue as to whether or not it is right to allow others to answer these questions for themselves. Consensus? I don't think so.

"Now, let me ask if any of you know who was the largest individual campaign contributor to both President Thorpe and his opponents' campaigns a few years ago."

Grant looked around the room. "Didn't think so. It was Donald Ames, president and owner of Hatch Industries, the largest processor of soybeans, corn, and wheat in the world. Mr. Ames and his employees, and his corporation, contributed heavily to the campaign of every other office holder chosen in the last election. Owners and officers of every other grain processing company contributed likewise during the election. It's a matter of public record. You can look it up in all the candidates' campaign finance information.

"Why would these men give money in this manner? Wouldn't we expect them to support one candidate and oppose the other based on each candidate's policies, and then contribute money accordingly?

"Well, we all know why these contributions are made. It's so that no matter who wins, that candidate is beholden to his supporters … OK, special interest groups. And it isn't just the other party's guy who's beholden to special interest groups, it's your guy, too. Whoever he may be.

"In this case, these 'lobbyists' are then called upon to help create farm policies. Legislators who have been paid by special interests then wrap themselves in the flag and cry out to save the family farm. That is a noble cause, by the way. But what they're actually doing is begging for monstrous subsidies that are designed to make farmers dependent on the government and just solvent enough to stay on the farm another year. But the bottom line here is that these farm policies guarantee a low price for the raw materials, which Hatch Industries uses to create an immense private fortune. And once again elected officials have given special interest groups the key to government coffers and duped the public into feeling good about it all.

"Take a look at this model of government being twisted to serve only a few. Maybe you disagree with the scenario I've just created. That's OK. It just may be all wrong. But ask yourselves if you think that something like this could happen in this country. Now substitute your medical insurance company for Hatch Industries in this equation. Do you feel good about the future of your healthcare? You shouldn't."

Grant paused and looked around him. "Now, having said all of this, suppose I'm all wrong. Most of you are already certain of that fact anyway." Grant smiled. Small grins appeared all around the room. "Suppose national health care is an idea whose time has come. Whoever it is that draws up a framework for a national health care policy must be certain to determine exactly what we, as a nation, expect from our health care system. We cannot enter into a system of socialized medicine without a clear vision of where we expect our system to take us — you know, 'just do something different than we've done because it's different and different must be better.'" Again Grant paused and looked around the room. "The men who framed our constitution did a great thing. They created the greatest nation in history with that document. But they neglected to deal with one thing — slavery. They left that issue for later generations to resolve, and it almost destroyed this nation. Before we create a National Health Insurance Program, we need to know what we expect of this program as a nation — and I don't believe we're even close to consensus yet. I don't think it matters what we say here today, the rest of the country isn't interested in listening to someone else's feelings on these issues. We need to get it right the first time on this issue. Can we do that?"

Grant appeared to be finished, but he lingered for a moment and remained standing. "Before I sit down," Grant continued slowly, "I'd like to return to something I said a little earlier ... and confess." The room settled into deep silence. "My self-interest — my bias here — is that I want to protect the past. It may not have been perfect, but it was good, and much will be lost if we simply turn away from something that was built on the lessons of our past. Let's remember to hold onto what is good from the past before we consider the future. Thank you, Dr. Bailey. I'm finished."

When Grant sat down, there was no applause, only more silence. Charles Sanders, the black author who sat across the table, caught Grant's eyes. Sanders smiled and gently nodded his head up and down. Grant had liked Sanders from the very first day the committee met. Then Sanders showed Grant his right hand, palm down and extended over his notebook. He raised his eyebrows and flip-flopped his hand gently — the universal gesture for "not bad." Grant smiled a little smile.

He had not intended to address his own bias when he began speaking, but the further he went with his address, the more he recognized that all of them needed to do so. Strangely, for the first time since he'd been meeting with these people, he felt some self-doubt when he said the words, "I want to protect the past." He wondered to himself, as he listened to the others, "Just how important is the past?"

Others took their turns and spoke. Some committee members had remained enthusiastic supporters of any form of socialized medicine, while others retained a bit of caution regarding the potential for excesses and abuse.

When Charles Sanders stood, he said only, "I agree with just about everything Dr. Thorson said. Also, I'd like for this group to remember that the system we've built over the years isn't really that bad, and the problems most of us have identified have come as a result of fairly recent third-party (insurance company) and government involvement – things we've added to the old system. Maybe our patient is sick because of the medication we're giving. Perhaps more of the same medicine will kill the patient." Then Sanders sat down. Grant gave him the "not bad" sign immediately but made a face suggesting he could have done better. Sanders returned a bigger smile.

When Darrell Osterquist rose to speak, Grant could feel his original disdain for this group returning. As Osterquist spoke, it became clear that some things never change. He spoke of vision and the future and chastised those who supported the failed system of health care. Grant could hear the familiar air of indignation. Anyone who could disagree with Osterquist was obviously stupid, or possibly just unenlightened.

Lunch break was nearing. Grant was growing tired of this refrain from Osterquist. As he grew impatient for a chance to stretch his legs, his mind began to wander. His contempt of Osterquist grew. He began to see Osterquist as a comic figure, and suddenly the memory of an adolescent prank came to him. He knew Will Campbell would enjoy what he was about to do.

On a small piece of paper, Grant wrote ZIPPER! in large letters. When he'd finished writing, he looked up and just by chance caught Charles Sanders' glance. Sanders had seen what Grant had written and knew what he was about to do. He looked at Grant with a look that asked, "Are you sure you want to do this?" Grant only smiled in reply. He then slid the note slowly into Osterquist's line of vision.

He held the paper where Osterquist could see it. For almost a minute he watched for recognition in the eyes of the strangely dressed man. Osterquist stumbled briefly, almost imperceptibly, when he caught sight of the note. Grant pulled it back and placed it in his pocket immediately. As Osterquist continued to speak, his right hand slowly crept toward his zipper. Grant, seated on Osterquist's immediate right, noticed that most of the other committee members weren't looking anywhere but at their own notes. He coughed as loud as he could in a deliberate attempt to draw attention to himself and then stared at Osterquist. The speaker's hand returned to his notes. His delivery seemed confused now. Osterquist quickly ended his comments and sat down. He never looked at Grant. Grant watched as he checked his zipper immediately after he sat down.

~

When the group finally broke for lunch, Charles Sanders waited for Grant with a smile. "Haven't seen that one for a while."

"Got kicked out of social studies in eighth grade the last time I did it," Grant replied.

"Join me for lunch?" Sanders asked.

"Love to."

As the men walked toward the door, a short, serious-looking gray-haired woman stepped toward them. She positioned herself in Grant's path, and when he stopped she said, "Dr. Thorson?"

"Yes?"

"I'm Petra Vanderhoft. We met at Susan Wells' speech at Georgetown a while ago."

"Oh, yeah. I'm sorry. I didn't recognize you. Nice to see you again.

"It's nice to see you, too."

"You aren't here ... working, are you? Your paper wouldn't send an editor over here ... for this? Would they?"

"No, this committee is old news. It'll get a paragraph or two somewhere about page four tomorrow," she smiled. "I'm here to meet a friend for lunch." She paused again. "The reason I came to find you is that Susan asked me to pass along a message."

"Oh?" Grant felt his pulse quicken just a little.

"She said she was disappointed that you hadn't called her, and that she'd planned to call you and see if you had plans for dinner one night this weekend."

"Oh?"

"Yes. But she had to accompany the President on his visit to Montreal for a few days. She tried to call you before she left town, but she missed you. I'm guessing that she'll call you tonight. In any event, she asked me to extend her personal apology for missing your visit."

"Thank you."

"You're welcome. I hope you enjoyed your time in Washington." She turned and left.

When Petra Vanderhoft was out of earshot, Charles Sanders ventured, "She sounded like she was dismissing you."

"I thought so, too. Like when the principal reamed you out and then sent you out to stand with your nose against the wall."

"You would know," Sanders added.

When the final session of the final meeting ended, Grant went directly to his room and ordered a pizza. He watched hockey on TV and waited by the phone.

He pounced on the phone when it finally rang at 9:30.

"Hello?"

"Dr. Thorson?"

"Yes." It wasn't Susan. It wasn't anyone he knew.

"Can you hold for President Hutchinson?"

"Yes." 'Must be some traveling secretary instead of Jessica Wickham,' he thought.

"Grant?" Thom said briskly after the line clicked.

"Yes, Mr. President."

"Done with all the meetings, I understand?"

"Mercifully, yes!"

"Well, I wanted to thank you for serving. You did fine!"

"I just proved that you have low standards for people you chose to be your friends."

"Not true! You performed as I hoped you would."

"Well, thank you."

"So how is everything back home?"

"Pretty quiet, Hutch, pretty quiet. You're in Montreal tonight, huh?" Grant made an attempt at small talk and felt embarrassed immediately. He could hear other voices in Thom's room, and he assumed Thom had no time for chit chat.

"Yes. Hmm? Yes." The President had been interrupted and was talking to someone else. "I have to go, Grant. I will be in touch. Thank you again for serving."

The line was already dead when Grant said, "Keep your powder dry!"

The phone rang again in a few minutes, and Grant picked it up quickly once again. "Hello?"

"Hello, Grant." This time it was Susan. He was excited to hear her voice.

"Hello, Susan. Are you trying to avoid me? Is that why you're always out of town?" He tried to smile.

"Quite the opposite. I was set to call you and see if you wanted to get together and talk about great authors or dental floss or some such thing. Then this came up, and here I am! I have been traveling a lot recently, though."

She made him feel good. He could see she had some attraction to him or she wouldn't have called, or visited him to apologize two months earlier. "How was the final meeting today?"

"Just more bullshit. There will be no sweeping solution. Some crisis will have to come along and cause the whole thing to implode. Then maybe a new system will arise, or maybe the old one will reappear as it used to be. Who knows, it's all just overwhelming."

"Did you make anyone hate you today?" she smiled through the phone.

"I tried, like always. Oh! I had a warm chat with Ms. Vanderhoft."

"I'll bet."

They really didn't know each other well enough to sustain a long phone conversation, and when they'd exhausted everything they had to talk about, Grant stepped out on a limb. "Hey, Susan?"

"Yes?"

"I really had hoped to see you this weekend. We're all done with the committee, you know."

"Yeah, I know. We'll have to keep our friendship alive over the phone for a while." She paused as if she were about to let him in on a secret. "The President told me last week that he was making a trip to Minnesota in May. I'll be there for at least part of that trip west."

"He's coming to Spider Lake, you know. My home!" Grant recognized the excitement in his voice and knew immediately that he sounded like a schoolboy.

"Yeah, I know. He was telling me all about it the other day. He's really looking forward to it! So am I."

"Well, that's great. We'll see you then. Is it OK if I call you before then?" Now Susan could hear the excitement in his voice.

"Absolutely. Who knows — maybe we'll even see each other before spring!"

"That would be nice." 'What a change a few hours can make in a man's outlook,' he thought when he hung up the phone.

chapter *NINETEEN*

During the night, about three inches of heavy, wet snow had fallen on Spider Lake. It was late March now and heavy snows were common, but no one really cared because spring was coming soon. Now, as Grant's cross-country skis plowed new tracks in the fresh snow, he felt strong. He was pulling the plastic toboggan that he'd bought for Ingrid many years earlier. Loaded on the toboggan were fishing tackle, an ice auger, two thermoses of coffee, and two plastic buckets to sit on.

"Did you bring minnows?" Will called out. He was skiing immediately behind Grant as they crossed Spider Lake on the way to Christian Island.

"Wax worms!" Grant turned his head and answered quickly. They were on their way to search for the drop-off at the south end of the island. During late winter, just before the spring breakup of the ice, they always found perch there.

When they reached what Grant thought looked like the right spot, they stopped and began to line up the surrounding landmarks that they'd used for years to put themselves directly over the most productive fishing hole.

"OK, let's see … we line up the two big tombstones in the cemetery and then the big white pine across the bay and the scrub oak on the tip of the island." Far across the lake from Christian Island, a small bay was littered with large stones that protruded above the surface. From a distance they looked like tombstones. Hence, the little bay was called the cemetery. "This look good to you?" Grant asked as he looked all around.

"Yup," Will answered. He took his skis off, lifted the old ice auger off the toboggan, and began to drill a five-inch diameter hole in the ice. The auger ground the ice into powder as Will twisted his hands in opposite directions while he powered the auger through the frozen surface of the lake. Finally, it plunged through, and water and crushed ice gushed up onto the surface.

"Looks like about twenty-four inches of ice. Don't wanna drill too damn many holes. Hope we're in the right place." Will paused to get his breath as he spoke; he was overheated from the work of drilling the hole. When he took his hat off, steam rose from his head.

By the time Grant had drilled a hole for himself, Will had rigged his fishing rod, seated himself on one of the buckets, and lit his pipe.

Will had phoned Grant earlier in the week because he always called Grant first when something bad or good happened in his life. Molly, his oldest daughter, had announced to Will and June on Monday that she was moving in with her boyfriend … and Will was crushed. He'd argued with Molly, then he'd argued with June. Now he sat on the bucket with a forlorn look on his face and stared off across the lake.

Grant poured himself a cup of coffee and remained standing after he'd rigged his fishing rod and rested it on the other bucket. "So talk to me, buddy," Grant coaxed.

Will didn't look up at Grant. He just started talking. "Remember the night Molly was born?"

"Yes." Grant smiled at the memory. She'd been born while they were still in dental school.

"I stopped by your place when I left the hospital. I wanted to tell you all about what I'd just seen." Will turned toward Grant now. "You got up out of bed and fixed me a drink. We sat up most of the night and you listened to me tell you all about it over and over again. Remember?"

"Yeah, you were pretty animated." Grant's smile widened.

"We had way too much to drink, remember?" Will asked.

"You did!" Grant replied.

"When I got to the hospital the next morning, the first thing I did was puke in the little bathroom in June's room, and then I laid in the bed next to June's ... major hangover. She knew what had happened right away. Man, she was really pissed at you."

"You know, I never understood how that whole thing worked. Every time you screwed up, she hated me a little more." Grant's eyebrows furrowed, and he appeared confused as he took another sip of coffee and handed the cup to Will.

"Yeah, I was never too clear on that either. But I was damn thankful to have you around to blame shit on!" Will laughed out loud. "If I even hinted that you were involved in something that went bad, or that June didn't like, she locked onto you and directed all of the hate and revenge your way." He sipped at the coffee and passed it back.

Will started to laugh all over again. "When I called my folks to tell them Molly was here, they were convinced that something was wrong with her — you know, two heads or something — because I sounded so bad. June took the phone out of my hand and told them that 'that damn Grant got Will drunk last night.' I wish you could have seen it." Will smiled at Grant.

"So what did you say then?" Grant asked.

"I hurled again ... it was like throwing gas on a fire. She was so pissed at you!"

"Well, hell, I guess that's what friends are for." Grant laughed and finished the coffee, then put the top back onto the thermos.

Will looked away for a brief moment, and his voice carried anger and disappointment when he said, "I never thought that beautiful little child would be shacked up with some asshole. She could be something if she wanted to. I'm afraid she's gonna piss it all away and make life really difficult for herself."

"Do you have shit in your ears?"

"Huh?" Will looked puzzled.

"You should be able to hear your father's voice echoing the same words, and not that long ago. I think Yogi Berra said it: 'This is like déjà vu all over again.'"

"June and I never lived together!" Will said indignantly.

"I know that. But you got married young, and you chose a different career than your father wanted." Grant stopped, bent at the waist, and brought his face close to Will's. "And it all worked out pretty well ... didn't it?"

"I still don't like it!" Will's face tightened.

"Maybe everything isn't about you!" Grant raised his eyebrows when he spoke, and he looked directly into Will's eyes.

Will did not respond to Grant's comment. He held eye contact with his old friend for a moment and then began to nod his head slowly.

When he did speak again, he'd let go of his sullen mood of a few minutes earlier. "Looks like you set us up on a red hot fishin' hole. Gimme some more coffee, will ya?"

"Hey, this is ice fishin'. You know as well as I do that this is some sort of Norwegian/Zen brain torture! It's not about catchin' fish! It's about staring down a hole in the ice until your IQ and the air temperature are in harmony."

Just then, Nellie trotted over to them. She'd been playing in the small trees on Christian Island. Will reached an open hand toward her and she wagged her tail as she came to him.

"Man, she's getting a gray muzzle! How old is she now?" Will asked.

"Almost ten," Grant replied.

"Pete would have been thirteen this spring," Will said quietly as he looked at Grant again. "Wow … time flies."

Will had purchased a black lab puppy almost thirteen years earlier. "Pete" had been a great athlete with a chiseled appearance. He had the classic look of the labs on the duck stamps. He was the most handsome, most athletic dog either of them had ever known. He should have been a great hunter except for one huge flaw: Pete was gun shy. He was terrified at the noise or even the sight of a shotgun. All efforts to heal him had ended in failure. His training sessions with throwing dummies were beautiful things to behold. But as soon as a gun was revealed, he began to whine and roll on the ground. Then he'd hide under a car or take whatever cover he could find.

But one strange, improbable, unbelievable event had made Pete a legend. Will and Grant had tried everything to help heal Pete's flaw. Nothing had worked over his first three years. One day, they decided to take him out hunting one last time and see what might happen. They had to drag him on a leash to a small duck blind on a small pothole in northwest Minnesota. When they reached the pothole, they took Pete off the leash. He immediately raced back over a hill toward their truck. Both hunters assumed he was gone for the day, and that he'd be waiting for them under the truck when they were done hunting. They'd decided that this was Pete's last chance.

Almost instantly after Pete had run away, a large flock of ducks sailed directly into the pothole, and the hunters killed seven ducks with their first volley. As they looked out over the water, they began to wonder how they'd retrieve the dead ducks. Then, suddenly, Pete appeared. He was racing toward them like a greyhound. He hit the water after a huge leap and retrieved all seven ducks, one at a time, to Will's hand. He then hunted with them until they'd filled their daily bag limit, retrieving every bird perfectly. The gun shy behavior was gone! It was as if something had snapped in Pete's soul. He was suddenly "complete." He was spectacular! He had it!

That was the last day of the season, and Will spent the winter bragging about his dog and waiting for the next year. The following spring, however, Pete died of cancer. He never hunted again. He'd had only one day, but it was an awe-inspiring day. Will was distraught at Pete's death, and he vowed never to have another dog.

Both Will and Grant spent a minute now reliving Pete's special day in their minds.

"If he'd been a ball player, he'd have thrown a perfect game that day or hit five home runs. That one retrieve was the single greatest thing I ever saw any dog do ... a septuple blind retrieve ... unreal!" Grant shook his head in disbelief as he spoke.

"So what are you gonna do when Nellie dies?" Will asked bluntly.

To another man the question might have sounded insensitive, but Grant knew exactly what Will meant. "Well, I'm never gonna quit the life I love so much. A big share of the joy in all of this comes from her. I think I need a friend to love, and I think the love we give to old friends comes from some endless source. I'll probably feel bad for a while, then find a new huntin' buddy."

"No broken heart?" Will asked.

"Absolutely, but I think it will heal," Grant shrugged his shoulders.

Now that he'd heard himself say those words, Grant couldn't help but think of the loss of his wife. He finally sat on the other plastic bucket. He reached for the thermos and began pouring more coffee. "Cold out here," he mumbled to himself.

When Grant had a drink of coffee, Will extended his hand to ask for the cup. Grant passed it and began speaking, but it was as if he was speaking to his own feet.

"You know, one night after Kate got really sick, I came home from the hospital and just sat there with the lights out. The thought that she might die became real for me at that moment. I felt sort of overcome by a fear that I'd never felt or heard anyone speak of before. I worried that if she died now, she'd take her love for me with her and I could never replace that. She'd shared the very best part of my life, my youth, and she knew me in a way that no one ever could again." Grant looked at Will now. He wasn't pleading for understanding as he'd done other times. He was just emptying one of the private places in his heart.

"Certain words, names, songs, whatever would cause her to look at me and smile. Without speaking a word, we could say everything to each other and relive some old joke or special time. When she died, all of that was gone forever."

Grant's voice was firm when he continued. Now it was as if he was pressing Will for an answer that he knew Will couldn't give. "So was it selfish for me to think of her death as losing part of myself, too? Is it really not about me? For the first time, I understand why old people sometimes just give up the ghost and die when they lose their mate ... their life just died and left them." Grant paused and looked away again. "She took me — my past — with her."

Through all their conversations since Kate's death, Will had not seen Grant shed a tear or show any real emotion. He thought briefly that this would be the moment when Grant might vent his grief. Will waited for several minutes, but Grant did not speak.

Finally, Grant interrupted his own silence with "the fishing sucks. Let's go stoke up the fire in the cabin and get something to eat. Or do you wanna sit on that bucket for four more hours and see if anything starts to bite around sundown?"

~

"OK, here's the deal," Grant said as he bent over to strike a match and light the gas barbecue grill. "Spring training opened last month so we're eatin' ball park food tonight ... brats 'n sauerkraut and beer 'n ice cream!" Both men looked ridiculous. They wore fur hats and sweatshirts, but a few minutes earlier they'd stripped down to their boxer shorts in the heat of the cabin. Now they'd stepped into their heavy boots and walked onto the porch to start the grill. They each carried a beer in one hand, and steam rose from their bare legs in the ten-degree weather.

"All right, then, we'd better get our lineups set. Are we talking fifties, sixties, all time?" Will replied as he twisted the top off of a beer bottle.

"All time," Grant responded as the gas in the grill flashed when it caught fire. It was another ancient game the old friends played while they passed time together. Each of them would select a baseball team, one player at a time, and then justify his choice. Sometimes they'd choose their teams from the fifties, sixties, thirties ... it didn't matter. Tonight they were choosing their all-time teams again.

"Who you got pitchin'?" Grant started.

"Gibson. Lifetime ERA 2.91 ... 251 wins."

"I know." Grant acted irritated at Will's choice. "I'll throw ... The Babe!"

"You think you're so clever!"

"Yes, I do. I now have the greatest hitter of all time in the nine hole. And you'll have to pick another right fielder." Grant seemed to gloat.

"No problem, I'll take Aaron."

"A poor choice – no charisma, no flair, he never seemed to love the game ... but don't get out of order. Who's catchin'?"

"Bench! Your turn."

"Shit ... Campanella. I wanted Bench!"

"No Yogi tonight?"

"Nah, Campanella's fine. First base?"

As the brats cooked slowly and the managers sipped at their beers, the choices moved around the diamond until center fielders needed to be chosen.

"Mays," Will said. "Your turn."

"Mickey Mantle," Grant added slowly, with satisfaction. "The Oklahoma kid!"

"How come you always take him? Casey Stengel even left him off the all-time Yankee team. The guy came up short by any measure."

"Yeah, but when Big Ole used to hit me fly balls, I'd stand with my back to the old corncrib and go back for the ball like it was headed for the gap in Yankee Stadium. Sometimes I made great backhanded running catches, sometimes I didn't. But I always tried to run like Mickey Mantle. I had my mother sew a number seven on the back of my shirt, and I wore that shirt whenever we played ball in the barnyard. I don't care what he woulda, coulda, shoulda done. He was there with me then and he's my guy now."

Will could only smile, and their game lasted all through supper. As their celebration of the new baseball season wound down, Will turned to Grant and asked, "Ever hear from Anne?"

"Not a word. We should have been right ... but we weren't." Grant looked at Will and smiled a funny smile. He wasn't angry or upset. He held the odd smile for a while, but he said nothing more about her. After a short pause and a sip of beer, he smiled again and said, "The Prez will be here in six weeks. I wonder what that's gonna be like."

"Yeah, I'll bet the security around here is gonna be interesting. I wonder if there's gonna be a huge media presence. You know, Thom is gonna overnight at the Ordway house. Where will all the security and press and other people stay?"

"Thom told me that would all be taken care of. I assumed they'd have some sort of mobile quarters for the security types and then take the media into town," Grant added.

"Hey! Thom told me you've been seeing that babe from the *Post!* Were you just gonna let that slide or were you gonna tell me about it?" Will demanded.

"I just spoke with her a couple of times when I was in Washington for that ridiculous committee. She wasn't even in town the last two times I was there. But we've sort of become friends."

"Right!" Will said sarcastically.

Grant returned a huge smile to Will as the phone rang. Grant rose to answer it and pointed at Will, implying he had more to say about Susan Wells after the phone call.

"Spider Lake Duck Camp," Grant said, still smiling.

The voice on the other end of the phone was Gladys Thorson. "Grant, you'd better come home. It's Dad."

chapter TWENTY

The grass was mostly brown, but there were traces of green beginning to show here and there. On this morning there was a chill in the air. But the afternoons of late March were beginning to carry the feel of spring. Most of the recent snow had melted, except for the small drifts on the north side of the road ditches and buildings.

As Grant walked along the sidewalk leading into the nursing home in Halstad, he looked to his right and noticed that the ice in the little pond was honey-combed with air bubbles and growing dark. There was open water around the edge of the duck pond, and now there were some mallards and several dozen Canada geese waddling around the edge of the pond and begging for passersby to feed them.

'Won't be long – maybe three weeks – and the ice will be out at home,' Grant thought to himself as he reached to open the glass door that led into the lobby of the nursing home. As soon as he was inside the building, he noticed his mother sitting at a table. Seated next to her was Big Ole.

Ole Thorson was slumped over in his wheelchair. Someone had tied a dishtowel around his chest and then around the back of the chair so he wouldn't fall out of it. Grant was stunned by the decline his father had undergone in one week.

The previous Saturday had been Ole and Gladys' sixty-third wedding anniversary. Ole had ordered Grant to buy sixty-three red roses and have them delivered to his room in the nursing home so he could surprise Gladys when she came to visit on their anniversary. He'd sat up and bragged to everyone within earshot that he'd "married the prettiest girl in town sixty-three years ago today, and she's sittin' right there."

Gladys laughed and cried off and on all day. She cried whenever Ole was asleep or wasn't looking. Ole became an instant folk hero for all the women who worked in the nursing home. They came in one at a time and told Gladys they were going to take her man away. Gladys only smiled and nodded when they spoke to her.

Today was terribly different, however. Grant kissed his mother hello, but when he held his father there was no response. Ole was breathing, but he was otherwise lifeless. When Grant sat at the table, he took his mother's hand and looked into her eyes. "Tell me about it, Mom," was all he said.

"He's been like this for about three days. I was gonna call you last night anyway." She turned her head and looked at Ole again. "All of a sudden yesterday, he looked at me with those old sharp eyes and smiled like he used to. He'd snapped out of the fog that he'd been in. He looked perfectly fine. He said he was going duck hunting with Little Ole." She smiled an odd smile.

"No!" Grant's voice registered disbelief. Then he wrinkled his eyebrows. "Really?" Little Ole Hokanson was Big Ole's neighbor and long-time hunting buddy. Little Ole Hokanson had passed away twenty-two years earlier.

"Really!" Gladys nodded. "He also said that Grampa was there, along with a couple of men whose names I didn't recognize. And then he mentioned ... Pastor Aamot. Said he was there, too."

"Who's he?" Grant wrinkled his eyebrows again.

"He was the minister at Red River Lutheran Church where your dad was confirmed in 1927. He's been dead for fifty years! He really liked your father. They hunted together a little bit when your dad was young, too."

"Wow." Grant leaned back in his chair and smiled at his mother.

"I asked him if you were there, too!" Gladys added. "He looked me right in the eye and said, 'No, he's a good boy!' How about that?" She shook her head and smiled.

"So what do you think, Mom? Was it a vision of Heaven, someone waiting for him on the other side?" Grant asked with a curious expression.

"I don't know. I guess that's what I was thinking, but I was hoping you would say the words first."

Grant got his mother and himself cups of coffee and sugar cookies, and they sat together holding hands and looking at Big Ole. Grant asked if he should call his brothers and let them know what was happening. Gladys said she'd already done that. They talked for a while longer — mostly small talk and talk about relatives and old friends around Halstad.

Gradually, it began to bother Grant that he was treating his father as if he didn't exist anymore. Sometimes he would speak of Big Ole as if his dad was not seated right there to hear it. When his mother referred to a recent visit with the minister and the funeral home director, Grant could feel himself recoil. His father needed to be the center of conversation — not anyone or anything else.

He knelt on the floor beside his father's chair and pressed his cheek against his father's face. Then he kissed Ole and whispered, "I love you, Dad" while he stroked the back of Ole's head. He was certain his father could not hear him and didn't know he was there. Grant was about to stand up when Ole's eyes opened. Grant was taken aback by the clarity in his fathers eyes. He looked like he'd just returned from someplace faraway.

Big Ole gently took Grant's hand in his, kept his face near Grant's, and said very clearly, "I love you too, son." Then he began to weep. He cried mournfully. Grant had not seen anything like this yet from his father. He wasn't certain if his father was weeping due to pain or because he sensed that his death was near. But there had been an eerie quality in the way he'd said the words. Somehow, Grant knew in his heart that it meant 'goodbye.'" Big Ole leaned close to Grant's ear and whispered, "I'm gonna miss you, boy." And then he slowly stopped weeping. It was the best — and worst — thing his father had ever said to him.

Ole turned away from Grant and gestured for Gladys to come near to him. When she drew close to him, Grant let go of Ole's hand and stood so that Gladys could be close to him. "You're still the prettiest girl in town," Grant heard him say. Their faces were touching and they were talking quietly while Grant stood beside them for several minutes.

Then Gladys stood up and said, "He's asleep. Let's put him in his bed for a nap." She was wiping tears away from her eyes as they rolled Ole's chair back to his room. When Ole was resting in his bed, Gladys took Grant's hand and led him into the hall outside Ole's room. "He told me not to start a feeding tube or anything like that. He said, 'Just let me go!'"

Grant held his mother while she wept quietly. He thought it was strange that none of his life's experiences had prepared him for something like this. He didn't know what to say to his mother, and he didn't know what to do. He felt like he was being carried along in a current that could not be stopped.

Grant dropped his mother off at the farm that evening and didn't really know what to do. He wondered if he should return to the nursing home and sit with his father. He wondered if he should stay with his mother. He'd seen fear in her eyes. She knew she was about to lose the love of her life. He decided to go home but to visit Ingrid on the way, to tell her Big Ole was slipping. He tried to convince himself that Ole would rally.

But the call came much sooner than expected. Grant was in Ingrid's dormitory room when the phone rang.

"Hello? … Hi, Gramma! … Yeah, he's right here." Ingrid's voice lowered when she gave the phone to Grant. She already knew what the call was about.

"Yeah … OK, Mom. OK. I'm on my way back." He never looked at Ingrid while he spoke on the telephone. "Grampa is dead," he told her after he'd hung up. He walked to the easy chair by Ingrid's bed and sat down. Ingrid approached cautiously, then took her old seat on his lap. She was just his little girl once again. Grampa was gone forever; the world had changed again. She rested her head on her daddy's shoulder and wiped away her tears. She could feel her father trying to swallow the pain.

Grant thought he'd been prepared to hear the words, to say them. But that could never be. 'I should have been there with him at the end,' he thought. "But what difference could it have made? He was in another world, wasn't he?" Now, as he sat quietly in the gathering darkness, Grant had the strange sensation that he couldn't remember what his father looked like. In only a moment he grew desperate to see his father's image, so he began fumbling through his wallet. He found a tattered, wrinkled old black-and-white photo of himself and his dad. Grant was eleven when the picture was taken; his ears were pushed down by his hat, and Ingrid thought he looked ridiculous. He and his father each held a large Canada goose and a shotgun. Ole Thorson stood tall and straight, his dark eyes gleaming in a huge smile. Ingrid smiled and cried at the same time as she looked at the photo.

~

Twenty minutes into the flight, a small man began making his way toward Susan Wells' seat. She thought he looked young – too young to be an assistant for the First Lady. When he reached her seat, he told Susan that Mrs. Hutchinson would like to speak with her. Susan rose immediately and followed the young man from the press section to the section of the plane that had been partitioned for privacy for Ellen Hutchinson and her staff.

As she made her way through the relatively small group of writers and photographers that were accompanying the First Lady on this trip, she thought she knew why she'd been summoned.

The President had been in Europe for only a few minutes on Monday when Ellen had called to tell him of Ole Thorson's death. In the back of his mind, he'd planned to attend the funeral if it were possible, but he could not leave a European summit for Ole's funeral. So he'd asked Ellen to go in his place.

Susan had chosen not to cover the President's visit to Europe and had remained in Washington. When she heard of Ellen Hutchinson's plans to travel to Halstad, Minnesota, to attend the funeral of Grant Thorson's father, she was glad she'd stayed in town. Susan decided to accompany the First Lady as part of the media on this trip. She'd quickly grown to like Grant Thorson, and she wanted to pay her respects in person also. She felt terrible that she'd been unable to see him during his last two trips to the capital.

"Hello, Susan," the First Lady said when Susan stood in the aisle facing her. "Please sit down with me."

"Thank you, Mrs. Hutchinson." Susan sat in the seat facing Ellen Hutchinson. There was a small table between them.

"It's Ellen. I asked you to sit with me because Will Campbell told me that Grant was fond of you. Will says he speaks of you often. You've become friends with him?"

"I guess so. Initially I didn't think I'd like him, but as I've come to know him … I've grown to like him. I guess we're friends." Susan was holding back a little; she didn't want to give away too much information.

"Thom likes him very much. He admires his candor." Ellen was smiling.

"Yes, I know what you mean. He hides it very well sometimes, but he's actually a pretty bright guy, too." Susan was smiling now.

She sensed that Ellen Hutchinson was offering to get to know her on a personal level.

"That's what Thom says, too. Thom also really admires the friendship that Will and Grant share."

"Yes. Grant gets a silly smile on his face whenever he mentions Will Campbell. I've only met Will once; it was at the White House party in October. I really don't know him at all."

"He was Thom's roommate in college. You'll love him. Everyone loves Will. He introduced Thom and Grant when the boys were all in grad school. I don't think Thom and Grant liked each other very much to begin with. Thom certainly likes Grant now, though, even though they're quite a ways apart philosophically. I think they grew up in different worlds." The discussion of the three men allowed Ellen and Susan to get to know each other somewhat. There was no talk of politics or issues — just friends and the experiences they had in common.

After about an hour of conversation between Ellen and Susan, the First Lady's young assistant approached cautiously and told her there was a phone call for her.

"I'll excuse myself," Susan said as she rose to return to her seat.

"Will you sit with me at the funeral, Susan? I hate to do funerals alone!" Ellen asked when Susan had stepped into the aisle.

"Certainly," Susan said. She then turned to walk back to her seat in the press section of the plane.

There were still patches of melting snow around the little church in the country, but it was unseasonably warm — almost fifty degrees today. April 2nd would be a good day for a funeral. A grave had been dug between a row of pine trees in the old cemetery surrounding the church. Patches of green grass were beginning to show amongst the brown winter-kill that covered most of the ground.

The brick steeple of Six-Mile Valley Lutheran Church was visible for several miles in every direction. It rose out of the tall pines, which surrounded the cemetery, which surrounded the little old country church. The church had been built just before the Sioux uprising in 1862. Martin Thorson was Grant's great-great-grandfather and the patriarch of one of the original five settler families that came to Six-Mile Valley to raise a family, a community, and a church.

Several black limousines pulled up to the little country church together. There was a very visible Secret Service presence, a moderate number of media, and a few photographers. The media and photographers were kept outside the small church when the First Lady, along with Susan Wells and several Secret Service agents, entered Six-Mile Valley Lutheran Church.

A large crowd of family and friends filled the church and spilled over to the church basement. An entire church pew had been reserved for Ellen Hutchinson. When she and Susan and two agents had taken their places, an elderly man and his wife were seated next to them. Several agents had arrived earlier and now remained relatively inconspicuous as the funeral was about to begin. An entire community had come to say goodbye to Ole Thorson.

A solemn procession of family members walked from the back of the church to the front. Gladys, her five sons, and their wives and children filled the first three rows. Then about three dozen other family members filled the rows behind the immediate family.

Ellen looked to her left and saw Will and June Campbell and nodded a "hello." Then she turned to Susan and whispered, "This looks like a Norman Rockwell painting." The old men in the church were mostly farmers. The tops of their heads and faces were pale, due to a lifetime of protection from their hats, while the bottom halves of their faces were dark and worn from a lifetime of wind and sunburn from working the land. The young men were also mostly farmers, and they had a rugged look about them, too. Among the older women there was a generous amount of blue hair and bad dentures.

Susan smiled. She remembered she'd told Grant that Gordon MacQuarrie stories made her think of Norman Rockwell, and Grant had thought that was good. She turned to Ellen and said, "Is that Grant's daughter sitting next to him?"

"Yes. She looks just like her mother," Ellen replied.

"Beautiful girl," Susan whispered.

Ellen nodded in agreement. As the service progressed both Ellen and Susan noticed the stoic nature of the Thorson family. Grant and his brothers all touched a handkerchief to their eyes from time to time, but no one in the family ever made a sound. The minister spoke repeatedly about how much Ole Thorson had loved his family. The pastor obviously knew Ole Thorson very well. He talked briefly of Ole's war experience and then told several stories about him that brought smiles and a few chuckles to the mourners. Then he raised his eyes to the congregation and said he wanted to tell of one special visit he'd made to the Thorson farm. "I pulled into the barnyard just as Ole was walking across the pen where Grant's pony was kept. Grant was a toddler. The pony apparently knew that Ole usually kept sugar cubes in his pocket because he sneaked up behind Ole and bit him right on the ... pocket." Everyone in the little church began to laugh quietly – they knew of Ole's temper. "Big Ole swung around and grabbed that horse by the neck. His eyes were like hot coals." The laughter was getting louder now. "He spun that horse around so that all four hooves came off the ground, and then he let go. When the horse hit the fence, he splintered all three boards and rolled over twice." The laughter was so loud that Pastor Fred Jacobson had to raise his voice to be heard. "Ole stared at me as though he was about to throw me through a fence next. Then the anger in his face disappeared instantly, and he smiled sheepishly and said, 'He bit my ass. Hi, Fred!'" The little church shook with laughter. "It's probably not the way I'll remember him, but every time I think of that day I laugh out loud." The pastor took his glasses off and wiped his eyes.

The solemn nature of a funeral gradually returned when the congregation sang "Amazing Grace" and then "Holy Holy Holy," two of Ole's favorite hymns. Pastor Jacobson finished his message by relating to the congregation one of Big Ole's final concerns. "Perhaps the best way to share with you all of the love that Big Ole Thorson had for his family would be to tell you that the last concern Ole voiced to me was that he felt bad because when he was gone there would be no one to have devotions with Gladys before bed at night." Fred Jacobson turned off the little light in the pulpit and walked to the back of the church. As the pastor, and then Ole's family, found their way to the back of the church, the congregation sang "Faith of Our Fathers." It was the last of the hymns Ole had chosen, and the words moved everyone who knew Ole's story:

> *Faith of our fathers, living still*
> *In spite of dungeon, fire, and sword;*
> *Martyrs chained in prisons dark,*
> *Were still in heart and conscience free.*
> *And blest would be their children's fate*
> *If they, like them, should die for thee;*
> *Faith of our fathers, holy faith, we will be*
> *True to thee till death.*

When the service was over, six of Ole's grandsons carried his coffin out the door of the church and directly to the grave that had been dug between the pines.

Ellen remarked to Susan that she'd never seen this done before. Susan said she hadn't, either.

When all of the family and friends were gathered around the gravesite, the minister said one final prayer. Then the honor guard from the American Legion post in town fired a salute and presented Gladys with a flag. There were only six men in the honor guard, and most of them looked to be about Ole's age. One old soldier carried his rifle on one shoulder and an oxygen tank on the other. The little old man that had sat next to Susan saluted and then wiped his eyes.

Then came a moment that neither Ellen nor Susan would ever forget: Ole Thorson's immediate family all gathered around his grave as a canvas cover was lifted from his gravestone. It said simply: "Ole and Gladys Thorson, parents of John, James, David, Paul, and Grant." The stone was big and red; it looked so new in the green grass and patches of wet snow. In one corner, a small cross and the date of Ole and Gladys' wedding had been cut into the stone. The dates of Ole's life were completed; Gladys' dates were not.

As the sons of Ole Thorson read the stone, they saw once again that Ole wanted to be remembered for only one thing: his family. Each of the brothers began to weep and embrace their wives. Grant looked to his left and saw Ingrid holding her grandmother. Grant was all alone with his grief. Now, he looked stricken for the first time. Everyone read the pain on his face; he was beginning to break.

Susan grabbed for Ellen Hutchinson's hand and squeezed it. Grant Thorson was lost and alone and about to burst. There was a gentle stirring among the mourners, and then the crowd parted as Will Campbell walked through them quickly toward his friend. It was the moment that defined their friendship. Will took his friend in his arms swiftly as if he were a scared child, and then Grant Thorson let an ocean of grief spill out of him. It was the moment Will had expected for over a year. Grant sobbed loudly, and his tears covered Will's shoulder and back. He grimaced in pain for several minutes and continued to weep. Will had never seen anything like it from Grant, nor had anyone else. He was always a rock, never showing much emotion – at least not pain. But now, there was no controlling his grief. June Campbell found her way to Ellen and Susan, and they all stood together and watched and wept and held hands. The only sounds in the cemetery were the loud sobs coming from Grant.

The two friends just stood and held each other as the others began to filter back into the church for the customary meal and fellowship following a funeral in the Midwest.

Grant's family all touched him as they walked past him into the church. His mother and Ingrid each stopped for a long, silent embrace before they returned to the church. Eventually, only Will and Grant remained at the grave.

"I can't let him go," Grant said through gritted teeth.

Will did not reply. He just kept his arm around his friend's shoulder.

"Doesn't seem right. I want everyone in the world to stop what they're doing and know that the best man I ever knew just left me forever." Grant wiped his eyes and blew his nose. "God, I didn't know there could be pain like this. I feel so bad for my father ... watching him slide into a hole in the ground ... and I feel like such a big part of me is lost now, too."

~

When Susan and Ellen and June had moved through the buffet line in the church basement, they sat together at a table somewhat apart from the other tables but with several available seats. As the others chose their places to sit, their table remained empty. It seemed that everyone was too intimidated to sit with them. Soon enough, the old man who had sat with Susan during the service and saluted during the burial walked over and sat at their table. His wife followed close behind him carrying both of their meals since the old man had to use a walker to move about. There was a small oxygen tank connected to the walker as well, and a small, clear hose ran to the little man's nose.

The old man took a seat and nodded hello when he sat down, as did his wife. Susan smiled quickly at June Campbell. She wondered if either the old man or his wife had any idea they were sitting with the First Lady of their country.

"Hello, I'm June Campbell."

"John Fortuna, and this is my wife, Hazel." The old man's voice was high pitched and just as unsteady as his walk. John shook June's hand.

Ellen and Susan introduced themselves. There was no special sense of recognition from the Fortunas when they greeted Ellen.

"Did you know Ole Thorson, John?" June asked with a smile.

"Jumped out of an airplane with him once!" John Fortuna answered quickly. As he spoke, food gathered at the corners of his mouth. Hazel reached a napkin around his face — and the oxygen hose, which extended into his nose — and wiped the debris from his mouth. She smiled quietly as she took care of him.

"You were with him, on that plane and as a POW?" Ellen asked.

"Yep. We spent a lot of time prayin' together! I'm the last one of the crew left. Came from San Diego to say goodbye. A drip of coffee emerged from the corner of John Fortuna's mouth and began to slowly move down his chin. Hazel reached a napkin to his face and smiled while John appeared not to notice her. Then he asked, "So how did you girls know Big Ole?"

"Our husbands are friends of one of his sons," June answered.

"Which one?"

"Grant!" Susan surprised herself with her quick answer.

"That apple didn't fall too far from the tree!" They were all laughing when Grant and Will walked in from the cemetery. The men walked directly to the table, and Grant put his arm around John Fortuna. Grant's eyes were swollen and red, but he wore a large smile as he approached his father's friends.

"John, Hazel, how are you? It was so nice of you to come!" Susan, Ellen, and June could tell immediately by the warm expression in his eyes that Grant admired John Fortuna and was happy to see him. "How was the trip?"

"Fine," John answered. "But I would've crawled all the way here over broken glass to say goodbye to your dad!" John Fortuna's face remained expressionless, but Grant's features tightened and he began to blink tears back.

"I know it, John," Grant said quietly. He put his face next to John's and patted his back softly. He appeared ready to burst again, but he gradually recovered with a smile.

"Did you talk to the other boys yet?" Grant was referring to his brothers. "They'll all want to say hi and tell a few lies." Grant was smiling again now as he walked around the other side of the table.

"Send 'em over here," John said. "I'll talk to you later."

As Grant approached June Campbell, his face tightened once again when she extended her arms and held him gently. "He was such a great guy," was all she could say before her voice began to waver.

"Thanks, June." Grant stepped back from her, took a handkerchief from his coat, and wiped his eyes. "Didn't think I had this many tears in me." He tried to smile.

Ellen Hutchinson opened her arms and embraced Grant next. "Thom was so sorry he couldn't be here! I feel like I really missed something ... I never met your dad." She was running her hand across his shoulder and smiling at him.

"You did miss something. But my family is thrilled that you're here. I'd like to introduce you to everyone. OK with you?" He raised his eyebrows with the question.

"Certainly. I've been looking forward to meeting them," Ellen replied.

Grant let go of Ellen and turned to Susan Wells. He said nothing at first; he just stepped toward her and put his arms around her also. When his cheek was touching hers, he whispered, "I didn't think I could have a pleasant surprise on a day like today ... it's so nice of you to be here!" He held her close for a moment, and just before he stepped away from her he let his arms and hands pass her something very subtle. "Perhaps it was just a gentle squeeze," she thought, "but perhaps it was something more."

When he stepped back from her, Susan no longer felt so much like an outsider or an intruder. She understood that Grant Thorson had let her come a little closer.

"Will you come and meet my family?" he said to both Ellen and Susan. They smiled and followed him over to the crowd of relatives. Will and June remained at the table, and Will began asking questions of John Fortuna. Grant could hear John's description of the guards at the POW camp when he began to walk away from John's table.

When he found his mother, he said, "Mom, I'd like you to meet …." He stopped and turned to Ellen. "Do I introduce you as the First Lady … or … what?" He was smiling at Ellen.

"Just Ellen Hutchinson," she replied as she extended her hand to Gladys and smiled.

"Well, Ellen, this is my mother!" Grant said as he presented Gladys to the wife of the President of the United States. He smiled another huge smile and glanced at his brothers as they looked on.

Then, without hesitation, Grant held his mother by the hand and said, "Mom, this is my friend Susan Wells!" Gladys Thorson extended Susan the same smile and warmth that she had to Ellen Hutchinson, and Grant felt a surge of satisfaction as he watched Susan greet his mother.

Susan and Ellen spent the next ninety minutes meeting and visiting with Ole Thorson's family and friends and sharing stories as if they were part of the extended family.

Grant greeted other old friends of the family. Susan watched him from a distance and noticed him using his handkerchief to blot away tears several times during the gathering in the church basement. But he, too, continued to observe Ellen and Susan through the crowd in the church basement, as if to watch over them. He was impressed at their social skills as they moved through a group of strangers and made new friends at every turn. He wanted his family to notice Susan.

Eventually, Grant's oldest brother, John, found his way to Grant's side and said quietly, "So what's the story with the blonde?" He raised his eyebrows when Grant turned to him.

"No story, bro, she's just a friend," Grant lied. He didn't want to explain anything to his brother today.

"Oh." John intentionally let his reply drip with disappointment. But he sensed that his little brother was hiding something.

"Sorry to let you down," Grant smiled.

"That's OK, think she'd go for me?" John stood straight up and sucked in his potbelly.

"If she'd been off the planet for a couple years and you were the only man left when her spaceship returned." Grant paused and looked John up and down. "No, probably not even then."

"Well, she's comin' this way. I think she's hot for me!"

"Hi," Susan said when she reached Grant and John. "You have a nice family, Grant," she added with a smile.

"See!" John said as he raised his eyebrows and walked away.

"Just ignore him. No one really likes him." Grant spoke louder as John moved farther away. John turned his back, put his fingers in his ears, and walked to another small group of friends a few feet away.

"Would you like to step outside for a little fresh air?" Grant asked Susan.

The sun was shining brightly as they walked among the pine trees and tombstones in the old cemetery. Grant told stories about playing in the cemetery during countless church activities through the years. He found Martin Thorson's gravestone. He told her how his great-great-grandfather had immigrated to the prairie and fought with Indians. He told her about neighboring farms and pointed to a hill about a mile away where he'd searched for arrowheads and Indian artifacts as a child. He pointed out the farm where he grew up. Susan said she'd never seen any place like this. She listened while he rambled and told her everything he could about his home. For the first time, he didn't turn the conversation to her. He just went on and on about this little place. She sensed there was something cathartic for Grant in all of this. And she began to feel good that he'd chosen her to talk to.

By the time they returned to the gathering in the church basement, Ellen Hutchinson and the security people were preparing to leave. Susan spoke to Ellen briefly about their return to Washington, and when she looked back for Grant he was no longer standing where he'd been. She thought nothing of it and began to say her goodbyes to Grant's family. When she felt it was time to say goodbye to Grant, she walked up the stairs that led outside and looked out onto the gravel road in front of the church where all of the cars were parked. Reflex caused her to step quickly back inside the small church when she saw Grant.

A beautiful woman with black hair was holding both of Grant's hands and talking to him while they stood beside the road. It was Anne Robertson. Susan recognized her when she turned and spoke. Anne was dressed in black. Susan found herself staring at Anne. She could not look away from the dark lines of Anne's figure or the beauty of her dark eyes. A sense of disappointment crept over Susan. She didn't know for sure what she was seeing, but it was clear that these two had feelings for each other. In that moment, she became aware that she, too, had begun to feel a deeper attraction for Grant Thorson.

As Anne spoke, Grant nodded his head from time to time. He never smiled, but he did appear to speak several times. Susan began to feel like a Peeping Tom, but she could not turn away. Anne put her arms around Grant, kissed him, then turned and walked to her car. When Grant turned back toward the church, his eyes were red and swollen again and he was reaching for the handkerchief in his pocket. His eyes revealed an old hurt that had been re-opened. Susan decided to hurry back to the crowd in the church basement.

Grant did not return for a few minutes, but when he did it was as if he'd never spoken with Anne. He did not mention her to anyone.

The security people in the black suits were beginning to move toward the limousines parked on the gravel road in front of the church when Grant found Will and June talking to Ellen and Susan.

"Looks like those guys are getting ready to take you home." Grant stepped toward Ellen and put his arms around her. "Thank you for coming, Ellen. Please greet Thom and tell him that we're looking forward to your vacation at Spider Lake in a few weeks." He smiled as he stepped back.

"I can't say that I had a good time, Grant, but I enjoyed meeting your family, and I'm so sorry that I never knew your dad," Ellen said.

Grant nodded his "thank you," then turned toward Susan and held her for a moment. "I'm glad you came, Susan. Thanks."

"I've never seen anything like this, Grant. This place, these people ... this has been quite an experience for me. Is it OK for me to say that I had fun?"

"Yeah, I think Dad would like it that someone had a good time at his funeral," Grant smiled softly.

"OK, Mrs. Hutchinson. We're ready to go whenever you are," said a large man with short gray hair. He was obviously one of the security people in charge of transporting the First Lady, and he'd approached the small group from behind Ellen Hutchinson.

"All right, then," Ellen said with authority as she turned. "Goodbye. We'll see you in a few weeks." She waved, Susan waved and smiled, and they turned to leave.

When the First Lady's group of cars had disappeared down the gravel road in a cloud of dust, John Thorson found his way to Grant's side. Other people were beginning to leave now also. The brothers said goodbye to a few old friends, and when they were alone for a moment, John turned to his little brother and asked, "Did you ever manage to get the old man really mad at you?" He turned and raised his eyebrows to emphasize his curiosity.

"Well, yeah," Grant answered slowly. "Once, when I was about fifteen, we were outside in the yard and I backsassed when Mom told me to do something. Dad heard it." Grant shook his head and smiled. "He came around the corner of the house and took me by the back of my neck ... so hard and so fast! He made me apologize to Mom, and then he made it clear my head was comin' off if he ever heard me talk to my mother again like that. I didn't even think that what I'd said was so bad, but I never did it again." Grant paused. "You know, you'd think I'd get angry at Dad and resent that sort of treatment. But all I can remember is feeling bad about maybe hurting Mom's feelings ... like he said. Seems like he was always right when he got angry." Grant smiled and looked at John once more. "How 'bout you ... ever get him really pissed off?"

"We had a beer party one night ... you were probably about five years old." John smiled at the distant memory. "I came home drunk and heaved all over. He got me out of bed at 6:00 a.m. the next day and we made fence. You know, with that big damn hammer and the steel posts?"

"Did you have to apologize to your girlfriend's parents?" Grant tried to maintain a serious demeanor.

"How the hell did you know about that?" John asked in disbelief.

"Well, let me tell you ...." Grant put his arm around John's shoulder and they started to walk toward their family. "Maybe we should check this out with the other Thorson boys ...."

~

"I saw some things today I've never seen before," Susan Wells said quietly as she leaned across the small table separating her from Ellen Hutchinson. Any lingering doubts she may have had about the character of Grant Thorson were gone forever. He was a man of substance, and she wanted to know him better. She shook her head and looked at the First Lady. Their shared experience at Ole Thorson's funeral had allowed a friendship to begin between them, and they both sensed it. They'd enjoyed each other's company during this long day, and now they had some time to reflect on the unusual nature of the day as they flew back to Washington.

"Like what?" Ellen asked.

"Well, I grew up in a small, really dysfunctional family, so I never saw a funeral service quite like that."

"What do you mean?" Ellen leaned forward.

"People laughing, crying, telling stories. Some celebrating, some mourning ... and then they'd switch. I've never been inside a little country church like that, or walked around a little cemetery like that. And that little town, it was just a wide spot in the road. And all of those people had such ... reverence ... for the place. They all knew each other and shared a common past. And when Grant wept so hard, that was tough to watch!"

Ellen nodded in agreement and smiled.

"You know, I don't think John Fortuna knew that you're the First Lady, either," Susan smiled in disbelief.

"I noticed that, too," Ellen said. "But then I began to wonder if he just didn't care. I wondered if he saw me only as a friend of Ole Thorson. That was odd, wasn't it? But it was good ... says a lot about their friendship."

"Grant's father must have been quite special. Everyone talked about him like he was John Wayne."

Ellen turned a quick look at Susan and said, "Thom says John Wayne spent his life trying to convince people that *he* was Ole Thorson."

Susan looked back at Ellen in surprise. She didn't know what to say, but she could sense that Ellen Hutchinson admired the strength and character of men like Ole Thorson.

As if to change the pace of the conversation, Susan leaned back in her seat and asked, with a quizzical look, "You want to know something kind of charming?" Then she said, "Grant and I took a walk around the little cemetery today and he told some stories.

Then he said something I still can hardly believe." She looked at Ellen and then put both of her elbows on the table. "Now, here's a man who can pick up the phone and get the *President* on the line with one call, and he says, 'I'm almost fifty years old, and all I ever wanted — the only goal I ever had — was that I wanted my dad to think I was a good boy!'"

Susan looked at Ellen with a strange stare, a look that said she didn't understand. Then she said, "After a moment he looked at me and said, 'What am I gonna do now?'"

Ellen said nothing. Susan stared straight ahead. She was attracted to Grant Thorson. She had seen strength and humor in him from the beginning. But today she'd seen a quality about him that invited intimacy, too.

chapter TWENTY-ONE

Saturday, May 14th, dawned clear and warm in northern Minnesota. The forecast called for temperatures in the mid seventies with clear skies and a gentle breeze. The opening day of the walleye season in Minnesota is something of a religious holiday throughout the state – perhaps not quite as important as Christmas, but close. All of those who fancied themselves as fishermen would be on the water for most of the weekend, and a party atmosphere always developed in the small, lakeside communities as the week before the opener unfolded.

Actually, the season had opened at midnight on Friday night. Grant and Will had managed to be on the water at midnight several times during their younger days in order to greet the opening moments of a new season. The fishing had never been much better at midnight than it had been the next morning, and the novelty of the "midnight thing" had worn off years earlier, however. Now, as darkness began to lift on the east side of Spider Lake, they talked quietly over coffee in the kitchen at the Ordway house.

They'd risen early in anticipation of the President's visit, and now they waited for the sun to rise over the trees across the lake.

"Shoulda been here this week, Will, when they came and set all this stuff up. I had a Secret Service guy visit and go through my house ... and Nellie's kennel ... and all of the outbuildings. They took six guys through this place!" Grant said with a smile, referring to the Big House. He knew, however, that Will was already aware of the security procedures prior to a presidential visit.

"Yeah, I guess they've got shooters in the woods, a pile of electronic surveillance, and divers in the lake, not to mention all the snoops in the area," Will shrugged. Then his face brightened with another memory. "The cardiologist from Bemidji called me at the office yesterday ... really pissed! Seems he has to be in the ER all weekend with a trauma team. Just in case! Messed up his plans for the opener," Will laughed. "Oh, yeah, and Thom has to travel with a physician now ... think your vacations are expensive?"

"I guess it'll be interesting to see if this place can maintain the wilderness feel with so many people around here." Grant leaned forward with his elbows on the table and pointed a finger at Will as he smiled again. "I think you should do that clever thing that you do in my boat – you know, whip it out and pee over the side of the boat, or in the boat! That would really be funny. I don't think anyone would notice either!" Then Grant leaned back and smiled at Will.

"Well, you might have your dick on the cover of the *Enquirer*. But you'd be a star!" Grant added.

Will's expression didn't change. "No, they'd need a wide-angle lens to get all of that on the cover." He took a sip of his coffee and was about to speak again when June walked into the kitchen.

"Jesus, you guys really scare me. You're both gonna wind up looking like Jimmy Carter's brother," June said as she walked to the coffeepot and filled a cup for herself. Usually she'd still be wearing pajamas, but today she was dressed and ready for an event.

She walked slowly back to the table and sat next to Grant. She squinted when she looked at him. "He has enough trouble making good decisions as it is. He doesn't need any suggestions from you!"

Grant leaned back and tried to look innocent. "What?!" he said as he shrugged his shoulders.

~

At 8:30 a.m., Will Campbell and Grant Thorson stood on the small dock in front of the Ordway house and admired the fine boat that had been supplied to them for the weekend by one of the marinas in Walker. The Secret Service people had said that Grant's little boat would not be acceptable for the President. They needed one of their own people on the boat with the fishermen, and they needed a motor of at least 150-horsepower to provide escape speed in case of a "situation." The marina had also made several other boats available to the Secret Service for an escort around the lake.

"Pine Island Marina" was painted down the side of the glistening new boat. Twin 150-horsepower motors powered the eighteen-foot beauty. Will and Grant could smell the new smell of the red carpet and vinyl upholstery as they looked down at all the built-in amenities it featured. Will's coffee cup was empty. He reached for Grant's and said, "We gotta have him visit more often."

Both men noticed the faraway sound of a helicopter at about the same time and looked beyond the Ordway house into the western sky just as the President's helicopter came into view. There were already about thirty Secret Service agents and people from the President's staff milling around between the Ordway house and the meadow just to the north of it where the helicopter would soon land.

Will and Grant walked up the long slope from the lake to the Big House as quickly as they could, and they arrived at the meadow just in time to watch as Thom and Ellen Hutchinson departed the huge helicopter.

The surface of Spider Lake sparkled in the morning sun as the President and the First Lady exchanged greetings with Will, June, and Grant. They spoke softly and renewed their friendships on the large screened-in porch on the east side of the Ordway house. But Grant was aware of bustle and activity in the Great Room of the house and around the outside corner of the porch. Several trucks with electronic communications gear and a few security vehicles had been moved onto the grounds on Thursday, and a large crew was required to man all of the equipment.

Grant was peering around the corner, trying to see what was going on, when the President said, "It's OK, Grant. Once they get settled in they'll be as unobtrusive as possible. I told them I need this to be a vacation, nothing else."

Grant was slightly embarrassed. He wondered if his curiosity about the activity had come across as disdain for the crowd. "It's no problem, Hutch. I'm just not used to so many people around here."

"Well, the media people should be here any minute, so there will be even more of a crowd for a while. Martin told me there were a few photographers, some writers, and a couple of TV crews coming for a while. Then they'll all be taken off the grounds so we can relax." Thom Hutchinson smiled a sly smile.

"I thought they'd all arrive with you," Grant replied. Just a hint of anxiety spread across Grant's face.

"She's coming!" the President said in an overly reassuring voice. "I promised her an interview on the flight back to Washington also!" Now everyone smiled at Grant, and he was mildly embarrassed. He was excited to see Susan Wells, too, and he hadn't been able to hide his excitement very well.

~

By the time the media arrived, agent Mike O'Neil stood on the dock with Thom, Will, and Grant. The media people were led onto a large, covered pontoon about twenty feet from the

President's boat. They had arrived a few minutes earlier in several vans. The familiar members of the press began to call out with questions for Thom Hutchinson as they boarded their pontoon and watched the President's party climb aboard the shiny new fishing boat. Grant waved when he made eye contact with Susan.

Will and Grant were impressed immediately as their old friend turned on the Presidential persona and charm that he'd acquired over the past months. He waved and posed with a fishing rod and quipped about the big ones not getting away today. Mike O'Neil began to ease their boat slowly away from the dock, and Will turned to Thom with a smile. "Jeez, you're good!" he said with admiration dripping from his voice, teasing Thom as only an old friend could.

"Yeah." Thom returned the smile and sat back in his chair while they sped across the lake toward Christian Island.

Grant waved to Susan once more as their boat roared away from the pontoon. He'd only spoken to her briefly when she'd first arrived, and now he wished he could talk with her more. He watched her face grow smaller and then disappear behind several large men as the pontoon followed well behind them.

Two speedboats occupied by serious-looking men kept fairly close company with the fishing boat now. When they reached Christian Island, Grant turned to Mike O'Neil and asked, very politely, "Mike, would it be OK with you if I drove the boat? I know where the fish should be, and I promise I'll behave."

Agent O'Neil nodded and changed seats with Grant. "Now, Mike, you'll have to let me know," Grant started seriously, "if the CIA or someone has scuba divers out here planning to hook some fish on Thom's line. I'll be glad to drive directly over them whenever you want." He looked straight at Mike O'Neil. "I think everyone knows what a terrible fisherman he is. It's OK with me if he needs to use the United States government to make him look good."

"Now, when I start catching fish you're gonna wonder, aren't you?" Thom asked with a smile. Both Will and Grant noticed that Thom's countenance had changed already. He leaned back in his chair and looked very comfortable. Then he reached his hand over the side of the boat and put it in the water. "Water's still pretty cold," he said to no one in particular.

When Will had rigged three rods, each with a jig and a minnow, he gave one to the President and then extended one toward Grant. But when he saw that Grant was fumbling with the depth finder and trying to pour himself coffee while he steered the boat, he turned toward Mike O'Neil

"Here, Mike, you fish for a minute while the commodore pours coffee."

Grant never looked up. He just continued to fumble with his projects. Agent O'Neil instinctively grabbed the fishing rod and then immediately grimaced, set the rod down, and looked around. "Oh, jeez, I'm sorry, Mike. You probably aren't supposed to do stuff like this while you're on duty."

"That's correct, Doctor. Sorry." He smiled sheepishly; he was embarrassed when he answered. Then he added, "I've never been fishing before, either."

"No?" Will, Thom, and Grant all said in unison — and disbelief.

"Jeez, you are working this poor guy way too hard, Thom," Will said. Then he began asking questions of Mike O'Neil. Will asked about his childhood, his hometown, and his parents. Soon, Will was asking about Mike's plans for the future and then promising to take him fishing someday. As agent Mike O'Neil began to share his life story with Will Campbell, Thom looked at Grant and winked. This was what Will did; he made friends with everyone — he made them feel special.

~

The pontoon carrying the media had lingered for a while along the western shore of Spider Lake in order to photograph Spider Lake

Duck Camp from the lake, while the warm May sunshine turned the water's surface into a million diamonds, and reflected the deep green of the Minnesota forest.

When the pontoon eventually approached the President's boat, Susan Wells could actually hear the men's laughter over the noise of the outboard motor. When she looked closer, she saw Will Campbell standing and waving his arms. The President was rocking back and forth in his chair, slapping his knee. Grant was turned sideways in the pilot's chair, laughing out loud. And in a most unusual scene, she watched while Mike O'Neil, a Secret Service agent in charge of the President's personal safety, laughed so hard he had to wipe the tears from his eyes.

Susan had never seen Thom Hutchinson like this before. None of the people on the pontoon had ever seen any president like this before.

"What the hell do you suppose they're laughing about?" one of the men in the media asked out loud.

"Must have been a helluva story!" one of the photographers said as his camera clicked. Susan couldn't help but smile as she watched Will gesture with his hands and continue talking. She walked to the front of the pontoon just as Grant turned to look toward the media group. When their eyes met, he waved to her again, and she could read very clearly in his eyes that he wanted to talk to her. She motioned with a quick tilt of her head and a smile. The gesture said, "Well, come over here and talk to me, then!" Grant's face lit with pleasure.

The pontoon inched a little closer to the President's boat, and one of the photographers called out, "How's the fishing, Mr. President?"

Thom took the cue and stood up with a stringer of fish for the cameras. "Walleye for lunch, boys!" he called back to them with a proud smile.

"Somebody's gonna be pissed at you for killing fish, Thom," Will said in an attempt to bait his friend.

"Yeah, I suppose so," Thom shrugged.

"Hey, Hutch! You wanna have an old-fashioned shore lunch on Christian Island for the media? You know, the way we used to do it in the boundary waters?" Grant asked.

"Yeah! That would be great! Does that work for you, Mike?" Thom asked.

Agent O'Neil spoke into his radio for a few minutes and then answered, "Sure! We've got two men on the little island already."

"OK, then, if you'd have one of those drag boats take me back to my cabin, I'll pick up everything we need and be back in ten minutes," Grant said.

A short time later, Grant was returning from his cabin in his little green duck boat, with Nellie and a large wooden box in the front of the boat. The small motor whined and pushed his boat directly toward the media pontoon. He pulled up alongside the media boat, stalled his motor, and doffed his baseball cap when he stood up. "Would you join me, Miss Wells?" he called out.

When Susan had taken a seat in the little boat, Grant pulled on the starter rope and the boat lurched toward Christian Island. "I'll get a fire started and clean the fish!" he called to Will as he steered toward the small beach.

The sun was high in the sky on a beautiful spring day as the green boat slid onto the beach. "We're gonna have a little party now," Grant said with a warm smile. He was staring at Susan. He couldn't take his eyes off of her as she sat several feet from him and smiled back at him. Just the sight of her made him want to put his arms around her and hold her, but he wanted to show off just now. If he'd been a little boy on the playground, he'd have stood on his head or lifted some heavy thing to impress the pretty girl. The way she'd gestured to him from the pontoon and the way she looked at him now sent a thrill through him that made him feel just like an adolescent boy.

"Have you ever had a shore lunch of fresh fish over an open fire?" he asked.

"No," she smiled.

"Well, good. Then this will be the best one you've ever had!" And with that Grant started picking up driftwood and dried leaves along the shoreline. When he'd built a fire and had extra wood to fuel it stacked neatly beside it, he walked quickly to the boat and lifted a canoe paddle and the stringer of fish.

Susan's eyes popped open as Grant took a walleye off the stringer and laid it on the canoe paddle. The fish was about twenty-two inches long and weighed about three and one half pounds. He took his fillet knife from its sheath and held it in his right hand while he held the fish steady with his left. When he made the first cut, behind the fish's gills, its tail flapped involuntarily. Susan could not look away now. Grant cut along the backbone, then the belly. Then he deftly cut the skin from the fillet, turned the fish over and repeated the cuts on the other side.

She watched while he filleted five walleyes. When he was done, he had blood all over both hands. He placed ten fillets into a pan, then threw the fish guts out into the lake for the turtles and gulls to eat. She stood silently and watched Grant wash his hands and the fillets at the same time, swishing them in the clear, shallow water along the shore. When he'd finished washing the fillets and his hands in the crystal clear lake water, he stood and smiled at her.

"Amazing," she said quietly. She'd never seen anything like this before, and she hadn't dreamed that Grant Thorson or anyone else might possess the skills she was witnessing.

As the President's boat and the pontoon drifted onto the beach, Grant went about preparing the rest of the meal. He filled a coffeepot with lake water and put it directly into the fire. He opened the tops of several cans of baked beans and put the cans near the fire to cook.

A small crowd had gathered around the fire now. Two more boats carrying Secret Service agents that Will and Grant didn't know about began circling the island. Grant reached into the wooden box with the lunch supplies and removed a huge can of Crisco. With his fillet knife, he lifted several chunks of lard about two inches by two inches and flipped them into the huge frying pan. "Heart medication," he smiled as a crowd gathered around the fire. "The trick here is to get the oil just about to the temperature of the core of the sun." He smiled again and turned his head to avoid the wood smoke rising from the fire.

The fillets hissed as hot oil splattered when he dropped several pieces of fish into the large frying pan. While Grant tended to the fire and the fish, Will opened a cooler and started passing cans of cold beer and soda to everyone around the fire.

Two men carrying video cameras walked around the fire and filmed the shore lunch from a distance. Eventually, Grant called to them, "You guys are working way too hard. C'mon over for a taste of fresh walleye!" Both men sat their cameras in the tall grass and found a place around the fire.

A strange thing happened next – a thing that no one would have predicted, and none of them really took note of, until the moment had passed. There was a brief moment, shortly after the two cameramen had helped themselves to fish and baked beans, when the gathering of people around the small fire fell into silence. Several men stood, staring into the fire. Most of them sat with paper plates on their laps. From a distance they looked like they were posing for a photograph. They all sank into the comfortable little world around the campfire.

Thom Hutchinson ended the silence with, "This is definitely the most informal press gathering I've seen yet." Everyone laughed politely, but the thing that everyone would have expected to happen next didn't. The President did not instantly become the center of the conversation. It was an invitation to chat with the President, and no one noticed. The people around the fire only relaxed more. Someone asked for salt and pepper. One of the men that Grant had not seen before commented on the nice weather.

Someone else asked about the fishing. Will shared some stories about the history of Spider Lake Duck Camp. The campfire – and not the President – was the center of the group's attention for just that moment. During that brief time when everyone tasted the fish and sipped at the cold beer and nodded to each other, the President was just another man sitting by the fire.

Grant made an effort to keep Susan near him, and now that Will continued to entertain the whole group, he turned to her and asked quietly, "How's your lunch?"

"Delicious! Even the beans are great!" She smiled another full smile and leaned toward him when she answered.

"Yeah, shore lunch is always pretty good," he said as he threw his empty plate into the fire. "I'll do the dishes!" he added, leaning back against a rock.

"This is my first time ... city girl, you know." She smiled again.

Grant looked at her and wondered how any woman wearing a baseball cap and eating beans off a paper plate could look so beautiful.

The smell of wood smoke and frying fish still swirled around them when Susan looked at Grant's little boat and asked him, "How did you come to call your boat 'Silverheels'?"

"Oh, it's from an old Gordon Lightfoot song. Actually, I think the boat in the song is a beautiful sailboat, not a floating toilet. But I really like the song, and I really like my boat ... so it's 'Silverheels'."

"Susan?" He waited until she looked at him. "Would you ... could you ...," he stumbled a little trying to find the words, ... "spend the afternoon with me? You know we'll just be in my little boat, right around here next to Will and Thom ... er, the President." He stumbled again.

"Aw, hell," Grant started anew. "I'm probably gonna blush again, but I've got to tell you something." He looked directly into her eyes. "I'm afraid that if I let you get on that pontoon with those other people, I'll never see you again. I felt cheated when I missed you at my last two visits to Washington, and I was proud of you, like you were an old friend, when I introduced you to my friends and family. I'd really like to be with you today. Is it OK for me to ask that of you?" His demeanor was straightforward, but now he feared that he'd asked a question she might answer with a "no."

"Yes," Susan said, but she didn't smile. "I'd like that. Well, to be perfectly honest with you ..." She paused, and Grant feared she'd suddenly take back her "yes" answer. "I was trying to figure out a way to stowaway on your little boat if you didn't ask me pretty soon." She smiled and touched his arm.

Her touch was so soothing, like Kate's, and he wanted more. "Terrific." He smiled a relieved smile at her. Each of them could see the attraction in the other's eyes now. Grant stood up immediately, as the others were all beginning to stand and throw their paper plates into the fire before they returned to their boats. "I'll be right back," he said as he turned and walked toward Thom Hutchinson.

Will Campbell was holding a paper plate with a golden brown walleye fillet resting on it and extending it toward Mike O'Neil. "OK, Mike, I know you can't have a beer or go fishing, but you can try this fish when you're on duty," Will said as he held the plate out.

Agent O'Neil used his fingers to break some of the flaky white fish flesh apart and then raise it to his mouth. He smiled after a second and reached for more. Will, Grant, Tom, and O'Neil stood in a small circle as the young agent smiled and said "really good!" with a mouth full of fish.

"OK, guys," Grant said as he leaned forward and changed the subject. He looked as if he had some important secret to share, but then in an uncertain tone of voice he asked, haltingly, "S'pose it would be OK for me to have Susan spend the afternoon in my boat? We'll just fish right around here, too." He looked right and left, his eyes asking for approval.

Both Will and Thom looked to Mike O'Neil as if he had the final say. Then all three of them smiled simultaneously, slowly, and said "yes" very slowly. They were teasing.

"Hutch thought you'd bring that up before lunch," Will said dryly.

"OK." Grant seemed unfazed by the way Will acknowledged the fact that they'd recognized his attraction to Susan and predicted this question.

"One more thing." He stopped and looked at each of them again. "You know the little party that we have planned for tonight? Any reason I can't ask her to stay ... stay overnight? You know, when the media types get sent back to their accommodations, I'd like her to stay. Can she stay in the Big House? It might look bad if I ask her to stay with me. There's gotta be a spare room up there somewhere." Grant looked nervous, and he tried to hide the anxiety in his voice. He raised his eyebrows and nodded his head, once again asking for approval.

And once again Thom Hutchinson looked slowly toward Mike O'Neil, giving him permission to answer the question. "It's already done!" Mike said with a dry look. "We made the call to have all of her gear brought to Spider Lake right after you plucked her off the pontoon."

"Good ... thanks," Grant said as he turned to return to Susan. He was trying not to smile, not to turn handsprings. He felt just as he had when pretty girls smiled at him a lifetime ago.

"You rascal," Will called out as Grant moved away. His remark was clearly intended to tease his friend. Thom Hutchinson and Mike O'Neil chuckled and covered their faces.

Grant turned on his heels and walked straight back toward Will, trying not to smile. When he stood face to face with Will, he took the cold beer from Will's right hand and took a swallow. Then, with no facial expression whatsoever, he said, "You're a jerk, and I never liked you." He took another swallow of Will's beer and handed it back to him, then spun again and started walking toward Susan.

"Now I suppose you're gonna ask about my dog and then start throwing fish, or ducks, in my boat… you're a funny guy!" he called loudly to Will as he walked away from him. Just before he reached Susan, he stopped and turned to Will once more. Now he smiled at Will, opened his eyes wide, and smiled with his lips pushed firmly together. It was a silly, familiar smile, and Will could read it perfectly. It said: "I know that *you* know that I like this woman … and I know that you're pulling for me. Thanks, old friend."

Will simply raised his beer as if to salute, to affirm Grant's assessment of things.

~

An hour later, Grant's little green boat rocked gently in the warm breeze. The sky was clear, and the small ripples on the surface of the water made tiny splashing noises on the aluminum hull. Grant had cleaned and washed the inside of his boat earlier in the week, and it actually looked presentable now. Nellie paced back and forth between Grant and Susan, begging for attention first from one, then the other.

The pontoon carrying the press had been taken ashore, and the reporters had been taken to their hotel. Some of the press had simply returned home. Now the President and First Lady were actually alone, on vacation. At least they were as alone as they could ever get.

The shiny new fishing boat passed close to Grant's boat off and on as they both trolled and drifted around the point on the southwest corner of Christian Island. Everyone, including Susan, caught a fish from time to time, and each fish was celebrated just loudly enough so the occupants of the other boat could witness the success. Since lunch, every fish had been returned alive to the lake.

Grant lifted the minnow bucket out of the water. Nellie came to attention and stared intently at the yellow plastic bucket. Grant stuck his hand into the water in the bucket to grab a new minnow, and Nellie wagged her tail excitedly. Grant put the minnow on Susan's hook. "There you go," he said as he flipped the jig and minnow over the side. "Guaranteed to catch a fish." He wiped his hands on his blue jeans and smiled. "Hey, I met Petra Vanderhoft again on my last trip east. She's not exactly *warm*, is she."

"Well, she's my boss, and my friend, and she's become sort of a surrogate mother. She's actually pretty nice."

"Could have fooled me."

"She just doesn't want me to like you," Susan smiled.

"Oh?"

"She thinks you're just a cowboy," Susan shrugged. "She's afraid I'm attracted to …." She stopped herself.

"Losers?" Grant volunteered.

"Yeah, that's it, pretty much," Susan admitted. Grant loved the smile she couldn't put away.

Grant reached for the gunwale to adjust his weight, and Nellie snapped to attention again.

"So why does she do that?" Susan asked quickly.

"Hell, I don't know. She's your friend," he replied.

"No, Nellie! Why does she start to drool every time you reach for that bucket?"

"Oh, I thought you meant …." Grant and Susan both laughed out loud. As he chuckled, Grant reached into the bucket and Nellie sat straight up again.

He pulled his hand from the bucket and threw a minnow into the air. Nellie's front feet came off the floor of the boat and she caught and swallowed it in one smooth move. Then her eyes begged for another. "She just wants a treat," Grant smiled. "Fish diet makes her coat look like patent leather, too."

"Does this all strike you as kind of odd?" he asked, as if he were frustrated with the conversation.

"Well, yes. Well, what do you mean?" Susan asked. She was a little confused by the question.

"Think about it. Here I am, some dentist from Minnesota. I bump into you at the White House, of all places, amongst hundreds of other people. When we meet again, you make me blush. I can't remember the last time that happened. Then we meet again! And every time we meet I think to myself, 'There's a beautiful, smart woman who makes me feel really good when I talk to her.' But every time we meet, I'm right in the middle of some personal crisis, and then I don't see or talk to you again for weeks. I travel across town to see you speak and you're embarrassed by my presence, but still I can't stay away from you. The high point in our friendship so far has been my father's funeral. And here we are today, feeding minnows to my dog while the President of the United States is sitting in a boat fifty feet from us. But you're so pretty I can't take my eyes off of you. I think this is odd."

She was delighted by his words, but she was only partially successful when she tried to hide her feelings. "OK, I'd agree with that, I guess. Let's see, I've been to a few parties at the White House, and it isn't every day that I bump into some handsome guy who introduces himself as a waterfowl processing technician, so I remember that guy. It's clear that this guy has a thing going with a nice woman, but every time I bump into him I think he's clever and I'm attracted to him. I see enough special qualities in this dentist/waterfowl processing technician that I recognize that I need to break up with the man I'm dating because he has none of these qualities that I'm so attracted to. Then, on the night that I plan to break up with this man — that would be Jason Vincent — this other man shows up out of nowhere and surprises me almost into shock. I find myself wanting to call this man and talk to him, but I'm afraid to. I'm afraid of rejection, I guess, but I sneak over to his hotel anyway. Then I have a wonderful time on the worst day of this guy's life. And now we're sitting here feeding minnows to his dog while the President sits fifty feet away. I think you might be a special man, and I've wondered all along just what you think of me because we never seem to connect. Yeah, I think this is weird."

"So there was a little more to it than what you told me that night at my hotel?" Grant asked softly. He'd picked up on that part of her story and he leaned forward.

"Yes."

"And you felt something ... for me ... all along?"

"Yes."

Grant extended his hand to her, and when she took it he raised her hand to his face and kissed it. He looked like he was relieved. "Doesn't seem quite so strange now, does it?" He felt calm and comfortable now holding her hand. "This was all I wanted," he added as he lifted her hand a little higher and squeezed it.

"Well, it's still strange ... it's what I wanted, too." Susan smiled now. As they'd spoken, they'd each admitted something to the other that they'd wanted to for some time but hadn't been able to verbalize.

chapter TWENTY-TWO

Susan Wells looked into the small mirror in the second-floor bathroom and shook her head. As she finished putting on her makeup, she thought once again about how strange this all really was. Her growing attraction to and friendship with Grant Thorson was one thing. They had met and developed feelings for one another under unusual circumstances — that was true enough. But now she was dressing in a tiny bathroom with knotty pine walls and loons on the shower curtain, so she could walk downstairs and have an informal evening with the President of the United States. The President: the one whom she'd had to wait for earlier after he'd showered because he'd used the last of the hot water. She was just thankful now that she didn't actually have to share a bathroom with Thom and Ellen Hutchinson.

She blinked and then began speaking to herself in the mirror as if she were reading her own column. She couldn't believe the situation she found herself in. "In addition to weak or no leadership on environmental issues and military spending, President Hutchinson continues to use all of the hot water when he showers — and he leaves the toilet seat up after he pees!" She stopped and contorted her face. "Now there's a door no journalist has opened yet."

Susan shook her head as if to clear it and stepped into the upstairs hallway. Grant had taken her to the Ordway house in the late afternoon when they'd finished fishing so she could clean up for dinner. June Campbell had shown her all around the huge old lodge before she'd washed up.

June had begun to treat Susan as a mother might treat her children's friends. She oozed hospitality and took every chance to make Susan feel at home now. June had felt good about Susan from the beginning. During their visit at Big Ole's funeral, she'd noticed Susan's wit and poise when she was introduced to the people in Grant Thorson's life.

Susan walked quickly down the open, wooden staircase into the Great Room of the Big House. A fieldstone fireplace stood at one end of the room and enormous windows lined the opposite wall. A spacious screened-in porch surrounded the Great Room on two sides. The log walls were covered with canoe paddles, old shotguns, and fishing rods that had been retired for several generations. Of course, the obligatory trophy fish — in this case several large northern pike — covered the prime wall space. A deer head looked over the room from above the fireplace. The big buck had been shot by Victor Ordway in the 1920s in Wisconsin, and it was the first thing he'd moved to the lodge. Evie Campbell always said she felt like the old buck was watching her, and she'd talked about throwing it out for years. But no one else in Will's family would hear of it.

Two men wearing black suits stood in the doorway of the downstairs den and tried to be invisible. Susan saw two other men sitting in the den at a desk beside a bookshelf, and each of them was speaking on the phone. The odd nature of the day continued when she reached the floor of the Great Room and looked to her left. Through the open door of the Great Room, on the screened-in porch, she could see Thom Hutchinson and Will Campbell, each with a drink in his hand, chatting while Will kept an eye on something that he was cooking on the barbecue grill. It was enough for her to have the bathroom-sharing thing going on and the security people wandering around, but now she'd be doing the north woods equivalent of tailgating with the Chief Executive of the land.

"Even that wouldn't be so awkward," she thought as she looked at the men on the porch, but she knew the President's staff viewed her as something of a minor adversary, and that fact made all of this a little bit uncomfortable for her. She stood briefly and looked at Will and Thom while they spoke quietly with each other, about the fishing, she presumed. Until recently, she'd seen Thom Hutchinson as a presence, a force, perhaps not even a person. She didn't agree with his position on many issues. In fact, she liked to joke that she didn't even know what his position was on many issues because he was so evasive. Now she simply saw a man chatting with an old friend.

"Hi, Susan. Did you find everything all right?" June called as she walked into the Great Room from the other direction. Ellen was a step behind her.

Susan jumped when June called to her, then put her hand on her chest and smiled. "You startled me," she said as she leaned forward. "I was just staring out the window and didn't hear you coming."

"Sorry. I'll stomp my feet louder next time!" June was enjoying her role as hostess tonight, and as she spoke she gestured to Susan to join them when they stepped onto the porch. Once again, June made Susan feel welcome, and the three women joined the men on the porch.

"Whoa, you look nice!" Will exclaimed to Susan. He'd glanced over his shoulder when he heard the women coming and then done a double take. Susan did look nice. She was stunning even in khaki slacks and a salmon-colored cotton sweater. Thom Hutchinson only smiled.

Will began to backtrack instantly. He wore a huge smile when he turned his face toward June. He knew he'd committed a faux pas by exclaiming that one woman in a group of three was somehow more attractive than the others. "But *you*, however, honey, are radiant, even more beautiful than usual." He furrowed his brow, pointed the barbecue tongs at his wife, and continued. "In fact, Susan and Ellen look plain . . . no, shabby when compared to you." He let a smile show through a sincere façade when he faced June.

"Shut up, Will," she said calmly.

"OK," he said. He turned to Thom and shrugged his shoulders to admit failure, as if to say, "I tried to recover."

Thom Hutchinson was still smiling when Ellen took his hand and kissed him. The lake and the sky were a pure blue as the early-summer sunset was beginning to cast a golden hue across Spider Lake.

"Did you have a good day?" Ellen asked Thom.

"Oh, yeah," Thom answered with some enthusiasm. Then he looked out over the lake as the colors of the north intensified during the sunset. Ellen put both arms around his waist and pressed her head against his chest. They had the look of a couple who had just recently fallen in love.

When Will and June caught each other's eye, they both looked like the proud parents of a child who had just won the spelling bee at school. They were gloating. They were thrilled, and maybe a little relieved, that Thom and Ellen were relaxing and enjoying their vacation so much. June in particular was getting a vicarious kick out of Ellen's visit. She'd taken Ellen for a long walk in the woods after they'd had lunch at the Big House, and then she'd left Ellen on the large porch for a while in the afternoon so she could read, or nap, or just enjoy the view by herself.

"Hey, I can smell the rumaki way down here!" Grant surprised them all when he called to them from the trail between his cabin and the Ordway house. He'd gone to his cabin to clean up before dinner. He walked up the wooden stairway to the porch and entered through the old screen door. As it slammed behind him, like old screen doors do, he looked at Susan, raised his eyebrows, and said, "You look nice!" He put his right hand on the small of her back and touched her softly.

"So do you," she replied, putting her arm around his waist.

When Susan pulled herself close to Grant and then stood next to him, he felt the same soothing rush that he'd felt earlier, only it was better this time. Her touch was wonderful enough, but she'd let the others see her hold him like a boyfriend or lover. She smelled exquisite. He felt proud of the way she touched him. He wanted his friends to see it.

The vicarious kick that June Campbell was feeling only intensified now. She'd begun to feel like a matchmaker for Grant and Susan, and she wore the same silly grin as a few minutes earlier when she'd watched Ellen embrace Thom.

Will could not let it pass. "Jeez, honey, make up your mind! I tell her she looks good and you wanna drive a stake through my heart. He says she looks good and you drool on yourself."

"Shut up, Will!" She squinted and looked as if she were talking to a fly buzzing around her head.

"Right, honey," Will replied quietly. Neither of them smiled until they'd turned their backs to each other.

"So what are you cooking, Will?" Susan asked after a short pause.

"Duck rumaki." He raised the big black lid of the grill to show her several dozen bite-size pieces of duck breast and water chestnut wrapped in bacon.

"I've never tasted duck before," Susan said. "What does it taste like?"

"Wait and see," Will teased. Then he added, with a confident tone, "You'll like it."

"Every duck recipe my mother ever made tasted like liver. My mother even called it flying liver!" June interjected. Her face was contorted when she started again. "But Will and Grant have actually found several ways to prepare it that everyone seems to like.

If you hate these hors d'oeuvres, though, don't worry about it. Grant's dog loves this recipe."

"Thank you for that ringing endorsement, honey! I know she's gonna like it now."

Susan smiled and asked another question. "I've never understood how the men who claim to love the ducks so much can shoot them ... kill them. Do you guys ever wonder about that?" She looked at all three men.

Grant cleared his throat and turned to the others. "I'll handle this one," he said, looking into Susan's face. All three men had grown a little defensive toward the anti-hunting lobby. Grant spoke up first because he always did. "I have asked myself that question ...." He raised his eyebrows to exaggerate the importance of his words. "Many times, as a matter of fact. The only answer to it is that you're either a hunter or you're not. One person can't make the other understand or agree with his side on that issue, no matter how forceful or articulate he may be in presenting his case." Grant paused and leaned away from Susan. "And don't forget, we eat all that we kill here at Spider Lake." Grant paused again and assumed the posture of a statesman, an orator, as he moved his hands about and continued. "But there is something else here. Some deep, ethereal thing that hunters get and others just don't." He looked at Ellen now. "I never love my friends more than when we're together, out there." He gestured toward the lake. "And when I see the scratches on my gun stock or marks on my boat, the golden memory of how these trophies were won play themselves over and over in my brain ... and I know I'm tied to my friends, and my father, by the richest of all traditions.

Grant looked to Susan again. "If I may quote Gordon MacQuarrie — you remember him, Susan, the greatest writer in the history of the English language: 'The outdoors holds many things of keen delight. A deer flashing across a burn, a squirrel corkscrewing up a tree trunk, a sharptail throbbing up from the stubble — all these have their place in my scheme of things!'" Grant stopped for a breath, and his voice became only a firm whisper. He leaned forward when he began to quote MacQuarrie again: "'But the magic visitation of ducks from the sky to a bobbing set of blocks holds more of beauty and heart-pounding thrill than I have ever experienced with rod or gun. Not even the sure, hard pluck of a hard-to-fool brown trout, or the lurching smash of a river small mouth, has stirred me as has the circling caution of ducks coming to decoys.'" Grant nodded for punctuation, as if to say, "I'm finished now." There had been real emotion in his voice as he'd spoken the last sentence.

Thom Hutchinson raised his eyebrows and smiled at his wife but remained silent.

Susan's face broadened slowly into a glowing smile, and she said nothing. Instead, she nodded back to Grant as if to say, "I can accept that." She put her arm around him and pulled him close once again.

"Good one, pard!" Will tried to sound awestruck — to tease and compliment his old friend simultaneously.

"Thank you, Doctor," Grant nodded to Will.

~

The night air was soft and cool when they moved back out to the porch after a long, informal meal in the dining room. When June offered chocolate cheesecake and coffee, Grant thought reflexively of his dinner with Anne in Washington. He still thought of Anne some. He wished it didn't bother him so deeply that things hadn't worked out with Anne, but it did. He wanted to understand what had been missing in his relationship with Anne. She was beautiful, too, and he'd known her and liked her his whole life. 'It should have worked,' Grant thought. He had nothing — at least no shared past – in common with Susan, but she caused him to feel that wonderful little twitch way down low in his belly when he watched her laugh or when she smiled at him and touched him. Anne had been correct: Susan made a spark come to Grant's eye.

"What a peaceful place this is," Thom said while they all sat on the darkened porch, staring into the still night. "In a moment like this …." Thom paused and tried to compose the end of his thought, "… this place becomes the only place … all there is in the world. Does that make sense?" he asked to no one in particular.

"Yes," Will and Grant answered in unison.

"You know, I've been thinking about that, too." Susan spoke now as she looked out onto the vague, blue-gray outline that was the surface of Spider Lake reflecting moonlight. "There was a moment today that struck me as unusual. Did you notice it, Mr. President?" She stopped herself and checked his reaction with a smile. She still felt obliged to call him Mr. President. "We were sitting around the fire today. You spoke up and basically made yourself available for small talk – personal conversation with those guys – remember? And none of them picked up on it. They were so taken, so busy with that moment, that place, that they overlooked the President of the United States in order to ask for more fish or talk about the lake. I guess I'm not exactly an old timer, but I've had a personal audience with three presidents and I've never seen anything like that."

"Yes, I noticed that, too … never seen it before, either. Most of those guys can't wait to ask a question back home," Thom replied as he rocked in his big wicker rocking chair.

When Grant began to speak, it was clear that he was once again quoting someone: "'Something happens to a man when he sits before a fire.'" He raised a finger and pointed into the air; he was showing off again. "'Strange stirrings take place within him, and a light comes into his eyes which was not there before. Once a man has known the warmth and companionship there – once he has tasted the thrill of stories of the chase with the firelight in his eyes — he has made contact with the past, recaptured some of the lost wonder of his early years and some of the sense of mystery of his forebears. Around a fire, men feel that the whole world is their campsite, and all men are partners of the trail.'" They all stared in Grant's direction when he finished. He looked out at the lake for a moment, then turned to face them. "Sigurd Olson, 1956." He gave credit for the quote. Then he looked at Susan. "Tell *that* to Shakespeare."

"Well said, Doctor," Will added. There was a childlike joy in his voice once more.

All of them sank into the quiet of a summer night.

"Thom?" Will broke the silence after a few minutes.

"Yeah."

"Grant said he wants to be on some more committees."

Grant stood immediately. "Gotta go." He was laughing as he extended his hand to Susan. "Would you like to go for a walk along the lake?"

"Love to!" Susan said as she stood and took his hand.

When they reached the trail, Will called to them, "We'll work out this committee stuff. You kids behave … be back in an hour or I'm sending some of Thom's friends to look for you!"

Will turned back to Thom, Ellen, and June and in a much lower voice added, "That boy's in love again!"

~

The moon shadows danced slowly across the ground. The rustling noise of the cottonwood leaves flipping in the evening breeze was the only sound as Grant and Susan strolled along the path toward the lake.

Susan crossed her arms in front of herself and shivered when they neared the small pier where the boats were all tied. Grant seized the opportunity to put his arm around her and pull her closer. The cedar planks creaked when they reached the end of the pier. A huge reflection of the moon was broken by the tiny ripples across the surface of the lake.

A loon called ... one lonesome call stretched all the way across the big bay. "That was a loon?" she asked.

"Yeah. Pretty cool, huh?"

Susan moved closer to Grant and turned toward him. She was thankful that the cool air gave her an excuse to move closer. Grant understood the not-so-subtle message as she pressed against him.

One more loon called, a tremolo this time – several notes, like yodeling. The sound was, as always, mysterious, mournful. It was the signature of night on the northern lakes.

"Wow," Susan whispered.

"Ever heard that before?" Grant asked.

"No. Not where I live!"

Grant waited for a silent moment and then said, "You know, earlier today when you said you'd broken up with the guy you were dating? Remember the things you said?"

"Yes."

"That was the best part of this day. Made me feel special ... like I haven't felt for a long time."

Susan slowly raised her lips to his and kissed him. It was a rich, warm kiss, like all the first kisses of his youth. They both knew they needed this small, silent moment together – some things were better left unspoken.

"No ... that was the best part of this day," he whispered when their lips separated. They stood together for a while with their arms around each other, their faces nearly touching, kissing and talking quietly until Susan shivered again.

"Maybe we'd better go on up and get warm," Grant said.

The two couples on the porch were laughing, and Grant and Susan could hear a woman's voice as they approached the stairway leading up to the porch. When they opened the old screen door and stepped in, everyone on the porch turned their head and looked at them. Will started talking immediately. As usual, he was trying to tease Grant, and the others could hear the playfulness in his voice.

"Jeez, it must be cold down there by the lake. We could see you guys huddling up trying to get warm, I suppose, and then ..."

"Shut up, Will," June interrupted.

"OK, honey," he replied in the same childish tone, faked contrition in his voice.

Susan left to get a warmer sweater, and when she returned the party was breaking up. Will and June, and Thom and Ellen said goodnight and went inside to go to bed. Susan stood in the doorway by the staircase while Grant stood one step below her. They were looking directly into each other's eyes, as they were about to say goodnight to each other.

"I have to ask you something," Grant said seriously. His eyes were probing hers, looking for permission to ask a question.

"OK."

"Remember that night when you came to my hotel in D.C.?"

"Yes," she replied. She had no idea where he was going with this.

"Well ...," he paused. He looked embarrassed, uneasy with the question he was about to ask. "What were you doing hiding behind the ice machine on the fourteenth floor?" His face stretched into a grin.

"Shit." Susan shook her head slowly. He'd known about it all along and said nothing until now. She covered her eyes with her left hand.

He reached his hands behind her waist and pulled her forward, just a little. While her hand was still over her eyes, he stole a kiss — just a peck on the lips. "That was a nice thing to do, coming to my room. But kissing me like you did down there?" He pointed to the lake. "That was nice! It was like ... it was like opening a package of baseball cards!"

"You lost me on that one." She moved her hand away from her face, and his playful eyes pulled at her.

"Well, try to remember one of the great pleasures of childhood. You know you have something good in your hands, you just don't know how good." He tried not to smile, but he was enjoying his own explanation. "You start to open the package and then all of a sudden there's a Mickey Mantle staring at you – life just turned out to be *so* much better than you had any right to expect – but nonetheless, it was just what you hoped for. That's how it felt when you kissed me."

He stole one more soft kiss and then walked away into the darkness and down the hill toward his cabin.

"See you in the morning," he called over his shoulder.

Susan watched him as far as she could, until he disappeared into the night. *No* man had ever spoken to her the way Grant did.

chapter TWENTY-THREE

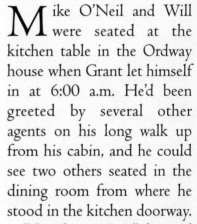

M ike O'Neil and Will were seated at the kitchen table in the Ordway house when Grant let himself in at 6:00 a.m. He'd been greeted by several other agents on his long walk up from his cabin, and he could see two others seated in the dining room from where he stood in the kitchen doorway.

"Good morning!" he said as he closed the door behind him. There was a light mist falling, and the morning was very dark and overcast. Grant was dressed in blue jeans and a rain jacket. He wore a hat that said "May the forest be with you" across the front. Will and O'Neil were holding coffee cups.

"Coffee's hot!" Will said with his usual smile. "How come you're up so early, anyway?"

Grant didn't answer at first. Then he held up his old thermos with the dented cap on top to show Will that he'd already made coffee. He tried not to smile when he asked, "Susan up yet? I thought we might go for a walk."

"Jeez, I shoulda known!" Will tried to look disappointed, to tease Grant about his attraction to Susan.

Just then, Susan entered the kitchen from the Great Room. She was dressed in blue jeans and a light rain jacket also, and the same baseball cap she'd worn the day before.

"Good morning!" she said cheerily to all three of them. But she brought her eyes to Grant's and passed a special greeting. The twinkle in her eye triggered that familiar little feeling, low in Grant's stomach. He always thought that feeling had something to do with how a man could tell he was in love. Whatever it was, he liked it. And he was pretty sure Susan felt it, too.

"You guys planned this last night, didn't you?" Will asked, as if he'd just figured out some cosmic mystery.

"See you later, Sherlock," Grant said as he held the door open and Susan stepped past him into the mist.

Grant held the thermos in one hand and Susan's hand in the other while they walked directly to the pier where the boats were tied. The morning was very still. Not a leaf moved on any of the trees except when droplets of mist fell from them and caused them to bob when relieved of the water weight. The air was warm, and the glassy surface of the lake was broken only by the gentle impact of a billion tiny raindrops. A loon called from a half mile away and sounded as if it was at their feet.

Grant produced a coffee cup from his pocket and filled it for Susan. Then he filled the dented cup for himself. She noticed that he didn't share a cup with her. "What a place to take your morning coffee!" Susan said after she'd raised the cup to her face.

"Yeah, every morning is good here," Grant said without looking at her.

"So why do they call it Spider Lake?"

"I don't know. Lots of islands and bays and peninsulas, I guess. Probably looks like a spider from above. They say the Indians even got lost on some of these lakes. The one just north of here is called 'Mantrap' for that reason. You know, the Indians said if you were lost out there, the lake took part of your spirit." He paused and looked at her. "I think that's all wrong. Once you've been lost and then you've found your way, your spirit is stronger than ever. And I've been lost a few times," he admitted.

"Hey! There's a fish!" Susan pointed to a tiny sunfish beside the dock. She was excited by the arrival of the fish. "What kind of fish is that?" She smiled a smile like a small child.

"It's a sunny ... a sunfish. There's millions of 'em around here." Grant began to take his shoes and socks off and then sat on the dock so his feet could dangle in the water. "Wanna see what we used to do when I was a kid?" He was surprised at his own behavior. He wanted to share something from way down inside of himself, and he wasn't afraid that she might see some measure of weakness in him. He hadn't done this since Ingrid was a toddler.

"What are you doing?"

"Well, if you put your bare feet in the water, sometimes the sunfish will come up and kiss your toes."

"No shit!" There was wonder in her voice. Then she raised her hand and covered her mouth. "Oops." He thought the lack of decorum was charming. She began to take her shoes and socks off, too. Then, before she sat down and lowered her feet into the water, she looked intently at Grant. "Is this some kind of practical joke? Are these fish gonna bite me or something?" Grant only smiled and wiggled his own toes.

There were already several more fish inching toward Grant's feet when Susan dropped her feet into the water and spooked them away. "Ooh, water's cold!" she said.

More sunfish were moving toward them, and Susan began to squeal softly like a little girl who was about to get a shot from the doctor and didn't quite know what to expect. A fish finally swam up to her and put its mouth on her foot. "It tickles!" She twitched her feet and laughed and spooked the fish again. Soon she was narrating the whole experience to Grant as a dozen sunfish continuously tapped her feet with their lips. "Here comes another one!"

"Well, this is a new one!" she said finally as she held her cup out for a refill.

As he poured more coffee, Grant said, "If I was a fish I'd be kissing you, too. You even have pretty feet!"

She looked at him as if she couldn't believe, or understand, what he'd said. Then she kissed him softly on the lips.

"Susan," he started slowly, "you know I'd be lying if I said this was all a surprise. I hoped we'd be able to be together some, like this, and I think you did, too. But we live in different worlds, and I just don't want this to be all there is. We've been forced to get to know each other under pretty uncommon circumstances. When you leave today, I don't know when I'll see you again." He tried to smile at her. "Will and June are celebrating their twenty-fifth anniversary in a couple of weeks. Would you like to come back and be my guest for a few days?" He stopped and looked at the little fish around their feet. "I think of you all the time, and the more I'm with you the more I want to be with you. I just want to see you again." His face, his eyes, seemed to be asking permission to share what he'd just said.

The rain began to fall a little more heavily. Susan turned away from him and looked at her feet now. She continued to stare forward. Then she slowly faced Grant. "This bud of love, by summer's ripening breath, may prove a beauteous flower when next we meet." Her face was serious, expressionless. "William Shakespeare, 1599! Tell *that* to Sigurd Olson." With these words, her face lit up in a radiant smile, and Grant could not keep himself from returning it.

"I'd love to come back for their anniversary!" she added, triumphantly.

The rumble of distant thunder rolled over them, and the rain continued to intensify. They stood and began walking barefoot as they returned to the Big House, carrying shoes and socks and coffee cups as they hurried.

"Hey! Just out of curiosity," Susan said when they'd reached the path that led up to the house. "What were you guys laughing so hard about when we pulled up in the pontoon yesterday?"

Grant coughed and laughed at the same time. Her question had surprised him. She could tell he was protecting someone when he answered, "I'll never tell!"

~

Thom and Ellen Hutchinson sat together on the porch, each in a redwood rocking chair but still reaching toward the other and holding hands while they took their morning coffee. Grant and Susan hurried up the twelve steps on the outside staircase and burst onto the porch in order to escape the rain.

"Good morning!" Grant stomped his feet and took off his rain jacket while Susan did the same. "It's gonna be a wet one if we're gonna fish today, Thom!" Grant added.

"No such luck!" Thom looked up at Grant. "I was just told that there's lightning all around us and I won't be fishing today." The rain was falling steadily, but because there was no wind it was very quiet in the woods. The only sound was the unremitting pat, pat, pat of raindrops gently pelting green leaves and the roof. "But that's OK, I can't remember when Ellen and I had such a peaceful morning." Thom pointed at the lake with his cup just as another loon called.

"Yeah, I don't suppose you get much of this at home, huh?" Grant asked. He recognized that Thom and Ellen might appreciate this quiet time to be alone together.

He took Susan's hand, led her into the Great Room, and closed the door behind her. There was a bit of an increase in the "buzz" surrounding the President today, and Grant took it upon himself to protect Thom from it as best he could, if that was possible. He looked back over his shoulder through the glass in the door and saw that Thom and Ellen remained quietly rocking as they watched the rain fall.

The smell of fresh biscuits drifted out from the kitchen and filled the Great Room. June was holding a coffeepot and pouring refills for two men in black suits standing just beside the fireplace while a third man talked quietly on the phone. Will was still talking to Mike O'Neil, and there was another man in the kitchen now who seemed to be making breakfast preparations.

The man working in the kitchen had already provided something of a special surprise for June Campbell. The previous day, Thom had introduced June to Hal Huffman. Hal was the President's personal attendant when he traveled. He did things like prepare or assist in the preparation of meals. If the President needed an aspirin for a headache, Hal would get the aspirin, then call the President's physician and check with the doctor before he gave Thom the aspirin. If the President or the First Lady needed anything — from reading material to a clean shirt — Hal took care of that, too.

Hal was proving to be the one person that Will Campbell couldn't make friends with. "Hey, Hal," Will had asked on Saturday evening. "Do you taste the President's food to see if someone is trying to poison him?"

Hal didn't answer. June looked at her husband and rolled her eyes.

"Well, it's a legitimate question, honey." Will looked to Grant for approval and then continued. "And then, what if the President got some rare disease from sharing his food with someone else like Hal?"

"You should have someone check your food for poison," June said to Will. "But I guess you might know something about rare diseases, or maybe brain damage, from sharing your food with Grant all these years!"

Hal Huffman served everyone a late breakfast on the porch, and they spent the entire morning watching the steady rainfall.

~

"All right, Susan, what would you like to talk about?" Thom Hutchinson asked as he looked across the small table between them on Air Force One.

She had many questions she'd wanted to ask the President for some time, but she started with something more personal. "Well, first of all, I'd like to thank you for allowing me to intrude somewhat on your vacation. My friendship with Grant has sort of come out of the blue, and I hope it hasn't caused any problems for you. Were you uncomfortable with my presence this weekend?" Her question was sincere, and he gave her an honest answer.

"Not really. I do read what you write, though, and I know you've been unhappy with my leadership on most issues. I hope you weren't uncomfortable with my presence. I hope you can allow me, at times, to simply be a friend of Grant Thorson's.

"Absolutely, if you can allow me the same!"

"That's a fine starting point. Now, where do we go from here?" Thom Hutchinson asked with a satisfied smile.

Two hours later, as their visit was drawing to a close, Susan leaned back in her chair and said, "OK, one last question: What were you guys laughing at when we pulled up in the pontoon yesterday?"

A wide smile creased the President's face, and then he laughed out loud. "Never ... I'll never tell. Don't even ask."

chapter TWENTY-FOUR

The subtle sounds of the city were not subtle for Susan anymore. The roar of cars revving their engines and honking their horns had appeared for Susan to notice for the first time in her life. It wasn't really an irritant, but it was now something she'd become aware of, just as she'd become aware of its absence while she was at Spider Lake. In fact, she'd begun to notice all of the commotion and bustle around her since her time in Minnesota — things like telephones constantly ringing or large numbers of people milling past each other and making the dull noise of human traffic.

Susan had enjoyed the way things were at Spider Lake. She leaned back in her desk chair now; she thought of Grant while she looked at the small wooden duck he'd given her when she'd left. No man had ever treated her the way Grant had. When he touched her, she could feel strength in his hands and arms. Yet she recognized some sort of softness when he'd put his arms around her. She thought he'd touched her as though he was afraid ... afraid he might break her.

335

But when Grant spoke to her, that's when she knew she'd met a better man than she was accustomed to. His voice and manner were tender, almost pleading with her when he asked what she was thinking. Then, suddenly, his eyes could carry an uncommon humor when he teased and joked with her.

Susan had noticed a paradox within Grant. In many areas of his life he struggled for control; he worked so hard to create order where he could. He needed control in his work, his relationships with his loved ones, and the material things around him. But he reveled in the disorder of nature, of his life outdoors, and the spiritual part of his life. She'd begun to notice that he sometimes tried to find order where there could be none. Sometimes his need for control forced happiness just beyond arm's length.

Working at this job over the last ten years, she'd become cynical and suspicious about men. Men misled her, or outright lied to her. Sometimes they did it for political reasons, often just to impress her. So why had she lowered her guard so quickly and completely for Grant Thorson, she wondered. He was just some guy who made her feel like ... like a girl. Susan tilted her head back and smiled even more when she remembered Grant calling her a girl.

She had also come to see the President in a more favorable light since her trip to Minnesota. He'd explained to her on their flight back to Washington that he was well aware that he'd been no one's choice for President, and that he was trying to consolidate his power somewhat. Susan could see the human side of Thom Hutchinson now, and she found herself feeling less critical of his administration.

Once, in passing, after a press conference during the week after the Spider Lake trip, Thom and Susan had a brief exchange and she'd commented on her change of heart. His reply had reminded her of something Grant might say: "Yeah, that's why kidnappers aren't supposed to talk to their victims ... maybe they'll start to like 'em and be unable to do their job!" Then he winked at her and walked away.

Susan was still leaning back in her chair and stroking the little duck in her hands when her phone rang. She'd had a blank stare on her face while she'd tuned out the rest of the world for a few minutes. She smiled now at the memory of the place where her thoughts had taken her as she leaned forward to answer the phone.

"Susan Wells," she said. Petra Vanderhoft stepped through Susan's open door at the same instant and stood, staring at Susan. Susan waved hello.

"Hi, Susan." It was Jason Vincent, and Susan was surprised to hear his voice. He'd tried not to let it show, but he'd been angry and hurt when Susan told him she didn't want to see him anymore.

"Hi, Jason." She was polite but cautious. Petra raised her eyebrows suspiciously. Susan answered her with a shrug.

"I wasn't sure if I'd catch you at your desk. I just wanted to see if you'd like to go out for a bite to eat after the staff meeting tonight regarding next year's lecture series?"

Susan paused. She'd been clear about not wanting any more involvement with him.

"No strings; just coffee and a chance to chat about next year. Not a date!" He sensed her hesitation.

"OK, but I need to be home early tonight." She wished she'd said no as she hung up the phone.

"Seeing Jason again?" Petra asked.

"No."

"Well, I walked past your door and noticed you swooning."

"I wasn't swooning."

"Oh?"

"I wasn't."

"Were you revisiting the Land of 10,000 Lakes?"

"Maybe," Susan smiled.

"Be careful. That ... dentist ... makes me nervous. I just can't see you with a ... dentist." Petra used the word "dentist" as if she were holding it with one hand and plugging her nose with the other. She turned and left.

"He's a waterfowl processing technician!" Susan called.

~

Jason Vincent was the antithesis of Grant Thorson in many ways. He was the product of an elite East Coast education. His family was moderately wealthy. He'd become an ultraliberal on all social and political issues. He'd had many articles published in various magazines and periodicals, and most of his work reflected his liberal values. He'd started, but not finished, three different novels. Jason avoided confrontation with his antagonists. He chose instead to speak of them behind their backs while he maintained a friendly façade.

Susan watched Jason from the back of the small meeting room as he led the staff meeting for the English department and then moved on to the schedule for the next year's lecture series on American writers. Almost immediately after she'd met Grant, she'd come to see that Jason was missing something – something huge and important. She realized what it was that Jason was missing when she began to notice the way Grant's eyes shone when he joked with her and when he'd spoken about his family and friends. Jason had lost a childlike joy, but Grant had not; Jason thought the wrong things were important.

Jason did, however, do a nice job with the English department, and she'd always felt he was interesting to talk to. When the meeting ended, she waited for everyone else to leave while Jason crammed papers into his briefcase. When they were alone, he looked at her and asked politely, "Where to?"

"How about Santo's? The college kids all hang out there. It's supposed to have atmosphere." She smiled and walked out the door with Jason. Their conversation on the walk to Santo's was all small talk. Susan knew Jason wanted to restart their relationship; she could feel it. His feelings had been hurt during their breakup, and he felt obliged to address what he felt was the source of their problem.

As soon as they'd been seated at their table, Jason asked her bluntly, "How was your trip to Minnesota?"

"Great," she replied with a smile. "Got an exclusive with the President!"

"I heard you got to be friends with John Birch, too. Or is it Billy Bob? I forgot." He couldn't hide the contempt in his voice.

Susan leaned forward and put her elbows on the table. "It's Dr. Thorson!" She could feel her anger beginning to rise, too.

"Oh, yes, your dentist," he replied smartly.

"You got me there." She leaned back and smiled – which only brought more contempt, or arrogance, or perhaps jealousy, to Jason's face.

"I saw him make an ass out of himself on the TV news that night. He's just a shit kicker from down home who thinks he has all the answers." Jason laughed. He wanted to be sure that Susan knew he'd been aware of what was happening all along when she'd broken up with him.

"No, that's not true," she said slowly. She knew this conversation, this evening, was over before it got started, and she was happy with that. But part of her wanted to say something terrible to Jason, to hurt him. She remembered what Grant had said about liberals who think that everyone who disagrees with them is stupid. She wanted to defend Grant. But then she thought about what he would do if he were here, and she smiled.

Susan sighed and looked at Jason. "He's really a sensitive, intelligent man, and it's too bad he isn't here to respond himself."

"Oh, like he'd take the toothpick from his mouth and then enlighten me?" Jason glared at Susan.

That did it for Susan. "No, as they say at Spider Lake, he'd kick a mud hole up your ass and then stomp it dry! Don't call me anymore." She was smiling when she turned and walked away.

~

Spider Lake Duck Camp was alive with a party atmosphere when Grant and Susan drove into the long driveway. Balloons and "Happy Anniversary" signs marked most of the property. Will and June both came from large families, and Susan could hear the laughter and voices of a crowd coming from the Ordway house as she stepped out of Grant's Suburban in front of his cabin.

"Would you like to freshen up before we walk up to the Big House and meet the others?" Grant asked.

"Sure," Susan replied.

When she entered Grant's cabin, she stopped just inside the doorway and turned to him. "This place really is *you!*" she said with a warm smile. She'd seen his cabin during her brief visit in May, and she thought it was charming. "Same decorator as Will's place, huh?"

Grant led her through the big room that basically was the cabin. She left his side and strolled around the room for a minute, inspecting his home while he watched. When she came to the big northern pike on the wall, she looked closely. Then she puffed her cheeks and blew. A small cloud of dust rolled off the fish, and she looked at Grant. He shrugged. "It's been a dry summer ... decade."

Big Ole's straw hat and his cane rested on the mantle above the fireplace. When Susan saw them, she looked back at Grant and asked about them with her eyes. "I like the cane ... and his hat, well, it smells like him ... aftershave and tobacco. I just hold that old hat up to my face and smell. Then I have my dad back for just a moment." Grant shrugged with his answer.

Then he took her onto the small porch overlooking the lake. Susan shook her head and smiled again. "I would have known this was your place." Several fishing rods hung from a homemade rack by the screen door, and a dish with "Nellie" written on the side rested between two old wicker rocking chairs. She thought of the mauve and teal color scheme and the accessories at Jason Vincent's apartment and had to turn her face away from Grant. She knew what Grant would think of Jason's place, and she wanted to hide her smile, not explain it.

Just then, Ingrid stepped out of her bedroom. Her long, dark hair was pulled back, and she was smiling. "Hi," she said, walking over to shake hands with Susan. Susan thought she was even taller than when they'd met at Big Ole's funeral.

Grant introduced them again and then added, "You met at Grampa's funeral."

"I remember," they both said at the same time.

"Well, I'll show Susan where to put her things and we'll all walk up and say hello to everyone at the Big House," Grant said.

"Why don't I just meet you up there, Dad? Molly's waiting for me. We're gonna go for a boat ride. I think she wants to dodge a few of the 'rellies'." Ingrid was talking as she opened the door. She seemed in a hurry to get away from Grant and Susan.

Molly Campbell had moved out and moved on from her relationship with her boyfriend. Will and June were relieved, and Ingrid was enjoying the racy, mature way she felt when she hung out with her experienced, older friend who'd lived with a guy.

"Behave yourself," Grant said as Ingrid disappeared out the door.

"Pretty girl!" Susan said when Ingrid was gone.

"Thanks. She's reached the age where she thinks her father is the village idiot. They say kids grow out of it in their early twenties … I'm hoping." Grant shook his head to show that he didn't understand.

When Susan had put her things away and was ready to join the growing party, they stepped toward the door together. But Grant stepped in front of her and stopped her. He reached both hands around to the small of her back and pulled her toward him softly. He kissed her gently on the lips – just a "hello, I'm glad you're here" sort of kiss. The instant their lips met, Ingrid burst back into the cabin.

"Forgot my ...," She stopped, not more than two feet from them, and looked at them briefly. "Eeeooo," she said, as though she was changing a bad diaper, and backed out the door, closing it behind her. Susan was embarrassed immediately. Grant thought it was somewhat funny. Ingrid just didn't quite know what to think.

"Give her a few minutes to let it settle," Grant said. "I'll talk to her. It'll be OK." He could see some anxiety in Susan's eyes. "Don't worry, we weren't thrashing around on the floor or anything like that."

"No, but that's what it felt like when she looked at us," Susan added.

Laughter and children's voices could be heard again all the way from the Big House when Grant and Susan started up the long hill toward the party. They emerged into the clearing around the Ordway house and saw about three dozen people standing around the old log lodge. There were more on the porch.

Grant began to introduce Susan to those people that he knew. "OK, here's the deal. I'll introduce you to everyone I know. The majority of these people are family, the rest are mostly dentists. Remember, if we get separated and somebody introduces them-selves as a dentist ... you probably have a geek on your hands, so lose 'em. You know, put your finger in your mouth and start talk-ing about some terrible thing your dentist did to you ... dentists hate that." Grant took her hand and winked, then began introduc-ing her to virtually everyone they passed.

When he found Evie and Frank Campbell, he made a special point to make a formal introduction. Susan could see that Grant held them in high esteem. "Ah, Evie and Frank, this is my friend Susan Wells!" he said, with a special emphasis on "friend."

"Yes. Will and June have told us all about you, Susan," Evie said. Then Frank started right in asking questions of Susan regarding friends of his in Washington. As it turned out, Susan knew several of them, and Frank and Susan spent a few minutes discussing common acquaintances.

As Grant and Susan left the Campbells and moved toward the house, Frank called to Grant, "Hey, we drew our elk license in Colorado … September … you'll be there?"

"Wouldn't miss it, Frank," Grant called back to him.

"How did you and Will come to be such good friends?" Susan asked as they walked across the lawn.

"We studied together in dental school … well, actually he helped me study … saved my bacon, to tell the truth. It's odd, people told him he was too smart to go to dental school. And they told me I was too dumb." Grant paused; he seemed to be remembering things long forgotten. "June used to say he just kept me around because I laughed at all the stupid things he said." Now Grant was smiling.

~

The summer weather was perfect – not too warm and not too much breeze. A beautiful, sunny late afternoon turned into a warm, clear summer evening. Family and friends continued to laugh and eat and drink. There was music from the sixties and seventies playing on the porch while some of the smaller children chased each other around the outside of the Ordway house. Occasionally a parent would be summoned to comfort a crying child who'd fallen during the rough play.

When Grant and Susan finally found June, she greeted both of them with a hug. "What a summer so far, huh?" She was clearly having fun.

"Have you seen the girls?" Grant asked June.

"Yeah, they were over there a minute ago." She pointed to the table on the porch where several cases of beer sat in an ice bucket. "It's nice to see them playing together like they did when they were little!"

"I don't think they're playing the same games they used to. I'll be back," Grant said as he left in search of them.

When Grant was out of earshot, June turned to Susan. "It's been a rough couple months for him … with Ingrid. She's had two speeding tickets, she's lost two summer jobs. Not that they were such great jobs, but ... a bit of an attitude has developed. She's begun to treat Grant poorly, too. It really hurts him. Probably hurts him more than it should, though. All kids seem to go through this stage when they separate from their parents. He always thought he was doing such a good job with her. Now he feels like he's failed. You know, it's hard enough to raise children when you have a good partner. Now he's got no one to share the responsibility with."

Susan told June that Ingrid had seen them kissing and what her reaction had been.

"Oh, well, that's no big deal! Is it? At least you weren't ... you know," June smiled. Her face brightened even more as she remembered something. "Will walked in on Frank and Evie once when he was in high school. He was on his way to pitch in some baseball game and stopped at home to pick something up. *Bad* timing," June laughed out loud. "It was the worst game of his life ... said it was impossible to concentrate because, well ... you know ... he had this really distracting mental picture that he couldn't shake. He laughs about it now, though, as much as a man can laugh and cringe at the same time." June was laughing uncontrollably now. Susan could not help but join her.

"What's so funny?" Will sidled up next to June. "Hi, Susan! Nice to see you."

"I was just telling Susan about the time you walked in on your parents."

"Ooo," Will covered his eyes, then looked at June. "Why?"

"It's a long story. I'll be right back. I need to say hello to someone."

Will and Susan shared an awkward silence for a brief moment. As always, Will made the awkwardness vanish. "Never thought I'd see you here, like this, when we met at the White House last fall."

"Really?" Susan tilted her head with the request for an explanation.

"Yeah. Life seems to take us around a bend in the water sometimes, you know what I mean?"

"Yes, I guess so. But I saw something in him right away." She knew Will was referring to her friendship with Grant.

"Yeah, he's an easy guy to like. But he can be an odd one, too, but I guess that's one of the things I like about him."

"What do you mean?"

"Well, I saw him go at it, bare knuckles in a fight, with some college stud in an amateur baseball game two years ago. He was forty-five years old and still playing ball! Got his ass kicked, too! But he made me come down out of the bleachers and put eleven stitches over his eye so he could finish the game. Those young boys on his team gathered around in the dugout and watched every stitch. He finished the game, too. Those kids think he's twisted steel," Will laughed. "All he wanted was to show them that you just never back down. Hell, I've seen him go out on the lake and challenge the weather, for God's sake."

Will took a sip of his beer. "But he's also the guy who cried every time one of my dogs died. He had to leave the room when he heard Mickey Mantle died. This tough guy thing is a handy shield for him to hide behind sometimes. He just stuffs his emotions ... doesn't want to appear weak. I never saw him cry through the whole thing with Kate. Can you imagine that?"

~

Grant had been unable to find Ingrid and Molly. After fifteen minutes, he gave up the search and began to make his way back toward Susan and Will. As he approached them, he noticed a third person talking with them. He didn't know the other man, but as he drew near he could see through the twilight that Will was smiling, then laughing silently with his mouth open, looking at Susan. The stranger turned and walked away as Will's laughter increased. Susan turned slightly, and Grant could see that she had her index finger in her mouth and she was still talking, and laughing along with Will.

"Friend of yours?" Grant asked when he reached them.

"He's a geek!" they both said simultaneously.

"Bruce Backstrom. Practices down the hall from me in Duluth. Nice guy, June likes his wife, but …." Will smiled again.

"He's a geek!" they both said again, laughing together.

"As soon as your girlfriend stuck her finger in her mouth, I knew you'd been coaching her. I have to mingle. See you later." Will wandered off into the crowd.

~

Grant and Susan held hands and strolled through the crowd until just about sunset, when Evie Campbell produced a bullhorn and stood with her other arm around Frank's waist. They both sang "Happy Anniversary" to June and Will. The two of them looked totally undignified; the sight of them singing raised a laugh from the crowd. Evie Campbell apparently liked the bullhorn because she continued to address the crowd with it after their song. Frank whispered something into Evie's ear as she held the bull-horn, and instead of putting the thing at her side and responding privately, she turned to him with her finger on the trigger and said, "WHAT DID YOU SAY?" into his face at full volume. Frank grimaced, covered his ears, and made her put the bullhorn down, and that was the end of the formal program.

When the party began to reach its peak, about two hours after dark, Susan and Grant found themselves standing alongside Will near one of the two kegs of beer that had been set up in the yard. Will was a little "altered," as he liked to say. Grant knew Will had been drinking for a while even as he approached him – his hair was mussed, and that was always the sign. As Will was standing by a campfire entertaining friends with jokes and stories, Susan and Grant walked over to him and stood around the small fire. "Hey."

He turned to them and beer splashed over the rim of his glass. "Good party, huh? Glad you could come, Susan. Little different atmosphere than last time you were here, huh?" He reached around to his hip pocket and produced a bag of chewing tobacco.

"It's quite a bit different, that's for sure," she replied. Will introduced her to the other people around the fire as "Grant's girlfriend." She covered her mouth as if she were surprised or embarrassed, but her eyes made it clear she liked the introduction. "I have a question for you regarding my last visit," Susan smiled at Will.

"Shoot," Will said as he loaded his lip full of brown leaves. Susan was totally relaxed, and her exceptional powers of persuasion were in high gear. She leaned forward and asked, "What were you laughing at when we pulled up next to you in the pontoon last month?" She smiled a smile as if she were one of the good ol' boys and Will should naturally want to tell her all about it.

At first, Will made a face as though he couldn't remember. Then his eyes cleared. He extended the bag of chewing tobacco to Susan. The implication was clear: "Have a chew and maybe I'll tell you." She could see there might be an opening here. The only thing she didn't do was bat her eyes.

Grant was pretty sure that Will would never tell, no matter what. But suddenly, Susan reached for the open bag and pulled out a wad of tobacco. Grant thought it looked like worms when she placed it in her mouth. She smiled at Will, then raised her eyebrows as she packed it inside her lip.

Will's eyes widened, and Grant realized he was going to tell. Susan had taken the dare, and Will was about to reward her.

"Well, we were duck hunting one time years ago, you know — Thom and Grant and I." He paused and looked at the lump in Susan's mouth and shook his head. "Grant was driving, like he always does — it's a power thing with him. Thom was having a bit of a stomach cramp if you know what I mean, and he hollered 'PULL OVER!' So Grant looks at him and says 'huh?' and Thom hollers 'pull over!' again. Grant says 'Why?' and Thom hollers from the front of the boat. 'I think a gastrocolic event is about to happen in my waders ... judging from the pressure.' He held his belly and made a face. 'I'd say I've upgraded from Defcon Two to Defcon One – the missiles are fueling and about to fly.' He was talking like the President and he wasn't even in Congress yet. 'We have a Code Brown here!' he said, and his voice was getting pan-icky. Now, we all think this is pretty funny, and we start laughing, which makes the whole thing harder to stop."

Will looked at Susan now. He could see that she was laughing also, but spit had begun pooling in her mouth and she just didn't know what to do with it. He shrugged his shoulders and said, "We made it to shore OK, but as soon as his foot hit the beach he lost his grip ... shit his pants. It was nasty, too ... like his ass threw up in his undies."

With that Susan laughed, then coughed, then swallowed all of the saliva she'd been unwilling to spit *and* the plug of tobacco leaves. Every one of the half-dozen men standing around Will was laughing hysterically now, just as Susan had been ... briefly.

Suddenly, Susan was ashen colored. Even in the moonlight she looked terribly pale. Her smile disappeared as if someone had pulled a shade over her face. She had the look of someone who knew her time was limited – like a convict waiting to walk from his cell to the electric chair. The other men were laughing at Susan's nauseated expression as much as Will's story. Grant realized what had happened. He said only "uh oh!" The others continued to laugh as Will looked on sympathetically. Grant took Susan by the arm. He steadied her and began walking toward his cabin immedi-ately. He knew all too well what was about to happen.

"I'm really dizzy!" Susan said weakly. They continued to walk along the path. She slowed noticeably and said, "I don't feel ... " She never finished the sentence. She began projectile vomiting as Grant held her by the waist from behind. After several truly disgusting-sounding dry heaves, Grant was relatively certain that Susan's stomach was empty. He picked her up and carried her, like a baby, to his cabin.

He put Susan in his bed, took her sandals off, and laid her on her stomach in his four-poster bed. Then he got an empty one-gallon ice cream bucket and put it beside her bed just in case she had to vomit again. He wanted to walk back up the hill and say goodnight to Will and June and a few others, but he didn't feel he should leave Susan. She began to dry heave two more times, then lay quietly for a while.

About an hour later, Grant was sitting on the couch where he'd planned to spend the weekend, nearly asleep, when Ingrid came in the porch door and walked directly to her room. As she passed by she giggled and said, "Heard Susan got the flu," then closed her bedroom door.

Grant decided to let that one slide. 'Perhaps Susan had that one coming,' he thought. He was nearly asleep on the couch a second time when he was startled by another voice.

"Grant, Grant." He jumped, and when his eyes focused he saw June, sitting next to him on the couch. "Is she OK?" June asked.

Grant rubbed his eyes. "Yeah, she's sleeping. It's OK, June. This is gonna be funny in about twelve hours," Grant laughed.

"Susan might feel fine tomorrow, but Will's gonna have a whopper of a headache. He's upstairs driving the porcelain bus right now. He really overdid it tonight," June said as she got up and walked to the door. "Know what he said when I told him I was gonna come and check on Susan? He said, 'Tell Grant I'm sorry.'" She put her hands on her hips. "Here's my husband on our twenty-fifth anniversary, and he wants me to apologize to you. So when can a woman expect a man to grow up?"

"I don't think the good ones ever do," Grant replied.

"Yeah, I suppose not," she sighed. "Well, we're gonna go out for our private anniversary dinner tomorrow night. So you two have a nice time tomorrow!" And she turned to leave.

"Hey, June?" Grant called. "Wait."

June turned.

"You wanna have a drink, just you and me? I don't think in all these years you and I ever sat down ... just the two of us."

"Yeah," she said. She plopped heavily into the leather chair. "Brandy," she added as she held out her hand.

Grant smiled and made them each a drink. He handed her an old-fashioned glass with brandy and ice and sat back on the couch where he'd been. He put his feet on the coffee table so they were touching June's feet. Then he nudged her foot with his. "He loves you, June!"

"Yeah." She shook her head and grinned. "I know."

"Thanks for sharing him all these years."

June only looked deeply into the ice cubes in her hand. She did not reply. Then, after a moment she nudged his foot and looked at him.

"So how come your wife never got mad at you?

"I'm pretty wonderful."

"No, really, she was never angry at you?"

"A couple of times."

"OK, name one time. What happened?"

"Remember when we had to study for national boards during the summer after our junior year?"

"Yes."

"Well, I had to. Will didn't. Anyway, we're walking around school and we bump into Dr. Schafer and Dr. Ruminsky, and we start talking with them about fishing, then fly tying. Next thing you know, Will invites these two over to my place to tie flies that night. That wasn't so bad, but I'd told Kate that I couldn't go to her family reunion that day because I had to study.

"We didn't think they'd really show, but they did. Will mixed a pitcher of martinis, and one thing led to another. When Kate came home, we were all in the bag. She had to drive Dr. Shafer and

Dr. Ruminsky and Will home. When she came back, she was so pissed ... not at Will for causing that train wreck, but at me. And then the next day I find out you're mad at me for getting him drunk. How does that work? Everybody gets pissed at me and he's cute and funny?"

"That's just the way it works for you, but don't forget ...."

"What?"

"Dr. Shafer and Dr. Ruminsky's wives were pissed at you, too!" Grant did not reply. He only looked at his feet and smiled.

"Getting cold in here." He got up to close the door that opened onto the porch. When he returned to the couch, he let out a sigh.

"You're in love, aren't you?" she asked.

"Feels like it," he answered. He stared at his ice cubes.

"Well, here's to the love of a good woman!" she said as she raised her glass.

"I'll drink to that."

~

Morning light was coming in through the windows, and Susan was already awake when Grant let himself into her room.

"Good morning," he said softly. "How do you feel today?"

"Terrible!" Susan replied as she put her hand over her face in a gesture to show Grant she was ashamed. "I haven't done anything like that since I was in high school."

"I thought that was just good investigative reporting ... you got your story."

"Yeah, that part was pretty good, but I don't know if it was worth the effort!" She smiled, then laughed and shook her head.

Susan sat up in bed now and looked at Grant. He put his hand on her thigh and stroked it gently. He touched her like a small child might touch a sleeping puppy. She'd been touched by many men in many different ways, but never like this. "I came in here to see if you'd like to see the white horses run."

"What?" She was confused.

Grant knew she would be, and he smiled but offered no explanation. "If you'd like to see something special, come with me. I'll even pour you some coffee."

"Well, give me a minute and I'll be there, but I don't think my stomach needs any coffee. Thanks anyway."

~

Walking slowly along a smooth path between some small white pines, they came upon, what looked to Susan, like a giant pickle barrel with a chimney sticking out of it.

"What's that?"

"Hot tub."

"Really?" She demanded the truth.

"Really." You have to build a fire in that little fireplace to heat the water ... takes a few hours."

"A wood-powered hot tub?"

"Sure. I'll show you later."

The air temperature had dropped significantly during the night. This morning, even though the sun would rise into a clear blue sky, the surface of Spider Lake was covered in a thick, white fog. The warm vapors from the lake rose up and condensed into a cloud, which lay across the water to a height of about thirty feet.

Grant led Susan to a wooden bench by the lakeshore, and they both sat down. He put one arm around her shoulder and pointed toward the lake with the other. "See the white horses running?" he asked in a satisfied way, as if he thought she was fortunate to see such a rare thing and he was proud to be the one showing her.

The gentle morning breeze was beginning to blow the cloud of fog off the lake in puffs. Each small fragment of the fog seemed to tumble and gallop across the water before it disappeared. At first she didn't see it. 'He got me out of bed to watch fog,' she thought. For a moment she wasn't sure if he was serious. Then she saw the horses.

"Oh, yeah … white horses!" Susan said as if she suddenly understood a riddle.

They watched in silence for a moment, and then Grant spoke up. "I wait most of the year for the white horses to run on these chilly mornings. I love this. It's like the lake and the sky have decided to get together and give something up. These are the most special times here. It's like everything must be just right for the lake to share this.

Susan's head and her stomach felt fine now — much better than she'd expected when she'd first arisen. As she watched the white horses running, Susan was moved by the beauty of the morning. She took Grant's hand but said nothing for a moment. "You think Heaven looks like this?" she asked after a few minutes.

"Yup!"

While she watched the morning cloud peacefully melt off the glassy surface of the lake, she wondered about the man sitting next to her. She was beginning to have deep feelings for Grant Thorson. She recognized a strong man who sought — no, demanded order in most areas of his life. But at the same time, he was a man who reveled in the mysterious, ethereal nature of the things he loved. He wasn't the inflexible, opinionated cowboy that she'd suspected months ago. She thought it was touching, romantic, that this man thought it was special to hold her hand and watch the fog roll off a lake. The beauty of this man and this place were tied together.

"Thanks for having me here this weekend," she said as she squeezed his hand a little.

"I'm glad you came!"

"Didn't get a very good start on the weekend, though." Susan curled her face into an apologetic sort of grimace.

"Whadya mean? It was great. My best friend overdoes it on his twenty-fifth anniversary, and somehow it gets to be my fault in his wife's eyes … once again! We probably should have been celebrating the twenty-fifth anniversary of that phenomenon. And then this babe that I've been bragging about for weeks shows up and swallows a wad of tobacco the size of a tennis ball ... then sprays vomit over half of Hubbard County. You sounded like you were going to turn inside out, by the way. The guys were all impressed with the way you sort of holler when you vomit." He was teasing her, raising his eyebrows as a small boy would do while bragging about some great thing that his favorite baseball player had done.

"God, that's enough." Susan lowered her forehead onto the palm of her hand to admit shame. "What do I have to do to make you forget it?"

"Let me buy you breakfast?"

"Done!"

~

All of the regulars were seated in their usual booths at Emil's Café when Grant and Susan entered. She stopped one step inside the door, turning slowly to her right and then her left. She knew immediately that she'd been brought to a place with special importance. She exaggerated the act of noticing the ambiance.

"Nobody beats Emil's meat?" she said with a smile when she read the sign above the door.

"Yeah, it's kind of a play on words. You might think it means ... well, you know. But it really means ..."

"I know." She cut off Grant's sarcastic explanation, but she could not hide her smile. "This place is awesome. I didn't think places like this still existed. When I visited my grandfather's farm there was a place like this in town — but that was ... well, it was a long time ago."

She stopped and looked at the odd combination of items for sale in the old display case. "See that?" Grant said. "Hoppe's #9 gun oil. Most women don't know it, but all real men find that to be an aphrodisiac. Put a little of that behind your ears and real men come running. You can only find it in the cosmetic or firearm section of most fine restaurants." She shook her head in disbelief and kept looking.

"Look! You can buy live bait in this restaurant!" Susan exclaimed.

"Yeah, it's a bait and breakfast," Grant added. He was able to stifle a smile when she looked at him. "Hey, the corner booth is open. Let's go." The men at the breakfast counter had their backs to Susan and Grant as they walked past. Grant reached in front of Susan and pointed at one of the men as Susan passed behind him. Exposed between the bottom of his shirt and the top of his blue jeans was an enormous white ass split by about eight inches of cleavage. The man wasn't wearing underwear.

"Hi, Geno," Grant said.

The man at the counter kept both elbows on the counter and did not bother to turn around. "Hi, Doc," he replied.

When they passed by the man, Grant whispered, "How's your appetite?" Susan merely closed her eyes as if she'd seen enough.

When they got to the corner booth, Susan looked at the animal mounted above them. Before they took their seats, she grabbed Grant's arm and asked, "What is that?"

"I think it's a river otter. Will thinks it's a gargoyle. Nobody wants to ask Emil ... might hurt his feelings."

Men were shaking dice at two of the other booths. The loser was to pay for coffee for everyone at the booth. The smell of bacon and coffee filled the air. Susan smiled as she scanned the whole restaurant. The conversation at every booth concerned the fishing on Leech Lake.

Susan was looking behind herself, out the window, when Hilda Krause ambled up to the booth to take their orders. Hilda was huge. She wore a white shirt with a white apron. The apron was peppered with hundreds of grease stains, and it was tied just below her large breasts. She was about sixty-five years old, her hair, short and gray, was combed straight back. Her ruddy face was sweating when she turned to Grant and said, "Hi, Doc!"

When they'd given Hilda their orders and she'd left the table, Susan began to chuckle all over again. "Did you read the button she was wearing?" she asked Grant.

"You mean, 'If you can't see your reflection in it, it ain't breakfast'?"

"Yes," Susan laughed out loud.

"Emil plans to have that on his tombstone," Grant said seriously.

Still giggling, Susan asked, "That was Mrs. Emil?"

"Well, we don't know for sure. There is some speculation that Emil and Hilda may be identical twins."

Susan's head spun reflexively to look again, to check the resemblance for herself. When she saw Emil standing next to Hilda, she gasped, "Oh my God!" Emil was also huge, he wore a white shirt and white apron, and had short gray hair, a sweaty face and big breasts.

"I *think* Emil's a little cuter, though," Grant added. "He has man boobs ... but a nicer tush."

Susan laughed like people who start laughing in church or at funerals and then can't stop, and they don't want to be seen laughing, either. The more she tried to hide it, the more she laughed. "This place is great!" she coughed through her hands as she hunched over to hide her face.

Grant was finding her playful nature to be very attractive. She had the same joy and enthusiasm that he'd seen only in Kate, and Will. Anne had merely tolerated this place, and now Susan seemed smitten with it. The difference in Susan's and Anne's responses to Emil's Leech Lake Café was not lost on Grant. He couldn't say why, but Susan's laughter made him feel good about his home, himself.

~

When they returned from breakfast, Grant and Susan spent the rest of the day either on the lake or walking the trails through the woods and talking.

Grant had never liked the phrase "falling in love," but he knew it was happening to him. He sensed it in Susan, too. Everything he said to her seemed to prompt the perfect response. She saw the world as he did, for the most part. Her quick wit made him laugh, and she enjoyed his sense of humor, too.

During the hottest time of the afternoon, they went for a boat ride in Grant's little green boat. Susan liked to refer to it as 'Silverheels' now. Grant shut the motor off and let the wind blow them across the open water. While they bobbed in the breeze, Susan spoke and Grant watched her. His eyes moved over her long legs, her hands, and the delicate features of her face. She kicked her shoes off, and he stared at her feet. "She's sleek," he thought. "She isn't sexy in the way that a centerfold is, but she is *so* attractive." Grant even thought the way she wore her baseball hat with a pony tail coming out the back made her look pretty.

When they tied the boat up on the pier and returned to the cabin, it was almost 6:00 p.m.. Ingrid was getting ready to leave for a concert in Bemidji, and Grant suggested that she take the cell phone in case of an emergency. As Grant was extending the phone to her, she rolled her eyes as if she thought her father was a fool and snapped the phone quickly from his hand as she stomped out the door to her car. Her actions were rude and disrespectful, and Grant stifled an urge to stop her at the door and discipline her.

The little scene embarrassed Grant and hurt his feelings. The one person on earth whom he wanted to love him and respect him clearly thought he was not worthy of common courtesy. Grant looked at Susan and shook his head. He wanted Susan to be impressed with his daughter, not embarrassed for her.

"She's just a kid. She'll out grow this stuff," Susan offered.

"Maybe," Grant shrugged, then sighed.

"Think she's still struggling to understand what she saw yesterday?" Susan asked.

"Maybe ... that was no big deal, though," he replied.

"Her father was kissing someone who wasn't her mother. Has she seen that before?"

"No."

"Are you sure she's OK with it?"

"No" Grant admitted hesitantly.

Susan stepped close to Grant and put her index finger on his chest. "Try to imagine what must be going on in her head right now ... regarding you and me. In addition to that, you have all the parental separation stuff that a twenty-year-old feels. Talk to her about all of this."

"Yeah, you're right." He put his head down. "I was hungry a few minutes ago, but not anymore. How 'bout you?"

"I can wait."

Grant took a beer from the refrigerator for each of them. He slouched into one of the wicker chairs on the porch, and Susan sat on the one facing him.

He was barefoot and wore swimming trunks and an old golf shirt. She wore a revealing two-piece swimsuit and cotton shirt with the tails tied at her waist. When she sat down, she deliberately put her bare foot on top of his. Instantly when she touched him, he could think of nothing else but the unmistakable rush of sexual energy her touch generated.

He took a sip of his beer and smiled at her. He was feeling that little twitch inside himself now. He looked at her and wondered just where that little glow came from in his foot, his brain, and his crotch. He didn't know. He didn't care. He just smiled at Susan as she rubbed her foot softly on his.

"You are a beautiful woman," he said as he raised his eyebrows and continued to grin at her. "And you know that I'm in love with you, don't you?" he confessed.

Susan said nothing. She made an innocent face and then nodded her head "yes." Only a moment earlier, when he'd reached into the refrigerator and then stood to face her, she'd caught herself staring at his back and shoulders, and then the tight lines in his legs, as he moved.

"But Doctor," she said quietly, finding great joy in the words. "You are a beautiful man, and you know I'm in love with you, too, don't you?"

Grant looked away but smiled a broad smile. Her words were all pleasure for him, too. He'd never heard those words spoken quite like that.

She ran her bare foot up his leg until he looked at her. Her eyes were waiting for him with a very warm, seductive smile.

Several months earlier, Grant had confessed to Will that he feared he'd never know this feeling again. Now the excitement, the comfort of another person's laugh, and touch, had returned.

He stepped out of his chair and toward her. As he drew close to her, both of his knees were resting on the floor in front of her chair. He reached his hands behind the small of her back and pulled himself close. She spread her legs and brought her bare heels around to the back of his legs.

Both hearts were pounding when their lips met. Their kiss was wet and full. After several seconds, Grant lifted his mouth from hers and then briefly rested his cheek on hers. He kissed her cheek, her ear, then lifted his face away from hers. The smell of her sunscreen reminded him of other summer days and other pretty girls long ago — and whatever it was inside of him continued to warm and quicken. He knew what would happen soon if their embrace continued.

"Susan, I have to tell you something, and I guess it's a little inappropriate to say it now."

She tried not to appear puzzled as she leaned back and continued to hold her hands on his sides.

"I know what it seems like we should do — what I want so much to do. But I have to tell you ..." He paused. "I think I got sex and love confused once before. Everyone got hurt. I do love you and I think it's the 'take her home to meet the parents' kind of love. I don't want anything to ruin what I'm feeling right now. I can't believe I'm saying this, but I think we ought to hold off on this for a while."

"OK," Susan said with an accepting smile. She was truly puzzled. No man had ever held her the way Grant was holding her now and then offered to hold off on sex.

When they both stood up, they embraced each other and Grant's erection pushed solidly against Susan's stomach so that they both were aware of it.

He looked down into her eyes and added, with a broad smile, "But not for ever."

Susan smiled a sheepish smile; she looked embarrassed. She lowered her eyes for a very deliberate look at his member, which was straining at the front of his swimming trunks, then took a breath and looked into his eyes as she sighed, "Whew. I thought for a minute there you were gonna tell me you'd been injured in some sort of waterfowl processing accident." Her eyes twinkled when she said "injured."

~

"OK, the water's hot."

Susan dropped her bathrobe over a small branch on a poplar tree, and Grant helped her step into the rustic-looking hot tub. "Feels good!" She dropped steadily into the water until only her head was above the water. Grant followed close after.

"See, in the time it took us to watch *Jeremiah Johnson*, we got a fire stoked up and the hot tub is ready." He smiled at her. Their evening meal had been the beer and popcorn they'd shared while watching the movie.

"I think I've heard you say most of those lines to Will. I felt like I'd seen it before," she said.

"Yeah, we do have some fun with the dialogue."

The sun had disappeared behind the pines a few minutes earlier, and the sky was turning to deep blue. The lake was quiet and flat, as it often is at sunset. Off and on, loons called from all over the lake.

"We figure there are nine pairs of nesting loons on the lake," Grant said.

"Are they talking to each other?" Susan asked.

"Who knows?"

Steam was rising off the surface of the hot tub as the night air began to cool. "Hey, we've got white horses right here!" Susan called as she gently blew the small vapor trails across the water.

When she looked up to see if Grant was watching the small white horses, she was grinning. Grant was staring at her and stirring the water gently in front of him.

"What do you dream about?" he asked. He wasn't concerned about the white horses now.

"Pardon me?"

"What do you dream of? What do you hope for? You know, when you're all alone and everything is quiet. What do you dream of?" Grant still stared at her.

"Oh. Hmmm. Well, I guess I hope for peace, and …."

"No. What do you hope for, for you?" He squinted at her. "Know what I mean?"

"Well, I used to hope for a big house in the country and a handsome man and beautiful kids. You mean stuff like that?"

"Maybe. It's your dream."

"What do you dream of?"

"You'll laugh." He paused. "When I was a kid, I dreamed of home runs and strikeouts. Then I dreamed of girls." He smiled a sheepish smile. "For a while I dreamed of success at the office. You know … money, status — being somebody, I guess. But through all the years, the dream that comes back the most has stayed the same. I see water. I see myself in my little boat. Ducks are gliding toward me with cupped wings, or maybe fish are rising all around me. More and more lately, I see myself sitting on the porch here at my cabin. It's just sunup … and I can smell coffee … and …." He stopped suddenly. "That's enough. You tell me now!"

"I don't know if I think like that. I don't know what I dream of."

"Everyone needs to hope for something. It's what keeps us going."

"I'll have to think about that one for a while."

Grant let her answer be good enough for now. He raised his arms out of the water and rested them on the rim of the tub. Susan could see steam rising from his arms into the cool night air. He leaned his head back and changed the subject.

"Hear the pine knots crackling in the fire?" he asked with a grin.

"Yeah. It's a peaceful sound ... has a calming effect," Susan added.

"Hmph!" Grant's smile widened and he looked away. "Can I tell you about a special memory in this old tub?"

"Sure."

Grant continued to stare off across the lake. "Will and I hunted hard all day long one time a few years ago. We got back to the cabin late, and the weather turned a little foul." Grant looked at Susan and swished the water in front of him. "It was after dark and the snow was coming sideways ... big flakes ... but strangely quiet." He paused, then started again. "It was cold, so we had our lids on and we were ..."

"Lids?" she interrupted.

"Fur hats. Your IQ goes down about thirty points as soon as you put one on ... and they look even dumber. But they're warm!"

"OK, I understand. Continue."

"So anyway, we're sitting in a hot tub, in a snowstorm, naked except for our fur hats. The snow made everything *so* quiet ... all we could hear was the fire crackling and the faint noise of the wing beats of all the northern ducks. They were migrating ... just above the treetops. We just took turns dashing out of the tub and putting more wood on the fire."

Grant stopped. He was looking into the water in front of him when he spoke again. "Neither of us said a word for two hours ... and we had a great time together ... just the fire, and the ducks, and the snow, and this old tub."

Susan thought he seemed a little embarrassed that he shared the story with her, but she liked it when he could just open himself up and ramble. She swished the water and smiled back at him.

"So what do you think Petra Vanderhoft would say if she could see you now, sitting in a wash tub in the dark, listening to loons?" Grant left the story of the snowstorm behind and changed the tempo of the conversation again.

"I think she'd like it." Susan was beginning to love the place now, too. She felt peace here – peace like she'd never felt before. She wondered also if Grant was an extension of this place. Susan wondered silently if she could be happy living here.

She thought Grant was reading her mind when he spoke up. "This is how you know you're alive – when you feel the things this place makes you feel. Maybe it's a warm summer night, with loons calling and stars flickering and a breeze rustling the cottonwoods or swooshing through the pines. Maybe it's the cold wind blowing down your collar when you cross the lake with a boat full of decoys. Sometimes I wonder if it's the fear I sense when I'm out there in a storm." His voice trailed off a little. "Maybe it's what I feel for you."

He could see her eyes smile in the moonlight. He straightened his back, pointed his face toward the treetops, and said, almost in a whisper, "Only got my dad over to see this place once ... he was getting pretty sick and feeble when I moved in here. It was a nice spring day, and we walked out onto the small pier ... I had to hold onto him so he could keep his balance." Grant lowered his eyes back to Susan's. "After a few minutes, he turned to me and grinned a little grin. Know what he said to me?"

"What?"

"'You're gonna be happy here, boy!' It was odd. He never said things like that," Grant shrugged.

"So are you happy?" Susan asked seriously.

"Yeah ... I am. But it's so hard for me to hold onto it."

chapter TWENTY-FIVE

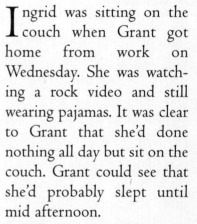

Ingrid was sitting on the couch when Grant got home from work on Wednesday. She was watching a rock video and still wearing pajamas. It was clear to Grant that she'd done nothing all day but sit on the couch. Grant could see that she'd probably slept until mid afternoon.

"What time did you get home last night?" he asked.

"I dunno," she said without looking up.

"Make any calls about a summer job today?" he asked calmly, although he could feel himself beginning to boil.

"No," she said, once again without looking up, but this time Grant read a disrespectful snip to her voice.

"OK, that tears it!" Grant raised his voice and walked quickly between Ingrid and the TV. He turned the TV off when he was in front of it. His face was flushed with anger, and his hands rested on his hips. "Get your ass off that couch and go get a job. I know that the past year or so has been tough for you, but it's time to get on with things now! What do you think? Just because something bad happens in your life you have the right to absolve yourself of your responsibilities to yourself and to others? You act like a spoiled brat — like you're above the rules of decent behavior that the rest of us have to follow."

"What about you and your girlfriend!" she snapped back at him. She was angry, too, and the focus of her anger caught him by surprise.

"Oh, so that's the issue here," Grant said slowly. Then he sat down in the leather chair and rested his elbows on his knees when he continued.

"I think there are actually several things going on in your head right now, Ingrid, and you're having trouble sorting them out. Let's save the thing about my girlfriend for a minute. First and foremost, you're a young adult trying to separate yourself from your parents and find your own way. That's all pretty normal, except your sep-aration from your mom was tragic and traumatic — and it can't be changed. Your separation from me — this anger you feel toward me — is pretty normal, too. I've tried to give you some room ... some slack. Remember, honey, this is hard for me, too. It's my first time down this road as a parent. I really don't know the best way to help you through this time. It's OK for you to sort of separate your life from mine."

He stopped, took a deep breath, and started again. His tone was harder now; he meant for there to be no mistake in what he was about to say. "But by God, you'll respect your father, and yourself, and the rules of this house. You'll get a job to help pay for your college, *and* you'll get a job because work is good — it's what we do, it's how we find respect for ourselves. Now, you have a job by this time tomorrow or I'll find you one — and it might be shoveling shit somewhere, so I'd advise you to find something *you* like before I get involved. Understand?"

"Yes." Her anger from a moment before was gone. Her father had, as usual, been pretty clear, and she knew exactly what he expected.

"Now, about Susan … " His voice was much softer now. "I don't understand why your mother had to die, but she did. I wish she hadn't left me, but she did. I don't think someone your age can imagine the void it leaves in a person's life when their spouse dies. Soon you'll be leaving my life in many ways, too, because you'll be moving on to your own life. I'll be all alone. Your mother made me happy when I was with her, and when she died I thought I'd never know that sort of happiness again. I think Susan might be the one to let me feel like that again. I need for you to let me try to find happiness. Can you do that?"

Her knees tucked under her chin, Ingrid was looking at the floor in front of her. "What about your hot little fling with Anne Robertson?" The anger in her voice had returned.

Grant was caught off guard. He didn't know how much she knew, and he was embarrassed at the prospect of discussing his relationship with Anne. It was painfully clear that he'd been unsuccessful in hiding much from Ingrid. "I guess that just wasn't meant to be. That's a longer story than you know …." He decided to stop any explanation.

"But you're just going to throw me out the door for your women?" She still looked at the floor.

"Oh, jeez no, honey. I thought you were throwing *me* out … for your friends. You can't seem to get away from me fast enough. I thought I was just trying to make it easy for you, so you wouldn't feel bad about leaving me."

"You're the one who's leaving *my* life. It's like you died, too, just like Mom." Her words hit him like a punch in the chest. Only minutes before, he'd been the head of the house, explaining just how things were to his daughter. Now he was spiraling away from her, confused and hurt by what she'd said. He was disappointed with himself like never before. He was a poor father. Big Ole would never have found himself in a conversation like this. He backed slowly toward his bedroom.

"I love you, honey," he said quietly when he reached the door to his room. All he could think to do was to give her some room to grow.

~

Susan's answering machine indicated that there were two messages waiting for her when she plopped onto her couch after a long day at work. She put her feet up, kicked her shoes off, and checked the messages. Both were from Ellen Hutchinson.

Ellen had called several times since they'd returned from Spider Lake. Susan sensed that Ellen's gestures of friendship were genuine, and she'd begun to enjoy her conversations with the First Lady. She'd called Ellen once, just to chat, and she'd been invited to the White House once, just for coffee with Ellen and a visit.

Susan picked up the phone and called the number she'd been given, even though it was after 10:00 p.m. A White House secretary asked her to hold, and momentarily she was greeted by the First Lady. "Hello, Susan?"

"Yes. I just got home and thought I'd return your call."

"Thank you. It's nothing important. Thom and I were just talking earlier. He laughs every time he talks about Will and Grant, and our visit to Spider Lake. Anyway, we were talking about you and your most recent visit there, and I just decided to call and chat for a while. Did you have a nice time?"

"Certainly did." Susan went on to tell Ellen about the boat rides and the hot tub. She felt like a college girl giggling with her dormitory roommate as she described her experiences. She started to tell Ellen about Emil's Café, then the chewing tobacco and the information she'd uncovered because of it. Her own laughter, and caution, slowed the story as she searched for just the right words. Then she just decided to quote Will.

Ellen laughed out loud when the story was complete. "So they were duck hunting when that happened?" she asked.

Susan heard something in the background on Ellen's end. "Ellen?" she asked.

"Yes?"

"The President is right there, isn't he?"

"Yes."

"And he knows what I just told you?"

"Yes."

"Does he look angry?"

"No. He's mumbling about it not being much use to you. Says it's not a secret with national security concerns, not a picture the public wants painted, either." Ellen's tone was still light hearted.

"Would you ask him an unrelated question, Ellen?" Susan wanted to offer something of an olive branch as she changed the subject.

"Yes."

"Ask him if he's ever been to Emil's Café."

Susan could hear a man's voice in the background. Ellen sounded confused when she repeated the answer. "He wants to know if Emil still has the critter that looks like he wants to fight you for your breakfast."

"Tell him yes!" Susan thought the conversation was beginning to take on a very strange character. She asked haltingly, "Ellen, is the President, like, standing there in his boxers listening to you as we speak?"

Ellen covered the phone, and Susan heard laughter on her end. "He says you know too much already! But he wants to know if you're planning any more time in Minnesota."

"Yes! I'm going to take a week's vacation there next month."

After more muffled conversation on Ellen's end, she returned to the phone. "He just raised his eyebrows and smirked!"

"I'll tell you all about it when I get back, Ellen!" When she hung up the phone, she couldn't help but think how much she'd changed since she'd met Grant Thorson.

~

Petra Vanderhoft sat rigidly in a high-backed chair designed for a sitting room and covered in a floral pattern. Her office was neat and tastefully decorated. There was a feminine feel to it but Susan always felt obligated to maintain proper decorum when she entered. "I've noticed something different about the President recently," Ms. Vanderhoft began.

Several staff writers considered their reply but waited for someone else to begin.

"He seems more confident, but I couldn't tell you why," one of them offered.

"Yes. He seems to answer questions more quickly ... his posture seems to have changed. He looks taller. Sounds funny, doesn't it?" another added.

"He's been spending a lot of time with the Joint Chiefs, and some meetings with the other military brass, but that's all I've got for now," the final member of the meeting shrugged.

Susan also felt she'd seen Thom Hutchinson change. But she didn't know if the change was in her eyes or in the President. "I don't know. I'm not sure what I see." She elected to abstain for now.

Ms. Vanderhoft briefly discussed the direction of several breaking stories and how she wanted them examined. Then she dismissed the group from her office.

"Please wait just a moment, Susan," she said.

Susan lingered by the door of the office. When the others had left, Petra Vanderhoft said, "Surely you see a change in the President."

"Well, yes. But I have to question my own objectivity a little bit. You know, I've gotten somewhat involved with a friend of the President's."

"Yes." Petra Vanderhoft did not hide her disdain. "And be careful there, Susan ... if I may offer an opinion."

"It's all right. He really is a nice man."

Ms. Vanderhoft turned her head and asked in a sly voice, "Is he a good lover?"

"I can't tell you — I don't know." Susan raised one eyebrow as she stared at her boss ... her friend. "He said everyone got hurt once when he got love and sex mixed up." Susan enjoyed sharing that comment with Petra Vanderhoft.

"Hmm ... I don't think I've heard that one before."

chapter TWENTY-SIX

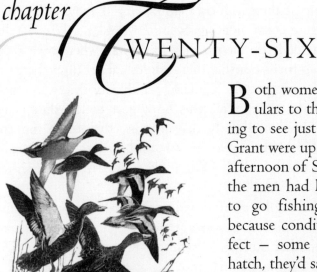

Both women raised binoculars to their eyes, straining to see just what Will and Grant were up to. On the first afternoon of Susan's vacation, the men had left them alone to go fishing for a while because conditions were perfect — some sort of insect hatch, they'd said.

Grant stood in the front of the little boat, fly casting and occasionally catching a sunfish. Will sat with his feet over the gunwale, his weight back in his chair, throwing minnows into the air for Nellie to catch. They were both talking and laughing from time to time.

"I wish we could hear what they're saying," Susan said.

"I don't know if you'd really want that," June added. They both stared at the green boat in the distance.

~

"Hey, I've got one for you," Will said as he reached for another minnow. A rambling conversation had slowly drifted to the business of dentistry. "I had one of the guys that work at the Duluth water filtration plant in my office the other day for a post-operative check. You won't believe what he told me."

"Oh yeah?" Grant threw a small sunfish back into the lake. "You want to fish for a while?"

"No, you go ahead. Anyway, my patient tells me that some clown showed up at the filtration plant asking if maybe the guys had seen a denture come floating by in the sewage. My guy tells him that they actually do have a shelf on a wall where they keep all the trophies. It turns out that there are several dentures there on the shelf. Apparently people regularly get drunk, throw up, and flush their dentures away. Well, this bozo goes to the shelf, says 'there it is!' and tosses one of the dentures directly into his mouth! It had been plucked from a river of shit, and the guy just put it in his mouth and walked out!" Will looked over his shoulder at Grant. "You believe that?"

"Yeah. Good thing he didn't accidentally grab the wrong denture ... might have picked up some germs," Grant smiled as he set the hook on another sunfish. "Reminds me of something Dr. Ruminsky said to someone once in clinic at dental school."

"What was that?"

Grant false cast the fly line several times. As the small white fly hit the water along the weed bed, he said, "The first thing you learn in dentistry is to always wash your hands before you go to the bathroom!"

Will only smiled, then added, "I always liked that guy."

"You know, things have really changed since his day." Grant continued to fly cast.

"Whadya mean?"

"He practiced his whole life with no interference from insurance companies or state bureaucracies!"

"Yeah, dentistry was better then."

"Everything was better then." A fish struck at Grant's fly, and Grant missed when he tried to set the hook. He stripped the line in slowly and decided to change flies.

"OK, Doctor, with all of this in mind, you know we work way too hard. We need to get into something more profitable," Will opined.

"Yeah?" Grant sensed that Will was headed somewhere with this. He took a small popper from the fly box and tied it to his line.

"Yeah. I'm thinkin' we should publish a men's magazine – a sportsman's magazine with universal appeal to all real outdoorsmen." Will's words oozed sarcasm.

"Sort of a huntin', fishin', porno thing I suppose?" Grant guessed. He didn't look up from the small knot he was tying.

"You got it, pard!" Will pointed at Grant enthusiastically.

"Got a name and a format picked out?" Grant asked. Again, he assumed he was to be the straight man. He pulled the knot tight with his teeth.

"Oh yeah." Will looked up into space, put his hands together, and separated them as though he was reading his magazine's front page at that moment. Grant stopped and looked at him.

"*Guns and Pussy,*" Will said proudly, with wonder in his voice. He radiated satisfaction, like a TV evangelist who'd just delivered his best line.

Grant burst out laughing. He knew Will secretly enjoyed the redneck element that shared his interest for the outdoors. Will kept a straight face. "Yeah," he continued as if he were really onto something now. "We'll have intellectual articles about deer rifles, bass lures, and four-wheel-drive vehicles. Probably have an interview each month with someone famous. I'd stick with tournament walleye fishing champions or porno stars to start with – of course, we'll be the only outdoor journal with a centerfold. I'm thinking something unique … like some babe wearing nothing but GORE-TEX boots and camouflage ass thong while she stands on the bow of her new bass boat and throws plugs into a weedline, casting for muskies." Grant was nodding his head and trying to appear to be listening seriously.

"Of course, you'd be in charge of the literature and editorial content," Will continued.

"You mean stuff like letters to the editor? 'Dear *Guns and Pussy* ... Last fall I was in the woods guttin' this deer I'd just blasted with my new .90-caliber assault rifle and all of a sudden these two chicks drive up alongside me in a shiny new three-quarter-ton, four-wheel-drive pickup truck with fog lights and a winch on the front. The driver was a blonde with some nice bumpers herself. She said she thought her rear end needed some attention, and would I crawl underneath and have a look. Well, after a few minutes under her hood ..." Grant stopped and raised his eyebrows. "You mean stuff like that?"

"Yes! Meaningful contributions by actual readers, from their real-life outdoor experiences ... you just have to make 'em all up!"

Both minds were racing with ideas for their magazine for a while. But soon enough they were both staring silently at their hands again.

"You wanna keep any fish?" Grant asked.

"No, I hate to clean those little peckers you catch. ... You ever think about Anne?"

"Some ... that was a really bizarre sentence, Will." Grant continued his casting, still not looking at Will.

"She was pretty." Another minnow sailed through the air toward Nellie. Will pushed Grant for an answer. "Do ya?"

"Yeah ... I still have feelings for her."

Will looked back. "You do seem to attract beautiful women."

"Yeah, that is true," Grant said as he landed and released a sunfish. "Women do find me irresistible. I think it's my big ... boat."

Will belched a loud belch with his mouth open — "right" — then looked over his shoulder at Grant. "Need another beer?"

"Sure!" Grant replied.

"Get me one, too, will ya?"

Several more minutes passed before Will ended the silence with "how many?"

"Huh?"

"How many women?"

"You're asking me how many women I've had?"

"Yeah."

"Why would you ask me that?"

"Just curious."

"Kind of personal, isn't it?"

"Remember, I am a doctor."

"OK. Well, let's see ..." Grant looked off into the sky after he'd rested the fly rod under his arm. He began to whisper to himself, and when Will looked at him he began to tap his fingers and whisper numbers just under his breath. "No, that doesn't count except in several western states." He backed up one finger and then resumed mumbling his count. When he'd tapped every finger on both hands twice, he stopped: "Two."

"I'm disappointed." Will turned around. "I was hoping for something more spectacular. What about Susan?"

"Sorry, pard."

"It's OK," Will sighed.

"You know, when I was with Anne, like that, it seemed like we were each taking something from the other. That make sense to you?"

"I'm trying to imagine it all right now." Will flipped another minnow to Nellie.

Grant could only smile at Will's expectations. "So how about you? How many women for you?"

Will mumbled something.

"Pardon me?"

Will mumbled again, still facing Nellie.

"Didn't catch that," Grant begged.

"ONE!"

Grant turned back toward the fish that were rising to the surface in front of the boat. He started false casting once again. Then he began to laugh out loud.

~

Will and Grant returned from the lake with no fish. They showered for dinner and met again on the porch of the Big House.

June and Susan were standing just within earshot of them when the men started the barbecue, and the women then overheard a common conversation.

Will opened a beer and said, simply, "'57 Braves."

Grant responded with "'65 Twins."

"Gonna kick your ass," Will said.

"No way," Grant replied, then took the beer from Will's hand and tossed back a big swallow.

"Who's pitchin'?" Will took his beer back and finished it.

"Mudcat Grant."

"Love that name. I'll throw Spahn. Behind the plate?" He opened another beer.

And they continued through their lineups like they always did.

Eventually Susan and June moved to the kitchen, and Susan asked, "Is that some sort of male bonding?"

June shook her head. "I think it's just penis envy."

For Susan, dinner at the lake had now become the casual thing it was for the others. With her frequent visits and deepening friendship with Grant, she'd become one of them ... almost. Will and June treated her as an insider now. All four of them sat on the porch and chatted while they watched the potatoes and the rib eyes cook on the grill. When the steaks were done, they all sat at the table on the porch and ate dinner slowly. The conversation restricted itself to the four of them, to Spider Lake, and to the little world around them. They ate with their elbows on the table, they sipped at cold beer, and they laughed together.

Susan enjoyed sitting on the porch of the Ordway house and listening to banter that ranged from the duck hunting in the old days to the current duck population. The boys were beginning to plan hunting days in the autumn already.

"I guess I don't understand the fascination with hunting," Susan said while they leaned on the table and finished dinner. "I mean, I don't have any real objection to the killing. I just don't understand what it is that would make you get up in the middle of the night and sit in a freezing wind and think you're having fun." She kept eating; she really hadn't been calling for an answer. Her question had been mostly a rhetorical one. She continued a moment later. "Wouldn't it be a lot cheaper just to go buy some liver?" she asked as she smiled at June.

Grant slid his plate forward and put his elbows on the table. He was smiling a faint smile and staring at his plate when he started talking. "I shot a hole in my dad's car once, when I was a kid." He was still looking at his plate ... something in Susan's words had jogged a memory loose. The others all turned to him.

"Little Ole Hokanson and my dad took me pheasant hunting when I was nine years old." Grant looked at Susan. "Ever wonder why they called my dad "Big" Ole? He wasn't that big you know." He raised his eyebrows with the question. "His best friend – I guess he was a father figure for my dad – was a little old man who lived just north of us, named Ole Hokanson ... so they just became Big Ole and Little Ole." Grant looked back at his plate and continued.

"Anyway, I shot a pheasant." Grant turned to Will with a big smile, "Ground pounded him ... I could never have hit a moving rooster! When dad picked up that bird, he was so swollen with pride, he looked at little Ole and held up the bird. "'Nice shootin',' he said to me." Grant's eyes were focused several decades in the past as he continued.

"They were both making a big deal of my shooting and naturally I was excited. When I got back in the car, I put my gun, a little old 410, in its case and rested it between my legs. We'd driven about a hundred feet when there was an enormous "BOOM!" in the car. Both of their heads almost spun off when they turned to look at me. The barrel of my gun was about six inches from my dad's butt, pointed at the floor, and I'd forgotten to unload it ... it went off. Dad jumped out of the car and whipped open my door to see if I was all right." Grant shook his head a little and smiled.

"Boy, his face was busy. I could see anger, relief, fear ... everything. Little Ole was pretty calm, though. He told me to get out and unload my gun. When I got out, Dad was already on his knees looking under the car. There were carpet strands hanging down through the hole I'd made. I could feel the back of my throat tighten, and then I started to cry. Dad was so pissed. I'd forgotten all of the gun safety stuff he'd been preaching. The anger was rising to the top for Dad. 'Let's go home,' he snapped. He sure wanted to say more. Little Ole was trying to calm him down.

"When we reached Ole's place to drop him off, no one had spoken for a few minutes. The car was full of dust, which was coming through the hole I'd made and making Dad even more pissed." Grant put the palm of his hand on his forehead and rubbed it for a moment. The others waited for him to continue.

"When the moment came for Little Ole to get out, he turned to Dad and said, 'Wanna see if there are any ducks on the pond?' His eyes were pleading with my dad ... pleading for a chance for redemption for me. Dad looked at Ole, then at me. He didn't give up the angry look, but he said, 'OK.'

"We all walked down to a small livestock pond in Little Ole Hokanson's pasture. It was surrounded by tall grass on three sides, and Little Ole had built a duck blind there. We all sat down on the wooden bench inside the blind and began to talk after a while. Eventually there was a sense of forgiveness in that little blind. Then the Oles even began to joke a little. There was not a hint of a duck in the sky, though, and they were laughing and talking about lunch.

"We were sitting in the little blind, talking and not paying much attention, when Dad suddenly ducked and said, 'Shhh.' Off in the distance were two geese heading our way. They were real low and coming straight toward us. Little Ole kept a sandwich in his hand and motioned for me to get ready as we all shortened our necks and hid. My hands were a little shaky as I slid a couple of shells into the 410. I had no idea what a waste of time it was for me to take a shot at these big honkers with such a little gun.

"Dad and I were shoulder to shoulder and peeking through the grass as the two geese approached. He was whispering to me to stay still and stay calm. The honkers were silent as they sailed up to us, but they were so big that I wanted to shoot when they were still about six hundred yards away. I'd only shot at pheasants that were rapidly moving away from me, and waiting just didn't feel right. 'Not yet, not yet, not yet … when I say OK, you take one and I'll take the other,' Dad whispered." Grant looked at Will and smiled.

"Finally he said OK when they were almost on top of us. We fired a barrage, and one goose folded immediately. The other one fluttered and glided toward the tall grass on the other side of the pond. Dad turned to me and hollered, "You got him!" The guy was a genius. Took me about fifteen years to figure out that he'd shot them both. 'You take one and I'll take the other.' Right! But I fell for it, and then I was on top of the world again.

"Way across the pond, we could see the wounded goose running in the grass. Little Ole took the gun from me and growled, 'Go get him!' – just like he was talking to a dog. So I took off like a shot without giving it much thought. It never occurred to me that the honker would do anything but surrender, just put up his hands and then be dead.

"I was in for such a surprise." Grant still stared at the table in front of him. "As I raced around the corner of the pond where the cattle had flattened the grass, I could see that honker was still making his way through the tall grass as he headed for the pond. I decided to position myself in his path, then crouched in the grass and hid. About three seconds later, the goose burst through the grass right in front of me and I grabbed him. The whole process of fetching the honker had happened so fast, and this was my first close encounter with a goose. Maybe the way my pheasant had died had led me to believe that the goose would give up the same way.

"No such luck. What happened next absolutely terrified me. The instant I got my arms around the goose, I was surprised at how big he was. But before I had time to think much about his size, he turned his head, opened his mouth, and clamped onto my nose. It scared the hell out of me, and it hurt. He was making funny noises and shaking his head. Initially, I thought he'd just give my nose a good squeeze and then run away when I let go of him. But after I released my grip on him, the horrible reality of the situation hit me.

"The whole thing had been a trick. He'd just faked injury to draw me out of the blind. Now the brute had me, and his plans were very clear: He intended to swallow me head first and then fly off ... or maybe he'd shake me senseless and then fly away while clutching me in his webbed talons, only to eat me when he got back to his nest high atop a rocky cliff." Susan and June were chuckling now. Will smiled a wide smile.

"So this was the end for me? Life had been so short. I just wasn't ready to go yet. I'd been letting the goose push me around out of some sort of timid resignation. But now, suddenly, I was really angry – or maybe I was scared ... I can't always tell the difference. A wild feeling sort of flooded through me, and a guttural scream began to erupt from deep inside of me. My right hand was around his neck, and my left was on the top of his right wing when I felt my strength come to me. He was pushing me backwards and shaking me when I squeezed both hands as hard as I could and flipped him backwards over the top of me. It was a move that I'd seen Chief Wahoo McDaniel use on Scrap Iron Kadaski once. Although I hadn't had the benefit of throwing him off of the top turnbuckle, the move worked for me, too. When I landed on my back, I heard my attacker sort of splat. He sounded like a bag of water when he hit the ground, and the impact caused him to lose his grip on my nose. I was up and ready for a fight to the death now. The goose was up again and looking at me, too. I was crouched and slowly circling as I wondered what Wahoo would do next? The pile driver? The airplane spin?"

Grant seemed animated now. He smiled and looked at all of them. He gestured with his hands and continued his story. "Suddenly, Dad had the honker in his big right hand. He'd just walked right past me and quickly wrung the neck of that evil bird. Then he smiled an enormous smile and said, 'Nice work.' There was softness in his eyes, and his hands were so tender as he knelt in front of me and began to inspect my nose and wipe the blood away from it. It must have been sort of a curious exchange as we beheld each other. He was on one knee and we were nose to nose. I was so serious, almost breathless, after my battle with the killer goose. And Dad seemed so ... I don't know ... amused. He was reaffirming his love for a child who was sort of lost in that time between man and boy. He had me cleaned up in no time. As we walked back toward the blind, he held up the goose for Little Ole to see, just like he'd done with the pheasant.

"They both smiled and then laughed out loud when I told about my fight with the big bruiser. I thought they were laughing *with* me, but they were laughing *at* me." Grant looked away from the table sheepishly. "This time there were no distractions like lunch or accidental shootings. We all sat together by Little Ole's pond and told stories for a while as the afternoon shadows lengthened. I was part of the group when that day ended. I belonged. I'd drawn blood and been bloodied."

Grant was staring out the window at Spider Lake; his smile was gone. "Sometimes now, I can't remember what my dad's face looked like. Isn't that odd?" His tone became mournful. "But then I remember how he looked at me after I'd been wrestling with that goose." Grant's eyes were filled with tears when he turned to Susan. "I see his eyes ... I see it all every time. That's my special memory of my dad." Grant began to wipe the tears from his face. He did not speak for a moment, and then he turned to Susan. "Answer your question?" He was working hard to stuff his emotions again.

She reached her hand to the back of his neck and nodded. Susan hadn't felt this sort of pain at her own father's death.

~

The dented aluminum canoe still slid smoothly through the flat black water. A nearly full moon was about to rise over the eastern tree line, but for now the lake was dark. Their voices were the only sounds on Spider Lake.

"So how did you come to name Nellie?" she asked.

"I wanted a baseball name."

"And?"

"Not many good female baseball names."

"And?"

"There was a second baseman for the White Sox when I was a kid ... Nelson Fox."

"And?"

"Nellie Fox ... Nellie! Her AKC-registered name is Misty's Nelson Fox. Nellie ... see? I still have Nellie Fox's baseball card. He always had a chew in his cheek — a big chew. I loved his card."

"You really haven't let go of your childhood."

"Don't plan to, either." Grant could see Susan's silhouette against the moon on the horizon. The water gurgled gently over their paddles. "He died of lip cancer you know."

"Who?"

"Nelson Fox ... Nellie Fox. I just thought I'd share that to help you make a healthy decision about continuing your use of tobacco."

"Thank you, Doctor."

"You're welcome."

Usually Grant liked to point out wildlife or share some of the lore of the north woods, but tonight he kept silent for a while as the canoe moved across the lake. Susan always seemed interested in the things of the outdoors. He was impressed that a city girl took such an interest in the wild. Susan was enjoying the quiet of this night also, and neither of them spoke again until they'd finished their circle of the lake.

Susan lifted herself out of the canoe and then let her feet remain on the canoe seat while she sat on the dock.

"Hey!" she called to him as he tied his end of the canoe to the dock.

"Yeah." He placed his paddle under his seat and looked at her.

"I need to ask you something. Remember a while back when we talked about the things we dream of … hope for?"

"Yeah."

"You didn't finish your dream. What was the end of it? You know, the one about sitting on the porch in the morning?"

"You're the one who had a pretty lame answer to the dream question. You tell me first."

"I dream of you … all the time. This place, too," she blurted as she tried to read his eyes in the starlight. With his elbows on his thighs and a canoe paddle still in his hands, Grant only looked at his hands. Then he began to speak, very slowly.

"You probably don't know it, but when you touch me I get butterflies in my stomach … still. The time you rested your foot on mine and told me you loved me … unbelievable." He shook his head slowly but did not look up when he started again. "I dream about those mornings when the sun peeks over the pines and into my room. I dream that I'll wake up and feel your toes touching me."

"My toes?" She smiled with her question.

"Other things, too … I've got butterflies just telling you about it." Now he looked up at her with a huge smile.

When they returned to the cabin, only the light above the kitchen sink was on, and they left it that way. While Susan was standing at the sink rinsing a glass, Grant found himself staring at her back. She was barefoot, wearing cotton shorts and a T-shirt. He felt a rush inside of himself and walked directly to her. Ingrid was in Minneapolis and would be there for the week; they had the place to themselves.

The instant she felt him behind her, she knew what he wanted. Slowly, he reached both hands under her shirt and brought them up to her breasts. When she raised her head and leaned back in a submissive posture, he kissed her cheek. His right hand slid down her stomach and inside her pants. She spread her legs to let him explore and purred softly.

"Remember that stuff about having sex and love mixed up?" he whispered.

"Yes."

"Well, forget that!"

She turned her face slowly toward his. He could see a smile, but he could also see pleasure and desire on her face. Her eyes were closed when she brought her mouth to his. She whispered "good" and then shuddered as he caressed her.

The blue light of a summer evening poured through the large window in the bedroom. Grant raised himself to his knees and looked down at Susan. She lay on her back, with her arms extended above her toward the headboard. He moved himself slowly in and out of her, and she moaned softly. He touched her legs, her breasts, her face, her arms. She moved her hips slowly, as if to pull him into her more deeply. Her eyes were closed, but in the dim light he could read the intense pleasure in her beautiful face.

To be sure, this was sex — as good as it could ever be. But this was love. This angel, writhing with passion underneath him, was in love with him, too. She laughed and joked and cried with him. It felt soothing when she rubbed the back of his neck or touched his arm. Just the feel of her bare foot on his sent a thrill through him. He even felt himself get dreamy eyed sometimes when he watched her walk or talk. This union with her was so good it was nearly unbearable. He sensed that in her submission, her taking him in, they were each giving each other something — something powerful.

She opened her eyes and saw that he was looking at her. Only the hint of a smile mixed with the ecstasy on her face. Susan brought her hands to his sides and pulled him onto her. Her tongue was waiting for him when their mouths met. She clutched his back tightly and they held an intense, exploring kiss. She shuddered and moaned loudly as he spent himself inside her.

"I love you," he whispered into her ear when their passion began to ebb.

Almost on cue, a loon called from far away. Just one long hail call, one lonesome note, as if the loon were trying to say he felt the same way. They both began to laugh at the timing, and then laughed even more at the odd sensation of laughing while they were still one.

chapter TWENTY-SEVEN

The celebration was called Muskie Days. Most small communities in the Midwest have some sort of celebration or promotion just like it. All resort towns like Walker have them. There were floats with bizarre-looking papier-mâché fish being pulled by tractors and old cars driven by local merchants with kids in the back seat throwing candy to smaller kids along the street.

Walker had a square dance club that sponsored a float with four couples square dancing on a flatbed trailer to faint music coming from a too-small boom box on the flat bed. One of the women dancing on the flatbed was about sixty — at least that's what Grant guessed by looking at her from a distance. But he couldn't look away from her as the trailer rolled by. She had a black wig with a large "afro" look to it. Her legs were lean and muscular, and she wore a very short skirt. Grant thought her legs made her look about thirty. When she smiled, Grant almost laughed out loud; she had a terrible upper denture that made her appear to be in her eighties. He could not take his eyes off of her or stop smiling.

389

"That one has some hard miles on her," someone said from the crowd just behind Grant. He turned and saw Frank Campbell smiling at him. "She's been around for a while."

"Hi, Frank!" Grant said when Frank stepped up next to him. "She a friend of yours?"

"No. Let's just say a contemporary. She's not much younger than me. I've seen her around town forever. Looks like she needs to meet you ... but then maybe you did that fine work?"

"No, definitely not," Grant shook his head in denial. "So what are you doing in town? You didn't come in for the parade, did you?"

"Evie sent me to the store for some groceries. I gotta go. See you later."

"Bye, Frank."

Two marching bands came after the square dancers float, and as always the marinas were showing off shiny new boats in the procession.

Grant stood on Main Street with his hands in his pockets, watching his friends, both in the parade, and watching along the street. He'd closed the office for ninety minutes to enjoy the Muskie Days parade. He wished Susan could see this little slice of Americana; he knew she'd love it.

It was a warm, late-summer day. Grant thought he might go fishing after work, or maybe do some work on the duck blind. He thought of the passionate weeks he'd had with Susan recently. She'd returned to Spider Lake for a long weekend, and they'd met for a few days in Chicago. She made him happy. He loved her.

He greeted his neighbors when they passed and chatted politely with whoever stopped to talk. And for a while he thought of nothing but his little town. This was what he'd wanted for his life to be. It was what he'd had for so many years, before all the changes.

Suddenly there was a hand around his shoulder. When he turned to look, Ingrid's smiling face was only inches from his. "Hi, Dad!" She was leaning on him and smiling. A quickly melting ice cream cone rested in her other hand. She'd found a job in one of the many gift shops on Main Street. She was working with some older woman and some college girls, and she seemed to be liking it. She'd made a few new friends, grown up a little, and appeared less annoyed by her father all the time. He thought she was still far more concerned about her friends, though.

"Hi, honey!" Grant smiled. He began to feel his chest swell. He was happy that Ingrid had sought him out and acknowledged him ... in public. If only all of these people could know that this beautiful, charming young woman with her arm around him was his daughter! He wished he could holler and tell everyone in town to look, quickly, to see that his daughter liked him. Grant wanted to tell her how much the small gesture meant to him, but he knew it would be better left unsaid. He wondered briefly if she might be proud of him, too. 'Probably too much to ask for,' he thought. "Better not get my hopes up too high, could be she's only here because she's about to ask for money."

Grant was scolding himself for being so cynical when Ingrid spoke again.

"Whadya hear from Susan?" He tried to hide his surprise — Ingrid had never asked about Susan before.

"Talked to her last night ... samo, samo. That's good I guess." He was glad she'd asked, but he tried not to show his pleasure. When he turned to face his daughter now, he saw a little girl. She had ice cream on her chin, and she'd be embarrassed when he told her, but he just looked at her for a moment and grinned. He knew that others, especially men, saw her as a voluptuous woman. And that was OK, he reasoned, the way it was supposed to be. But he still saw a little girl, or at least someone stuck between child and adult. He was grinning at her when he wiped the ice cream from her chin.

"I knew that was there," she said with a big smile. She'd had no idea. He stared and smiled a corny smile. Grant wondered if what she saw in his eyes was what he'd seen in big Ole's all those years ago. "Parade's over, Dad, back to work!"

"Got a kiss for your dad?"

"No!" She stepped back, then looked left and right like a burglar. "Eeeyooo. Someone would see." She shook her head in disgust.

Grant was embarrassed at her response; he thought everyone around them had to have seen it, too.

"Gotta go." She turned and walked away.

Grant raised his chin. He was about to call out "I love you, honey." But suddenly he was afraid she'd ignore him. He froze and watched her walk away from him. She'd hurt his feelings again.

~

The sports page was spread out on the booth table in front of him. A gentle rain fell on the sidewalk outside the window of Emil's Café while Grant drank his coffee and read. Hilda Krause moved as she always did — not really waddling but perhaps lumbering toward Grant. She held a telephone in her hand. Grant thought for sure it was going to be bad. It was always bad when someone brought a phone his way.

Once again this morning, a patient had cancelled her appointment at the last minute, leaving Grant with an hour to waste, so he'd walked across the street to Emil's for coffee. Summer would be winding down soon, and the conversations at Emil's today were mixed between late-season walleye fishing, early-season duck hunting, and the Vikings' chances for a winning season.

He took the phone from Hilda, thanked her, and put it to his ear. "Dr. Thorson," he said almost defensively.

"It's me. I had to call you right away and tell you ... or did you hear the news?" It was Susan.

"The Twins traded for a left-handed starter?"

"You haven't heard, have you?"

"No, who'd they get?"

She ignored him. "You would not have believed it. The guy has nerves of steel. I was so wrong about him on that score."

"OK, maybe you should start again." Grant folded the newspaper and leaned back.

"Well, I was at the White House last night for another one of the President's parties ... like the one where I met you."

"Yeah? Was Myron Bentley there?" Grant interrupted.

"No. I don't know. Who cares?" She wanted to continue.

"How 'bout John Lewis?" he interrupted again, rubbing his eyes.

"I'm trying to be serious!"

"Sorry."

"Remember when the President had his hunting buddies join him for a moment in the Green Room?" Susan continued, back on track again.

"Yeah."

"Well, he invited me in with that bunch. He smiled and said that since I knew so many of his personal hunting anecdotes, maybe I'd like to join him. He can be pretty charming, but that's not why I called. Anyway, he laughed and joked and acted like he had all night to party with his pals." She stopped.

"Yeah?" Grant was still rubbing his eyes.

"Then he said he had to go upstairs for some business when the party started to wind down."

"Yeah?"

"Well, he excused himself politely and then went upstairs and invaded Columbia!"

"Huh?"

"No kidding! Turn on the TV. It's on every channel. Looks like some limited strike against the drug cartels and a response to the murder of some of our drug cops. Our government apparently found some way to view it as legal, and in we went. They passed a law down there a few years ago making extradition of criminals to this country illegal, you know.

"So what's gonna happen?"

"We'll be in and out in a couple of days and claim some sort of victory."

"Doesn't sound like you agree with the decision to go in."

"Oh, I don't know. That wasn't my point. I just couldn't believe how calm he was when he spoke with us ... while his people were planning an invasion! Balls of steel! I was wrong about him."

"So do great men rise to greatness? Or is greatness thrust upon ordinary men?" Grant asked rhetorically. He was looking at Spider Lake when he spoke.

"Well, I don't know that Thom is a great man, if that's what you mean. And I certainly don't know that he's done a great thing. But I actually have thought about that question quite a bit. I believe greatness is thrust upon ordinary men by outrageous fortune. The greatness of the man is measured by the strength of his response."

"Good answer."

"It was pretty good, wasn't it? You know, I was going to call you today anyway," she added.

"OH?"

"Yeah. I can get really good seats for the Orioles/Yankees series on the second weekend of September. Box seats. Interested? Besides, you haven't been out here since the health care committee broke up.

He knew he was interested; he knew he wanted to go with her. But he knew that Will and Frank were counting on him for the elk hunt in Colorado that weekend.

"I'll be there!" His world had shifted to a very tight orbit around Susan.

"OK, great. I have to get going. Talk to you later!"

"Hey!" He didn't know if she'd hung up or not.

"Yeah?

"That's only a couple of weeks away ... we're gonna have a good time!"

"Yeah, looking forward to it. Love you. Gotta go! Bye!"

"Hey!" Once again he didn't know if she was still on the line.

"WHAT!" She was in a hurry to go somewhere — the White House, he presumed.

"Did you say 'I love you'?" Susan could hear him smile.

"Yes." Now she spoke the one word very slowly and let him hear her smile.

"I love you, too," he said in a loud voice. He then hurriedly hung up on her. He laughed out loud, and a self-satisfied smile curled his entire face. Then he looked to his right and saw that Hilda Krause was standing by his booth with a coffeepot. She was staring at him, and so was Emil from behind the counter. He knew he looked like an idiot now, judging by the expressions on their faces.

"More coffee, Doc?" she asked.

"Yeah, that'd be good." And he held his cup out toward her and tried to recover his composure.

~

It had been several weeks since Grant and Will had last spoken. June Campbell wore a sly, satisfied grin when she handed the phone to Will. "It's Grant," was all she said. Will had noticed that she'd been talking to someone for quite a while but never suspected that it might be Grant Thorson. Grant had just told June what he was about to tell Will.

"Hey, pard," Will said with a questioning look on his face. Grant and June never spoke for very long on the phone.

"Hi, Will. Some bad news, I think."

"You OK?" Will was truly puzzled now.

"Yeah, fine. But I'm gonna have to pull out of the Colorado trip." Grant's voice was level.

"Well, how come?"

"I'm going to D.C. to see Susan."

"Well, hell! See her some other time. What's wrong with you ... we're going hunting!"

"Gonna ask her to marry me."

Will did not respond.

"Still there, Will?"

June was sitting by Will, waiting to see his face when Grant told him. She knew when Will went silent that Grant had told him. She smiled even more broadly. Will shook his head and began to grin.

"Good for you!"

"Gonna be OK in Colorado without me?"

"Hell, yes!"

"Sure?"

"Hell, yes! So when did all of this happen?"

"Been thinking about it all for a while. I love her, Will. It's the real deal."

"We could see that a while ago," Will said, smiling at June.

"Seems like some smooth water on that long river, Will."

"Well, you were due for some."

"Yeah, we'll be fine ... if she'll have me."

The men talked for an hour — about everything that had happened in the last year, the last twenty-five years. Grant had an odd feeling, like a strong déjà vu, that they were repacking their gear as they did on canoe trips, before they ran rough water ... like they were checking to see that all was in order.

"Well, I guess we're all going different directions that weekend. You're going east, I'm going west, and June's going to the lake. Molly and Ingrid have some sort of weekend slumber party planned ... a bunch of girls for one last weekend of water skiing at the lake. You heard about all the plans, didn't you?"

"Yeah. That's why I was talking to June for so long ... wanted to be sure she was gonna be around to supervise the whole thing. Sounds like a party I would like to have crashed when I was a college boy."

"That's for sure!" Will changed his tone to say goodbye to Grant. "Hey, pard, I'm happy for you, you know that. I love you, buddy ... my best friend."

"Me too, Will ... my best friend, always. Keep your powder dry!"

"And yours!"

Several weeks passed, but very slowly, as summer faded and Grant marked the time until he could be with Susan again.

~

Standing with his hands in his pockets, Grant surveyed the small backyard of Susan's home in Georgetown. As he waited for Susan to get ready for the ball game, Grant felt the same as he had so many years before during the standard waiting period that all young men must oblige their girlfriends before a date. He liked the feeling.

The brick home was built around 1920, Grant thought. The style of that time had called for a driveway that extended behind the house so that a small car, like a Model "A" or "T," could be driven around to the back of the stately home and parked in a separate detached garage that usually looked like a stable.

The small yard was very green and neatly kept. He smiled when his eye came to the blue of a neighbor's hot tub. He wondered if anyone in this neighborhood would find charm in a pickle barrel hot tub with a wood stove built into it. The place did seem comfortable, he thought, and there was definitely a feel of affluence that didn't exist in Walker, Minnesota. But something else was there, too. It seemed suspended above him. It was something indefinable, but something that hovered over him and seemed to hold him in the small yard. Eventually he guessed that what he felt was the distant noise of engines ... and people. Airplanes and automobiles and industries left a muffled clatter of noise just beyond or above him. Back home, the song of a purple finch would carry all the way to his porch from the bird feeder by the lake. A loon's call would carry for a mile on a calm evening.

"What are you thinking about? Missing Spider Lake already?" Susan interrupted his thoughts when she appeared at the screen door that opened from her kitchen onto the small patio.

"No, not really," he smiled. "I can tell you one thing I noticed right away that's nice!"

"What's that?"

"No mosquitoes! I've been out here for ten minutes and haven't had to defend myself once. That would never happen at home."

"So there's something here that's better than Spider Lake?"

"I didn't say that."

"Well, let's go," Susan said as she walked onto the patio and kissed him. "There won't be any mosquitoes at the ball park, either, and maybe we'll even be there early enough to see batting practice." She wore shorts and a T-shirt with Cal Ripken's picture on it and a Baltimore Orioles baseball cap. Grant thought she looked great. She smiled what he thought was a mischievous smile, but he didn't think much of it. As they walked to her car, she passed close by him and he caught an odd scent in the air.

Each of them carried a light jacket but wore shorts, as they intended to stretch every moment that remained of summer. A clear evening began to turn golden as they rolled onto the highway.

Susan drove her car to the ball park and pointed out some landmarks as they drove. Grant was, as usual, lost in the big city and intimidated by the mass of humanity that swarmed around them. 'Man, there's a lot of people out here!' he said to himself. Susan only smiled. Several times he thought he noticed an odd odor while they were in the car. But he said nothing: His conscious brain made him disregard what his nose was telling him.

They stood in line to enter Camden Yards. Susan glanced at the hair on his legs, the way the muscles moved when he walked. When he could, Grant let his eyes linger on her hair, her legs, the soft skin on her face. He tried not to stare.

There was excitement in the air outside the ball park. They watched and listened as the crowd around them grew. Little boys pounded their gloves in anticipation while their fathers talked about starting pitchers. Grant bent over to say something to Susan.

He put his lips closer to her ear than he needed to; he intended to tell her he loved her.

"You look great. I love ...." He stopped suddenly and stood straight up. Then he bent over at the waist and sniffed her again. His brow furrowed for a moment, and then he began to smile. "Hoppe's #9! You've got Hoppe's #9 gun oil on, don't you?!"

"Thought you'd never notice!" she said with a sly grin. "They keep this stuff under lock and key down at Bubba's Assault Rifle Emporium. It must be good."

Grant laughed out loud. He could not stop chuckling. This intelligent, successful woman had remained playful enough to go to a gun shop and buy gun oil, then wear it as perfume just to make him laugh. He put his arms around Susan's waist and lifted her off the ground. With his nose behind her ear, he drew a deep breath for everyone else in line to hear and see. "You are the one. I love you," he said into her ear.

Camden Yards impressed Grant immediately as a fine ball park. It was a new park, but the beauty and grace of an earlier, simpler time had been built into it, and he loved that. Their seats that night belonged to some big Washington law firm. They sat in the front row, so close to the field that they could hear the players call to each other from around the dug out. Susan said she got the tickets from a friend at work.

The sounds of the ball park were all around them. Bats cracked and line drives flew from the cage at home plate while players took batting practice. Gloves popped as the players loosened their throwing arms. Food venders were calling to fans to buy beer and hot dogs. They'd come to the game earlier than most of the other fans, and they sat together eating bratwurst over napkins spread across their knees and watching the players warm up.

A very bowlegged black player with a potbelly that seemed out of place among the young players walked out in front of them. Grant lowered his brat and stared. Judging from his physique, he was too old to be a player. 'He must be a coach,' Grant thought. He wore catcher's shin guards and a facemask but no chest protector. The coach took his mask off and exposed a row of very white teeth.

"Nate!" Grant called. "Nate!"

The black man looked at Grant with a blank stare. Grant stood and waved and gestured for the man to come over to him.

"Nate!" Grant called once more. He stood and raised his arms to show himself. The black man's face spread into a huge smile, and he pointed at Grant. It looked like the man had twice as many white teeth as before, and he ran slowly to the railing in front of Grant.

When they shook hands, the black man said, "Been a long time. Last I heard you were a doctor or something and moved back to the woods." He smiled.

"No, I struck it rich in the lumber business ... bought the Orioles today. You're my catcher from here on. I don't care how old and shitty you are ... you're playing every day." Grant seemed serious. Susan didn't know what was going on. The man looked cautiously at Grant for a moment, and then he looked around the box seats where Susan and Grant were seated. For a moment, he almost believed Grant. "You're still full of it, too," he said, and he smiled again. "Bring your daughter to the game?" He gestured toward Susan.

Now Grant returned his smile. "Nate, this is my friend, Susan Wells. Susan, this is Nate Monroe. We were friends in college ... teammates!" Grant smiled and looked back and forth between them.

Nate Monroe had been a star catcher at the University of Minnesota when Grant was on the team. He'd been drafted high all those years ago, and he'd spent over a decade bouncing around the minor leagues. He'd been called up to the majors twice for several weeks each time. But he'd never caught on with anyone. He'd spent the last several years as the bullpen coach for the Orioles, and he had hopes to manage someday.

Susan watched Grant and Nate Monroe exchange stories about their college days. She read the happiness in Grant's eyes as Nate told about his life and then told a few stories about current Oriole players. She thought Grant looked happier tonight than she'd ever seen him.

"Hey, I gotta go to work. Nice to meet you, Susan," Nate said as he backed away from the railing. "Will I see you here again, Grant?" he asked.

"Yeah, I'm pretty sure. Bye, Nate!" Grant waved, and Nate ran to the bullpen with two very young-looking pitchers.

"He was the greatest player I ever saw," Grant said to Susan. "I thought for sure he'd make it in the big leagues." Grant shook his head as if he couldn't believe Nate Monroe had come up short.

"Maybe he just wasn't in the right place at the right time. Maybe greatness wasn't thrust upon him?" Susan smiled with her lips together.

"Yeah, maybe," Grant answered. "All he ever dreamed of was the big leagues. Funny how things turn out sometimes, huh?"

As the players were finishing their warm-ups, Grant couldn't help but think back to the Twins game he'd taken Kate to twenty-five years earlier. He'd told Kate that surely someday they'd see his friend Nate Monroe playing in the big leagues. He thought it was ironic, maybe sort of amusing; that once again life had reminded him that it had symmetry. His memory of Kate did not trigger any mournful feelings or misgivings about unfaithfulness. His memory of her was only happy, and he could let it be that way now. In fact, he smiled when he thought that once again love could turn a base-ball game into foreplay.

"Maybe you could have made it in the big leagues?" Susan asked it as if she believed what she'd said. Just that thought made him feel special all over again.

"No, no chance of that. I just wasn't that good ... barely made my college team." He raised his eyebrows and confessed his lack of talent. "But you know, when I played ball, I never needed to win ... to win the big game or even be in the big game. I suppose that really hurt my chances. But every swing I took in batting practice, every ground ball I played in the infield, every pitch I threw ... it was all great, just like it was the seventh game of the World Series. It was all joy for me." He looked down at his feet and then out across the park at Nate Monroe. "When I did get in the game, it was only that much better. It was the playing of the game that made me happy, not the winning. This game is like ducks over decoys, like life: It will humble you if you play it long enough. You play because you love the struggle, not the winning. Understand?" he asked Susan.

"Sure," Susan smiled, shrugging her shoulders. After a moment, she looked back at him. He seemed to be a thousand miles away, lost in his own thoughts as he stared across the infield.

"What are you thinking?" Susan cautiously interrupted what appeared to be a dream.

"Just thinking about Will. Don't know why, I guess. Maybe because he's the only other person I talk with about that sort of thing." Grant looked at her and grinned, almost sheepishly. She knew he was only smiling as he always did when he spoke of Will Campbell. "I'd run through Hell in a gasoline suit for him," Grant added, and then looked away. He was still smiling.

"Play ball!" They were close enough to hear the umpire call it out, and their attention quickly shifted to the action in front of them.

Susan held Grant's hand as the game began. She thought it was cute that he still enjoyed this game and the other games of life so much. She pretended to understand while he explained how the designated hitter had ruined the American League. She actually did understand somewhat when he told her about curveballs and fastballs and righty/lefty matchups that managers tried to create and avoid, and who should cover what base in what situation.

Grant could see that she was pretty ignorant of the subtleties of baseball, but he loved that she found adventure in the action, the crowd, and the color.

It turned out to be a good game, too. The Orioles took the lead in the bottom of the eighth, gave it up in the top of the ninth, and won on a throwing error, a double down the first baseline, and a play at the plate in the tenth. "Safe at home! That's the way all great games should end!" Grant said. He took her hand and smiled during the celebration at the end of the game.

~

When they returned to Susan's apartment, Grant was still talking about the mistake the losing manager had made in the defensive positioning of his players when the phone rang. As Susan went to answer it, he called after her, "That's the great thing about baseball; even some dentist from the outback can manage!"

Grant knew that sometime in the next hour he'd ask Susan to marry him, and he knew she'd say yes, and he knew everything was going to be fine again.

Susan returned with the phone. "It's for you." She looked reluctant to give it to him.

"Hello?"

"Grant?" It was June Campbell.

"Hey, June! How are things at the lake?" he said cheerily.

"I have some bad news for you." Her voice was empty, and it turned him cold.

Everything stopped for Grant Thorson. The whole world went silent. He knew there was death on the other end of the phone. He knew it was Ingrid. His little girl had been killed water skiing or drowned; he knew it before June said it.

"Oh, Jesus, June. What is it?" His voice trembled as he spoke. His legs were heavy and weak.

"Will is dead." Her voice was strong, which only made it all the more unbelievable.

"What?!" Grant's face contorted. Susan could see that something was dreadfully wrong.

"I don't know all of the details yet, but Frank accidentally shot him. He died this afternoon." June's voice remained solid, unwavering. The news was all the more terrible and unbelievable because of her strength.

"I can't believe it. I'm so sorry," he whispered. "I'll see you as soon as I can get there." He spoke the words as though he was trying to understand a riddle.

When he hung up the phone, he turned to Susan. "Will is dead … killed in a hunting accident … Frank." Susan put her hands to her face and began to cry. Grant felt weightless and heavy at the same time; it was all so unreal. He hoped this was a bad dream. He waited to wake up. He sat at the kitchen table and stared straight ahead. Susan was crying when she followed him into the kitchen. She stood beside him and said nothing. She wanted to touch him, to hold him, but he seemed to move or turn away from her whenever she approached him. When he did take her in his arms, she thought he felt weak, like a bad handshake. He still did not show any emotion, and he wasn't trying to hide anything now. A hole had opened up, and all of his feelings had just fallen out. He waited for tears, for some sort of anguish to come. But nothing did. "I can't believe it" was all he could say.

chapter TWENTY-EIGHT

Grant's Suburban rolled to a stop across the street from the church. He took a deep breath and let it out all at once. The days had passed very slowly since the accident. It had taken several days to bring Will's body back from Colorado. Grant could only wonder about the agonizing phone conversations June must have had while arranging the return of her husband's body and the planning of his funeral. Grant was sickened by the certainty that Frank saw something unthinkable every time he closed his eyes.

The day of his best friend's funeral had dawned gray and cold. Grant, Ingrid, and Susan arrived before everyone else. Will's body had been prepared for reviewal in a large room just off the narthex of a big Catholic church in Duluth. As the three of them entered the church, Grant became increasingly pensive. The place was silent except for some muted conversation coming from somewhere down a long hallway. He wasn't sure if he wanted to look at Will in his casket. The last time he'd seen Will was during Susan's vacation at Spider Lake, and he thought he'd like to preserve that memory along with all of the other happy memories he had of Will Campbell. He didn't want to have his last vision of Will be the way he looked in death. He imagined Will in a black suit with his hands crossed and resting on his stomach. He was afraid to see an unnatural look pushed onto Will's lifeless face. He knew that psychologists advise family members to look at loved ones in their coffins in order to bring closure, but he just didn't think he wanted to do it.

The question of looking or not looking was decided early for Grant. They stepped slowly around a corner, and sitting on an easel in the narthex was a large photo of Will. He was holding a stringer of ducks, and he seemed to be talking to the photographer. It was the perfect picture for that place and time. His smile was bright, and his warm personality seemed to jump from the photo. Grant recognized the photo immediately — he'd been the photographer! Will was talking to him.

For the first time since he'd heard the news of Will's death, Grant felt the full weight, the reality of it all. He went outside and put his face in his hands. Until this moment, there had been no need to hide his feelings. There had been no emotion. Now he sat there and choked back the anguish and the pain. He swallowed hard and grimaced. Several times he thought he might break, but he sat stiffly on a wooden bench beside a little fountain and fought back everything that wanted to bust out of him. Susan and Ingrid left him alone for a moment while they made their way to the little room just off the narthex where Will Campbell's family stood around his open casket and greeted visitors.

Death was so silent, Susan thought as she took her turn and looked at Will.

Susan returned to Grant in a few minutes. She stood beside him, then touched his shoulder. "He looks nice. Do you want to see?"

"No. I won't see him again." Grant never raised his head, and he never did look at his friend in death.

The huge Catholic church was full for the funeral. Will Campbell was one of the most universally well-liked men Grant had ever known. Ellen Hutchinson entered with several Secret Service agents and then sat with Grant and Ingrid and Susan. The President was unable to attend; he'd spoken with June on the phone for nearly an hour two days before. Grant barely spoke to Ellen ... barely spoke at all. He knew that an embrace with Ellen, or anyone else for that matter, would cause him to lose the handle on his grief. He would not give God or anyone else the chance to see him weep, to lose control, ever again.

There were so many young people at the funeral, Grant thought. More than half of those teenagers were girls – probably friends of Will's daughters. All of the young girls were crying. Then Grant began to notice couples ... couples of all ages ... gray-haired couples, middle-aged couples, what looked like young married, and a few that seemed to be high school sweethearts.

The priest spoke about what a fine man Will Campbell was. Several people got up and sang, and someone read some verses from the Bible. For Grant, the service began to pass like a TV movie that he wasn't really paying attention to.

Grant looked around at all of the couples. He looked at June, sitting beside Molly. He looked at Frank and Evie. Exactly half of these people would someday be grieving like June was today ... like he'd done himself not that long ago. They'd sit there and feel like their insides had been removed. The best thing in their lives would be ripped away. Then they'd just find someone new to love and wait to have their insides ripped out all over again. Or maybe they'd watch their father's life ebb away in a nursing home that smelled like shit. Maybe there would be an unspeakable accident and their best friend would be killed by their own father.

It all seemed inevitable. That same old current, the unstoppable current of that long river, was still carrying Grant Thorson.

He was staring at his hands when he heard it. The first few notes of "Christian Island" rang slowly through the sanctuary.

Then the lyrics:

> *I'm sailing down the summer wind*
> *I got whiskers on my chin*
> *And I like the mood I'm in*
> *As I while away the time of day*
> *In the lee of Christian Island*

Grant turned to look at June. She was already facing him from across the aisle. She brought a handkerchief to her face, and through her own tears her eyes told him everything. She was letting Will say goodbye to him now, like this. June looked away. Grant closed his eyes:

> *Tall and strong she dips and reels*
> *I call her Silver Heels*
> *And she tells me how she feels*
> *She's a good old boat and she'll stay afloat*
> *Through the toughest gales and keep smilin'*
> *But for one more day she would like to stay*
> *In the lee of Christian Island*

Goodbyes were always terrible. Kate had been ashen colored and gaunt. She had been too weak to speak when she'd wanted to say goodbye. All she could do was try to squeeze his hand. Big Ole had sat with a dish towel around his chest and whispered, "I'm gonna miss you, boy." And now this. Everything fell away from him. It felt like he'd lost something he was expected to protect – like something very valuable had fallen over the side of a boat and was gone forever. Will had always been there for him. But he never would be again. Grief was crushing Grant Thorson.

Grant swallowed hard. He would not break down and weep. He tried to fight what he was thinking, to think of something else. His chest heaved when he held his breath and then held it again. He would not allow any more goodbyes, ever:

I'm sailing down the summer day
Where fish and seagulls play
I put my troubles all away
And when the gale comes up I'll fill my cup
With the whiskey of the highlands
She's a good old ship and she'll make the trip
From the lee of Christian Island

Susan reached her hand to his shoulder to comfort him. He wanted to push her away, but he didn't. 'Please, God, let this music be finished before I break,' he thought.

When the summer ends we will rest again
In the lee of Christian Island.

The end of the song, and the service, finally did come. Grant had to hold his breath several times in order to push back the heaving sensation that was welling in his chest. He tried not to hear the words to any more songs, or speeches, or prayers.

After an emotional service, there was no trip to any cemetery – just a meal in the church basement. Grant remained very quiet. He just wanted the funeral to be finished. He had not spoken to Frank since the accident, and when he saw Frank he decided not to speak to him today, either. Will's parents both looked dreadful. Friends would look briefly at Frank and then begin to think about what must have been going on in his mind, and then they'd look away. But Grant could not take his eyes off of Frank. He assumed Frank wanted only Evie at his side, so he left them alone.

Only a short time after the meal had begun, Grant went to June and shared a quick and painful visit, then did the same with Will's daughters. Then he found Ellen and spoke to her briefly.

"The family is planning a service at Spider Lake next Saturday. Can you make it?" Grant asked.

"Yes," Ellen said. She expected more conversation.

"See you then," Grant replied, and he left the church quickly.

He could not bear another word of conversation. Susan waved to
Ellen and then followed Grant out the door.

~

The Suburban was quiet on the drive from Duluth back to Spider
Lake. Susan held Grant's hand part of the way. No one spoke.
About halfway home, Grant finally spoke, "Should've been me."

"Don't say that, Grant. We need you. We love you," Susan said.
Ingrid had not spoken all day. She had a scared look on her face
when she looked at her father now.

"No, I meant it should have been me who pulled the trigger. I'd
trade places with Frank if I could."

His comment stunned Susan.

"Why would you say that?" Susan sounded upset. "Your life
would be ruined."

"Because then I could take away what I saw on Frank's face
today. NO man should carry that ... no man."

"And you could?"

"It wouldn't be the same — he wasn't my child. And besides that,
my life is ...," his voice trailed off, and he didn't finish his sentence. Susan was worried by his words, but Grant never looked at
her and never tried to explain more.

Only a short distance down the road, Grant pointed to an abandoned farm site. The buildings were mostly falling down, but the
lines of the old house still looked straight. The glass in the windows was all broken out, and the paint was worn off the siding.
Gray, weather-worn siding gave the place a lost, ghostly look. The
trees and shrubs were gnarled and overgrown.

"Somebody used to live in that place. In fact, when it was new,
somebody pounded the last nail into that little house and then
stepped back to admire his work. Musta been filled with pride when
he looked at his family's new home." Grant looked back and forth
between the road and gray buildings as he drove. "People loved each

other in that house. Babies were made and born there. People had happy times … Christmases, weddings. People loved each other there. Now look at it." And the place was gone, behind them.

A short while later, he took a deep breath and let it out with a loud rush. "If I'd known … if I'd understood … if I'd known the pain could be like this … I just never would have … let myself in for it."

~

The days had ground along slowly as the week between the funeral and the memorial service passed. Today, family and friends would gather for a final goodbye.

Grant was stacking driftwood in the brand new cedar-strip canoe when the guests began to arrive at Spider Lake Duck Camp for Will's memorial service. As he piled wood into the canoe, he remembered his conversation with June.

A week earlier, on the day before the funeral, June had asked to see Grant privately. "I don't know if I should be angry at you or happy, really! Remember a while back when your dad got sick and you and Will talked about a Viking funeral?"

"Yes."

"Well, he came home and was very adamant that if he should die, he wanted to be cremated and then have his ashes placed in a new cedar canoe filled with driftwood and then burned as it was set adrift at the lake. What do you think about that idea?" She wasn't angry. Grant could see that she was just asking him if he thought she should honor Will's request.

"It was my idea … so, sure, I like it … but for my dad! Did you think he was serious?"

"Absolutely. I just don't know if I should do it."

"Well, this will probably be the last time we'll cover this ground, but I'm sorry if I said something to get Will in trouble with you." He smiled at June and then hugged her. "I think it's perfect to bury him like a Viking warrior – like a great man – especially if that's what he asked for."

"OK. Will you help me?

"Of course!" And a sad smile curled his lips.

~

Car doors began to slam now as more people arrived. A warm September breeze barely ruffled the surface of Spider Lake. From where he stood along the lakeshore, Grant could hear more people all the time. But he just didn't want to visit much, so he stayed by the lake, far away from the growing crowd.

Warm and pleasant, today looked to be a fine day for a service like the one June had planned, but the evening was supposed to bring a chill, maybe a hard frost. She'd rented a tent and set out refreshments in the shade that it offered. Friends and family would have a chance to visit for an hour or two before the ceremony, which was scheduled for sunset.

Grant was standing beside the canoe, making final preparations, when he noticed three figures walking down the hill toward him. He put a hand up to shield the sun and saw that Ellen Hutchinson was walking his way, along with two Secret Service agents. She walked directly to him and held him firmly in her arms. She squeezed him and then patted his shoulders. "You OK?"

"Yeah," he whispered. The back of his throat was tight with emotion.

"Thom says hello. He really wanted to be here, but ..."

"I know."

"People are asking about you up there." She gestured toward the top of the hill.

"Yeah?" It was clear to Ellen that he didn't want to talk.

"Having a hard time with it all?"

"Yeah," he replied. Ellen could see that he had some resolve to remain apart from the others. She extended her hand.

"C'mon, other people need you." He took her hand and walked up the hill to the little tent. He didn't want to be with the others.

When Ellen and Grant reached the gathering, there was subdued laughter and light conversation among the growing crowd of Will's friends and family. He knew almost everyone there, and he began greeting all of those he recognized. For Frank, he had a warm embrace. He didn't say very much to Frank, but rather stood with him briefly and stroked his hand along Frank's shoulders.

As the sun dipped behind the treetops, the breeze died down and Spider Lake became a green and gold and blue jewel, as it did every day at sunset. A priest called everyone together for a short prayer, and they all walked together down to the lakeshore. The priest spoke again – just a short message about Will's life. Then June stepped out in front of everyone and welcomed them and explained the little ceremony they were about to see. She gave Grant the urn that held Will's ashes, stepped back, and wiped her eyes.

Grant sprinkled the ashes over the driftwood that he'd placed in the canoe. He dragged the canoe off the shore and into the water. He was wearing a gray sweatshirt, khaki shorts, and sandals as he waded knee deep into Spider Lake. The air temperature had been dropping as darkness had approached, and the lake water felt warm. Little pebbles from the lake bottom found their way between his feet and the soles of his sandals; he liked the familiar sensation. The sky above the lake was almost purple now in the growing twilight. Grant straightened his back and held the gunwale of the canoe in one hand as he turned to face the crowd.

"Will Campbell was my best friend. He was always there for me … always." Grant's voice was strong. "I've heard it said that the definition of a friend is someone who makes you like yourself better when you're around him. You all know that describes Will Campbell perfectly. As I speak, I see a couple dozen other men who called Will their best friend. Will and I talked a lot about life and death while we played out there." He pointed toward the lake. "He thought that life was like a long river and that he had to enjoy the calm waters when he reached them. I thank God that I had such a fine friend as Will Campbell."

Grant struck a match and dropped it into the canoe. He'd soaked some of the driftwood in diesel oil so that it would start burning slowly and then fire would engulf the entire canoe. He'd also weighted the canoe so that whatever didn't burn would sink to the bottom.

As the fire began to spread inside the canoe, Grant pushed it very gently out toward the middle of the big bay. "Bye, Will," he said quietly, so no one else could hear. But his own words let another wave of sadness wash over him. He raised his hand to bid Will farewell. Everyone stood in silence and watched the canoe slowly turn into a fireball, then disappear below the surface. June stood with her family. Susan and Ellen and Ingrid stood together. Grant remained alone, knee deep in the lake with his back to the others.

'So just what is this mystery I'm looking at? What's really happening here,' Grant thought as he stared at the quiet lake. 'Death? What is it? Are they just gone now ... all finished with me? Are they watching me from somewhere beyond all of this? What am I ever going to do? How can I ever go on from here? It's nice to be alive, but ... I'm so all alone.'

Some people cried quietly, some spoke softly, some raised their hands like Grant, and then after several silent moments, they all began to move gradually back up the hill.

Finally, when Grant turned from the lake, he saw that everyone had moved back up to the Ordway house, except for one person who stood alone in the near darkness, waiting for him. It was Anne Robertson.

From the midst of the friends and family who were talking and laughing quietly once again at the top of the hill, Susan and Ellen held hands and watched Grant walk up the slope toward Anne. He walked directly to her and they embraced each other immediately. They stood together in that way, not moving for many minutes. Susan felt something in her chest; she recognized the feel of jealousy. She could see Anne reach up and touch Grant's face.

Since the moment of Will's death, Grant had been different — detached and cold. Susan felt he'd been moving away from her. She heard him speak to Anne and then laugh softly. She saw them hold hands as they walked to Anne's car, and they embraced one more time before Anne drove off. Their conversation had been so warm ... but so brief. Susan didn't know what she'd seen.

Ellen and Susan looked at each other, and Susan tried to pass a clumsy smile. Ellen could feel the stress and anxiety that Susan tried to hide.

When Anne left, Grant made a half-hearted effort to mingle with everyone. But he was just not himself any longer.

~

The drive to the Fargo airport on the day after the funeral was very quiet. When they passed another abandoned farm site like the one Grant had pointed out a week earlier, he turned to look at Susan, then looked away. Grant dropped Ingrid off at Concordia and said his goodbye quickly. Then he continued to Fargo with Susan. She thought Grant was extraordinarily quiet, that he seemed depressed. She tried to cheer him up, but he remained indifferent to her. All he said to her at the airport was "I love you, I'll call you later this week."

"It's going to be OK, Grant."

"No, it isn't. Nothing will ever be OK again." Then he turned and walked away. He drove home silently.

Susan felt as though she'd been sent away like a disobedient puppy. She'd never seen anyone behave as Grant had. She wept and worried all during her flight home.

The mid-afternoon sun was warm when Grant returned to the cabin. He grabbed Nellie's throwing dummy from its hook and stepped off the porch. A walk with Nellie was always a good time to think and get some fresh air. He began walking toward the Ordway house and then he saw Frank. Frank looked twenty years

older than he had a week ago. He was sitting in a lawn chair, staring at the lake. Grant walked over to him and pulled up another
chair. He said nothing. He just reached over and touched Frank's
forearm.

"It was terrible," Frank said with no feeling when he looked up.
Grant did not reply. The two of them had not spoken of the accident until now. "It was so hot ... really hot. Will was coming to
get me for lunch. He'd rolled the top of his blaze orange coveralls
down to his waist because he was so hot. He was in the tall brush
and I couldn't see his orange pants. He was wearing a camouflage
shirt underneath his coveralls." Frank stared straight ahead for
another moment. "I drew a bead and shot when I saw him in the
brush. I thought for sure he was an elk." Frank turned toward
Grant, then back to the lake again.

"I think I knew as soon as I pulled the trigger ... what I'd
done." Grant remained silent. He just let Frank go wherever he
would with the moment.

Another long silence came over Frank. Then he continued the
terrible story.

"Will started calling right away. When I got there he was already
ashen colored. There was blood everywhere; it rose out of the hole
in his stomach like a leaky boat. You can't know the horror."

Yet another long pause. Grant stroked Frank's forearm and
waited.

"He called for his mother ... then slowly stopped talking;
stopped moving." Several more minutes passed in silence.

"I never told my boy that I loved him." Frank looked like a dead
man when he spoke.

"He knew. We talked about that all the time." Grant could only
whisper. He meant to somehow reassure Frank of something. But
he knew he could never give Frank the peace he was seeking.
"But *we* never did. I wish I could say it to him, just once." Franklin
Campbell had aged incredibly in the past week. He brought a

handkerchief to his eyes and wiped them. His hand trembled slightly, and he said nothing more.

~

Work was the best part of Grant's week after the ceremony at the lake. It offered at least some distraction – some diversion from the thoughts that came to him at all other times. He was able to treat patients and staff as he always had, at least during the performance of his job. He found himself retreating to his private office as often as possible, though, to avoid talking to his staff about his personal life. Insurance companies and government health care policy seemed really unimportant now.

Little things now triggered new, unkind thoughts. A patient might comment about his farm, and Grant would recall images of his own family farm in Halstad. And then – eventually but inevitably – he'd want to warn the patient about the heartache coming his way ... surely someone back home would die soon and crush his heart. Perhaps his assistant would share a story about her preschool children. Grant would find himself wanting to tell her that her boys would just grow up and think she was stupid in a few years. One morning over coffee at Emil's, he found himself wanting to tell an old friend to just wait: Someday some doctor would be telling him that his wife had cancer, or he'd find her gasping in bed and then his life would be shit, too. Life would just keep on bringing a painful emptiness around to him.

Sometimes when he returned to his cabin he felt bitter and angry. He didn't understand it, but he was angry at Will for dying and he was angry at the loss of his friend. He was growing bitter about the frustration and pain that life kept piling on him.

As the days wore on, he started to feel fear – a deep dread that began to creep into every other part of his life. In his quiet times, which were plentiful now, he began to fear that death was going to steal everything from him. He thought he'd lost the fear of his own death, but he truly feared the death of any more loved ones.

He did miss Susan. He resented her, oddly enough, for now she seemed to be the next most likely person to be taken from him. In the same way he was angry at Will for dying, he was angry at Susan because ... because she just might die, too. He hadn't asked Susan to marry him. He just never got around to it before the phone call came that night. Now he was glad he hadn't. It would only make what he had to do that much more difficult.

~

He waited ten days before calling Susan. She'd called twice and left two messages on his machine. In the second message, she had sounded concerned, almost panicky.

"Hello, Susan," he said flatly when she answered her phone.

"Oh God, I'm glad you called. I was getting worried. Are you OK?"

She was relieved to hear his voice.

"Yeah, I'm fine. Well, not really." He stopped.

"What's the matter, Grant?" He could hear the concern in her voice, and he didn't want to get into a long, argumentative phone call. All of this stuff was hopeless, but he knew a way around it.

"I won't be calling anymore, Susan. Not because I don't love you – I do love you. But I'd rather not anymore. I've had enough grief and heartache. I just don't want to open myself up for anymore of it!" He sounded businesslike, not angry – not the way one would expect a man to sound when he broke up with his lover. She thought he sounded absurd.

"What! I can't believe it! You tell me you love me, and then you say you don't want to see me anymore! That's not how love works!"

"Well, how does it work? I'd like for someone to explain that to me." An angry edge came to his voice. "Every time I love some-one, they drop dead. I guess I don't need any more if it. Do I need to draw you a picture?"

"Don't be silly. We've all lost loved ones. I lost both of my par-ents twenty years ago. How do you think I felt?"

"I don't know how *you* felt, God damn it! But you're talking to the guy who cried when Mickey Mantle died … *he* took a part of me with him. How the hell do you think it feels to put the three best friends I ever had in the ground all in the last year and a half? Every one of them took a big chunk of me with them. You think I want to stand number four up and wait for the fall?"

"Grant." Susan's voice had a calm, reassuring quality now. "You told me all about how you know you're alive … you know, when you feel something — a cold wind, a summer breeze, love. But you're telling me now that you're dead, too — that you've already let death steal your whole life. This is just the nature of life, Grant; you expect the pain that comes your way along with the joy. *That's* how you know you're alive! I know you. I know you really wouldn't, couldn't have it any other way."

Grant was silent for a moment, but it was clear that he was determined when he did speak again. "Look, Gordon MacQuarrie even wrote about this: 'Don't feel bad for the man who hunts and fishes alone' …."

"Don't shovel that romantic bullshit my way!" she interrupted angrily. "'Cowards die many times before their death, the valiant never taste of death but once.' I've seen qualities in you that I've never seen in other men. I love you, so much that it aches. But I never took you for a coward."

"Well, I may be a coward then." Grant paused briefly. "I love you, too. But I've learned that it's possible to love someone and know that you just can't spend your life with them. Goodbye, Susan."

"Grant! Wait! I love …" her phone went dead.

He was filled with resolve not to revisit the issue. He rose from his chair, turned off the answering machine, and went outside. If she called back, he didn't want to be tempted to pick up the phone. The first hour went by and Grant began to feel like he wanted to call Susan. But he resisted, and he struggled with himself several times during the night when he wanted to call her. When the sun came up, he felt defiant. He tried to shut out all thoughts of Susan, and he went to work. Each day he thought of her a little less. To be sure, he did think of her every day. But he was able to hide from his thoughts. Gradually, he got better at hiding from himself.

Opening weekend of the duck season followed on the heels of Will's funeral. In other years, Grant would have had his boat ready early in the week before opening day. The decoy cords and weights would be checked and all of the decoys bagged and waiting in the boat. But this year, he stalled until the night before opener to start preparing. He laid his clothes and waders out by the porch door and found the thermos just before bedtime. He decided to check the boat and motor in the morning.

When his alarm rang early in the morning, he simply rolled over and shut it off — then went back to sleep.

chapter TWENTY-NINE

Grant Thorson had exiled himself. He intended to remain apart from others, isolated from the potential for pain.

Hunting on the opening weekend without Will had seemed more than empty. It struck Grant as a downright painful experience. So he just avoided it.

After deliberately missing the opener, he did begin to hunt again. But he made a point to hunt by himself now. He never called other friends to invite them. Initially, he'd expected to feel miserable or lonely when he took to the lake alone, but he didn't. He told himself that he enjoyed the solitude. But it was actually something more than the solitude that he liked: It was the doing of things by himself. No one to question, no one to please, he had only to keep his own schedule, and he could remain in control of his world.

As the days grew short and cold, the northern waters froze. Grant ventured farther and farther south in search of ducks. He hunted the Missouri River in Nebraska, then the Platte River. In December, he hunted the flooded timber in Stuttgart, Arkansas.

After the holidays, which he spent alone, he flew to Mexico for a week of duck hunting on Laguna Madre.

He enjoyed Mexico enough to book a return trip for the following year. But during autumn's journey south, he felt that some of the joy was gone from it all. He'd sensed all along that something was missing, and he'd been willing to travel across North America to prove it to himself.

~

The end of her relationship with Grant had hurt Susan Wells more than anything in her life ever had. The breakup of her two marriages had been insignificant compared with the pain she'd felt when Grant left her life.

Smart and savvy, she was very experienced with men. She'd worked with educated intellectuals. She'd dated handsome celebrities. She'd been propositioned by rich and sophisticated older men. But she'd fallen in love with Grant Thorson. He had strength, humor, and a soft heart. She'd given him access to the most vulnerable places in her heart, and she'd given him a friendship that she didn't know she still had available to give.

Then he'd pulled the rug out from under her. He'd done the one thing she thought he could never do: He'd taken the most tender love that she had to give and thrown it back in her face. She was crushed.

Her phone rang one morning in early January. "Susan Wells," she answered.

"Susan, this is Petra. Can you come into my office please?"

"I'll be right there." Susan suspected the reason for their meeting. When she entered Petra Vanderhoft's office, she stood one step inside the doorway and raised her eyebrows.

"Close the door please." Petra was sitting behind her desk. Susan closed the door and looked at Petra once more.

"OK, what's wrong?" Petra asked.

"What do you mean?"

Petra said nothing. She folded her arms and waited.

"What do you mean?" Susan repeated. She knew exactly what her boss meant.

"We both know what I mean. I'm trying to give you a chance to talk about it. I'd be lying if I said your work has suffered, but in fact it might be better than ever. You, however, are not the same girl since you broke up with your friend."

Susan wanted to smile when Petra referred to her as a girl, just as Grant had. "Well, I guess I've been a little depressed, haven't I?" she conceded.

"Yes. And you're hurting, and I thought it might do you some good to talk about it." Petra waited again.

Susan let out a big sigh. "OK. Not much to say, really. I thought he'd call in the days shortly after the funeral. When he finally did, he told me it was over … just dropped the bomb. Said he couldn't stand any more pain."

"Are you sure he didn't just want it to be over anyway? Are you sure he wasn't just ready to move on?"

"I've wondered about that. I don't think that's true at all. In fact, I thought we were about to plan a future together." Susan began to cry softly.

"Marriage?"

"I don't know." She got up and took a tissue off Petra's desk and wiped her eyes.

"So what happened?"

"I don't really know. He had so much unhappiness in his life all in such a short time. His wife, his father, and Will Campbell all died in about one year. He was *very* close to all of them. He just gave up. He said love only made him vulnerable and he couldn't take any more losses. He has such a soft heart."

"You are talking about Grant Thorson, right?"

Susan smiled through her tears at Petra's sarcasm.

Petra continued. "The man who challenged everyone on the health care committee? The man who said the ACLU only protects the rights of dirtballs and murderers? The man who referred to the Russians as 'sons-a-bitches' and said they hadn't told the truth about anything for seventy years?"

Susan laughed and cried at the same time "You had to get to know him."

"Apparently."

"He told me that when I kissed him, it was like opening a package of baseball cards." Susan tried to laugh through her tears again.

"I'm sure if I'd known him better that would make sense." Petra stacked some papers on her desk and looked away.

Neither of them spoke for a moment while Susan sniffled in her tissue.

"Susan, everyone grieves in a different way. Maybe he'll call soon, when he's done grieving over all of this," Petra said hopefully.

"Perhaps. But he is strong willed. It's been three months ..." she sniffled again. "I thought he was the one."

As the winter wore on, Grant treated Ingrid like he treated everyone else: He spoke to her less and less. When she began to neglect her regular Sunday-evening phone calls, he did nothing. He told himself it was her way of separating herself from him. He would only think it through partway. He understood it was time for her to grow up, and that was where he stopped. Just as he could always suppress his emotions, he was now able to avoid the conscious understanding that he was setting his little girl adrift.

Every now and then, the realization that he was turning his back on someone who might be counting on him would come into his mind. He would understand, briefly, that Big Ole Thorson would never, could never, be such a poor father. Then he would make himself think of something else.

Three times during January and February, Ingrid came home to Walker for weekend parties at the homes of her friends and did not call Grant. When he found out afterwards that she'd slept on a friend's couch or in someone's guestroom, he convinced himself not to call and question her about it. He'd talked himself into believing that it was not really his business, and that he shouldn't be upset that Ingrid was choosing not to contact him.

~

Gladys Thorson was the only person whose relationship with Grant hadn't changed. Grant called her and visited her often. Each of them felt they were taking care of the other. Gladys was healthy and confident living by herself on the farm.

In the same way that he saw himself as his mother's guardian, Grant took it upon himself to call Frank from time to time. But he had mixed feelings about contacting Frank. On the one hand, he was concerned about Frank's mental health. He was worried that Frank might just give up and turn a gun on himself out of grief or guilt. At the same time, he didn't want to stick his nose in and offer compassion that the Campbells didn't need or that might come across as the kind of interest shown by motorists who drive slowly and gawk when they pass a car accident. When he did speak with Frank, he limited it to small talk unless Frank brought up something about Will. Then he just listened.

Occasionally, some acquaintance or maybe a patient would inquire about Frank. "Say, whatever happened to your friend's father? Boy, that was a terrible thing." Even those who'd never met Will or Frank knew all about it, and no one could disguise the pain they felt in discussing it. Everyone could sense the unbearable thing that Frank was dealing with.

June, like everyone else, heard less and less from Grant. She remained, however, the only person Grant spoke with about the accident. He'd been impressed all along by her strength. She talked openly about her own grief and her concern for Frank. She'd told Grant shortly after the accident that Frank was working hard to deal with his feelings. She said Frank had contacted a psychologist right after the funeral and was trying so hard to keep his life together. Grant was amazed at the way June and Frank could speak of it all. He certainly couldn't.

Grant saw an ugly scene that played over and over again in his mind's eye. It was like a song that he couldn't get out of his head; it just played over and over again. In his nightmare, which he saw at all hours, there was a hole in Will's stomach that kept leaking blood all over Frank while he watched his son slip away. The thought twisted Grant's face into a grimace every time it came to him. Then, after a while, he began to have a recurrent dream. He dreamed he was a young man again and none of his friends would talk to him. He'd call girls and ask for dates, but they wouldn't answer. He'd try to contact his friends, but they wouldn't answer. He had the dream so often that he began to think about it when he was awake.

~

The telephone was right beside his head, and the shrill noise scared Grant. Like any other middle-of-the-night phone call, this one had to be bad, too, he thought.

"Dr. Thorson," he said in a horse whisper.

"Dr. Thorson, this is Carl Wohlhuter." Wohlhuter was the chief of police in Walker. Grant wondered if there was a prisoner with a toothache. What else could it be?

"Yes."

"Your daughter was involved in a car accident tonight. Don't worry, she's all right, but her blood-alcohol is above the legal limit. Can you come and get her?"

"She's in college, in Moorhead."

"No, she's in Walker now. She was a passenger in one of the cars. No one was injured, except for a few bumps and bruises."

The night air was more than refreshing. It was minus eight degrees Fahrenheit when Grant stepped out of his Suburban and walked into the police station at 3:15 a.m. on a windy Friday night in February.

Ingrid and a young man — her date, Grant assumed — were sitting placidly in Carl Wohlhuter's office. Neither of them appeared intoxicated, but both were obviously scared.

"Hello, Carl."

"Hi, Doc."

"Can I take her home?" Grant stared at Ingrid with his hands in his pockets.

"Sure thing. She's been charged with consumption of alcohol by a minor," Carl added.

"Can I take her?" Grant's voice rose. He glared at Ingrid.

"Yes," Wohlhuter replied.

"What about Ryan?" Ingrid asked. She was almost afraid to speak, and she wouldn't look up.

"I suppose *this* is Ryan?" Grant asked. The young man nodded as Grant put his hands in his pockets and faced him.

Grant turned toward the young man. "Were you driving, Ryan?"

"Yes."

"Been drinking?"

"Yes."

"Well, Ryan ..." Grant stopped: The young man was looking at his own feet. "Hey! Look at me kid!"

"Yeah?"

"Well, just remember this: If you ever hurt my daughter, the last fuckin' thing you ever see is gonna be this face! Understand me?"

Ryan nodded yes. Grant took Ingrid by the arm. "Thanks, Carl."

"Good night, Doc."

As they moved toward the door, Ingrid jerked her arm from his grasp. Grant supposed she was angry at him for leaving her boyfriend — or whatever Ryan was — at the police station.

Grant was angry and disappointed with Ingrid. He was angry at the boy for driving drunk with his daughter in the car. He wanted to scream at Ingrid for getting in the car with someone who'd been drinking.

"So what the hell is wrong with you? Are you stupid? People *die* doing stupid things like you two did tonight. Don't you think we've had enough shit happen already?" The instant those words left his mouth, Grant clutched at the silence — and he was thankful Ingrid didn't know what he was thinking. The memory of his own car running all night in the barnyard with the doors open jumped at him. He saw the anger on his father's face as he made fence in order to serve his penance. His own life experience loomed in front of him as an obstacle now, and he simply stepped around it, as he'd learned to do with all obstacles.

"Someday you're going to have to learn to think!" he added, in order to make sure the problem was all Ingrid's.

Ingrid only stared at the road. She would not speak to him. "Fine," he decided, and he drove home in silence. When they reached his cabin, she went to her old room and he sat on the couch. He was alone, with his daughter.

The next morning, Grant and Ingrid returned to her dorm without speaking. She wore an angry expression from the moment she woke up. Grant made a conscious decision not to speak to her until she spoke to him. He left the radio off during the ride to Moorhead in order to emphasize his anger and his resolve to not be the first to give in and speak. When the Suburban stopped on the street in front of Brown Hall, Ingrid stepped out and slammed the door.

The instant the door closed in his face, Grant turned. He wanted to call to her, but it was too late. If she would have turned around, she'd have seen him waiting for her to return to talk. But if she had turned, he would also have seen her tears ... she kept on walking away from him.

He wavered briefly. He decided to run after her, then changed his mind. No, if she wanted to play it this way, then so be it. She could find out how hard things could be without her dad around. It was time to grow up anyway.

Something about it all just didn't seem right as he pulled away from the curb. But things would get better if he just stayed the course. She'd be fine by herself.

~

He'd grown to be self-sufficient, self-satisfied, maybe self-centered. He had no idea of the darkness in his heart until one warm sunny day in early May.

"Hilda, can I have a Styrofoam cup for my coffee?" he asked. "I'd like to walk down to the landing." He'd been eating lunch at Emil's Café and looking out over Leech Lake for about twenty minutes. The ice had gone off the lake several days earlier. The walleye fishing on Leech Lake would pick up now, and the bite would be on, better and better, through the spring. From his booth at Emil's he could see the floating pier at the public boat access, and he wanted to finish his coffee by the lake. He walked casually down the incline to the lakeshore and then out onto the pier. He leaned against the railing and looked out over the grand lake while he sipped his coffee.

At first he took no note of it. He was aware of a slight commotion about thirty feet away from him, but he paid no attention to it initially. Then he began to notice a tension in the words being spoken behind him, and several rapid footsteps.

He turned in time to see three fairly intoxicated local deadbeats standing around a neatly dressed elderly man. Grant had seen the scruffy-looking men around town for years but did not know their names. One of the men was pouring out the contents of the old man's minnow bucket onto the dock. One of the men was holding a gas can and daring the old man to reach for it. The old man's wife — Grant guessed her to be about seventy-five — sat in the little boat with an odd, fearful look on her face. The third low life, the biggest, was asking if the old man had any money.

When the old man turned, his eyes locked onto Grant's for only a second. Grant saw the fear on his face, and he understood immediately what had to be done. He walked very quickly across the pier and, with his left hand, spun the man doing the talking. Grant buried his right fist in the man's large potbelly. The big man wheezed and fell to his knees. By the time Grant turned, the man emptying the minnow bucket was holding a knife. Grant took one step and kicked the man in the groin. The force of the kick lifted the skinny, dirty little man off the pier. The man dropped his knife and coughed while he held his crotch and rolled around on the dock. He was wearing a dirty baseball cap over his greasy, matted black hair, and his cap came off when he fell.

The third man was still holding the gas can and staring when Grant drove his right fist into the man's face. His nose split and exploded with blood as the man fell.

The first man was getting up now and threatening Grant. "I'm gonna kill you!"

Grant grabbed the fat man by the back of his collar and his belt and swung him head first into an ice machine. The fat man's head made a large dent in the metal door of the ice machine, and Grant held his head there firmly in place with his forearm.

"If I ever see you here again, I'll take your buddy's knife and cut your greasy head off, and stick it on a pike on the end of this pier!" Grant was trying to holler, but his words only rushed out in a coarse whisper. He growled in a guttural voice that he'd never heard from himself.

The man began to talk and struggle again, and he tried to stand. Grant lifted the man by taking his hair in his left hand and then swinging his right forearm as hard as he could into the back of the fat man's head. The fat man's head bounced into the ice machine's door once more. This time, the now unconscious fat man slid down along the ice machine until he rested on the pier. He'd left a wide trail of blood all the way down the metal door.

When Grant stood up straight and turned, he was trembling. Emil Krause stood behind him staring, along with several patrons from Emil's and a police officer. They'd all seen most of the incident, and their mouths hung open in disbelief.

~

"Dr. Thorson, I'm not gonna charge you with anything because those men *were* threatening you and that old couple. Hell, we know who those dirtbags are; we get a lot of repeat business from them." The police officer on the dock had been Carl Wohlhuter.

"But I'll tell you something, Doctor, you had murder in your eyes when you looked at me, I know. I've seen it."

"I'm sorry, Carl, I just lost my temper," Grant said calmly. He looked at his hands while he sat on the metal chair next to Officer Wohlhuter's desk.

"You're not listening to me, get some help! You went way over the top today."

Grant made a face as if he disagreed.

"Dr. Thorson, if there had been a round two today, you would have killed any or all of these men, wouldn't you? You were ready, weren't you?"

Grant only lowered his eyes.

Carl Wohlhuter leaned back and flipped his pencil onto his desk. "Doc, this is a small town. Everyone here knows about what's happened to you. And everyone can see how you've changed. Take that for what it's worth. But what I saw out there on the pier today was not a healthy thing."

"Can I go now?" Grant asked.

As he walked to his car, he thought about what had happened, both on the pier in Walker and over the past year. He'd become aware of some confusion or perhaps conflict inside of himself. He'd always liked to be alone, and he thought that was good – a statement of his independence. He just didn't need anyone, and he thought that indicated strength. But he'd begun to feel that "alone" had changed to "lonely." There seemed to be such a fine line between alone and lonely, and now, for the first time, he sensed he was straddling that line and not really liking it.

chapter Thirty

"Hey, did you hear that?" Ingrid called to Melanie Willette. They were in the large kitchen of the Willettes' new home overlooking Leech Lake. French bread and all the fixings for deli sandwiches were spread out in front of them. Melanie's parents were in the kitchen, too.

"That was 'Lawyers in Love' by Jackson Browne." Ingrid smiled at Connie Willette, Melanie's mother.

"That's impossible!" John Willette's voice was gruff and mean spirited. John had been the Hubbard County Attorney for twelve years. He was one of those men that everyone spoke poorly about; no one liked him. He had a reputation for dishonesty at work and unfaithfulness at home. His comment had thrown a pall over the mood in the kitchen.

"That's impossible," he'd said. He'd really meant that it would be impossible for him to love his wife. It was a mean-spirited thing to say, especially in front of his own daughter and Ingrid.

Only moments before, the girls had been laughing and joking. Now Ingrid wanted to leave the room; she was embarrassed for herself and for Connie Willette because of John's words. John sat reading the paper and sipping a drink. He hadn't looked up from the paper, but they all knew he'd meant to hurt Connie. He always did that sort of thing.

Melanie's mother continued to arrange the sandwiches, but she kept her eyes down.

"C'mon, Ingrid, lets go for a walk," Melanie said.

"Why does he do that?" Ingrid asked when they were outside the house.

"He hates us."

"How can that be? That's not true."

"The only reason he stays with mom is that we're Catholic — and Grampa wouldn't stand for it if he divorced my mom." John's father was the senior partner in a busy five-man practice.

Ingrid knew it was true and didn't bother to argue. Everyone knew it was true.

"My dad is an asshole! He never tried to be a father. But what happened to your dad? I just don't understand that." Melanie shook her head sideways, then smiled and said, "Remember when he used to coach our softball team?"

"Yeah."

"Remember the time we got wiped out in that tournament in Bemidji?"

"Yeah," Ingrid smiled.

"Remember how, instead of yelling at us, he opened a cooler of pop, and we sat around it and had a belching contest?" Melanie asked.

"Yeah!" They both laughed. "Hey, Mel, thanks for letting me stay with you so often this summer."

"No problem. It's been fun for me, too. So is your dad really pissed at you, or what? You were always real close. What happened, really?"

"We had a big fight when I got busted last winter. We both got mad, and neither of us wants to be the first to give in."

"So go talk to him. It wasn't that big of a deal. You should talk to him, especially after what happened to your mom … and all that other stuff." Melanie worried that she'd said too much.

"I do go home every now and then. I even stay there once in a while. Usually I do a load of laundry or some such thing and just try not to start another fight with my dad. I know I should talk to him, but I'm afraid."

"Afraid of what?"

"What if he doesn't love me anymore?"

~

Nellie's paws reached up as she laid on her back and stretched. Her head rested in Grant's lap as they both reclined on the couch. Grant scratched her belly, and she groaned with pleasure. He held a paperback in his left hand and Nellie in his right.

He planned to go fishing for an hour or so before dark. But when he flipped his book onto the end table, the telephone caught his eye. On a whim, he decided to make a phone call. Several minutes later he was talking to Jessica Wickham.

"Well, hello, Dr. Thorson. I haven't spoken with you for a long time."

"Still chained to your desk?"

"Yes, sir! But it's OK. I like my desk."

"Well, is the boss around this evening? I just thought I'd call and talk briefly … nothing important."

"He is here. I'll see if he can speak with you. Just a minute."

The line clicked momentarily. "Doctor?" It was Thom Hutchinson.

"Hi, Hutch. Hope I didn't bother you."

"No, you picked a good time to call. So how are things in the big woods?"

"Pretty good. Well … pretty quiet, actually."

"I know. I speak with June every now and then. She says you've … withdrawn."

"That would be a fair way to put it."

"It'll all be OK. I still have a hard time understanding Will's death."

"I miss him, Hutch. It was like the straw that broke the camel's back. Nothing seemed right after he died."

"Yeah, life isn't always fair, is it."

"That's for sure." Grant paused for a moment, then blurted, "Ever talk to Susan?"

He was embarrassed at first, but once he said the words he knew he'd been wondering about her and stuffing his thoughts.

"Yes. I had a long chat with her several days ago. We've sort of begun to like each other. She's pretty good, you know?" Thom had been surprised by Grant's question. He knew Grant had shut her out.

"Did she ... mention my name?" Suddenly Grant had needed to know if she thought of him. He felt embarrassed by his own words again.

"No. She didn't. But we were talking about scandalous political things." Thom had heard the loneliness in Grant's voice.

"No matter, I guess." Grant sounded as if he were talking to himself. "Life sure deals some surprises, huh? Here you're President of the United States, Will is dead, and I'm ... well, I'm here."

"Yes. Who would have thought?" Thom was uncertain just how to continue.

"I better let you go, Hutch." Both men had started the visit with enthusiasm, but Grant's words had taken the proverbial wind from their sails.

"Are you OK, Grant?" Concern registered in Thom's voice.

"Yeah, I think so. Maybe we can talk about it all over a camp-fire someday."

"Definitely," Thom replied. Both of them knew that wouldn't happen for a long time.

"Bye, Hutch." Grant sounded as though he was fading away.

"Hey, Grant!" Thom called out.

"Yeah?"

"Watch your top knot."

"Watch yourn."

~

Another summer in the north had come and gone while Grant steadfastly kept his back turned to most of his old friends. As the days began to shorten and a chill returned to the night air, he went to the lakeshore regularly to train with Nellie for another season.

On a cool September Saturday, Grant took Nellie down to the edge of Spider Lake for her daily exercise. She was eleven seasons old now, but she pranced like a puppy at the beginning of every workout. She showed her age on her gray muzzle and the way her body had lost the athletic, angular look it once had. She was round, not fat ... she just looked like an old female lab. The practice games were always fun for her, but sometimes now, at the end of the day, her movements began to look feeble.

Nellie still hit the water with the same enthusiasm she always had. Grant made her sit and watch when he threw the training dummy as far out into the lake as he could. She trembled while she waited for the command. When it finally came: "Back!" Grant would hiss, and she exploded down the hillside and raced out to the end of the wooden dock. She launched herself like an Olympic long jumper into the lake. After a big splash, she paddled smoothly until she had the dummy. Then she returned the same way. She placed the dummy in Grant's hand and begged for another chance to retrieve. The game never got old for her.

As Grant worked Nellie back and forth along the shoreline, he noticed that Frank was sitting on the porch of the Big House. He raised a hand to wave. Frank returned the wave. "Hi, Nellie!" he called out weakly.

Frank Campbell had aged noticeably in the short time since the accident. He was slightly stooped over when he walked now, and totally gray. He wasn't handsome anymore; he was just old. He'd retired from his practice immediately after the accident, and Grant thought he'd quickly changed from being an imposing leader of men to just another unsteady old man.

When Nellie heard him call, she turned toward him and started to run up the hill. Frank met both Grant and Nellie at the top of the stairway and opened the screen door to let them onto the porch.

Nellie nuzzled up to Frank and began to beg him to scratch her wet ears. In short order, Frank's hands and pant leg were wet from the lake water covering Nellie. Grant asked, "How's it going, Frank?

"OK," he replied. "How 'bout you?" Grant noticed immediately that there was an edge to Frank's question. Frank seemed to be eyeing him suspiciously as he waited for his reply.

"Pretty good," Grant answered; he tried to sound upbeat.

"You're dying, boy." Frank looked at Nellie. His words came slowly, but they were very blunt. He seemed willing to be an adversary, but he looked and sounded so weak that Grant was caught totally off guard.

"Huh?"

"You're less of a man now than you were a year ago." Frank raised his eyes from Nellie to Grant, daring Grant to respond.

"Huh?"

"You know what I'm talking about." He was pushing, as best he could. "You quit. You can't quit!"

Evie was sitting on the couch just inside the cabin, reading something. She put her book down and listened to the talk on the porch. She'd heard what Frank said, and as she closed her book she waited for Grant's reply.

Grant leaned back in his chair. "Look, Frank, I've had enough. Everyone in my life keeps dying and taking part of me with them. I've got nothing left."

"Do you know who you're talking to here?! I feel like I'm made of glass." Frank stopped, drew a breath, and went on slowly. "People are afraid to talk to me. I know what people think when they look at me. They're afraid I'm gonna shatter if they talk to me. It's as if they think I'm ready to burst with the pain of what happened, and if they touch me I'll explode and get it all over them. You feel that way sometimes when you look at me, don't you?"

Grant nodded yes, ashamed that Frank had seen it in him.

"I wonder what poor Evelyn thinks. I killed her son. I wonder about what June and the girls think of me. I see that awful thing in my mind over and over again. I can't change it ... can't make it go away." Frank gave no hint that he might falter or weep. He was calm, but intent on saying what he had to say.

"I lost a brother several years ago ... Lou Gehrig's Disease. It wasn't pretty. About a year before the end, he was beginning to fail noticeably. I asked him one day if he'd like to be put out of his misery ... euthanized if it got too bad. I just wanted to let him say what he was thinking ... what he was afraid of. I want you to hear what he told me. He said he'd thought about that, but he felt that God had given him only one life — just one chance to experience everything that was to come his way — so he thought he'd do just that: ride it out!" Frank pointed a shaky finger at Grant. "Now there was a great man!"

Frank leaned back in his chair, and Nellie moved her head to his lap.

"So you've had some very bad things happen ... no doubt about your losses. But I want you to know that I get up every morning and relive my worst nightmare, then I look for *one* reason to live another day. And it's always the same reason: I need to see what life has for me today ... good or bad, it doesn't matter; I'll deal with it." He looked away from Grant, then straightened his back and continued. "Oliver Wendell Holmes had a great line: 'Life is passion and action, and each man must take part in the passion and action of his times, at peril of being judged never to have lived.' That sounds like something you would have said. You shouldn't have to hear it from me." Frank stroked Nellie's head and looked down at her.

"The people you've loved and lost had huge, full lives. When they died, they didn't take your life with them; they gave you their lives. They made you what you are ... or were." His voice dropped off with contempt. "They'd all be heartsick if they could see the way you shrank from a chance for true love. You told me once that death stole your past, your life, as if it had all been pulled down a hole in front of you. Well, you threw your future in after it."

"I gotta go, Frank." Grant rose to his feet and touched Frank's shoulder. "C'mon, Nellie." He didn't want Frank to know that he was getting angry at being spoken to in such a manner. But he didn't want to hear any more of it, either.

Frank called out as Grant reached the bottom of the steps, "Pain is the price you pay for someone else's love! If you're going to love someone, you're going to pay for it someday — and it's a heavy toll sometimes, isn't it? Other people are paying that toll now, too! But really, would you change the rules if you could? You always said that when you felt something, good or bad, that's how you knew you were alive."

Grant stopped and looked back.

"What do you think Will would tell you to do? Take yourself out of the game? Or step up and take your swings?" Frank asked.

If it had been anyone but Frank, this little confrontation would have offended and angered Grant. But he chose to simply turn and leave.

After Grant was gone, Evie walked out to the porch and sat with Frank. "Are you all right?" she asked. She reached over and touched his face.

"Are any of us ever going to be all right again?"

"Yes ... in time," she replied.

"Yeah ... maybe."

"Do you think he heard anything you said?"

"I don't know. It must be difficult when you're all alone." Frank took her hand and tried to smile. Evie thought he looked exhausted.

~

"OK, Elsie. Now remember, no using these new crowns for opening beer bottles or bending sheet metal ... you'll break them!" The woman with the new smile laughed and then smiled at herself while she examined her teeth in a hand mirror.

"Can I bite fishing line?" she asked. She wasn't joking.

"Definitely not. Use a clipper, and I'm gonna make a note in your chart that I told you that in case you ever come back and tell me I never warned you." Grant pointed a finger at her. He'd spent the last three hours finishing her smile, and he was just as happy as Elsie Strausser was that their visit was over. "Eat what you want, just don't be foolish. That's not a pair of pliers you just bought." He smiled and pointed at her teeth again.

"OK. Thanks, Doc."

"Bye, Elsie."

Grant walked quickly to his private office and took off his scrubs. He looked through his mail for a moment as he prepared to go home for the weekend. He'd just finished with his last patient of the day, of the week, and he was anxious to get home.

His thoughts had been with Ingrid all day long. She'd surprised him the night before. She'd called and asked if she could come "home" for the weekend. After a spring and summer of very limited contact with her, he didn't know what to think of her call – and he was uncertain about just what to say to her.

One of his assistants was emptying wastebaskets; the other was just walking out the back door of the office at the end of the day. Grant's receptionist came to his private office and said to his back, "There's someone here to see you." Grant slumped and made a face.

"Do I have to?" he asked. "Tell 'em I've left already." He wanted to go home. The last thing he wanted to do was talk to a salesman or someone with a loose denture or some such thing.

"You're gonna want to see this one," she said as she turned around and walked down the hallway to the front of the office. Grant followed close behind her; she'd aroused his curiosity.

Anne Robertson stood in the waiting room; she was as beautiful as ever. Grant's receptionist walked past Anne and locked the door. She turned and raised her eyebrows at Grant and said, "See you Monday." She then went home for the weekend, out the back door behind them once again.

"Hello, Grant," Anne said. They were all alone in his office.

"Hello." He stepped toward her and put his arms around her, then took a step back.

"Don't worry. I've come to say goodbye." Grant was embarrassed at the way she said it.

"I wasn't worried, Anne."

"I've met someone, and I'm getting married. I won't be seeing you again. Never. I promise."

"Don't promise me that."

"Well, I won't be back again. But I did want to say goodbye." She stared into his eyes.

"Do you love him?"

"Of course I do. I love you, too." She looked up into his eyes more intently now. "I always will, and I wanted to tell you that one more time so you'd remember it forever. It's odd, but it seemed important. I never thought I could have feelings like this." She smiled. "I want you to be happy, you know? If we'd been married and I ... and something happened to me, I'd want for you to find someone. I talked to June Campbell. She said you were struggling with ... well, with everything."

He nodded yes slowly. "I wonder why they all died," he said.

"Do you really need an answer to that question?"

"No, not really. I don't wonder much about the 'why' of death, I guess." He put his hands in his pockets and said very seriously, "You know, the thing that bothers me is that I don't know why they lived."

She raised her eyes to his. "Ahh, that's the one we all need to answer, isn't it." She stepped into his arms again and they stood in silence. "If we'd been able to talk like this, we might have made it," she said.

"Yeah."

"Spider Lake can swallow up a lot of tears, but it can't give you back your past. That's gone. It was the love you shared with others that made you happy. They needed you, too, you know."

They needed you, too. His head tipped to an odd angle, and he looked at her. Her words slid inside of him like water through a leaky roof.

"One kiss, for old times?" she asked. He brought his lips to hers for one gentle kiss. When she stepped away from him, he pulled her back and held her close.

"Always. Always know that I love you, too, Anne."

She stepped back, away from him, and unlocked the door. With her hand still on the door, she looked at his face one more time. "You know, when you love someone – I mean really love them – that love never dies or goes away no matter what happens to that person. I love you, too, and you are a good boy." She turned and walked out the door. Just like the other times when she'd left him, something inside of him wanted to run after her. He watched her cross the street, get into her car, and drive away.

~

It was too warm for a fire. The dry night air carried the smell of pine as it flowed through the screens on the porch of Grant's cabin. Anne's words drifted across the front of his conscious mind. They had for several hours. "They needed you, too," she'd said.

Grant thought that all along the problem had been that he'd needed others and they'd deserted him. Now he wrestled with the idea that they'd needed him. Had they? Yeah, probably. It seemed pretty clear now that she'd said it. "Just think of the people who needed *me*," he thought. "All of the people I was counting on to hold me up were looking to me for strength, too."

Things probably hadn't worked with Anne because the two of them didn't need each other. Anne had wanted him. Maybe she'd wanted him simply because she couldn't have him. He'd wanted Anne because she was part of his past. He'd wanted her because he thought she was what he should want. But they didn't need each other. He didn't need to make her laugh or feel her touch. He had never looked into her eyes and seen laughter.

The coffee in his cup had cooled to room temperature. He sipped at it anyway. When he rocked slowly in the wicker chair, it creaked and he listened to the noise it made. He hadn't heard that noise for a while. Then a loon called, and he thought it had been a long time since he'd heard that familiar noise, too.

Nellie came to him and bumped his hand with her gray muzzle. It was her way of begging for attention. She wanted him to scratch her ears.

A car door slammed and then the cabin door opened and slammed. Ingrid stepped onto the darkened porch and found her father staring at gently swaying pine trees and listening to the frogs down by the lake. The soundtrack from *Dr. Zhivago* was playing in the cabin, but Grant could hardly hear it on the porch.

"Hi, Dad," Ingrid spoke from across the porch. Both of them felt a vague uneasiness, but neither of them wanted to address it.

"Hi, honey."

"I'm gonna stay here tonight ... with you ... OK?" Grant could tell she was searching for his approval.

"Sure." He didn't look up with the reply. He wanted her to understand that that was what he wanted ... expected ... but he didn't want her to think it was a big deal to him. It would be easier for her to come his way if he didn't pull at her, he thought. "You want something to eat?" he added.

"No, I'm going over to Willettes' for a while … OK?"

"Yeah. Have a nice time." He didn't even try to persuade her to stay. 'Same old same old,' he thought. 'Not much of an olive branch.' He made supper for himself and watched an old movie on TV.

Hours later, Ingrid crept into the cabin and then tiptoed up alongside Grant's bed. "Daddy … Daddy." She shook him gently and whispered so she wouldn't startle him.

"Yeah?" he whispered. 'She never calls me 'Daddy,'" he thought as the fog from sleep lifted.

"Take me fishing in the morning?"

"Sure," he said, half awake. 'That was an odd thing to ask,' he thought. The fog lifted a little bit more. "Are you OK, honey?"

"Yeah."

"What time is it?" he asked, still thinking something was wrong.

"Midnight."

"Why are you home so early?" He turned and tried to focus his eyes.

"Just wanted to be home."

"OK, Good."

Grant felt a distinct relief. It was a familiar feeling, but one that had nearly been forgotten. He remembered how secure he'd always felt when his family all slept under his roof. If she was safe under his roof, then he could roll over and sleep soundly. Something seemed out of the ordinary, though. She'd said she just wanted to be "home" — she hadn't spoken like that for years. And what was that about going fishing? He'd have to talk to her about that in the morning. "Goodnight, honey," he groaned as he pulled the covers up to his chin.

She waited until she was pretty sure he was asleep again. "I love you, Daddy," she said. She needed to tell him. She said it again, "I love you, Daddy." He groaned in his sleep and rolled over. "I want you to take care of me again.

~

The muffled sound of kitchen pots and pans clanging against each other lifted Ingrid from a comfortable sleep. She woke up but did not open her eyes. Her dad made a lot of noise in the morning, she thought. He always had. He was banging things around in the kitchen and watching those stupid fishing shows on TV — that's what he always did. Even in her state of half sleep, she began to smile a little smile. She could imagine her father fumbling around in the next room while he pulled pots and pans from the cupboards and prepared for breakfast.

When she opened her eyes, she saw that he'd pulled her window shade so the early morning sun wouldn't wake her. But she could see bright sunlight around the edges of the window; it looked like a nice day.

She shuffled out to the kitchen, hefted the big enamelware coffeepot, and poured a cup for herself. Grant was reading one of his fishing magazines and watching two men hunting pheasants on TV. "When did you start drinking coffee?" he asked while he blew the steam clouds off his own cup.

"Helps me stay awake to study." Ingrid turned to the TV, and then she blurted, "The music on those dumb fishing shows sounds just like the music on the porn videos." Instantly, before the words were out of her mouth, she wished she could take them back. She crinkled her face and slumped, waiting for her father's response. If only she'd waited for the early-morning cobwebs to clear in her head before she'd spoken.

Slowly, Grant turned toward her. He looked like he had a bad taste in his mouth. "See a lot of porn movies, do ya?" He waited for a response.

Somehow, during the first part of a slow, apologetic explanation, a smile crept onto her face. "Saw one last night." She was smiling fully and couldn't hide it. She knew she'd been caught at something she was embarrassed for. Her smile had the same effect on Grant that it always had, he relaxed. "Mary Alice Knutson checked one out at the video store and brought it over to Willettes' house. We watched a few minutes of it after the other movie we rented."

Grant exaggerated the disgusted look on his face. He put his fingers in his ears and turned back toward the TV. She understood. He didn't approve. He didn't want to hear any more about it, either, and there would be no lecture. She was old enough to make her own decisions on such things.

After a long minute, he turned to her and asked, "Want some breakfast?"

"Bannock and bacon?" she asked with a smile.

"Sure." He hadn't made bannock since Will had stayed with him the previous year. Ingrid hadn't asked for it since they used to camp out together when she was in junior high. Bannock is a fried bread or biscuit that the voyageurs and Indians ate. Grant made it by mixing water and flour and slowly baking the ball of dough in a cast-iron Dutch oven. It was a staple of their diet while camping. This morning meal served as a ritual to help them recall the memory of other mornings around the campfire.

"That'll give you the thuds! You should be full for all day now." Grant swallowed the last bit of a bacon-and-bannock sandwich and washed it down with a swig of coffee.

"You still make the best bannock, Dad!"

"Yes, I do!" he smiled contentedly, then added, "Did you ask me if we could go fishing when you came home last night, by the way?"

"Yeah, can we?"

"When?"

"Now."

"Don't you have to study?"

"Nah! Plenty of time later."

Grant was turning over the soil by the garden with a potato fork and looking for worms when Ingrid approached him carrying an empty Folgers coffee can. She had on a well-worn pair of denim bib overalls, a red plaid shirt, and a Twins cap. Her hair was in long braids, and she had two fishing rods in her other hand.

He bent over and dropped to one knee when he turned over a large fork full of earth. Several large worms tried to escape back into the bigger clods of dirt, but Grant was soon busy crushing the clods with his bare hands. He threw dirt and worms into the can while Ingrid extended it to him.

"Ooh, there's one! Get 'em, Dad," she said several times as he turned over more dirt and then grabbed at worms and clods.

His knee ached a little from kneeling on it, and he leaned back to adjust his weight. White puffs of clouds drifted across the blue sky above Ingrid when he looked up at her. She smiled at him and shrugged ... she was enjoying this just as she had as a child. During the morning together, he'd sensed that she was looking for this — for something to return to, just as he'd always needed to return to the lake or the little farm where he grew up.

Grant sat back on his heels. "So why are you here, honey ... with me? What's happened? I thought you wanted to be out of my life." Then he wondered if he'd been too blunt.

Her eyes filled immediately. "I miss you, Daddy! I miss the way we were. I want my daddy back." She sniffled and her lip trembled. "I thought we were doing all right, but when Will died you dropped me, like you were angry at me. So I dropped you." Ingrid wiped her eyes with her sleeve. "Not so long ago, I had this wonderful family. Now it's all gone. You and Mom were better — just better in every way — than all of my friends' parents. She's gone now, and that'll have to be OK ... but can't I have *you* back?"

The long braids made her look like a child. It really hadn't been that long since she was a little girl, but it seemed like a generation had passed. In his mind's eye, Grant saw her now as a twelve-year-old waiting for her daddy to catch some worms. In the next instant, he saw a chubby toddler running through the lawn sprinkler with a black puppy chasing her.

The palms of his hands rested on his thighs as he took a long look at her, to see just exactly who it was standing in front of him. "I see your Gramma's smile ... she's so sweet." He took a deep breath and continued to stare at her. "I see your mother, too."

From somewhere deep inside of him, all of the things he'd been stifling for a year began to rise quickly. The back of his throat tightened, and his eyes filled. "And I can see in your eyes that you need me." Everything boiled over as it had at Big Ole's funeral. Grant began to sob and brought his dirty hands up to cover his face. "I'm so sorry I haven't been there for you." He could barely choke the words out before he began to sob again. "I'm so sorry I turned my back on you. I'm so sorry."

She meant to comfort her father when she dropped to her knees and hugged him. When she'd seen him cry, she felt weak and uncertain. The only thing for her to do was reach for him as a small child would. Whenever she'd held him like this, for her whole life, she'd felt his strength come into her – and this moment was no different. This was what she'd wanted ... needed ... for a long, long time. She felt love and forgiveness. She felt the unconditional love of her dad once again. Grant felt it all, too, and he thought about how he'd held Big Ole at the end of his life, and he wondered again about Big Ole's feelings when they held each other. He kept his arms firmly around Ingrid for several minutes and said nothing.

"I don't want you to grow up," he breathed into her ear. "I don't want you to leave me. I don't want you to take up with some dipshit who'll hurt you. I don't want you to get old and sick."

"Well, that's life, isn't it?" she asked.

"Yup. But it hurts so bad."

"Well, isn't that how you know you're alive?"

"You should only quote smart people." She knew he was smiling, even though his face was pressed against hers.

"I did, Daddy ... smartest man I ever met." He wept all over again because he knew she meant it.

They still held each other, comfortably now, each of them on their knees beside the little hole in the ground. Grant's face was covered with the black dirt from his hands and streaked with tears. They swayed gently with their cheeks touching; each of them only wanted to hold the other. All of the pleasure of Ingrid's childhood came back to her father. He loved how good it felt when his little girl had held him like this. Didn't matter if she'd been happy or sad ... just mattered that he'd been there.

"Dad?"

"Yeah?" They were still holding each other cheek to cheek.

"You were right."

"Bout what?"

"Everything."

Grant laughed out loud. Tears and snot covered his upper lip. He took a white handkerchief from his pocket and wiped his face. "Glad you think so, honey," he said as he held her close again.

"Dad?"

"Yeah, honey?"

"Are you getting my face all dirty?"

Grant grinned and stood up. He extended his hand to her and lifted his daughter to her feet. The left side of her face was smeared with her own tears and black dirt from his face. "No, you look fine."

She knew better than to believe him and started to wipe her face as she stood up.

Grant picked up the coffee can, stuck the shovel in the ground, and took Ingrid's hand in his. They walked together to the boat and started to get to know each other for the first time as adults. He asked about school. She asked about home. When they were ready to start out across Spider Lake, Ingrid asked, "Hey, can I drive?"

Grant simply moved to the front seat of the boat and whistled for Nellie to join him. He motioned for Ingrid to have at it and then watched her while she struggled to start the motor and move Silverheels away from the dock. Several times he tried to help with the rope start, and she pushed him away each time until she got it started by herself. As she opened up the throttle and accelerated out onto the lake, she asked, "Christian Island?"

He nodded yes.

When she arrived at the place where Grant thought the fish would be, he dropped the anchor and began to rig one of the fishing rods with a bobber and a worm. He flipped the worm and the bobber over the side and watched it for a second.

"You were right, too," he said, still looking at his bobber.

"About what?" she asked.

"The music on the fishing videos does sound like music on porn movies." He looked at his bobber, then smiled slowly.

"See a lot of porn movies ... do ya?" she asked reproachfully. Then her face bent into a smile, too.

He handed her the other fishing rod. "Today you can rig this yourself, worms and all." The hours passed easily. They talked about everything and nothing. They caught a few walleyes. They became friends again as the boat rocked gently on calm water.

Grant was fumbling around in the little tackle box he always carried when Ingrid poked him. "Hey, Dad. Look." When he looked up at her, she pointed to the cattails on the north side of Christian Island.

A drake and a hen mallard cupped their wings around the afternoon breeze and rode the wind into the still water along the shore. Grant heard himself utter, "Ooo, that was nice. Of all the things I see in this world, I love that the most. Even after all these years, there remains something enchanting in that sight ... makes my heart flutter every time — still."

"Yeah," Ingrid whispered, "I guess ... me too."

~

That evening, they stood in the kitchen waiting for the popcorn to finish popping once again. Ingrid put her hand on Grant's shoulder. "You OK, Dad?"

"Yeah. Fine."

"Honk! That was my bullshit-o-meter!"

He smiled at her. "Whatya mean?"

"Are you happy?"

"Yeah."

"Honk! I know that isn't true! But something *has* changed, more than all of the things we talked about. You're different."

"Anne stopped by yesterday." He didn't look up.

"And?"

"She said some things that made me think. She's getting married, too!"

"She's not the one for you, Dad."

"She's a good friend!"

Ingrid ignored him. "You have *Dr. Zhivago* playing again today!"

"So?" he asked

"Pretty hard to miss the symbolism there, Dad ... how appropriate," Ingrid smiled.

"What are you talking about?"

"Well, let's see. A politically naïve doctor gets caught up briefly in a political mess. He's in love with two women, one blonde and one dark. The dark-haired one ..."

"OK, write a paper on it and then show it to someone who's interested."

"Dad! Something has changed, you know it."

"I think I want to be me again," Grant finally admitted, "whatever that is."

"Ever hear from Susan?"

"No." Grant kept his eyes down and tried not to let Ingrid see the surprise on his face.

"I liked her, Dad."

"You could have fooled me." He wouldn't look up.

"You should talk to her."

Grant nodded yes but did not reply. Ingrid let that be the end of it. She took a beer from the refrigerator for each of them and walked toward the TV. Grant was relieved to be finished with the talk of Susan, but he grimaced at the thought of his little girl having a beer. He passed a disapproving look her way, and when she noticed it she said, "I've had a beer before, Dad. I've been away at college for awhile, I've been around a little, you know."

He put his fingers in his ears and turned away again briefly. He had nothing to say other than he really didn't want to hear any more. She moved to the little table by the TV and she was holding a video when she turned back toward him. "Hey, I've never seen this whole thing." She was showing him *Jeremiah Johnson*.

"Ah, one of the classics! Roll 'em." Grant held the popcorn on his lap and sank into the leather couch. Ingrid placed the tape in the VCR and then found a seat next to him. She smiled a satisfied smile when she settled next to her dad. She knew he wanted her to be there with him. They needed each other tonight.

chapter THIRTY-ONE

The relentless hammering noise made by the tiny ice pellets screamed in his ears. The storm quickened, and the hailstones hammered at the aluminum hull of the over-turned boat. He felt as though something was swirling just above him, searching for him ... with deadly intentions. The pressure he'd applied with his crumpled up face-mask had stemmed the bleed-ing from the wound above his right eye. The eye and the right side of his face were beginning to ache and swell. He slowly recoiled into the wet grass under the boat.

He lay still in the darkness, in the wet and cold, waiting ... for what, he didn't know. As the wind roared above him and the ice bullets drilled at Silverheels, he was thankful to have what small respite the little boat provided in order to collect his thoughts.

Only minutes earlier, he'd been preparing to leave. The wet, sloppy snowflakes had turned to ice and had begun to burn his face when they struck. That was when he should have made his run for home, but he hadn't — he couldn't. His last best friend needed him as never before, and he would be there for his friends, at all cost, from now on.

Two hours earlier, the ducks had come traveling on the cusp of a storm once again. They'd begun to kite into his decoys. Northern mallards sailed into his decoy spread in small groups, one group after another. They hung on the wind just above the decoys. They circled and sailed above him just as they had during a lifetime of pleasant dreams.

Grant killed one drake and sent Nellie after it, and she made the retrieve in fine fashion. But when she returned to the boat, she whimpered as she released the duck to Grant. She sat close to him and wagged her tail. The idea that something might be wrong with Nellie never occurred to Grant. He was lost in the spectacle of ducks circling Christian Island.

Her tail wagged slowly as she rested her muzzle on his thigh. Grant noticed Nellie turn her head toward the empty seat, and then she returned her muzzle to his thigh and let out a deep breath. "I miss him too, Nellie ...."

A small flock sailed directly toward the decoys with no hesitation. Their wings were cupped, and he hid silently. When they dropped their feet, Grant stood and fired twice. Two drakes lay dead — a classic double — a drake with each barrel. "Nellie, back!" he hissed. Nellie sprung toward the side of the boat, but when her feet rested on the gunwales, she stopped. She turned her gray muzzle toward Grant and apologized with her eyes, "I just can't do it anymore, old friend." They both knew it was the end of something great.

Grant retrieved the ducks himself and then put his gun in its case. He shared a peanut butter sandwich, some beef jerky, and two candy bars with Nellie while they watched the big ducks on the front end of the storm attack their decoys. 'Screw the storm, screw the weather, screw everything ... my old friend needs me,' he thought. He wanted to cry when he looked at Nellie. She was still wagging her tail and watching ducks. She just couldn't throw her old bones into the icy water anymore. "Man, we have been through a lot together, haven't we? Good times and bad," Grant sighed. And together they watched the northern flight migrate … for the last time.

Then the weather turned ugly about mid-afternoon. The raging storm had jumped on him from the north. Whitecaps boiled off the tops of three- to five- foot rollers shortly after the wind had shifted. Any hope of crossing the lake was abandoned at that moment. Silverheels could maybe handle the rough water. But if the motor failed, he'd be crushed on the rocks along the far shore.

Grant understood the danger around him as he began to pick up the decoys. Even on the lee side of the island, the boat was hard to control in the rough water. Most of the decoys had been bagged when the motor began to sputter. Grant didn't like what the motor was telling him, and he quickly turned the boat into the wind and gave the outboard some gas. It coughed again and then died. Now what? If he fumbled with the motor for a moment and couldn't start it, it would be too late. He'd be blown into deep water and be at the mercy of the storm.

He could feel the wind, or some force, turn his boat and wrestle it toward the maelstrom in the middle of the lake. Now there was real fear and confusion in his head. There was no time to think about his choices. He either had to stay on the boat and hope to ride it out, which did not appeal to him, or jump over the side immediately and hope he was still in shallow enough water.

In the deepening darkness, he could still see the shoreline. What to do? An undeniable force was towing his boat away from Christian Island. After an agonizing moment of uncertainty, he clutched the bowline and leapt over the side.

When he splashed clumsily into the lake, his feet felt the bottom come up to meet him. He'd jumped into four feet of water instead of forty, and the fear that had been overtaking him suddenly gave him strength. He dug in and horsed the little boat as far onto the shore as he could pull it.

The wind seemed to be throwing ice and fire at him at the same time. He'd lost the glove on his left hand, and his face and fingers burned in the screaming wind. He threw his gear out of the boat and onto the shore, removed the outboard motor and gas can, and untied the binding that held the duck blind onto the boat. The boat seemed weightless as he dragged it back into the small trees and brush a little farther inland and then flipped it over on its side.

While Silverheels rested on her side, Grant bent over slightly and tried to look at the ground before he turned the boat over completely and crawled under it. Just as he bent at the waist, a gust of wind blew a large branch out of a nearby cottonwood tree. The bough hit hard about fifteen feet from Grant and then fell toward Grant and the boat. He was completely unprepared for the force behind the heavy bough when it hit him.

The tree struck Grant's back and pushed him forward with a force like a small tidal wave. If Silverheels hadn't been in front of him he would have been knocked down with only a scare and some scratches. But the force of the impact slammed his head into the gunwale of the little boat, and everything went dark for him.

When he regained consciousness, Nellie was standing over him. He was face down in the wet grass and dirt, and rain was pelting his exposed head. His face hurt, and when he brought his hand up to feel for damage, he felt the open wound above his eye and warm blood running from it.

After he struggled to one knee, he reached into his pocket and found his facemask. Using the small nylon mask like a bandage, he applied pressure to his wound and then rolled under the boat.

In spite of the driving noise of the hailstones on the boat hull, there was an air of calm under the boat. For the first time since the crisis had begun he was aware of his own response. He was trembling. He could hear himself panting now that he was somewhat protected from the noise of the wind. He felt like he was cowering, as if a bully were standing over him.

Suddenly, the entire earth shuddered and the wind screamed through the pine trees above him with a new force. He wondered if the boat might be pulled off of him and tossed across the lake like a rag. Tree branches snapped, and he felt them hitting the ground around him. It was as if an angry God had been watching him struggle in the storm. Just now, when he'd reached safety, God had stretched out one arm and raked it across the lake as an angry man might reach across a dinner table, sweep all of the dishes off the table, and smash them against a wall. All Grant could do was flinch and pull himself closer to the wet ground.

Grant could see only darkness, but just after the trees around him snapped, he was aware of Nellie's presence. He could hear her whimpering and scratching the ground beside the boat. He lifted the boat slightly, and she crawled into the protective dome provided by the boat hull. She pushed herself close to him, and he could feel her trembling, too. Strangely, the smell of wet dog made him feel even more alone.

He tried to make himself comfortable and collect his thoughts for a moment. What if this was to be his end? After all of the heartache and loss and pain, to die this way? 'It's not fair ... it's absurd,' he thought. The world was totally out of control now. All he could do was watch and wait for whatever was coming next. The wind shook the trees again, and more branches and debris fell around him. Several times the ground trembled, and Grant thought it felt like nearby thunder. The only similar experience he could remember was the time he'd lost control of his car on an icy road. Everything raced past him at a terrifying speed, but he saw it all happening in slow motion. The memory brought a rush of uncertainty and fear, and Grant hated the feeling it caused in his stomach. He didn't like it, and he didn't want it to be happening again now.

The wind raged once more, and when it settled briefly, all of the fear in Grant's belly began to turn to an unusual sense of serenity. He began to understand that even if he died in this place, he'd be all right. Then, as the minutes passed, he slowly realized that he might live through the night. The peaceful sensation remained for many minutes while he waited for something – anything – to happen.

Shaken but relatively unhurt, he thought he had a reasonable chance to survive this night after all. But he knew that issue might still be in doubt. Now that he wasn't going to drown, it seemed that the things he had to worry about were hypothermia, the outside chance that another tree might fall on him, or the possibility that he'd had a serious concussion.

The fingers on his left hand were painfully cold and he slid his bare hand inside his waders. He gasped slightly at the cold his fingers caused on his own stomach. Then he remembered the goofy look on Will's face when he'd talked about grabbing his "weeny" with cold hands, and it made him smile.

For weeks after the funeral, he'd been angry at Will for dying. Then he began to miss Will in an unrelentingly mournful way. His home was filled with Will's things, and it seemed that every time he came across a possession of Will's, he was taken with a bittersweet memory. Photographs on the wall, nicks on his furniture, old songs, daily tasks – everything had reminded him of Will for months, and he felt the pain of his loss every day.

Grant thought of Anne's words as the memory of Will caused a smile to cross his face even now. Anne had been right, 'The love we have for people never goes away, even when the people do,' he thought.

What about Anne? What had been fair in her life? He himself had caused Anne plenty of pain. In fact, much of the happiness in his life had brought her pain. So just who, of all the people he loved, had life been fair with? Frank? Kate? Will? Big Ole? Anne?

The grinding shrill of the ice balls hitting the boat continued. Thoughts of survival returned, and he reached for his wristwatch. He found the small button on the watch and pushed it. The dial read 7:18 p.m. "It's gonna be a long night, Nellie."

June, Frank, and Evie were spending the weekend at the Ordway house. However, Grant had no plans to get together with them tonight or tomorrow. They probably wouldn't even notice that he hadn't returned from hunting today. If they did notice that he hadn't come home, he hoped Frank would not be foolish enough to venture onto the lake in a rescue attempt.

Grant also knew there was no possibility of the Campbells calling someone else to come for him. No boat could come through the shallow, rocky channels tonight. There would be no boat travel tonight between the public access, far across several odd-shaped bays, and through their small outlets, which opened toward Christian Island.

As he assessed the situation, it seemed to Grant that he had ten to twelve hours to stay alive – to avoid hypothermia – before he could be rescued or return home on his own. For now, at least, he was comfortable.

The blow to his head concerned him. He didn't know how long he'd been unconscious, but he reasoned that it couldn't have been too long because the steady rain would have soaked his clothes far more than it had if he'd been exposed for very long. The possibility of some sort of bleed in his brain existed, and he didn't like to think about it. But just the fact that he was thinking about it was good, he reasoned – his brain must be functioning all right.

His neoprene waders had kept the cold lake water out, but the neoprene would work both ways. He knew he'd worked up a little sweat while moving the boat and that the waders would keep that moisture in. If he stayed inactive and laid on the ground long enough, the perspiration inside his waders would cool and he'd begin to catch a chill. If he got up and moved around a lot now to stay warm, he'd only sweat more and have more moisture to deal with later. Just the fact that he could reason things out in this manner caused him to feel better about the possibility of an intracranial bleed. "Head's too hard," he said to himself as he readjusted his weight.

He was relatively comfortable now, and it seemed to him that the only prudent choice would be to remain calm and wait for morning. He pulled the hood of his hunting jacket over his head and bunched up some wet grass for a pillow. Grant was willing to allow himself to sleep for a while now. But as it turned out, sleep would not come easily.

Instead of sleeping, Grant lay on his side with his arm around Nellie, and while he stroked her wet fur and listened to the weather, he began to think about his life again. Bad things probably would continue to happen to good people. Life would not be fair, no matter how he thought about it. The words "outrageous fortune" came into his head, and then he remembered that the phrase had come from Shakespeare – which reminded him of Susan.

For the first time in months, he allowed himself to think about her. He admitted to himself that he missed her. She had been special. He supposed his love for her would remain now that she was out of his life, too. But he drew no comfort from that thought as he had when he'd thought about Will. In this moment, he allowed himself to miss her smile, and her touch.

His thoughts began to float. They made no sense. He drifted in and out of sleep. Once again he dreamed the dream about his old friends not returning his calls. He was startled when his own trembling awoke him sometime later. It seemed like much later, but he was disappointed to see that his watch read only 11:47 p.m. He was already very cold, and he'd need to stay where he was for at least six hours. The intensity of the rain and wind had diminished somewhat, but there was still a storm raging around him.

He propped the boat up so he'd have more room to sit upright underneath it. He prepared a much larger bed of grass and weeds and then settled his back into it. The extra insulation brought some immediate warmth. He wiggled his fingers and toes and slid the collar on his sweater a littler higher on his neck. He wasn't sure he could make it all night like this.

~

Frank Campbell had noticed that Grant hadn't returned from the hunt. He tried to believe that he'd simply not been looking when Grant came home, but after supper he took a flashlight and walked to Grant's cabin to check. The dark cabin and the waves splashing where Silverheels was usually tied told him everything.

June Campbell held the phone to her ear and looked at the rain streaming down the windowpane. She'd called the Hubbard County Sheriff's Department immediately when Frank returned with the news about Grant.

"There's no way we can get a boat out on Spider Lake tonight in this storm, Mrs. Campbell. We'll have our rescue boat at the public access tomorrow morning as soon as we can," the deputy told her. "But you people stay put tonight. There's no point in endangering yourselves, too. Besides, your friend may be all right."

"How can he be all right in *this*?"

"Happens all the time, Mrs. Campbell."

"Yeah, right," June said contemptuously as she hung up the phone.

"It will be OK, June." Frank stood beside her with his hands in his pockets. She thought he seemed to know something that she didn't.

June simply turned and walked into the kitchen. She poured a cup of coffee for herself and walked back to the Great Room. "I'm going to walk down to his cabin." She put on her boots and a slicker and took a flashlight out the kitchen door.

Evie had been sitting on the couch beside the door that opened onto the porch. As always, a book sat under the table lamp next to her, and just now she seemed isolated there in the yellow circle of light.

The concern in her eyes was unmistakable, and Frank went to her. Another mother's son was in danger, and she ached inside for all that this brought back to her.

"Evie." He took her hand in his when he sat next to her. He'd never recovered from the accident; he never would. Sometimes when he walked, it looked as if his arms and legs weren't working together. But when he spoke to her now, Evie could see a little of the old strength in his eyes. "I think he had something to work through, and it could only happen out there. I think he's going to be fine. Every man has to learn to deal with this way that life seems to carry us along. Does that make sense?"

"Not really."

"Yeah," he sighed. "Not really."

June returned slowly from Grant's cabin and spent the entire night pacing. Evie went to her room and tried to sleep. Frank sat in a big chair in the corner of the Great Room. He went onto the porch from time to time just to let the cold wind blow on his face.

~

An hour before sunup, June had had enough waiting. She got into her car and drove slowly toward the public boat landing on the far side of the lake. She turned on the gravel road that led to the county campground in the woods on the south side of the lake. The small campground was close to the place where the rocks protruded above the water's surface — the place the boys had always called the cemetery. She was hoping to find Grant sitting there waiting to be rescued. She walked the narrow beach and called out to Grant while she stepped over the small rocks and twisted pieces of driftwood.

A large old cork decoy lay on the sand. It rocked when the tiny waves bumped it. June picked it up and inspected it. The letters OT were painted on the bottom ... Ole Thorson. 'This is not good,' she thought. Then she found another ... then a life jacket. Then she heard a noise like a drum. The red six-gallon gas tank was almost empty, and the small waves rhythmically lapped at it and bumped it against a rock. It said "Thorson" on the side, and it was dented in several places from pounding into the rocks in the cemetery.

~

"Susan, this is June Campbell. I had to call you, I'm not sure if I should have."

"Hello, June. I was just leaving for work. What's the matter?"

June knew that Susan had been hurt badly when Grant had ended their relationship. She knew Susan had held on to strong feelings for Grant for some time, but she had not spoken to Susan for months. "I think Grant is in trouble. I don't know; he may be dead. I don't know ... I just had to call you." Her voice was strong, but not like it had been when she'd called to tell of Will's death.

"What happened?"

"He got caught in a storm last night, out on the lake. There's no sign of him on the lake this morning, and I found some of his things floating along the lakeshore. I'm at the public boat access now, with the police. Frank is here with me. We're going to help them search." Susan heard the stress begin to creep into June's voice. "The police think he probably drowned." June began to sniffle. "It doesn't seem like this can be happening ... it just can't be real."

"So you don't know for sure yet, just what has happened, right?" Susan asked.

"I guess not. But it doesn't look good. His gas can was all smashed up and floating on the far shore from where he would have been," June answered.

"In the cemetery?"

"Yes," June answered with a little cough, almost a laugh, at the macabre irony of it and the fact that Susan remembered the lake so well.

"Evie is waiting for word from us. She said she'd call Grant's mother and Ingrid if …." Her voice trailed off, then she started over. "I wanted to call you because, well, I wanted to call you … maybe for my sake."

"Thanks, June. Will you call back when … later?"

A year earlier, Susan had begun to wonder if she'd give up her career and move to Walker if Grant asked her to. She'd sensed that he was the one, the man she'd hoped for and then given up hope of ever finding. He'd made her laugh like no other man had. She'd known all along that he was smitten with her, and she'd loved the way that made her feel about herself. He was strong — a man's man, as Will Campbell had told her once. But he was weak, too. And try as he might to hide a soft heart, she'd seen it right away and been drawn to him by his vulnerable nature.

She'd had a year, though, to mourn his loss. It would have been almost the same for her if he'd actually died back then. She began to recall all of the pain and frustration and loneliness she'd felt when he'd first broken things off. She'd written several times, but he'd never responded. She'd called and left telephone messages, but he'd never returned a call. She'd tried e-mail a few times and then quit trying altogether when he never responded. Anger had filled her heart after the initial pain. When her heart began to heal, she'd dated others — she'd always had plenty of men interested — but Grant had become the standard for comparison, and others just fell short. At first she'd hoped that he'd call, but with each passing month that seemed less and less likely.

She began to wonder what his death had been like. Just what was it like to drown? Perhaps it had been something more violent. 'My God,' she thought, 'how would Gladys take the news, or Ingrid?'

Susan remembered how Grant had wept so bitterly at his father's grave, and how he'd sat quietly and stared when he'd been told of Will's death.

She raised the phone to her ear with one hand and dialed her boss's number with the other. "Hello, Petra. I'll be a little late coming in today. I need to wait by my phone for word on a personal crisis. I'll explain later." She left a message for her boss and hung up her phone.

~

Grant awoke for the twentieth time – or was it the thirtieth? He didn't know. But he noticed that the rain had stopped and the wind had died down considerably. As he moved his arms to roll onto his side, Nellie began to wag her tail. He peeked under the gunwale and saw that the blackness of the night sky was beginning to ebb to a light gray along the eastern horizon.

He lifted the boat off of himself and rolled out from underneath. His body moisture had condensed on the cotton shirt he wore under his waders, and it made him even colder when he moved and his clothes touched his chest. His breath had condensed into a thick layer of frost on his whiskers. His toes were numb, but at least his head only hurt when he reached up to touch it.

He knew he'd made it. He'd be home in a little while. The gathering light of the dawn seemed to signal a victory. He felt as though he'd crawled through a long, dark tunnel and emerged into the light here on Christian Island.

As he stood, he could see his outboard motor, lying on the beach where he'd dropped it. The duck blind was mostly intact but piled up next to the boat. Everything around him was coated with a clear layer of ice about two millimeters thick. All of the trees hung heavy with a coating of ice, but only a couple of feet of ice extended out from the shore at Christian Island. The lake was still open, and fairly calm. He walked a few steps and thought it felt good to move, to get some blood pumping. Walking slowly and looking in the direction of Spider Lake Duck Camp, he stumbled on the boat oars and nearly fell.

He stood and rubbed his hands together. Stiff and cold but otherwise all right, he decided to head for home.

It took him almost half an hour to reassemble the boat, and motor, and blind, and whatever gear he could find. His side by side had a big scratch on the stock where the boat had been dragged over it, but it appeared to be in working order otherwise. The duffel with shotgun shells and aspirin was still pretty much dry inside. He took four aspirin and washed them down with lake water. He wondered if the indestructible old Evinrude motor just might start up and carry him home, but the gas can was gone. So he'd have to wait to find out exactly what had been wrong the day before.

He could see the far shoreline of Spider Lake clearly when he slid his boat over the small shelf of ice and into the water. He was looking backward, at Christian Island, while he leaned on the oars and pulled himself toward home.

The little boat slipped quietly in one direction while Grant stared in the other. He used the sight of where he'd been to guide him home. A moment of awareness ... enlightenment ... came to him gradually. He leaned back on the seat and raised his head. He let the autumn breeze unfurl the things that had been wrapped around his heart.

In the gray dawn, an epiphany washed over him slowly. He'd never loved his life more than now, when he'd almost lost it. Life wasn't fair. 'OK, so who said it was supposed to be fair,' he thought. For a while there, during the night, death had been part of all the mystical, unknowable things he reveled in – the things that made him know he was alive, as he'd always said – and he'd liked that.

He understood now that there was no order to be made of some things, no control to be had over certain events. Death could not be the opposite of order; it had to be part of the ethereal ... of the great things that are to be pondered but never conquered.

His need to create order, to gain control, had kept much of life's joy at arm's length. Happiness could perhaps be found out there where order and ether met ... where the struggles with life took place. He could live with that. He'd be just fine with that! Deep down inside, he'd always known that was true, at least for others. Now, after the night on the island, he felt like something had been given to him, and he knew he could actually find joy simply in the struggle with life; he no longer needed control of it all. The oars creaked as he leaned on them. Nellie wagged her tail and watched the cabin come closer.

It was probably too late. He'd let the love of his life get away, and he had no right to expect her to come back now. 'She was actually the second love of my life,' he thought. Did people ever get to have more than one? He'd never heard anyone suggest such a thing. 'What a fool I've been all these years,' he thought.

~

Evie Campbell walked to the door, then onto the screened-in porch. It was cold outside — not quite freezing, but cold. She held a large coffee cup in both hands and looked out across the lake. She thought she'd seen something on the lake. She'd assumed it was the sheriff's boat. But it wasn't! Two oars stroked the water, then lifted, and then stroked again. The little boat was Silverheels.

She hurried to the phone and called Frank on his cell phone. "He's alive!" she exclaimed. "And he's rowing back across the lake." She hung up the phone, hurriedly put on her coat, and picked up the cane she used now when she walked. In her excitement, she tried to walk too fast, and she nearly fell several times.

~

Grant had been in the cabin for a few minutes when Evie finally reached it. She moved very slowly and deliberately now when she stepped onto the porch. She stopped on the doorstep when she heard voices. Then she realized he was on the phone.

"I know it. And I'm so sorry for the hurt that I caused you!" He was pleading when he continued. "If you ever loved me ... if you ever loved your mother ... if you ever loved anyone, please let me see you!" He paused again. "I was so wrong. I love you. I need to see you." After another pause, he added, "I'll come to see you then, if you'll talk to me."

Evie peeked in the window and saw him slowly put the phone down. He let out a long sigh. She let herself in without knocking, and Grant turned to the door immediately. He looked surprised when Evie walked toward him. 'I must look pretty bad,' he thought as Evie approached. The blood from his head wound was smeared and frozen all over his face and hands and clothes. Evie looked at him with the same concern that his own mother would have.

"You scared us all half to death!" she said as she put her arms around him. She rested her head on his chest and patted his back. Grant heard her begin to sob, and as she wept she clutched his back and pulled him close. She had to be thinking of Will ... and measuring the pain she'd just dodged. He put his arms around her and stroked the back of her head.

"I'm sorry I scared you, Evie. It was a long night."

"It sure was. What did she say, Grant?"

He looked out the window. "She said I'd hurt her enough already and she just couldn't come back for more. She said goodbye."

chapter THIRTY-TWO

Silent and still, the gray sheet of water and the forest that surrounded it lay as quiet as death in the autumn overcast. He'd lost his way out there somewhere, and oddly enough he'd never really left home. Love and grief had swirled over and through him like the chill in November's darkest winds … and left him here.

His legs dangled from the small pier as he stared across the lake. He was stranded, but he was finally home.

His eyes slowly lost focus and followed only the mercurial shine of the water's surface. Somewhere beneath it, or beyond it, he began to see the soft yellow light of his bedroom reading lamp. His wife lay next to him, warm under the covers and reading before bed on a cold winter night. She called to him. She wanted to read something for him. It was a quote from Shakespeare, and he saw her smiling as she read it. He'd heard it a hundred times before; she read it to him and smiled every time she came across it.

Here is a tide in the affairs of men
Which, taken at the flood, leads to fortune
Omitted, all the voyage of their life
Is bound in the shallows and miseries
And we must take the current when it serves
Or lose our ventures.

Before the image vanished, he wondered if he'd taken the tide as he'd always assumed, or escaped it ... for all his life.

His vision faded into the afternoon air, and after a moment — he didn't know how long, really — Grant knew it was time to get back to work.

The boat was actually no worse for the wear, even after spending a night upside down, he thought. Silverheels was suspended above the water on her little boatlift. He'd been making repairs on her for a few days now. When the new gas can was connected to the gas line, he lowered it under the bow platform where he'd always hidden it. He thought his boat looked ... not right somehow. "Must be the lack of empty shells and wrappers and such that we dumped on the island, huh Nellie?"

Nellie wagged her tail and lifted her head off the dock at the mention of her name.

"Hell of a way to clean your boat though," he mumbled to no one but himself.

Grant was bent over and fumbling with a wrench, trying to repair the framework of the duck blind on the little boat, when he heard footsteps on the dock. The footsteps stopped and Grant looked up.

Susan Wells stood at the end of the dock. She stared at him, unmoving ... rigid. She was well dressed, as if she was on a business trip, and she was carrying a small bag.

Neither of them spoke. Grant raised his eyebrows and tried to smile ... to draw a smile from her. He could not.

Spider Lake was still a familiar place to her. But it was not hers anymore, as it had been — or almost was — before. She felt like she had when she'd returned to her old high school ten years after graduation and found it the same, but different. It was just some-one else's.

Grant was wearing old blue jeans and a red plaid shirt, and when he climbed to the dock Susan thought he looked handsome, ath-letic. The attraction she felt surprised and irritated her. She was angry with him — no, she was way beyond angry — and she wanted him to know it. Now she felt she was being betrayed by her own feelings. He looked so handsome, and taken with the way she felt about not belonging here anymore, she began to resent her own decision to come. He walked toward her smoothly and put his arms around her. The row of fourteen black stitches above his eye and the discoloration on the right side of his face made the acci-dent real for Susan. He kissed her cheek and held her tightly.

"You said you'd never come back."

"I lied. Well, actually, I didn't really mean what I said. You can understand that, I guess."

Susan left her arms at her sides; she would not return his embrace or his kiss.

"You didn't come all the way here to hate me," he said into her ear.

"Yes, I did," she replied.

She wasn't certain if she'd intended to stay for an hour or overnight or to leave now, but something had drawn her here. Now she was here, and she felt very clumsy ... embarrassed at herself for coming. She felt compelled to turn and leave now, or scream at him, or say something really hurtful — anything but stand here like this.

"I'm so sorry, Susan. You were right ... about everything. I was a coward." He held her more tightly and she made herself more rigid. "It seemed right at the time. I'm so sorry. I'd like to tell you that I've changed. But I guess that would be too simple, wouldn't it?"

"Too simple? After what you did? I guess so! You hurt me …
more than anything ever hurt me!" Her voice raised in anger.

"I'm sorry."

"Oh, shit! Is that all you can say … 'I'm sorry'?" She was mock-
ing him, but he would not release her. She raised her arms around
him in a confused and frustrated embrace and began to hit the
middle of his back with her right fist. "Why?! Why?! Why did
you hurt me?" she hollered. Each time she said "why," she hit him
between his shoulders. She was crying now and still hitting his
back. She slowly stopped hitting and clutched his shoulders tightly.
She sobbed openly now and did not speak for a while.

"I was hurting, too," he said softly.

"Everything was so good. Friends are supposed to talk about all
those things that happened. How could you do that to me?" There
was a struggle in her voice; she was choking on the anguish that
spilled out with her words. Her nose was running, and tears
dripped off of her chin. She wiped her face on his shoulder.
"Sorry," she said. Then she started to hit at him again, although
gently now with her right hand, while she squeezed her left arm
around him tightly.

She could smell the familiar scent of his aftershave. His arms
felt strong again, as they always had before the night Will died. But
she did not want to put her arms around him as she had before,
when they were in love. He'd taken something from her and thrown
it away, and she wouldn't, or couldn't, forgive him.

He could feel her emotions colliding. Susan reminded him of a
mother who didn't know whether to spank or hug her child after
he'd done something dangerous like running through traffic. He
just held her for a while and said nothing more.

Her arms fell back to her sides, and she wiped her face on his
shoulder again.

"Would you come up to the cabin?" he asked as he took his
arms from her. She did not answer. She only turned and walked up

the path to the cabin. A string of pleasant but uninvited memories interrupted her answer as she walked past the old hot tub.

The weather had warmed after the storm several days earlier. Today was a calm, overcast October day, and there would be a few more duck days before this season ended. Grant took Susan's bag in one hand and followed her up the hill. He waited for Susan to speak as they sat facing each other on the porch.

"She's really gotten gray!" Susan said. She sat on the wicker love seat and scratched Nellie's ears.

"Yeah, I think she's reached the golden years," Grant replied as he moved next to Susan on the love seat and took her hand in his. He remembered Nellie looking at him when she refused a retrieve ... he told Susan how Nellie had faltered. Then he told her all about the storm and his night on the lake.

"Were you afraid?" she asked. Then she looked at his eye again.

"Yes," he laughed. "I was afraid for my life ... for a little while anyway."

"That was a pretty emotional morning, when you called me the other day," she said. "You were basically already dead to me, then you were really dead, then you were alive again!" Susan leaned back in her chair and questioned him like a skeptical attorney would question a hostile witness. "So what happened out there? You had some sort of vision and decided to patch things up with me, as if it was just some little tiff between us? What did you think I might feel?"

"I thought you might not want to see me ever again. But I decided to try because I was tired of giving up ... and because I love you and I had to tell you I did wrong, even if it was too late. More than that, because I need you ... and I know you need me."

She looked at him and tilted her head as if she was thinking about what he'd said.

"I didn't know whether to scream or cry ... there was so much I wanted to say to you." She stopped but continued to look at the lake. "I was so happy to hear your voice ... then I was angry and hurt all over again!"

"I know what you mean."

"Do you? Do you think you really do?" Anger had come back into Susan's voice, along with frustration. She hadn't really stopped being angry. "I would have quit my job, my career, and moved here if you'd asked." He knew she would have paid a high price for love. "And you just gave up," she added, contempt oozing out with her words.

"Look," Grant said, "I sailed through my small life in my small town and everything always went my way. Loving parents, lots of friends, no poverty, no incest, no drugs or alcohol ... everything was perfect throughout my entire little life. Then the wheels came off the wagon. I lost my wife, I lost my dad, I lost my best friend, and I was losing my daughter ... I was angry and hurting, too. What I did was wrong, stupid, and I've told you a thousand times I'm sorry. It isn't like I was unfaithful or something. I was just afraid to lose you the way I was losing everyone else. I was a coward. Maybe greatness was thrust upon me and I dodged it. Maybe I was afraid to run any more rapids on that long river Will and I talked about. I guess I was trying to control things that can't be controlled. It just seemed to me that the way to avoid any more pain was to stop giving my love so I wouldn't be vulnerable anymore. There's logic in there somewhere. It's not sound logic, but if you're already hurting it makes sense."

"So the next time something goes bad, are you gonna stop talking to me for a year?" she asked flatly.

Grant turned his face toward the lake. He was just beginning to really understand the hurt he'd caused her. He feared he might have pushed Susan so far away that she couldn't come back.

"You know, in every way I can think of to quantify success — or keep score in life, if you will, I've come up short. I never 'made it' at the university ... never turned out to be very good. I've never really been a success in my career … never made a lot of money anyway. In my only foray out into the world, everyone on the committee thought I was the village idiot from Walker, Minnesota." He paused. "No great shakes as a father, either." Grant lowered his head and took a deep breath.

"And I think you know that I always felt OK with that, because I had this little feeling that I somehow had a deeper understanding or appreciation of the little things, the special things in life. I thought I was living a better life than others because I understood all of those mystical principles about love and good friends. But when everyone died, I felt like I'd had that stuff all wrong, too. I just felt that I had nothing left to hope for … that everything would be taken from me."

He took another deep breath and let it out all at once, then he took her hand.

"Susan, on one of the last evenings I spent with Kate before she got sick, she read something from Shakespeare for me. That was one of the things that attracted me to you initially … that you quoted Shakespeare, too. But the piece she read to me spoke of a tide that comes along once in our lives, and if we catch it, it leads to great things. If we miss it, we have nothing. She said it made her think of me. Well, for all of my life I thought I'd been riding that tide to greatness. But over the last year, I've begun to feel that maybe I missed the tide … all along. Maybe *this* is my chance to catch that tide … maybe it's *your* chance."

Susan's face seemed to soften a little. This was the Grant Thorson she'd been in love with. But she would not let her guard down again so easily. She turned and looked at the woods.

The gray light of the afternoon surrounded the perfect green of the pines and muted the few yellow leaves still holding to the poplar branches. A few birds peeped around the bird feeders.

"I'm cold." She wasn't sure if she wanted the conversation to move in the direction it had been.

"OK, let's go on into the cabin and make a fire."

Susan stood by the kitchen table and watched while Grant built a fire. His back was turned to her when he began to stack paper and kindling and then small pieces of poplar in the fireplace.

"It's really been a warm autumn so far," Grant said. "Other than the big storm, it's been pretty nice. Some years, we're all iced in here by the end of October."

He struck a match and lit the fire. "Sit down and take a load off." He was smiling when he turned back to face her.

"I should call and get a room in town," Susan offered. Grant's face turned bleak and humorless. Now Grant was clearly frustrated.

"Look, Susan, I didn't call you for sex." He stood with his hands on his hips. "I want to restore what we had ... and I know we can do it. But you have to forgive me for letting you down. At some point you have to forgive me. What do you want to do ... kick me around for a while to get even?"

"Maybe," she said coldly. Then she looked at the floor and nodded her head in agreement. She was embarrassed for the way she'd sounded.

"We can't talk if you're not here." Grant waited for a response. She nodded again.

"Is Ingrid's room OK for you?"

"Yes." She looked at her feet, and then she raised a cold steel stare at him. "But you didn't let me down. You stuck a knife in my heart. You stole the sweetest, best thing I ever knew."

"And all I want is for you to let me give it back to you."

She only looked at him. She never replied. He took her bag into Ingrid's room, and when he returned Susan tried to let the conversation ease up. She sat down, and Grant did the same.

"How is Ingrid?"

"We had a rough year, too. I was a very poor father for a long time. I'm glad Big Ole didn't see me let my daughter down so many times." He rubbed his eyes with one hand.

"Everything is OK now?"

"It's very good. My little girl taught me some lessons about love."

"And your mother?"

"Fine."

"And Frank ... and Evie?"

"Frank has courage. So does Evie, I guess. I learned some things from watching Frank wrestle with ... all of this," Grant sighed. "I need to share something with you, Susan. There has been no one I could really talk to about all of this, until today. I need to say this." He stroked his chin and looked at the floor in front of him. "I don't miss Kate anymore." His eyebrows tightened slightly. "Maybe that isn't exactly the way to say it ... she was so good. But she's gone, forever. I can't bring her back. But you know, when I think of her now, I always feel good. I don't feel cheated anymore. That awful, heavy feeling doesn't weigh on me anymore ... when I think about her. She still makes me happy, that's all. I think that's good. Don't you?" And he looked away.

"Now, my dad ... that's a little different. I still get a little choked up when I think of him. I still want to be like him when I grow up! Maybe real heroes just never die, huh?"

Grant looked back at Susan. "And Will Campbell!" Grant's face brightened. "Will makes me smile!" Grant laughed and crossed his arms. "People say things to me, or maybe I'll see something happen on the street, or on TV, and then sure enough I'll see his smile and hear his voice. It's as though he's still with me." Grant smiled at Susan and raised his eyebrows. "It's good again ... know what I mean?"

She smiled a soft smile and nodded.

"An old friend told me all of this would happen," he said softly, to no one. Then he was ready to let their conversation lighten.

"So how 'bout you?" Grant leaned back once more. "Have you seen the President lately?"

"Yes, and Senator Bently, too. He said to greet you from all the other midlevel bureaucratic grunts who don't know or do anything!" Now she smiled for the first time.

"Really showed them a thing or two, didn't I?" he said sheepishly

"Especially the Russians. You know ... those lying sons-a-bitches who haven't told the truth for seventy years?" She smiled again. "My boss liked that one."

"I'll bet she was pretty happy that you were coming here."

"Not really." Susan couldn't seem to stop smiling now. "Hey! What about Emil and Hilda? Is anyone beating Emil's meat?" She covered her face with her hand to cover her own embarrassment.

"Nobody even wants to think about that." He leaned back in his chair. "Does it seem odd that we just discussed the President of the United States and Emil Krause in the same conversation?"

"Yes," she nodded.

"Are you hungry?"

"Yes, a little."

"Can you eat an Emil Krause Leech Lake left hander special frozen pizza if I open the freezer and cook one up from scratch?"

"I think so." She smiled and crinkled her brow ... asking him just what a Leech Lake left-hander special might be.

"You'll love it...beef jerky and pickled herring!" He nodded his own approval, straight faced and serious.

She knew he was joking. She lowered her eyes and smiled a bigger smile, she couldn't help it. He'd always had that power over her, just as Will had it over him, and now she remembered that little childish joy that always came with the smiles he drew from her.

Grant rose to preheat the oven for a frozen pizza. The cabin was dark now except for one table lamp and the yellow light from the fire in the fireplace. He had a beer in each hand as he turned away from the refrigerator and put the frozen pizza on the countertop.

"Hey, I forgot!" he said with a new delight. He walked quickly out the door and returned a moment later. A ten-week old female, yellow Labrador retriever tumbled in the door after him. The young dog was like a tornado, running and jumping and bumping into everything. Nellie was lying by the fire. She raised her head and looked at the puppy. Then she laid her head back down immediately as if to show her indifference.

"Susan, I'd like you to meet Mudcat. Currently Mudcat's only skills are eating and crapping, but Nellie and I hope to make a duck dog out of her!"

The puppy ran from one thing to another, first to Susan, then to Grant, then back around the couch. Susan's face bent into a warm smile. "Mudcat?" she said.

"Yeah, great name, huh?"

"Yeah." She smiled at Grant's enthusiasm, and Mudcat's.

As they shared the frozen pizza and beer, some of the barriers they'd been struggling with began to fall. Each of them knew it was happening, and they knew not to push too hard. Their conversation came easier; the rough edges on her comments went away. She saw that he was truly asking for forgiveness, and she began to wonder if they could really ever get back to where they'd been.

The cold beer reminded Susan of summer evenings at the cabin. She lifted a slice of pizza to her mouth, but before she could take a bite she stopped herself. "Hey, your friend John Lewis III made the news several times recently."

"Oh?"

"Seems he did a little insider trading. He won't be going away to visit the prison proctologist, but it's going to cost him plenty in fines."

"That's a shame." Grant tossed back a swallow of beer and shook his head. "I'm sure his actions warrant a thorough probing." He reached for another slice of the pizza that sat between them on the coffee table.

"The scary part is that I thought he was your date the night we met."

"Ooo. I'd prefer Emil Krause."

"Hilda would kill you!"

Grant leaned back on the couch and started to tell a story.

"One time, I saw Hilda throw a drunk out of the café … grabbed him by the belt and …" He suddenly sat bolt upright and stared across the room. He'd broken eye contact with her and was look-ing beyond her now. Susan looked where he was looking just in time to see Grant race past her toward Mudcat. The handsome puppy was hunched over by the coffee table, preparing to leave a message on the carpet.

"No, no, no!" Grant hollered, laughing as he ran to Mudcat. He picked the dog up as if she were a statue and carried her outside to do her business. A moment later, Grant re-entered the cabin, with Mudcat right behind him.

"That's when you find out just how much you love your dog — when you get up at 3:00 a.m. to get a drink and you step in shit! There's probably a message about lovers and friends in there too, huh!" He wore a great smile, and he stole a kiss on the lips as he walked by.

To her surprise — and somewhat against her wishes — she liked the kiss, and she tried to return it. This was the funny, clever man she'd been in love with. He made her like herself better just for being around him. It was exactly how he'd described his friendship with Will. He made her laugh. He sat across from her at the table and took her hand again. He kissed her hand. He smiled when he said, "I still love you, Susan. Will you try to love me again?"

She nodded yes, but she was uncertain if she could do it.

They talked for several more hours, and although they began to relax with each other, they still remained guarded — not quite able to find the easy comfort they'd always known before when they'd spoken with each other.

"You look tired. Would you like to get ready for bed?" Grant finally asked.

"I think so," Susan sighed.

"Can you stay for a few days? I took some time off work!"

"No, I have to leave tomorrow." She offered nothing more; she just couldn't.

"OK, what time do you have to go?" He didn't try to hide his disappointment.

"Early. I'll just have coffee and then go." Susan was actually far less compelled to leave him in the morning than she had been before. Part of her wanted to stay, to keep trying, and part of her saw that as giving in when she should be getting even. She still had a need to punish him — to not trust him.

When they were both ready for bed, Grant stood in the door of Susan's room. He would not enter. He wanted to kiss her goodnight, and she knew it. Instead of walking to him and kissing him goodnight, she simply climbed into bed and turned out her light. Then she called "goodnight" from the darkness.

Her message was clear, and she knew she'd hurt his feelings. She felt she had to ... she needed to ... but then she immediately felt bad about it, too. Grant walked silently to his room and crawled under the covers. He lay on his back thinking about how absurd this scene was. The two of them lay in adjoining rooms pretending to sleep, but each of them knew the other was wide awake. There was so much that still needed to be said and no way to find the words.

After many minutes of staring at the ceiling, Grant called to her.

"Susan?"

"Yes."

"Your life won't get any better if you turn into me."

Many long minutes passed again. Grant wondered if she'd fallen asleep. He felt sleep coming over him. He was dreamy and slow when he became aware that she was lifting the covers and getting into bed with him.

"Hold me?" she said.

When she slid under the covers and held him, he realized how much he'd missed her. He knew just how wrong he'd been. Her smell, the softness of the skin on her face, her small waist, the way she touched her toes on his legs — he remembered all the good things.

She thought he felt leaner, harder than before. And now she remembered his smell, the hair on his legs and his chest, the strength she'd always noticed in his hands and arms. How could something feel this right but still not feel like it belonged to her. She remembered once again that abandoned feeling she'd had when she'd visited her old school. This feeling she had with her arms around Grant like this was so good. Was she only teasing herself by doing this? Was she begging for something that could never be? She considered getting up and leaving ... but she couldn't do it. They held each other silently, their arms and legs entwined and their faces touching. Susan began to cry — very softly at first, then louder. Grant knew it was best to just let her cry. He held her close, began to gently stroke her hair, and whispered, "I love you, I love you, I love you."

Finally, through her tears, she said, "I love you, too." And she began to cry all over again.

~

When he awoke in the morning, he was alone in bed. He reached for Susan, but he couldn't feel her. He bolted upright in bed; she was not in the room. He feared the worst immediately; she'd left him. He stumbled to his feet and lurched through his bedroom door into the living room. He stubbed his toe, hard, on the doorframe when he burst out of his room. Hopping on one foot, he felt intense pain in the other. "Ouch ... shit!" he moaned for a second.

"Smooth!" came Susan's voice from the kitchen table when she looked up from the book she was reading. She was fully dressed, and she looked like she was waiting for something. When Grant's initial fear that she'd left for home was put to rest, he was quickly uncomfortable with a new fear. He thought she was ready to say goodbye and walk out the door at any moment. Her bag was packed and sitting by the door. But as his head cleared, he saw that she was wearing blue jeans and a sweatshirt. Didn't seem like traveling clothes, he thought.

"Good morning," he said as he limped over to the table and sat down beside her. He made an inquisitive face. "Gonna stay?" he asked, nodding yes to help her answer.

"I can catch a later flight," she said.

She folded the book and laid it down just as Grant rose and limped toward the stove to pour himself some coffee. The boxer shorts he'd slept in had little duckies on them. She watched the muscles in the back of his legs tighten as he walked. She'd always liked that athletic look about him, but she thought his boxers were absurd.

He turned and began limping back toward her. The T-shirt he was wearing said "The way to a man's heart is through his fly" and had an image of a rainbow trout striking a fly at the end of a fisherman's line. Grant's hair was messed up, and he looked like he'd just woken up. He tried to blow the steam off his coffee, but his limping caused him to spill the coffee and stain his shirt. "Ouch! That's hot," he mumbled while he walked.

From over the top of his cup, Grant could see that Susan was staring at him. "Don't stare," he said reproachfully, then smiled.

She smiled back at him. She had been caught staring, wondering about him.

"So you think I'm looking pretty good ... don't you?" He nodded yes, knowing full well that she'd been looking at his hair and clothes and limp and coffee stains.

Susan lifted the book she'd been reading; it was Gordon MacQuarrie's *Stories of the Old Duck Hunters.* "Ever take a girl duck hunting?" she asked with a smile.

"Not yet. Would you like to be the first?"

"Yes." She surprised him with her answer.

"Can I make you some breakfast first?"

"Sure."

"Spam and eggs?"

She shrugged. "Do I have a choice?"

"No."

"Spam and eggs, then."

He turned his back to her and set about his work in the kitchen.

"Do you want any help?" she asked.

"Nope." After a short pause there came the sucking noise of Spam exiting its can. He turned and raised his eyebrows as he met her smile. Then he returned to his work.

Susan had been glancing through the *Old Duck Hunters* book again for a short time when she noticed that Grant had put a CD in the CD player. "Christian Island" started to play, and Grant began to mumble along with the words. He never turned around, so she just watched his back and listened:

> *I'm sailing down the summer wind*
> *I got whiskers on my chin*
> *And I like the mood I'm in...*
> *Tall and strong she dips and reels*
> *I call her Silverheels*
> *And she tells me how she feels*
> *She's a good old boat and she'll stay afloat*
> *Through the toughest gales and keep smilin'*

Grant worked on breakfast and continued to accompany Lightfoot. Susan stared at his back – and his ridiculous boxer shorts. Was he still the same man she'd loved? She remembered how he'd grieved and struggled during Will's funeral. But there was none of that now. In fact, he sang along with Lightfoot:

> *And when the gale comes up I'll fill my cup*
> *With the whiskey of the highlands ...*
> *When the summer ends we will rest again*
> *In the lee of Christian Island.*

"OK, breakfast is served!" Grant turned toward the kitchen table with a frying pan full of scrambled eggs and small cubes of

Spam. "I left out Emil's secret ingredient though," he said as he dished up a plate for each of them.

"What's that?"

"'Bout a pound of lard."

~

After breakfast, Grant hurriedly set about feeding the dogs and preparing the duffel. He filled the old thermos with coffee and found Susan some warmer clothes. As he gathered the gear he always took along when hunting, he wondered about the way her voice sounded when she'd asked, "Ever take a girl duck hunting?" The question, and the veiled challenge within it, reminded him of their first conversations and hinted at the old joy and teasing that awaited just ahead in the conversation. It reminded him of the way she'd spoken to him in the hotel lobby so many months before. He thought that was good.

Susan watched as Grant launched the boat. The ride across the big bay, out toward Christian Island, was chilly, she thought as she covered her face. The smell of gas from the outboard was something she'd always liked. She looked at his bare hand as it rested on the tiller arm of the motor. She looked at his eyes as they searched the lake, and she felt secure in his care.

When they slid into the weeds along the shore of Christian Island, he coached the dogs, set the decoys, and readied the blind. Susan thought he looked like a man who liked his work.

When everything was ready, Nellie sat still in the bow, looking out across the lake. But Mudcat seemed to be everywhere. She tripped on the decoy bags, she chewed on empty shotgun shells, she put her wet nose on Grant's and sniffed at him. Grant held Mudcat gently and looked around her curious face when he spoke to Susan. "We're not gonna see any ducks today, you know."

"Why not?"

"Weather's too nice ... no new ducks moving south, and locals are decoy shy. We're getting started way too late ... the first hour is usually the best time of day." He pushed Mudcat away again.

Grant began to peer out over the blind in search of ducks, even though he knew it was almost hopeless. "Feels like we have a dozen pups in here, not one," he mumbled with a smile.

She looked at him and said, "I'm glad I came here. I missed this place."

"Does that mean ... you'll stay ... for a while?"

"I don't know," she replied.

"We don't have to be out here hunting to make me happy you know," he offered. The last thing he wanted to do was bore her with something she didn't care about.

"No, I wanted to do this, really. It was right over there on the island that I first began to have strong feelings for you. It was when I watched you clean those fish, of all things, and then I watched you make lunch around the fire."

"I was showing off just for you, you know," Grant admitted with a smile.

"I know you were. I loved it."

"Yeah, it is a fine place," he said as he looked all around. Then his face curled into a familiar smile. "Look at that — Mudcat likes the boat just like Will did!" The puppy was peeing on the floor. "She'll be a fine huntin' buddy!"

Grant reached for the thermos and started to unscrew the dented cup on top as Susan began to speak. "There was a special time when everything turned, though." It seemed safe to let her guard down a little bit now; she needed to know how it felt. She leaned back and folded her arms. She looked down at an old boat oar in front of her and recalled a special thing. "That time you kissed me when we sat on the end of the dock, when the little fish were nibbling our toes — that was it. Well, the first time we made love ... that was pretty good, too!" She looked at him and grinned.

"But that morning, sitting there on the dock ... you looked at me as though you were seeing something for the first time. You know, for some people it probably never happens. For others it maybe happens all the time. But I think if we're lucky, there will be one time in our whole life when we look into another person's eyes and see that they are in love with us. We'll see a dreamy stare on our lover's face. They won't speak; they'll just look back softly and seem to reach for us with their eyes. I saw you look at me like that on that morning. You looked at me and I knew! I was safe to give you everything." She stopped, like a song that ends when the radio is suddenly clicked off ... but there was more. Grant knew that what she'd left unsaid was just as important – "and then you took it away and wrecked it."

"I can't undo what I did. I just can't," he started slowly. She'd made it his turn to speak. "I can't change all of those things I've chased around my whole life. I can't. I can't make everything make sense, and I can't hide from life. But I guess I can accept the brokenness of the lives of the people I've loved, maybe the brokenness of my own life. I think now, for the first time, I can let the journey be the destination ... let the search be the treasure."

She looked at him and nodded her understanding.

"I need to tell you something else, too, Susan. Remember how we used to talk about the things we dreamed of, the things we hoped for?"

"Yes."

"When I turned my back on you, it was because I lost my courage, and I'm ashamed of that – I always will be. But more importantly, I lost hope. A man has to have hope – he has to have a dream – and I couldn't dare to dream anymore. I gave up all hope for happiness with you because I was afraid. A man without hope – well, with no hope for the future – he's as good as dead. "

"And now you have hope?"

"Yes! I guess I realized it when I thought that just maybe, I was dying ... over there." He pointed to Christian Island.

"I always had you figured as a guy who would find a safe way through a storm – a night on the island – and just not miss a beat, maybe even enjoy the experience," she interrupted.

"I had myself figured that way, too," he said in a low voice. "But I was afraid for a while there. It was dark, and cold, and I was hurt." He stopped, then shrugged. "I heard my dad say once that he found hope – he knew he was going to make it – when he was in a POW camp. Doesn't make much sense, does it? But I knew – I just knew ... after a while under that boat – that I wasn't ready to give up yet. I knew I wanted to live."

"Why, what happened?"

"Well, Ingrid ... and Frank ... and Anne planted some ideas, I guess. And maybe time helped heal me. When I was under the boat, and when I was rowing back across the lake ... that was when I let myself dream of you again. The thought of you, of what we had, gave me some hope." He smiled at her, then looked away. "Remember when I told you how I dreamed of your toes, and other things, touching me in the morning? Well, I remembered that, and I got that same wonderful feeling in my belly again. Can you understand that?"

She only nodded. Then she began to ask a question. She spoke as though she already knew the answer but wasn't sure if Grant did. She knew she was taking a huge chance in asking it, but now was the time.

"Ever think that the things your father taught you were meant to lead you to this moment? And that your life with Kate was meant to prepare you for our love? That your friendship with Will was meant to lead you to me? That your past was all meant to get you ready for what's coming, between us?"

The palms of his hands rested on his thighs, and he leaned back on his boat seat. Through a wrinkled brow, his eyes questioned her briefly. "Yes ... yes, I have wondered that ... and I think it might be true," he said slowly, nodding. Then he continued. "Now let me ask you something. Are you willing to take the risk that some-day one of us will be sitting all alone in this boat, mourning the loss of the other? Is this love worth that pain?"

"Yes, a hundred times over," she said with businesslike certainty and no hesitation.

"Me too, finally." He looked back into her eyes. "For a while there, I was sure I just wasn't entitled to any more … happiness, friendship, love … I don't know." He shrugged and scowled slightly. "It just seemed like I'd used up all of the good things I was entitled to for one life. I couldn't stand that thought … so I quit. But Frank was right, when you're willing to pay a heavy toll for love, that's how you know you're alive." He screwed the top back onto the thermos and took a sip, then another, from the cup.

Then he told her everything she needed to know with one small gesture: He passed the cup to her. She stared back at him … but he looked away and peeked out over the top rail of the blind in search of ducks.

The implications of his gesture were not lost on her. He'd passed the cup as he always had with Will. But he hadn't even noticed his own actions. And that was when she knew that some place had been reopened for her inside Grant Thorson's heart, and she knew nothing he could ever say to her could make it as clear as the little gesture of sharing that dented cup. She knew she'd been admitted to that place in Grant's heart where only his best friend was allowed. His gesture had told her something accidentally that was so certain and unmistakable it needed no oath or pledge for verification.

She raised the cup to her mouth and, while he was looking for ducks, she said firmly, "Coffee sucks!" She tried to put a sarcastic edge on it.

His face spun to meet her smile, and just then he, too, understood what he'd done. They both knew they'd found their way back to where they'd been. Grant bent toward her, and his mouth found hers with the most gentle, sublime kiss. They stared, not smiling … but smiling. Then he backed away and spoke, "Oh, I forgot. You're a connoisseur of fine tobacco products. Just a minute while I locate my pipe and special aromatic blend. Or would you prefer a chew? I have vomit bags too!"

They laughed like children, they loved each other again, and they both knew it. She removed her mittens and took his cold hands in hers, but she said nothing. After a moment, he asked her cautiously, "Gonna stay for awhile?"

"I've been lost, and I've been found, out here on this lake. And now I just want to stay here ... in the lee of Christian Island ... and wait for the white horses to run."

"Could be a long wait."

"Good."